I0664082

The characters and events in this book are fictitious. Any similarity to real person, living or dead, is coincidental and not intended by the author.

PHASE 1

THE

PLAYERS

CHAPTER ONE

The 04' Cadillac Deville DTS sat idling outside of the jewelry store, the four passengers inside wore black ski masks. Two of the men were armed with 9mm glocks, while the other two packed a .44 magnum and a .40 cal Desert Eagle respectively. Three of the men exited the car, leaving the driver to wait. The trio burst into the lavish store with guns set to kill. The two with the glocks held up the cashier as the other masked man ran collecting expensive watches, chains, earrings, and bracelets tossing them into a gym bag. One of the gunmen demanded the cash from the register and safe, both orders were quickly filled. In three minutes they were finished. On the way out, one of the gunmen shot the clerk at point blank range, killing him instantly.

Thirty minutes later, the Cadillac pulled inside a homemade garage. The occupants removed their masks before leaving the garage. With the guns and masks hidden away in an old tackle box, the crew quickly made their way up the stairs and into their apartment.

"Damn it Doug!", Linz exclaimed, "Why the fuck did you kill the clerk?" Doug, a young man of about 27 years old, pale as a full moon, said nothing. Instead he took a Newport from his pack, withdrew his Zippo, lit it and clicked his Zippo closed. Coming to his friend's defense, A.P. suggested, "Doug was probably considering that dude was finna call the muthafucking po-po! No witness, no chance of our identity being discovered." Linz, criminal yet a Christian, shook his head and said, "I feel sorry for your soul Doug." Finally K.J. spoke up, "Fuck all that shit!! Let's break out the chocolate tye, roll a spliff, crack the seals of this Henny, and get twisted!" With that and Lil' John's crunk music on the stereo, the party began.

This group of four has been together since childhood. Lionel Lindsey aka Linz was the leader of the crew. He was strong and fearless, standing over 6 feet tall and weighing in at a solid 200 pounds. He was nicely chiseled from working out while in prison. His presence was intimidating to almost everyone he met, but he was actually the soft hearted one of the group.   Next came Anthony Parr aka A.P, intelligent and quick to react in any situation.   He also pulled a light bid for selling drugs.   He lived by the old school code, "Never pull a gun unless you planned to use it", which he did with skill. Kevin Ward aka K.J. Was the joker, he kept everyone in good spirits with his wicked sense of humor.   He was also a loose cannon with a cannon, preferably the .44 mag. K.J. was also the best driver in the hood.   He was known as the Jeff Gordon of the ghetto.   Finally, rounding off the crew is Douglas Trupiano aka Doug.   His poverty stricken mother moved into the hood after his father was shot and killed by the police while they were trying to detain him.   Doug witnessed his father's murder at the tender age of four, something he will never forget.   Doug is not much of a talker, he often spoke with his pistol, which always seemed to get his point across just fine.   He kept his mouth occupied by chain smoking Newport.   The Zippo lighter he carried belonged to his late father.

Linz, not one to drink or smoke, cracked the cap of an Ocean Spray orange/grapefruit juice mix and began scheming on the next hit.   "Yo, I'm tired of this little money, what y'all think about taking on an armored truck.   Who's down wit me?", Linz said.   Doug, puffing on a blunt with a Newport still smoldering between his fingers, nodded not only to Linz, but also to the tune etched in his brain, Bone Thugs -n- Harmony's "P.O.D". He sung the hook out loud, "Let's get P.O.D'ded, Reefer and blunts is all that's needed." After taking a chug from the bottle of Hennessy (King Louie the VIII), A.P. said, "That's some big boy shit, but I'm down wit you."   K.J. rolling another blunt, also agreed to the idea.   The crew was lost in the thought of coming up in a major way.

Twenty minutes later there was a knock at the door.   "Who the fuck is it!", Linz shouted, grabbing his Desert Eagle from the table.   A.P. jumped under the table with 12 gauge Moss burg pistol grip pump loaded with double aut bucks, cocked and ready, aimed at the front door.   K.J. rolled up his bag of weed and stashed it in a cookie jar, then covered the gym bag full of jewels, along with a backpack filled with money. Doug reached under his jersey for his prized Ruger 9mm.

"Who's there?', Linz bellowed again.   "Lil Mac.", came the reply.   "Nigga, is you creepin or speakin?", Linz asked. "Nigga, I gotta holla at you!", Lil Mac stated almost in tears. "Shit, let that crying muthafucka in!", K.J. said laughing. "Man listen, something bad just happened to me about a half hour ago.", Lil Mac declared. "These dudes came busting in and shot my peeps. Then held guns on me and my girl. Niggas took all my weed and money! That shit wasn't even mine! They got 15 pounds of hydro and $35,000 in cash!!" Lil Mac was glistening with sweat. He is just a worker for Dee, and nigga's know that Dee don't take no shorts or believe in sob stories. "How long ago did this go down?", A.P. asked. "About half an hour ago, right before y'all showed up.", Lil Mac replied. "Them nigga's was on some other shit, like they were high on boy or something."

"Sounds like the work of Spyder and Abbs to me. Let's go holla at them nigga's.", Linz said. "Don't worry about your boy, if he believed in the good Lord then he will be alright. As for them two clown ass niggas, I'll help them bust hell wide open!" K.J. , always down for beef, shouted, "Dig that!!" The crew checked their weapons, and headed out the door. Once outside, they by-passed the 'Lac and went straight for the stolen Dodge Intrepid that Lil Mac had gave them a few months back.

Spyder and Abbs ran an exotic bar with a bad reputation for fights, drugs, and prostitution. The last three cops to go in there didn't come back out, so some officers decided to ignore the bar to prevent further loss. The Four Kings, a name given to the crew by their friend Grench, weren't intimidated. Strapping on Kevlar, they made their way into the bar.

With weapons concealed, they walked slowly through the crowd, searching for their victims. Doug tried an unmarked door and found it locked. He could hear voices and the clicking of lighters on the other side. "Yo, let's chill for a minute and watch the show so that nobody starts with an awkward eye.", A.P. advised. The four men choose a table near the front, then sat down to watch as the first girl came out, just as Luda, John, & Usher's "Lovers & Friends" leaked through the clubs speakers.

Linz caught her eye as she began to dance. She was tall, nearly 6 feet without heels, and very leggy, just the way he liked them, wearing only a bra and thong. Her breast were medium sized, with dime size nipples. Her almond skin glowed, as her alluring body swayed seductively back and forth, in tune with the crazy, sexy, crunk beat. As she proceeded to work the room, her eye's scanned the crowd, locking on the group of handsome strangers that just entered. Sensing new money and giving in to curiosity, she then strutted over to Linz and sat in his lap. "Hey boo, I ain't seen you here before. What's your name?, she purred. "Prezident.", he replied, recalling the moniker he went by in prison. He began running his fingertips up and down her silky skin, caressing her hips and thighs and across the softness of her stomach.

The next two girls came out shaking their twin apple bottoms to the tune of Mr Cheeks hit "Lights, Camera, Action", and performing they were! As set of twins Asian and Black-Cuban, a deadly combination. One tiptoed over to A.P. and the other slid over to K.J. After making their presence felt, the dames continued lap dancing for these two fortunate men.

Doug sat and watched, taking in the whole scene while smoking a cigarette, as the fourth girl came out and sauntered towards him. She was an albino, rocking a short hair cut dyed strawberry blond, with pierced nipples. He snubbed out his Newport and motioned with is finger for her to join him at his side. As she came into his lap, he started whispering in her ear.

The four women knew that the four men were new to the club and possibly new to the city. They were getting tired of the same old ugly ass niggas, coming in the club broke as hell, trying to cop a few cheap feels and not talking about nothing. The Four Kings were different, they had bread, but today they were here on business.

"My name is Tootie.", the six foot beauty told Linz, "These are my sista's, Diamond and Jade, and that's my girl Cristal, like the drink, she's smooth, bubbly, and sexually intoxicating." Getting comfortable in his lap, she felt the outline of the Desert Eagle that he packed. After a brief pause, she turned to Linz and said, "Y'all only here for two reasons, your either new in town, or them nigga's Abb's and Spyder fucked up and did some foul shit again. So, which is it?" Linz gave her a look that could melt steel, as did the rest of the gang. Diamond looked at A.P. and said, "Look, just give us a head start, we ain't trying to get caught up in the bullshit!" Jade added, "I don't know why but I'm feeling y'all vibe, especially you.", pointing at K.J. "Be careful, them nigga's know y'all here." With that said the four girls continued their lap dances, making them extra slow and sensual for the newcomers.

"Alright y'all listen up, this is how it's gonna go down, after the music stops them sucka's die. Ladies, that's your warning.", Doug said, taking a drag of his Newport. He blew out the smoke and asked, "So, what y'all gonna do, ride or die or BBQ or mildew, it's up to you?" K.J. busted out laughing saying, "The reaper speaks." Suddenly the music died, the lights came on, and two shots rang out. The crew quickly jumped under the table. The girls went scattering for cover, as several shots quickly followed the first two. "On three, jump up blazing!", Linz said. "1, 2, 3..." Linz and Doug fired at their opponents with the attitude of Billy the Kid in his prime, only this time armed with a Desert Eagle and Ruger 9. A.P. and K.J. crawled toward the unmarked door. Before the door could close, A.P. slide the Moss-burg in the doorway using it as a doorstop. That allowed K.J. to kick open the door and fire point blank range at the two in the room, high off heroin, with his nickel plated .44 Mag. The loose cannon was at it again! A.P. was a half step behind him sweeping the room with the loaded pump. What he saw was the aftermath of the big .44's wake, leaving bodies in a permanent lean.

Everyone's ears were ringing from the gun blast. All the other patron's had escaped unharmed. "Alright, let's grab the goods and get ghost!", Linz exclaimed. They went into the backroom and found the stolen loot and hydro. As they left the room, one final shot whizzed past A.P.'s ear. He turned clicking the pump, then fired, removing Spyder's head from his body. "Don't go in there.", he told the beautiful young dancers. "We weren't planning to!", Tootie, the almond skinned fawn, said. "Actually we were hoping to come with y'all. The cops will be here soon and we don't need to be here when they get here. Feel me?" She walked up to Linz and slid her arm around his waist, rubbing the small of his back. "That's cool wit me. Lets be out.", Linz decided. Diamond and Jade took the arms of A.P. and K.J. giggling. Cristal took Doug's right hand in her left and his Newport from his mouth with her right. With a sexy smile cooed, "My favorite." The group exited, jumping into the Intrepid, they saw the flashing blue lights just as they left the parking lot.

CHAPTER TWO

Back at the apartment complex, they hid the whips in the garage that is used by the maintenance man.   The eight of them ascended the stairs into the plush three bedroom apartment.   "So, y'all in trouble with the police, huh?   What y'all do assault a dick head?", K.J. joked.   A.P. added, "Looks like they got some killer coochie too!!"   The fella's busted out laughing, the women took it in stride.   Tootie waited until the laughter died down, then said, "Actually, my sista's and I did merc some people.. Financially. We do identity theft, credit card, and bank scams.   That's our specialty.", she proudly admitted.

"Shit! Y'all my type of bitches, I could fuck with y'all!", K.J. stated.   Then asked, "Y'all smoke because we about to get lifted."   The girls weren't too happy about being called bitches by some nigga's they didn't know, but decided to let it ride for now.

K.J. began to roll a couple of blunts and prepared them to be dipped in honey for a slow burn.   Doug grabbed a bottle of Crown Royal from the fridge and poured two shots for him and Cristal.   After downing them, they took turns drinking from the bottle.   He spilled some on her chest and licked it off, then kissed her passionately on the lips.

Diamond and Jade were doing their twin strip teach routine for K.J. and A.P.   The three blunts filled the room with smoke, blended with smells of honey and weed.   Jade had her full backside grinding into K.J.'s lap, while Diamond had A.P.'s head between her large double D's.

Tootie was giving Linz her undivided attention.   Her soft, hazel eyes were fixed intensively on him.   She began to wonder what was on his mind. because here she was, fine as hell, a natural beauty, wearing no make up expect for lip gloss, standing in nothing but a thong and a pair of 6 inch stilettos, and this nigga gave no reaction.   Tootie was a quarter piece even on her worst day.   It fucked her up because most niggas would be trying to touch and feel by now, but this nigga acted as   if it had no effect on him.

8

She knew then the this was a man worth getting to   know, and probably keeping.   Only time would tell.

Linz was taken back by Tootie's beauty and poise.   He had encountered a lot of bad bitches in his lifetime, but hands down, she was one of the baddest.   At least in the top three.   This siren was literally poetry in motion, something from the pages of a book by Maya Angelo or Saul Williams.   She had a body that would make a thug shed tears. He had to keep his poker face on because if his homies knew what this woman's mere presence was doing to him, they'd clown him something terrible.   He couldn't have that because them nigga's would never let up.

As the spliff's kept going around and getting shorter with each pass, everyone except Linz got higher and higher.   "Yo, let me holla at y'all in the kitchen for a minute.", K.J. said, exhaling a monster hit.   The women took seats on the sofa and love seat and began to talk as the men got up and went into the kitchen.

"What's up?", A.P. Asked. "Man I got an idea, let's put the armored truck thing on the back burner for a minute.   I got something a little less risky, but for sure money." The crew was all ears now.   "Let's hit a couple of these fake ass ballers around here frontin like they untouchable.", K.J. said.   "Man, most of them niggas don't fuck with us like that. We can't get close to them cats with the big chips, and I ain't fucking with the average street niggas.", Doug replied.   "True, we can't get close to them, but those hoes can." K.J explained.   He let those words sink in then continued on saying, "Nigga, them some top flight bitches, you know as well as I do that every baller's weakness is a bad bitch with a fat ass!"

"Nigga, is you stupid!" What the fuck you smoking?", Linz started to ask, but stopped short and said, "I think your on to something, keep talking."   K.J. continued to relay his plan to the rest of the crew.   He painted a picture that they could all envision. He summed it up saying, "Since that Tootie chick seems to be the leader, Linz it's up to you to convince her and her peeps to ride with us on this.   Can you handle that?"   Linz stated matter of factly, "I got this Nigga.   You know I'm something like a P.I.M.P!" The men gave each other a pound and departed back into the living room to focus once again on the fine group of females that sat in the living room half naked.

When they reentered the room, Tootie rose to meet the object of her desire asking "Is everything alright?" "Yeah, I just need to holla at you for a minute.:, Linz told her then led her towards the back of the apartment. "Babe, me and the crew got something in the mix and we kind of need your assistance to pull it off. You will be paid well if all goes as planned." "So, what we gotta do?", she asked. "Just be your beautiful self, that's all.", Linz replied. Tootie sucked her teeth and said, "That ain't telling me nothing!!" "Alright here's the deal, we want to hit a few ballers for that tax free cash that they holding. You feel me.", Linz stated. Tootie tossed the idea around in her head for a minute, then said, "Count us in, as long as we get a fair shake and y'all got our back if anything goes wrong, we're down." They exchanged pounds and then joined the others. Linz gave a nod to his peeps that it was all good, while Tootie pulled her girls together and laid the plan down to them. Diamond had some questions. "How we gonna do this, and who is the nigga's we gonna hit?" K.J. shot back, "Don't worry about who, all y'all gotta do is gain their trust and we will handle the rest, aight." This time Jade spoke, "But what about bodyguards? All the big nigga's with major figures roll with a deep crew and it's only four of y'all." Her twin nodded in agreement. "That's a risk that we're willing to take,. Me and my crew's pistol game is on point.", Linz stated with confidence. "Mmm huh, like Bush, huh?!? Fuck around and get us killed! This ain't Iraq Nigga! Fuck is really on ya mind, do we look like suicide bombers to you? Your plan better be air tight because I ain't trying to knocked off for nobody. Nigga, we don't know you from a can of paint!", Cristal exploded. "Babe, it's like Allstate, your in good hands, so calm down, aight.", Doug said.

"Look, everybody just chill for a minute. We already know who we gonna hit. We'll let y'all know soon, we still gotta scope out our victims a little more.", K.J. said while putting out the last of his blunt. "But for now, I'm bout to crash, I'll holla at y'all in the morning. Jade, what's up, you coming?" jade just giggled and followed him. A.P. stood and extended his hand to Diamond signaling for her to come with him. Both girls exchanged a look knowing what the other had in mind. Rumor was that they gave the best head in the western hemisphere. The twins were well skilled in the art of oral sex, both women shared an oral fixation. Jade would make it her duty to make K.J. beg like a bitch for her to let him cum. Then she planned on riding him until he pleaded for her to stop.   Yeah, he was in for the night of his life.   While Diamond, on the other hand was passive.   Her favorite position was from behind, that how she got off.   A.P.'s endurance would be tested on this night.

"Good night homie.", Linz said to Doug, who waved a cigarette holding hand in reply as he and Cristal reclined on the couch watching the end of a movie that was playing on the flat screen.   As Linz and Tootie made their way down the hall to where Linz's room was located, he asked, "You ready for this?"   She replied, "Whatever Boo, all men talk shit.   I just hope you ain't one of those types.", as they entered the bed room.

In the dark, dimly lit room, Linz ran his hands up and down her silky thighs as she lay back on the king size bed, totally nude, except for the bracelet she wore around her ankle and a toe ring that adorned her pretty pedicure toes.   This bitch was bad!   Tootie sat up on her elbows and said, "You've seen mine and what I'm working with, now let me see yours.", with a wicked smile playing on her lips.   Linz stood and began to unbutton his shirt and undo his jeans, taking his time slowly teasing her, as she sat up with renewed interest.   As the shirt came off, her breath caught in her throat, she was astonished at what was in front of her.   She could not wait to run her fingers and tongue across his chiseled chest and rock hard abs.   The kid had an 8 pack!   Her mind was taken to a whole other level when his jeans and boxer's came off.   Her eyes widened as she feasted them on his half erect member.   Clearly, she was surprised, mouthing a silent thank you.

As Linz approached the bed she rose slightly to meet him, one hand went to his chest to see if it was real, the other gently stroked his penis.   He began to cup one of her breasts in his hand, letting the other hand fall on her well shaped ass.   He laid her down and began to fully caress her lovely body, before reaching in the nightstand drawer for a condom.   Anticipating this moment, Tootie began to rub herself to ease the entry she was about to experience.   She spread her legs wide, welcoming him into her soul.

The first thrusts were gentle, but grew more aggressive with each stroke. "OOOHH.. AHHH.. Damn this feels good!", she moaned, bucking her body to match his rhythm.   He savored the feeling of his body against hers, soft against hard, smooth against rough. He loved the way her long toned legs wrapped around his torso, squeezing his lower back. He loved the way her perky nipples fit his mouth, the softness of her breast, the sweet taste of her skin, the look on her face as she moaned combined with the sparkle in her eye's told him that she was enjoying his work.

Tootie loved the feeling of his manhood inside her warm vagina, it was almost a perfect fit, no discomfort. She couldn't remember her pussy ever being this wet during sexual intercourse. This nigga is rocking her world. Her whole body tingled with each stroke, sending small explosions through her nerves. Linz's dick game was truly presidential. She dreamed that this episode would never end. Her eyes widened as he turned her over and entered her from the back, slamming it in while slowly dragging it out like a true cock smith on a mission. She knew that too much of this and she'd be addicted, so she searched for a way to flip it on him. She had to put her pussy game down because this wasn't no ordinary nigga. She was finding it harder to control her body with each stroke this nigga administered. Tootie's mind went blank as he massaged her ass with one hand and gently pulled on her long wavy hair with the other. She knew she was in for a long night. She prayed that she'd last, this nigga was dicking her down. He could walk the walk and talk the talk.

CHAPTER THREE

Kuan and Kuo, never knew their father.   He had met their mother, Tekoa, while in the service, when he was stationed somewhere over in South Asia.   Tekoa came to the states shortly after she found out that she was pregnant with twins.

Victor Santiago, half Black, half Cuban, died three months after Tekoa's arrival in a Miami whorehouse.   He was shot while getting a blow job.   His killer was never found. Life events left Tekoa to raise her two kids alone.   Miami   was a place of bad memories for her, so when the girls turned six she relocated to Columbus, Ohio to start anew. The twins were identical in stature, almost impossible to tell apart.   They wore the same size in clothing and shoes.   The Vixens stood 5'8" and weighed 144 pounds solid, but soft in all the right places, carrying it well on their size 9 frames.   They shared the same taste in food and clothes and often times dressed alike.   They even had the same tattoo's, the Japanese symbol for love inked at the base of their spines and a Tribal Dragon   that started just below the right knee, spiraling down around the calf, stopping on the top of their finely pedicured feet.   There was only two ways to tell the women apart.   One way required a real keen eye for detail.   Kuan's breast were a half cup size bigger than her sisters, while Kou's lips were fuller.   The second way was by the jewelry these raven haired beauties wore.   True to their names, each donned a 16 inch herringbone necklace, cast in platinum, with an elephant dangling from it.   Diamond's elephant was encrusted with diamonds, while Jade's was carved out of the finest jade stone.   They also had matching charm bracelets worn on the left ankle with the Asian symbol of their birth name, made in their trademark stone.   These two computer savvy freaks with an oral fixation, had the style and flair to mirror that of Hollywood's most elite.   One would never know that these two gems were mined in the ghetto.

Camille,aka Crystal was the product of a common nigga and a drunk german.Her father Franklin was killed in a back room brawl when he was caught skimming cards at a poker game.Her fathers death took a punishing toll on her mother Deanna's mental state, so much she had to be commeted to a mental hospital.Sending Camille to live with her aunt Tracey from the age of four.Crystal usually kept her hair styled in a short cut, similar to the one like Halle Berry.   Her high cheekbones and sleepy eyes combined with pillow soft lips that formed a highly seductive smile, gave her a dream like appearance. Although free spirited, she had a dark side, a violent streak inherited from her late father, that no man could match.   Although it was rarely seen, it was there oozing in her blood. Her height came from her mother Deanna, standing 5'2", weighing 112 pounds.   She was strapped with a modest B-cup, a slim waist, and packing enough ass to test the stitching on a pair of size 7 jeans, baby girl's body was banging!   Camille's only addition was Nike Air Max Sneakers.   She owns over 60 pair in all sorts of colors. Those were her brand of choice, nothing else.   She was not one for heels, boots, or sandals, but would wear them if the job required her to do so.   Her clothing was simple, mostly consisted of T-shirts, jeans, and various sweat outfits.   The only two pieces of jewelry she wore, or even owned for that matter, is a platinum box chain adorned with a small heart pendant, engraved on each side with both her parent's names. She also wore two small diamond hoop earrings that belonged to her mother.   Camille possessed and uncanny ability to add numbers quickly without writing them down or without the help of a calculator.   You could give her a group of numbers and in a few seconds she would spit out the answer.   It was a gift that not many people knew that she had.   Often an outcast because of her lack of pigmentation, she chose to stay to herself or running with the what some would say her only three friends, Kuan and Kuo Iko and this tall skinny girl named Toychica Williams, who lived a few houses down the block from her.   These girls accepted her as she was, coming to her defense whenever needed.   She was very thankful for them and loved them as sisters.

Toychica, just like the other girls, was a mixed breed.   She came from a long line of high yellow women.   Ajia, her mother, was very easy on the eyes.   She was tall, young, wild, and untamable before she fell for Dontello, Toychica's father.He was a short Italian businessman from Long Island, NY she met while working as a concierge for the Marriott at Chicago's International Airport.   It didn't take long for Dontello to entice Ajia, she had an eye for spotting the rich and wealthy.   She accepted an invitation for drinks one night, which turned into three weeks of wild unprotected sex.   After his business in the city was done, he hopped the next flight back to New York, home to his wife of ten years and two boys ages seven and ten.   He didn't even bother to say goodbye to Ajia.   All those nights of unprotected sex lead to the conception of Tootie, a nickname given to her by her mother.   Ajia spent weeks trying to track down Dontello to tell him of her pregnancy.   When she finally found him, he wasn't interest in what she had to say.   He claimed it wasn't his, but sent her $500 dollars for an abortion and told her to beat it and to never bother him again.   Ms. Williams never tried to contact him again.   Though hurt, she took it in stride and vowed to raise her child by herself. Money was often tight, a lot of times they barely ate, but they made it work somehow. A few years later when Tootie was seven, Ajia packed up and moved her daughter to Columbus, Ohio, hoping for a fresh start.   She stayed with her brother until she could get a place of her own.

Tootie grew up a tomboy, running the streets with the local kids getting into all sorts of fights, mainly with the boys.   She hung with three girls, a set of twins that lived four blocks away in the Asian community and a little albino girl that everyone picked on who lived a few houses down from her.

At the age of ten, Tootie stood 5'5" tall and lanky, seemed like she would be another Olive Oyl.   But, at the age of 17, puberty kicked down her door.   Her now 5'11" frame began taking shape.   First came the breast, followed by a set of hips that screamed for attention, and a pair of well toned thighs and calves that would give Tina Turner a run for her title.   Five years later, low and behold, her phattygirl was born.   Tootie has an ass the shape of a teardrop, perfectly sculpted by God himself, completing her size 10 frame. The end result was a shockingly beautiful goddess, with brains and   razor sharp street smarts to match.   She is fully aware of her beauty, her body, and the power it tends to yield over beings of the opposite sex.   Hell, even those of the same sex secretly and openly wished for a taste of her goodies.   Elbow length wavy black hair, and soft hazel eyes that seem to sparkle and hypnotize, were the only things she'd ever got from her father.   Toychica was a very sharp dresser, her style changed with her mood and surroundings.   The broad had outfits for days, everything from Old Navy to Chanel and beyond.   Like Camille, she had a shoe addiction.   Her shoe game was off the meter, ladies Timberlands in every style and color, along with custom Nike Air Max and Air Force Ones.   Her casual and dress assortment of footwear was just as mean.   She only rocked two pieces of jewelry, a diamond tennis bracelet, worn sometimes on her ankle but mostly on her right wrist. She also had a diamond crucifix which adorned her neck, lying elegantly between her breasts suspended by an invisible chain.

The four women pulled money together after graduation and set out to take the world by storm with their good looks and hidden talents.   The crew moved to the faster paced and constantly growing city of Pittsburgh, PA.   Each of these sirens longed to be loved by a man that truly cared and would give them their all.

CHAPTER FOUR

Below the apartment, flashlights shone in the makeshift garage, which housed the 2004 Cadillac.   Three voices argued back and fourth, someone knew who the crew was and what they did for a hobby.   They pinned the Four Kings for last night's shooting at the Red Devil Bar, but nothing would be done about it tonight.

Early the next morning, Doug, a light sleeper, awoke thinking he heard something late last night.   Lighting a Newport he went outside and peered down over the railing at the garage, but nothing seemed out of place or disturbed.   Shaking his head, he returned inside to retrieve a bottle of aspirin to relieve his pounding headache.   Cristal sat softly singing a tune by Jill Scott, " Looove... Raain... down on me.. I met him on a Monday, it was a cloudy afternoon..." waiting for the pot of coffee to brew.   Even though this apartment was just a crash pad for the Four Kings, it was nicely furnished.

Linz awoke with Tootie sprawled across his chest, kissing her softly, he quietly slid out of bed trying not to disturb the woman who lay sleeping peacefully in his bed.   He stood admiring her beauty for a moment before pulling on a pair of shorts, and going into the living room to catch the morning news.   Sure enough, the top story was the robbery and shooting at the Red Devil Exotic bar last night.

"Four black men are believed to be the shooters in last nights homicides.   The alleged suspects were seen leaving the bar in an unknown vehicle after the shooting witnesses say.   Also, there are rumors about some of the dancers at the club were kidnapped at gunpoint, but at this moment that is unconfirmed.", the anchorman continued saying, "Anyone with information about the two killings is urged to call Pittsburgh Police Department immediately.   Now back to Dan for your local weather..." Linz grabbed the remote and turned the volume down.   "You hear that bull?", he asked Doug, who replied, "You know how them news bastards are.", after taking a long sip of water and a pull from his Newport.   "What was that I just heard?", K.J. asked.   "That was us bro, we made top story!", Doug said with a smirk. "Dig that!!", K.J. shot back. Jade appeared behind him wrapped in a bed sheet asking what all the fuss was about. "Us" Cristal said between taking sips of her coffee. "They said we was kidnapped." Smiling Jade commented, "Shit, I don't know about y'all three but, I came on my own." A.P. and Diamond weren't up yet, it was only 6:30 am, and they were both late sleepers. Back in Linz's room, Tootie stirred awake, stretching out the tightness from last night's workout, looking around for the man she wantonly gave herself to. Forcing herself to leave the comforts of the beds warm sheets, she arose and went to the mirror to admire her reflection. She suddenly realized that all she had with her was a lavender bra and thong, a pair of cheap heels, and nothing else. The rest of her clothing was back at the club, which was now most certainly a crime scene. Oh well, she thought, I'll just borrow this, picking up the button down shirt that was thrown on the floor. It stopped just below her ass cheeks, barely covering them, but it will have to do for now she reasoned as she made her way to the living room.

The smell of fresh brewed coffee made her think of food, and she was starving. "I know y'all got something to eat in here, right?", she asked. K.J. responded, "Why, you cooking?" "I don't mind what y'all got?", Tootie asked. "I don't know look in the fridge and see, it should be something in there." K.J. replied. The three women converged on the kitchen to see what the men had in the fridge.

While the women worked their magic on the stove, turning the few items they had to work with into something edible, the men sat discussing the present situation and last night's events. It was decided that they'd shut down this apartment and find another, but in the meantime chill at their own cribs. Doug and Linz shared a condo, as did A.P. and K.J.

Tootie told the girls about her clothing dilemma. The others realized that they too were in the same position, stuck with just the clothes on their backs, which for the most part wasn't much. It consisted of just bras and panties or see through bodysuits. Cristal managed to grab her bathrobe and tote bag that all the women kept their personal belongings in while at the club, such as keys, cell phones, and wallets. The women shared a three bedroom duplex together and a 98 Nissan Maxima.

The smell of food greeted A.P and Diamond, they woke up ready to eat.   Last nights sexual romp had taken it's toll on their stomachs.   After eating, they were filled in on the day's happenings.   When the women finished cleaning the dishes, they filled the men in on their lack of clothing situation, which brought laughter and comments from the men.   "Seriously Nigga, we need something to put on.", Jade said.   Laughing K.J. said, "Wear what you came in."   "Oh, its like that Nigga! After y'all done fucked us this is how y'all gonna treat us?   Niggas ain't shit! Fuck you!!   I ain't begging no nigga for shit!   Keep your sorry ass clothes!   You a sorry ass nigga!", Jade exclaimed and stormed out the room.   All eyes were on K.J. now.   "Fuck y'all looking at me sideways for?   I was just playing.", then added, "If the bitch wanna get an attitude, then so be it!"   Her sister Diamond spoke up saying, "Now ain't the time to be playing Nigga!   And don't call my sister no bitch wit your punk ass!"   K.J. just laughed harder.   "It ain't funny nigga, we'll jump your skinny ass!", Diamond said as she got up to console her twin.   The fella's continued to laugh as they heard Jade say, "Naw, fuck him."   Cristal asked, "K.J. are you really gonna do my girl like that?"   Her eye's narrowing as anger began to over take her calm demeanor.   "Naw, I was just fucking with her.   I wouldn't do her like that.", K.J. calmly said, then got up to go holla at Jade.

Just as K.J. was about to enter the room, Diamond and Jade were coming out, dressed in the clothes they had on last night.   He grabbed her arm as she attempted to pass by.   "Get the fuck off me!", Jade demanded.   "Chill, let me holla at you for a few.", K.J. said.   "Naw, I ain't fucking with you.   I'm good.", she coldly replied.   She tried to pull away but K.J. was too strong for that.   "Get your ass in here.", he said shoving her into the bedroom and slamming the door in Diamond's face.   "Don't get fucked up about my sister!", Diamond warned.

K.J. still had Jade's arm in his tight grip even after the door closed.   "Calm the fuck down.", he said playfully.   "Fuck you and fuck calm, let me go.", she shot back.   Jade still had her mad face on and an attitude to match, but for some strange reason she found herself being turned on by his roughness.   Her juices began to flow.   "Look, I got you with something to wear, aight.   I was just playing with you, so just chill.", he said.   "Mm humm, don't be playing like that!"   She still wore her mad face.   He began looking at her with lust in his eyes while rubbing his penis.   "I don't know what you doing that for. You ain't getting none. After the way you just clowned me, Nigga please!", she stated. Her words had no effect on him as he began to caress her ass and stroke her moist coochie. Several minutes later, her bodysuit was around her ankles and she was bent over the dresser as he proceeded to pound her from behind, burying his manhood deep into her womb, trying with force to knock on her rib cage.

Jade was loving every stroke of this vaginal assault, urging him to go deeper, harder, and faster. He didn't need to be told twice. Her moans echoed throughout the apartment letting everyone know what was going on in the back bedroom. The fellas cheered their boy on, while the women sat looking stupid. They put up a big fuss about K.J. disrespecting Jade, and she was getting her back beat in by the nigga they were prepared to beat down on her behalf. The nerve of her slutty, horny ass they all thought. Still Jade was their girl and each of them knew that without a doubt, that she would go through the same extremes for them. Truth be told, they all wished it was them getting their back blown out. Nothing like good sex to start the day.

"Damn that bitch ain't gotta rub it in, didn't nobody want to hear you moaning and shit!" The rest of the girls laughed as Diamond continues, "Sissy, you making that little skinny nigga look like a champ in the sack. That bitch let the dick get her side tracked." While still laughing, A.P. said, "That's my Nigga! Hit that shit! Represent Nigga!", giving each other high fives because their boy was putting his thing down like a champ.

After the women were given some of the men's old sweats and t-shirts to wear and the fella's dressed, it was time to bounce. "What's up with that B-I we spoke about yesterday?", Tootie asked. Her mind was on getting paper. She had plans and things to do with the money they hoped to receive, as did the other women. They often discussed stepping their game up, just waiting for the big lick to come their way. Well here it was, opportunity knocking, along with some fine brothers. Things were starting to look good for the women. All they had to do was play their cards right. "We gonna get at y'all later and go over some things, but right now we got some loose ends to take care of.", Linz answered. Tootie wrote down her cell number and told him to call when they were ready. She hoped that it would be soon because she was dying to see him again, to feel him pushing inside of her. Not only that but she wanted to get to know him a little better, and to get that loot they spoke of.   All the others were exchanging numbers as well, making plans to hook up on their own time, not as a group.

"A.p, you and K.J ditch those two Intrepids, make sure you wipe them clean.   Also, get rid of those burners in the box too."   They nodded in agreement.   Linz continued, " Doug, you take the 'Lac and drop the females off.   Then leave it parked with the keys in it, some knucklehead will take it off our hands.   After you drop the girls off, take the loot and stuff and drop them off at the house.   We can all link up around 6 pm.", He instructed.   "What about the business with Lil Mac?   What we gonna do about that?", K.J asked.   "I'm about to handle that now.", said Linz.   "We gonna return it to him minus $10,000 for our recovery fee."   They all smiled at that.   "Plus, I need to holla at him about getting us some new whips for those other jobs.   Any preferences?", Linz asked.   K.J said, "As long as it's fast and black.   See if you can get a couple of them new Chargers, the ones with the Hemi in it."   A.P said, "That sounds cool.   How you gonna get home?"   "Shit, we still got that bike, right?,   Linz asked.   "Nigga you tripping, it's about to storm outside, you better look at the clouds.", K.J said looking out for this boy.   It was then that Cristal said, "Here," offering up a set of keys, "take our car, it's a maroon Nissan Maxima parked in the drug store lot across from the club. Tootie will get it back from you later."   Cristal was quick on her feet offering up their car.   She was sensing how bad Tootie wanted to see Linz again.   These girls knew each other as well as they knew themselves.

Doug lit a cigarette and balanced it on his lower lip while loading the duffle bag filled with jewels and the backpack with money into the Caddie's huge trunk.   The women piled into the car as A.P and K.J went to get the Intrepids.   Linz climbed the stairs to Lil Mac's apartment with a military style bag in hand.

Bzzzzz...... Bzzzzz..., the buzzer rang through the small apartment that Lil Mac shared with his girl Jeanna, prompting her to get her lazy ass off the couch and answer the door.   Looking through the peephole, she was relieved to see a familiar face, she quickly opened the door.   "Hey Linz.", she said, stepping aside allowing him to enter the apartment as she returned to her seat on the couch.   She was wearing a pair of tiny shorts, probably a size too small for her, even though she was on the petite side.

"What's good Jeanna, where Lil Mac at?", Linz asked. "I'm good. You heard about yesterday, right?" she replied. "Yeah, Mac told us about it. Where he at?" Linz commented. "Shit, hell if I know, he left without saying nothing. I could be feeling a lot better though. All you gotta do is stop teasing a bitch and let me hit that one time, na'mean." she flirted. "You crazy, Lil Mac gonna kill you one of these days." Linz warned.

Jeanna knew that Linz wouldn't tell on her because he knew how much Lil Mac loved her sneaky ass. All in all, Jeanna was a good girl and always down to ride for the cause. She was a keeper, just a freak, that was her only flaw. "Lil Mac will be back in a few. You want me to call his cell for you?" she asked. "Yeah do that." Linz replied. He watched as she got up to get the phone. Knowing that he was watching, she started switching a little something extra for him, trying to entice him. "Linz, you sure you don't want to sample a scoop of this double chocolate?" she teased. "Naw, I'm cool" he said. "Well, if you ever change your mind let me know, Lil Mac ain't gotta know." she offered.

Jeanna flirted a lot but only A.P called her bluff and fucked her in Mac's bed a couple of weeks ago. She didn't know that the crew knew, but they did. Besides, she probably wanted them to know so they'd want to hit also. Hell, she might be that kind of freak. A.P felt that since she didn't belong to no one in the crew she was open game, as far as he was concerned. But, the others declined out of respect for Lil Mac. Even though dude wasn't one of them, he was considered a stand up guy by the Four Kings.

The brief conversation ended almost as quickly as it started. The only words spoken were "I need to see you", and "Aight, I'm on my way." The two men had an understanding and stuck to the hustlers code, Say nothing about business over the phone.

CHAPTER FIVE

A.P and K.J arrived back at their condo about an hour after leaving the crash pad. Although everyone in the crew was tight like glue A.P and K.J seemed to click more with each other. They shared a common interest in the love of old school '60 - '78 model muscle cars and an ear for the blues music, they called pimpin. Maybe it was that they each had a parent from the south. K.J's father was from Memphis, Tennessee. His pops was a small time pimp back in his younger days, and part time bass player in a small band. He met K.J's mom while touring. He couldn't get enough of the little brown skinned thing he met while playing at a venue in Monroeville, a suburb of Pittsburgh, PA.

A.P's mother was a true southern belle whose mind was blown by some slick talker from Michigan, while attending the Art Institute of Pittsburgh. That's how they came to live in the Burgh.

A.P stood about 5 ft. 10 in, 190 pounds, brown skinned with a head full of waves. Niggas might get sea sick just looking at them. He possessed a Colgate smile that women loved. His nice, athletic build came from a two year prison bid he caught for a drug beef. He is an avid reader. He had read almost everything. He had the demeanor of a pretty boy and the confidence to match. He had one hang up, the only tennis shoe he wore were the Nike Cortez. They were called gangsta Nikes in the south and dope man's in the north. A.P, Linz, and K.J had always tried to out dress each other. They were always so fresh and so clean everyday of the week. The group often teased him because of the hard creases he put in his jeans. Doug nicknamed him "Heavy Starched". His most prized possessions was the candy yam colored '75 Chevy Nova sitting on 22" chrome Niche Bella's. The Chevy thang looked so sick when it rolled past. He didn't much care for the '06 Lincoln Navigator he drove. To him, it was just another car taking up space in his garage. Now the Nova, that was special, he had it stored for the fall, you wouldn't see it again until the summer. After this mission was over, he planned on getting this '63 Lincoln Continental convertible with kissing doors, and fitting it with 24" gold daytons.

K.J was the joker of the four. He stood 6 feet even. He also weighed 175 pounds. This skinny nigga is always humming a Willie Hutch tune and claimed to be a "certified PI", whatever that meant. He was the loose cannon of the group. His weapon of choice was any large caliber handgun, .41's, .44's, and the coveted blue steel .50 cal. K.J. Was a true soldier, he got the job done. Plus, the boy had mad driving skills, perfected from his car stealing days along with many night watching New Jersey Drive. The nigga only had six waves in his head, but you couldn't tell him that, if you did he'd swear you were hating. All in all, K.J was a good dude who would give you his last. If he liked you it was all love, but if he didn't then God help you. Like DMX said, "I got a good heart, but this heart could get ugly.", that's the best way to describe his demeanor. His only habit was weed. The kid smoked all day, everyday. Like his partners, he was a dapper fellow when it came to clothes. His old school ride of choice was a burnt orange '70 Chevy Chevelle SS, standing tall on 23" chrome 204 spoke daytons, with white guts and orange piping. He also had an '06 Ford Excursion on 26's. His dream car was a sun gold '07 Mercedes S600 which he'd surely get after these next few capers were done.

Both of these men had bread. The crew had a pact that they followed. They all save 50% of their personal take from every robbery that they committed. It was a code that they stuck to at all times, to be prepared for any situations that life in the streets threw at them. The condo that the two shared was very plush by anyone's standards. The decor was masculine yet supple. It had two huge bedrooms with walk in closets, two and a half baths, and skylights. A.P entered the house and went straight to bed, so he could be refreshed when he hooked up with Diamond tonight. K.J, on the other hand, sat back and rolled a dutch, so he could have something to smoke on as soon as he woke up. He then put a load of clothes in the washer. The boy was tired from his romp with Jade. He was starting to get a jones for her. She turned him on in every way, but he had another hoe to deal with tonight, Teresa, his college cutie. K.J and A.P were man whores, but Diamond and Jade could possibly change all that. Deep down, even though they would never admit it, they were tired of sleeping with a different girl every other night. They longed for one that they trust and settle down with.

Doug dropped the girls off at their house in McKee's Rocks, and then headed through the Liberty Tunnels towards the airport.   He and Linz shared a spacious three bedroom flat out in Robinson Township, complete with walk in closets and a fireplace. The place only had one and half baths but the main bath was huge.   It boasted a large spa tub, a very spacious shower stall with multiple shower heads, along with dual vanities and African pine floors.   Doug found the place a few years ago while working at his landscaping job.

Doug was the quite one of the group.   He was half black and half Italian.   He stood 6 ft. 2 in, 165 pounds, with dark curly hair.   Doug was more of a thinker, when he did speak his mind pay attention because wisdom was about to flow.   He and Linz spoke all the time at home, they exchanged wits and opinions on a variety of topics daily.   When Linz and A.P went to jail, it was Doug that sat down once a week to drop them a few lines and whatever money he could, even if it was his last.   He also made sure that they had a place to call collect for any reason.   K.J, not one for writing, sent photos and money weekly.   The crew looked out for each other to the fullest. Unlike the other three, Doug was a simple dresser.   He wore Coogi, Moeshe, Phat Farm sweat suits, and Roca Wear jeans with Timberlands.   He rocked a platinum link with a pair of diamond encrusted dog tags, with matching bracelet and one and half carat in each ear.   He drove a '06 Acura RL, white with 20" Sean John rims.   He also pushed a '05 Chevy Avalanche, it was also white fitted with 26" chrome rims and spinners, five screens and custom suede interior.   Although the truck was nice, he had his sight set on the new BMW 760 IL.   That was the next car he planned on copping once this was over.   He, like the others, followed the saving plan code, after all he's the one who advised it.   K.J called Doug "The Reaper", because crossing him meant death, or one step from it.   The boy had shooting skills like a sniper.

After leaving the 'Lac in the parking lot of Pittsburgh International Airport, Doug hailed a cab, loaded his bags, then gave the driver his destination.   He looked like a man who just got off a long flight.   Upon entering the flat, he fed his two Chinese fighting fish, put in a few cd's, and let the sounds of Bob Marley's Greatest Hits take his mind away.

Linz got out of Lil Mac's car at the drug store on Penn Ave, found the Maxima, and

drove off.   Rambling through the console he found Keyshia Cole's CD, The Way it is"
and threw it in the deck for the ride home.

Linz was the leader of the Four Kings, he stood 6 ft 3 in, 195 pounds.   He was 29
years old but could easily pass for 23.   His body was well chiseled compliments of a
five year federal prison bid he did three years ago.   The boy was highly intelligent.
Like A.P, he read everything and was well rounded in several areas.   Although his
presence was intimidating to most, he was the soft hearted one of the group.   Linz was
criminal, but still a Christian.   He found comfort in reading God's word daily and again
before he slept.   His favorite verse was Philippians 4:13.   Linz prayed for this crew
every night, thanking the Lord for keeping watch over them while they were out doing
wrong.   Linz was a sharp dresser, like K.J and A.P, he always looked like he just
stepped out of a magazine.   He kept his hair wavy all around with a temple taper cut.
His cut was always crispy.   His cye wear game was presidential, as was his shoe game.
He wore a platinum link fitted with a diamond encrusted replica of the King of Hearts
card pendant, with matching link bracelet, Ice Tek watch, and one and half carat in each
ear; compliments of a jewelry heist they pulled in Vegas two years ago.

In his spare time, Linz wrote poetry, something he was very good at.   He like to
frequent the open mic and poetry slams around the tri-state area.   He didn't drink or
smoke, and if he did it was champagne on special occasions.   His only addictions were
European cars and dime bitches with pretty feet.   He also had a thing for Lisa Raye,
Halle Berry, and Nia Long.   He had no kids, but wanted one or two.   He had it all it
seemed, but like the others, he had no one to share it with.

Linz drove an '05 Range Rover HSE, cream with rose colored Fendi interior, six 8
inch monitors and three 12 inch subwoofers.   The SUV sat on 24" rose gold Lexani rims
and the windows were rose tinted as well.   He also pushed a black 06" CLS 600 Bra Bus
Edition Mercedes Benz, on 20" Polo rims.   After this mission was over, he hoped to cop
this Aston Martin Vanquish that he had been lusting after for about a year.

If all went as planned, after these eight victims were touched, they should net about
eight to ten million each.   Each member of the crew already had $750,000 a piece put
away in offshore accounts and various banks, which were set up by their good friend Big

Rob.   He was one of the few people that they trusted outside of the crew.

As Ms. Cole sang to him, the woman that he spent the night with came to mind.   He had to admit that Tootie had some good pussy and more.   She definitely met his standards in what he looked for in a woman.   Plan and simple, the bitch was bad!   He wondered if she could be the one for him, the one to complete him.   He pondered on that question as he pulled into the driveway of their flat.   In just a few minutes, Yolanda Adams would be singing him to sleep with her soul shaking gospel music.

CHAPTER SIX

The girls were happy to be back in their own home. Jade was first in the shower, cleansing herself from the sexcapade she had a few hours earlier with K.J. The other three went to change into something more comfortable, getting out of those clothes that the Four Kings gave them to wear.

The place the girls called home was a very large three bedroom, one bath duplex with a basement. The proprietor gave them a discount on the rent because they have been renting for eight years from her. In those eight years the rent was never late, plus Ms. Dewiest took a liking to them, called them her daughters.

Since Diamond and Jade shared a room, they took the biggest of the three bedrooms, while Tootie and Cristal took the remaining two. Each room was lavishly furnished with items from IKEA and Pier 1. The walls were painted in their favorite colors complete with matching wall to wall carpeting. As Jade took her time showering, the others sat in the living room talking about the night before and what possibilities lie ahead.

Cristal admitted that she was really feeling Doug. "Was it good?", Diamond asked. Blushing Cristal said, "We didn't do it yet, but when it goes down I'll let you know." Diamond just shook her head, "You a lying bitch! You mean to tell me you ain't get no dick?" Cristal responded, "I'm being straight up, we ain't fuck, we just laid together." Diamond wasn't going for that, "Whatever hoe, I ain't going for that lie, you need to come up with something better than that.", she said. "Naw, I'm serious, I put that on everything, we didn't do nothing!" Cristal replied. Diamond came clean about her experience with A.P. She bragged about how she came three times, once while sucking his dick, the others while riding him, and that wasn't even her favorite position. She favored getting it from behind in the rifleman stance. Diamond and her sister knew the Kamasutra by heart. Tootie and Cristal knew that the twins did more than share a bedroom together, on some nights you could hear them pleasuring each other. It was no

secret that they owned a lot of sex toys, creams, ect.   Sometimes they bathed together.
The sisters only toyed with each other, they never approached the other girls in that
manner.

While Cristal and Diamond traded sex stories, Tootie sat with a silly look on her
face, lost in her own private thoughts.   "Tootie!   Tootie! Bitch, you hear us calling
you!", Diamond said.   As Tootie snapped back to the present, she looked at them both.
They notice that her eyes began to sparkle.   "What?", she said.   "Damn girl, that
nigga's shit must be like whoa!!   It got you zoning out.", exclaimed Cristal.   Diamond
just laughed, she remembered a time when a nigga had her wide open off the first stroke.

Tootie got up to see if Jade was out of the shower yet, but Diamond grabbed her
around the waist and said, "naw hooker, you ain't getting away that easy!   We want
details, and bitch don't hold nothing back."   Tootie just kept smiling.   "Don't make us
beat that ass!   Details hoe!", Cristal threatened.   "Aight chill, damn you bitches is
trippin.", Tootie said, sitting back down in the over-sized leather chair.   "Naw babe, you
trippin, over that nigga's dick! Get it right bitch!", Cristal shot back.   Jade overhearing
the conversation came in the living room saying, "I got two questions, is it big and can he
really work it like that?"   Tootie said, "I'll tell y'all when I get out the shower.
Diamond responded, Tramp, you gonna tell us now, then take a shower.   I can smell
rank cooch all the way over here."   The girls all laughed while Tootie rubbed herself
then smelled her hand. "Mmm, I do need to wash it cause it's not fresh", then began to
tell them about her sex session.

After a Tootie was done, Cristal said, "I could tell by the way you were acting that
you liked him, that's why I gave him the car, so you could see him again."   "Good
looking out, you was quick on your feet, I like that, I like that!"   Tootie said in her best
Bernie Mac voice.   "He was feeling you too.", Cristal said.   "How you know that, did
he say something to you?" Tootie asked.   "No, I'm just a good judge of character, plus I
can read people." Cristal said.   Standing to go shower, Tootie said, "I hope so, y'all just
don't know I'd slap my momma for another shot of that!"   The girls laughed and Jade
said teasingly, "We can see it's effects on you.   Shit, I might have to try me some of
that."

Tootie turned to Jade and said, "Bitch, don't get killed!", then turned and took her musty ass upstairs to the shower. The girls just laughed harder, they knew that their girl was really feeling this nigga who called himself "The Prezident", or as his boys referred to him as "Linz". Diamond looked at the time and realized that they had forgot to call their mother. Today, September 26, is their mothers birthday, she is 47.

Tootie got out of the shower and dried off slowly, rubbing her body down with coco and shea butter cream. She put in Sylena Johnson and Mary J. Blige cds and let them carry her off to sleep. In her dreams she she replayed the events of last night's rendezvous.

Royce was a rich nigga, a major heroin supplier out of Detroit. The nigga was sitting on some serious change, rumor had it to be about 20-30 million. That's not including the loot he got stashed in overseas accounts or the value of grade A china white that he possessed.

Royce got the name because the young nigga only drove Rolls Royce since the day he got his "L's". At the present time he drove an '06 custom drop top Phantom, along with an '06 hard top Phantom. Both whips sitting on 26 inch chrome Giovanni rims. The kid had cash in major way, he took over for his pops at the age of 15, which was twenty years ago. Royce was also a bitch nigga! His fight game was non-existent, but he didn't need one because he had a slew of real killers on his payroll. This nigga's loot made him a very dangerous man.

The plan was to knock him and his two most trusted soldiers, Ric and Roc. The brothers were responsible for holding his loot in one house and his product in another. Royce was also an arrogant bastard, he got off fucking other nigga's women, especially nigga's with bad bitches and no dough. He'd see you with your girl and if he liked what he saw he'd go holler, didn't give a fuck if you were standing there or not. His favorite line was, "I get what I want, plain and simple" and "I ain't met a bitch I can't fuck yet, my money too long for that!" Plenty of brothers hated Royce, but were too afraid to do anything to him because of his two side kicks. As a result plenty of nigga's shared their women with him. Rumor had it that he loved to eat pussy. The women say that he has a platinum tongue, he could suck a pussy for hours. Now what woman wouldn't want to try that, plus his money was long.

Royce was to be the last hit on the list. It was not out of jealousy that Royce was on the list. It wasn't his status either, in fact, the crew admired him and they respected his gangster, or at least pretended to. Five years ago, Royce fucked up and hollered at the wrong nigga's bitch in the club one night. Don't get it twisted it wasn't because of the broad, although she played a part, it was the blatant disrespect that put Royce on the list. The club was packed that night with wall to wall people. There was plenty of other bitches for Royce to chose from, but true to his nature, Royce wanted to steal this nigga's shine. That nigga swore he would get him back. That nigga was K.J.

The first on the list was this dude named Half-A-Mil. This nigga always bragged that he could put his hands on $500,000 in cash 24 hours a day, 7 days a week, 365 a year. Well his card would be pulled real soon. It was decided that Tootie would be used as bait for this one. Linz wanted to test her gangsta, see if she'd be loyal to the crew and down to ride. He knew that if she came through, then her crew would do the same. Trust was something that had to be earned with the Four Kings. Every name on the intended list was someone who had disrespected someone in the crew in one way or another.

At 5 pm, the crew met up at Linz and Doug's flat. There the list was made out of the eight victims that needed to be touched. Five of the victims were in the greater Pittsburgh area, the other three required the crew to travel to Atlanta, Memphis, and Detroit. They decided to tell the girls what they needed to know as each job came, just in case the plans needed to be changed. Linz was to get with Tootie and arrange for them to all hook up on Thursday to talk over dinner. It could have been done tonight, but K.J had to hook up with his college freak, this Mexican broad named Teresa. He also needed a day to recover from Jade's nympho ass. If he seen her, best believe that there was bound to be some fucking going on. What he didn't know was that she too needed a moment to recoup, her pussy was still sore from this mornings bashing that he handed out. That was the reason why she took so long in the shower, but she'd never tell him or her girls that. She just prayed that he was like most niggas and not call at least for tonight.

As the crew started to count the money in the backpack, Linz called Tootie. "Hello", Tootie answered. "May I speak to Tootie?", he asked. She was happy to be getting this call. Smiling from ear to ear she replied, "This is she, hold on for a minute.", trying to plug her cell phone into the charger so her battery would not die. "Look, my battery is low, so could you call me on the other phone?", she asked, giving him her home number. "Look, I just wanted to know if I could see you tonight?", he stated. "Yes.", she said. He then told her that he'd call back around 7:30 - 8:00 pm. Just as she was saying ok, her phone beeped, then cut off. "Shit!", she screamed, tossing her phone on her bed, but happy that she would be seeing him again tonight.

The total amount of money came to $87,000, including the $10,000 from Lil Mac. They split the money four ways netting $21,750 each. Not bad for three minutes of work. Now it was time to divide the jewelry. It was routine that before they turned it over to their fence they went through and took a few pieces for themselves. It was A.P's turn to go first. He selected a men's Rolex watch, a diamond encrusted bracelet, and a ladies Movado with diamond bezel. Next came K.J, he always took a chain, but this time he also took a few pieces of ladies jewelry also. Then Doug took four items. There were numerous watches, rings, bracelets, and earrings, only a few chains and pendants. Linz selected a woman's Cartier watch and a pair of yellow diamond earrings. It was clear that each of the men had a female in mind when they picked over the spoils. Doug figured that they'd clear over $250,000 for the jewels, as he made the call to Grench, their jewelry guy out in Vegas. The Grench said he would be on the next flight. Grench never second guessed the boys, they only brought him top flight shit. His agreement with the crew was that he would sell it then send them their cut once it was all sold. Grench's word was his bond; he owned a bunch of jewelry stores out west.

The men exchanged hugs and pounds before departing. Linz asked Doug, "What you getting into tonight?" Doug replied, "I'm probably gonna go to Frankie 2's tonight, it's reggae night." Every Tuesday night the club catered to the dreads. Caribbean beats pulsated all night long, the place was always packed beyond the legal limit. "I was thinking of asking Cristal if she wanted to go, she's cool peeps.", he said. "I know she seems real laid back. Did you hit last night?", Linz asked. "Naw, we just vibed and politiced for a while, but I could ." Doug answered, then added, "I'm kinda feeling her.", and stepped off to get dressed.

Linz pulled out his cell and dialed the number that Tootie gave him. Diamond answered on the third ring, "Hello" she said, using her Cuban accent. The twins could switch accents in a heartbeat. "May I speak to Tootie?" Linz asked. "Who dis?" Diamond replied. "Linz" was the response. "Hold on, I'll get her", a few seconds later Tootie was on the line. "Hello?" "You busy tonight?" Linz asked. "No I'm free, why?"she said smiling. "Cause I was wondering if you wanted to go out for a minute, grab something to eat, catch a late show, or something?" he told her. "What time so I can start getting ready?" she replied. "Bout 8:00, I'll come through and swoop you, aight." he stated. "That's cool, you got a pen so I can give you the address, cause you also have our car, remember." she said. "Yeah, go ahead, I'm ready." he replied, as she repeated the address. "Oh! Before I go, tell your girls we gonna link up on Thursday and go over the plans." he said. "Aight, I'll tell them." she stated and then hung up.

CHAPTER SEVEN

Tootie was happy as hell as she told the girls about Thursday's meeting. Then, she went to her closet to pick out something to wear before getting back into the shower. Cristal and Doug made plans to get together as well. Jade was sleeping like a baby and Diamond was on her cell talking to A.P.

Linz checked himself in the mirror, satisfied with what he saw, he grabbed his keys to the Range Rover, told Doug he was out, and bounced. He put his cell on the charger as soon as he got in the Rover and entered Tootie's address into the navigation system. Linz was feeling Ms. Tootie. He cued up Usher's Confessions CD, as he headed to get his new dime piece.

Upon arriving at Tootie's place, Linz parked the Range a few houses down, then walked to her duplex. Diamond answered the door, motioning for Linz to come inside. He liked what he saw, the girl's crib was laced! These hoe's wasn't joking, they shit was tight and well put together. "Have a seat, she'll be down in a minute." Diamond said, then went upstairs to get Tootie. "Girl, that nigga look good! He cleans up nice.", she teased. "That's him? What he got on, and how do I look?", Tootie asked. "Bitch, you tight. Now get down there, shit we got loot to get.", Diamond replied. Tootie peeped herself once again in the full-length mirror before going down to meet Linz.

Linz was speechless as Tootie entered the living room, he rose to greet her, kissing her cheek. He had to step back to take in the full view of her. She was rocking a pair of low-rise Apple Bottom jeans, cuffed at the leg, with matching cropped jacket. A silk caramel brown ladies tank top, with matching Dollhouse 3-inch wedge tie-up sandals. Her hair was parted in the middle with a ponytail on each side. Amber tinted Gucci Aviator shades covered her eyes. Knowing that she had his full attention, she did a half circle, letting him see how the jeans cupped her phatty, asking if he liked. All he could do was nod. Diamond whispered, "Girl, I told you that outfit was banging!", and gave her a high five. "What was all that for?", Linz asked. "Nigga, you know my girl look damn good!" Diamond said. Tootie just smiled because she knew the effect that she had on men, and it was started to show in him.   "Don't pay her no attention, you ready?" she asked.   He said yeah then followed her out the door.   Linz like what he saw, and especially the way her ass jiggled in them jeans.

Once outside she asked, "Where you park at?" "Down there.", he replied, pointing to the SUV.   She was delighted at his choice of truck, and the way the Range was customized.   Once inside, she fell in love with the softness of the leather seats.   Her mind was speeding as he started the truck Sade's "Love Deluxe" filled the cabin.   She reclined the seat back, closed her eyes and let the music take her away while he drove. As "Kiss of Life" started to play she sung along with it, Linz was surprised that she could actually blow.

Even with her eyes closed she could tell he was staring.   After the song ended she asked, "Where we going?"   He said, "I was thinking maybe Dave & Buster's, then hit AVI's After 5"   AVI's was a Jazz, R&B, and spoken word cafe that had live entertainment and held open mic sessions in a laid back atmosphere.   "Is that cool with you?" he asked.   Tootie just nodded her head and said, "Whatever, I'm with you.", and began to take off her jacket.   "Can I ask you something?" she said.   "Yeah, what's up?" he replied.   "About last night, was that a one time thing or what?" she asked.   Linz, feeling like a pimp, calmly stated, "I don't know, we'll just let things happen."   Tootie looked away feeling a little hurt, Linz felt her disappointment and said, "Why, what was you thinking?", rubbing her thigh.   "Nothing, I was just wondering if I was just another one of your bitches, that's all.", she replied looking out the window.   "Babe, it ain't even like that." he said.

After a few minutes passed, Tootie was internally arguing with her heart.   Her mind said "Fuck this nigga!" but her heart and soul said, "No, he's he one, just be patient!" As Mario's "Let me love you" came on, she sung along with it looking directly at him. "So, what you trying to say?" Linz asked.   "Just what the song says, let me love you." she replied.   After a brief pause she continued with, Look, it's no secret that I'm feeling you, trying to get to know you, and be in your world, so just tell me what I gotta do to make that happen.   What, I'm not cute enough or something?   My ass ain't fat enough for you?   Is it because I dance? Because if that's the reason, I'll stop right now if you want me to. I've only been doing it for a couple of months." Looking down at her feet, she felt stupid for letting that come out of her mouth, but it was too late to take it back. What's done is done. That's when she noticed that the flooring of the SUV was made of wood, Brazilian Hickory, just like the inserts in the dash, door panels, and other items inside the truck. Only the floor mats were carpet. Linz knew that Tootie wanted him, and the feeling was mutual. He decided to let her squirm for a few before answering her. "I'm gonna be real with you, you a dime no doubt and I'm really feeling you too, but I just don't trust women too much. About you dancing, if that's what you wanna do, then do you Ma." She turned in her seat to face him and said, "You can trust me." He just smirked and replied, "That's what they all say." Her reply was "I ain't them, at least gimme the chance to earn your trust. I promise I won't betray you." She reached over and brushed a piece of lint out of his hair, running her fingers over his waves a couple of times. Everything was cool until she broke Rule #1: DO NOT TOUCH THE RADIO!! She reached over and turned the volume down. "See you done started tripping already!" he said. "Chill, I'll turn it back up, I wanna tell you something." She then started to sing a verse from an Alicia Keys song, "I won't tell... Your secret's are safe with me.... Just think of me as the pages in your diary..." Linz was impressed, but kept his poker face on.

Dave & Buster's was crowded as usual, so the two headed straight to the arcade. There he gave her $100 and told her to get a card so they could play. As she waited in line, Linz stood by checking her out. Damn, baby girl killing that outfit!", he commented out loud to himself. Some brotha standing next to him said, "You ain't lying, shorty is right, and she got a fat ass!" Linz acting as if he didn't know her said, "Yeah, she do have a fat ass!", agreeing with the young playa next to him.

Tootie sensing several eye's peering her way felt good inside because it was mad dime bitches in the joint and she was stealing everyone's shine. That made her smile, along with the fact that she was there with a very handsome nigga, who was fresh to def in nothing but the best. Linz was rocking a Phat Farm denim hook-up with baby blue Timbs, to match the baby blue and white button down shirt he wore. He also had his Ice-Tek Chronograph with the diamond bezel. What she didn't like was the way this pretty little waitress was all up in her man's grill. He may not have technically been her man yet, but if things went her way he would be.   But anyway, this bitch was all up in his grill like a dentist and she didn't like that.

Natalie was a female that Linz gave the dick to every now and then.   Nat was fine, but she had some major issues and was ghetto as hell.   Linz felt that she was too much to deal with on a regular basis.   Plus, him and her were just bed buddies, no strings attached, that's how she wanted it, which was cool with him.

"Hey Stranger!   I ain't seen you in a long time.", she said.   "I've been chillin, what's good with you?", he asked.   "Shit, same ol', same ol', you know how it is." she said, stepping in to embrace him.   He was kind of hesitant.   "Oh, I can't get a hug?   I see how it is, it's cool for you to come fuck the hell out of me a few weeks ago, but now I can't get a hug.   Nigga stop playing!" she said while embracing him and kissing his cheek.   That's another thing that he liked about Nat, she had the softest lips in the country.   They felt good where ever she put them.   "I need to see you soon, so call me.", she whispered before breaking the embrace.   "Aight", Linz said giving her a squeeze and a tap on the ass before letting go.

Tootie was hot when she saw what transpired between Linz and Natalie, but she played her part.   When she finally got her game card, Nat was gone.   Linz and Tootie played all kinds of games, they even sat in the photo booth together.   She like being in his company.   They took turns beating each other in several different fighting games, especially Tekken 3, which Tootie was really animated in.   She took her anger out on him in the game, wishing that she could slap him for real.   After about two hours she used the last ten credits on the Simon Say's dance machine.   On this game you have to step on all these colored blocks that the screen tells you to.   She was good at it, a lot of nigga's came just to watch her ass and titties bounce.   Linz was feeling good, he knew that a lot of nigga's was lusting for Tootie.   He had to brush his shoulders off because he was truly feeling something like a P.I.M.P!

Linz stepped away to holla at a young playa he knew from way back in the days when he used to flood blocks with crack.   "What up Rello?", Linz asked.   "Oh shit, W-W-What's up Linz?, Rell said, as they exchanged pounds.   After some small talk, making sure his girl wasn't in hearing range, Rell said, "L-L-Linz, she hurting em!", pointing at Tootie.   Linz said, "I know."   "W-W-What would you do with that?, Rello asked.   Linz smiled and said, "I already did that.", then called Tootie over to where he was standing.   There was several females peepin Linz.   The boy was shining, you can tell he had a few chips.   Natalie was one of his groupies.   She wanted a piece of him tonight also.   She went over to holla at him once more to put her bid in for tonight. Her hopes were crushed because two seconds after she got there, Tootie slid over and put her arms around his waist and asked, "What's up boo?" kissing him lightly on the lips which caught him off guard.   She smiled and watched Natalie's face crack, as she walked away steaming.   After Linz introduced Tootie to Rell, he said" L-Linz where you find her at? She a dime."   Tootie smiled and said, "thank you".   Rell openly admired her, while some hoe's threw shade and looks of hate her way.

After talking with Rell, Linz asked Tootie if she was ready to eat, which she was. The girl was starving.   Once they were seated, Tootie saw Natalie go into the ladies room.   She excused herself and followed Nat.   She didn't know who this woman was or what she was to Linz, but she planned on finding out.   She entered the restroom and found it empty except for Nat, who was at the sink washing her hands.   Tootie approached her, not knowing what to expect, and said, "Stay the fuck away from my man, or our next conversation will not be so friendly.'   She then blew a kiss at Natalie, turned and left.   Natalie just stood there shocked, with a "No this bitch didn't" expression on her face.   When Tootie arrived back at the table, they ordered and engaged in small talk until the food came.   Once they finished eating, they left.

CHAPTER EIGHT

On the way to AVI's, Doug called and told Linz he was bringing Cristal to the house tonight, giving Linz a heads up that he'd be having company.   It's something that they always did if they were having a female over, not that they had to do that, it was just a thing between them two.   Tootie was feeling mighty comfortable now, looking in the glove compartment, being nosey, and came across his well worn Bible.   She cast a glance at him.   Before she could comment he said, "Yes, I read the Bible daily.   I place my trust in God's hands.   It's only fitting with the stuff I do and go through."   She was learning more about this man with every hour that passed.   She too believed in God, but hasn't read her word in a minute.   She told him to read Ecclesiatics 4:9-12, she then closed the glove box and relaxed as Maxwell's "Whenever, Whatever, Wherever" played, letting the bass from the three 12 inch woofers massage her back.

As they entered the cafe, an up-beat tune by Kindred greeted them.   Tootie had never been to AVI's, in fact, she had never even heard of the place, but she was truly digging the scene.   Tonight was open mic night, Horace, the jazz band's saxist, had asked Linz if he was going to bless them with some lyric's tonight.   Linz nodded in agreement.

The two found a couch in the sitting area.   This is a spot where you could chill on one of the twelve couches that were set up like a giant living room.   The soft lighting and scented candles were provided to enhance the mood, as the neo-soul sound of Floetry caressed the patron's ears.   As the song ended, the M.C. announced that the mic was open.   Tootie sat with her shoes off, feet curled up on the soft crushed velvet couch as her and Linz conversed.   After a few applause a woman took the mic and began to lace the crowd with her poetic wisdom.   The band strummed softly behind her intensifying her words leaving the listener's suspended on each one.   Tootie was mystified, this was a whole new world to her.   The spoke word movement was deep.

"When are you going up there?", she teased, not knowing that Linz was good at this. He said, "If I go, you go."   "I don't know how to do poetry!", she shot back.   "So sing, you did all that singing in the car." he stated. "That was just for you.", she said. "You said that you'd do whatever, and this is what I want.", Linz said putting her on the spot. He then got up leaving her on the couch to ponder his words. As he took the stage, a few applause's sounded. Linz gave a pound to the M.C. as he took the mic, then turning to his boy Horace, he said, "Gimme something silky". As Horace began to blow, making the saxophone sing, the cello player chimed in with its deep soothing bass, hypnotizing the crowd as Linz began to speak. The piece he recited was a new one that he'd been working on entitled "She sang a beautiful melody". He strode toward Tootie with the mic in one hand, putting her in the light as he spit words of wisdom:

Her voice was soft as silk
Almond complexion
Exotically and Erotically
Built,
Legs as long as the day
With a smile and stare
As piercing as the sun's ray
"She sang a beautiful melody"

As she opened her mouth words of love
And seduction flowed
Not only from her lips
But
Also from her hips

Pulses quickened
Hearts skipped beats
Throats went dry
As she brought the heat
"She sang a beautiful melody"

The song was passion
The tempo was lust!
As every man sought
The privilege of
Thrust!
Thrusting deep into her world
Exploring her inner most parts
Possessing her body,
But
Forgetting her heart

"She sang a beautiful melody"

Caught up in their
Owns desires
Never thinking the clock
Would expire
Or
They being Mandingo!
Would tire
But someone did....
It was her,
Tired of being used,
Tired of being abused,
Tired of being broken,
Treated not as a person,
But
As a token.
Worn on someone's arm,
Like a bracelet or charm
Often lost
Only to be found
And lost again
Picked up and discarded by
Many men!
As she says to herself
"Lord! Where does it end!"
She tilts her head
Looks above,
Cried out "FATHER! I just wanna
Be loved!"

As Linz began to walk away, Tootie screamed, "Do another one!" with a smile as the crowd blended in with her chanting "One more!". Linz, not one to disappoint, agreed to do another. He called this next piece "Ode 2 Black Women"

He apologized to the few white females that was in the crowd, they accepted by saying, "Speak on Brotha!". The few white women were there with black men anyway. Linz dedicated this to all the sista's in the club from all the brotha's, as he handed Tootie his jacket and began to flow:

You come in all shapes & sizes
Available in many different flavors,
From butter pecan, to sexy chocolate.
Your hair,
Long or short,
Nappy or straight
Braided or curled
Is like no other.
Your face is the canvas
That GOD painted
Beautiful!
With sparkling eye's
Full lips
Enticing smiles
That attracts 1000's
Of brotha's.
All this wonder
Sits atop
Your neck
Gracefully on display
Standing tall & strong
Like a tower,
Your breast
Yield strong sexual
Power.
They entice & excite
Like the pull of
The tide
In the midnight
Hour.
Those hips,
Slender or full
Dance & swing
Beautifully
When you walk...
Your butt...
Mmm.mmmmm
I don't care if it's tha'
Classic onion shape
Which brings tears to our eyes
Or
If it's the twin of those
Tears we cry!
Sometimes it's formed
Like the delicious, mouth watering

Apple!
Dubbed the Apple Bottom!
75% of y'all got
Em'
Legs as long as tha' day
Smooth & silky
Yet uniquely toned
Sometimes bare for all to see
Or
Covered in skirts, capri's, shorts, & jeans
Mules or sandals
Pumps or sneaks
All this founded
On 2 beautiful feet
LORD!
This has got me in a
Zone
This masterpiece,
Created by you
Of flesh & bone!

Tootie was mesmerized at his ability to weave words into poetic fashion. This man was nothing she'd ever experienced before. Her heart said, "I told you he was the one!" After Linz finished, he returned to where she was sitting, she was all smiles. "Your turn", he said taking his seat. She told him that she was nervous, but he did not care. He told her, "If you freeze up on something like this, just imagine what will happen when it comes time to handle this business." "But that's different.", she protested. "No, it's not. Look I ain't going to beg you to go up there, just know that your word means nothing to me.", Linz said with a tinge of attitude. Tootie remembered her promise and what was on the line, "Okay, you got me, but don't laugh!" She'd never done this before in front of so many people, but she was about to give it her all. She would prove that she could handle the pressure.

As she got up to fulfill his request, he playfully tapped her on her ass, causing it to jiggle and her to smile. He loved the way her cheeks shook in those jeans. Tootie was a nervous wreck when she took the mic. Her voice cracked as she whispered to Horace what to play. Taking a sip of water, she closed her eyes and blew a rendition of Rose Royce's classic hit from the Car Wash soundtrack, "Get Next to You". After overcoming her fears, she followed up with a sultry version of Vivian Green's

"Emotional Roller Coaster". The crowd loved her, Linz was truly impressed, and he could not wait to have her singing in his bed tonight.

Doug and Cristal were busy on the floor with the rest of the Rasta's as the selecta spinned Sean Paul's "Like Glue" blended with his "Shake dat 'ting/Duty Rock mix." Doug, true to his nature, sported a mustard colored Coogi sweatsuit with matching Timbs. He was laced with ice on his neck and wrists, the kid was right! Cristal, not to be out done, was looking tasty in skin tight Request Jeans, and a hot pink baby t-shirt with "GOT MILK?" airbrushed on the front, She sported a pair of pink and white Nike Air Max Shox's. Doug and Cristal was mashing it up with the other yute's.

The air in Frankie's was hot and sticky and smelled thick of sweat and curry chicken. The crowd began to "Pon Da River" and "Signal the Plane", as Sean Paul instructed. "REWIND!!", the Selecta screamed, as Macka Diamonds "Tek-Con" got the rude girls winding something fierce. Then he spun Richie Spice's "Youths so Cold, Blood Again, and Earth Run Red", then hit em' with a Benie Man's & Mya's hit song "Angel", as the Selecta slowed things down.

Doug grabbed Cristal from behind, as her body bucked and swayed to the rhythm. Her nipples were rock hard as Doug ran his hands up and down her sweat soaked t-shirt that clung to her body like a second skin. She was having a good time. It had been a minute since she had been out, except dancing at the bar, which she was tired of. It wasn't like they needed the money, the girls did ok doing their thing with the credit card and ID shit. Matter of fact, the dancing gig started off as a joke just to see if they could do it. They got a kick outta watching niggas trick cash in the club on girls thinking they was about to fuck. Now some of the other dancers were just as fine and got down like that, but these four didn't fuck around, especially with niggas who tricked off in the club they worked at. Cristal was letting herself go tonight, she ain't had no dick in like four months. Her pussy was dripping wet right now, and if the night kept going like it was Doug would be her sweet relief. She was truly digging this tall, lanky dude who rarely said anything. She told him on the way over to the club that he was too cool for her.

Across town, Diamond and A.P were in Blockbuster on Copley Road picking movies. A.P chose a foreign flick titled "City of God", while Diamond went for the comedy "Friday After Next". The two just decided to stay in tonight, instead of running the streets and club hopping.   Diamond wanted to be with A.P in a more quite and romantic setting.   She called her twin and told her that she would be spending the night with A.P at his place.   After several minutes of laughter and joking, she ended the call with her sister.   "Can we stop at the store on the way to your place, I gotta grab a few items?", she asked.   "Sure", he replied, pulling into the Giant Eagle.   There she bought a toothbrush, a fruit salad, and some fresh strawberries.   This girl loved fruit.

Once back at A.P's house, Diamond was shocked at the decor of the men's place. African art and figurines splashed the walls and adorned the coffee and end tables. Bone white Italian leather furniture provided the seating, in sharp contrast to the coffee colored carpeting, which was so thick her Manolo's didn't stand a chance.   Inside the door was a 5 foot half circle of hard wood pine flooring, she left her shoes there along with A.P's then headed over to the cozy little kitchen.   Diamond was dressed rather casual in a sleeveless turtleneck and plaid Burberry slacks.   She had her hair pulled back in a ponytail.   A.P loved the sight of what stood in front of him.   While she prepared the fruit salad, he got the movies ready.   "Hey Boo, you got a t-shirt or jersey that I can change into?", she asked, wanting to get a little more comfortable.   A.P went to his bedroom and returned with a 2X t-shirt for her to put on and then showed her the bathroom.

After changing, the two got cozy on the chaise lounge and began to watch the movies.   Diamond was making it hard for him to watch the movie, she kept grinding her ass against his manhood, sucking his fingers, and whispering nasty things to him in Spanish and Japanese.

As he began to run his hands under the shirt she wore, he discovered that it was the only clothing that she wore.   Her nipples perked at his touch, she closed her eyes and cooed, "Stop, let me watch the rest of the movie".   She had started it and A.P intended on finishing it.   "Damn!   Babe, you just going to leave me hanging like this?", pointing down to his fully erect penis.   She put her finger to his lips, "Ssssshhh.... I'll take care of him later.   I promise, he'll get my full attention.", she said smiling.   Then she placed his hands between her freshly shaven legs, against her warm pussy which was also freshly shaved, letting him feel it's slickness.   "Are you gonna take care of me?", she asked.   A.P knew what she wanted, Diamond wanted him to eat her pussy.   He didn't have a problem with that, in fact, he was itching to see what she taste like, but he'd never let her double scoop of rice and bean eating ass know it. So, he played like he didn't hear her. "Aight, act like you didn't hear me if you want to.", she said, repositioning her ass away from him and removing his hand from her dripping wet poo-poo. He wiped the juices on her leg, "Eeeewwww!!", she screamed, "Don't be wiping it on me!" "It's yours", he replied. "So what you made it wet", then gave him her sexiest look saying, "Taste it, I'm delicious." Then she stuck her finger in her pussy and licked it. A.P said, "You a freak!" She replied, "I'll do whatever to please my man, will that be a problem with you if you happen to be that nigga?" A.P just shook his head no.

K.J sat in Originals, the college hangout with Teresa. They discussed a few things that were bothering her, but his mind wasn't there, his thoughts were on Jade. He found it odd that he could not get her out of his system. Damn, the pussy was good as hell, but it was not supposed to be happening like this or to him. Teresa had no idea that after tonight he was done fucking with her for a while. He had to get his head on straight. He purposed a major plan and everyone was counting on it to fall through smoothly. The crew respected each others opinions and ideas. Even though Linz was the head of the group, they all played a role in the leadership and direction of the path the crew took

CHAPTER NINE

"Was that good enough for you?", Tootie asked sitting down next to him. Linz responded, "I ain't about to hate, you did your thing." She like the props that he gave and was smiling from ear to ear, she was feeling good inside. A waitress came over and offered them a drink, compliments of the house. He had a amaretto sour, she had a blue motorcycle. The couple exchanged small talk while waiting on their drinks. "You gonna bring me back here?", she asked. "Why, you like this spot?", he responded. "Yeah, it's different from the other clubs, it's mellow and laid back.", she replied sliding into his lap. With her face buried into his neck inhaling his scent she said, "Boo, you smell good, what is it?" "Polo Black", he replied. "I like it", she said in between kisses so soft he barely felt them, "Are you going to spend the night with me?" she asked. When he didn't answer she rubbed his chest and said, "Did you hear me?" "Yes, I heard you." he replied. "Well you ain't saying nothing, are you gonna stay with me tonight?" He nodded, "You gonna give me a private dance if I do?" he asked. "Sure and something else to go with it!", she replied in a whisper, as Jaguar Wright's voice seeped through the cafe's sound system.

"Your place or mine?", Tootie asked as they waited on the valet to bring the Range Rover around. "Yours", Linz said letting Doug have the crib to himself. It was several good looking couples out tonight. I could get use to this, she thought. When their truck came Linz opened the door for her like a true gentleman, tonight they were both shining.

Linz was feeling good on the way back to her place. The mood for sex was already set, so he took his time getting her home. For the ride, he threw in Jay-Z's "Blueprint: CD, increased the volume, smashed the gas, and was out. He and Tootie sang the lyric's word for word. How gangsta is that?

The two were in good spirits when they pulled up in front of her duplex, laughing and playing. He discovered that not only was Tootie fine as hell, but she was just as cool to hang out with, and had some good pussy. This was one night that he'd truly enjoy, because after Thursday it was strictly business. They had cash to get!   Making sure that Tootie and her girls were down to do whatever was essential, Linz planned on putting his thang down tonight.

As soon as they entered the house, she tossed her keys in the bowl at the front door, grabbed his hand and led him upstairs.   Her game plan was to put it on him something strong tonight.   Linz followed her upstairs as she showed him her room.

A queen size bed lay lavishly on one side of the room, the walls were mirrored as well as the ceiling.   The carpet was deep lavender color with curtains to match.   The bedding was just a shade lighter, but the same hue of lavender.   The dresser and vanity were made of burl wood.   A white leather casting couch sat in the corner, and a 36 inch plasma screen adorned the wall, with a stereo system tucked into the opposite corner. She kicked her shoes off and fell on the bed.   Linz sat on the edge taking it all in.

"It's 1:45 am already!", she said   "Why you got something to do in the morning?", he replied.   She smiled and said, "You!"   Then asked, "You staying for breakfast?" "Why? You cooking?", he asked.   "For you I am", she said and started toward the shower.   Stopping in the doorway she turned and said, "Have them pants off by the time I get back" and left for the shower.   While Linz just stared and mumbled, "She's Wild!"

Linz looked around her room and spent time going through her cd's instead of doing what she told him to do.   She had about 300 cd's piled on the floor next to her stereo. That was the only thing out of order.   He took his Timbs off and relaxed on the floor while looking for something to carry out the mood of what was about to go down in bed..

Tootie came in quietly wrapped only in a towel, still dripping with water, her unrestrained hair and moist, "You don't listen do you?   I see I am going to have to teach you some act right, huh?"   He turned around and saw her standing there, he got to his feet to help her dry off.   As he came close, she kissed him passionately full on the lips, sucking his tongue deep into her mouth.   He pulled her closer to him, feeling her body through the towel.   She broke the kiss, stepped back, and said, " Now drop em!", as she sat down on the bed watching him remove his clothes.   As she dried her hair, she asked him to rub her down with coco butter.   She turned over on her stomach stretching out across the bed.   Linz, now ass naked, pulled the towel off and began to gently massage the coco butter cream into her skin.   Leaving a trail of kisses down her spine, he caused her to wiggle as he licked and kissed at the base of her neck, down to her ass. He kneaded her back with his skilled hands. She wondered how many other bitches got this from him, and how could she keep them from getting it again.

As his hand gently caressed her ass cheeks, he placed a kiss on each one. Then he continued to massage and kiss first down her left leg, then back up her right. Spreading her pussy lips with his thumbs, he blew on her sex. Her body shook as his breeze touched her skin. He playfully tapped her ass and said, "turn over", and began on the front. First kissing her forehead, then eyelids, then on to her nose, lips, and neck. He continued down to her breasts taking his time on each nipple, all while massaging her still. He continued on down her stomach, licking her navel, running his hands over her perfectly trimmed pussy. Then resumed the kissing and licking down each leg. He stopped to suck on each of her pretty little toes. She began to get even wetter as his tongue tickled her toes. As her eyes rolled, she moaned and cooed.

He did something that she did not expect, taking one for the team and cause, he began to slowly caress the insides of her vagina with his tongue. Her back arched and bucked as her hands gripped his head. MMMMMM.....OOOOO....HHHHHH....SSSSSMMMMMMM was all that she could do, as her mind raced 100 mph. He had launched a counter attack before she even got a chance to put it on him. He was getting the best of her.

The tongue lashing lasted 20 minutes, she came twice and her eye's were glossy. She said, "Whew, that was the bomb!", while fanning herself. He just sat back and smiled. She cuddled up next to him, stroking his penis, while recovering from the oral assault her pussy just received. She began to kiss his chest, making her way down to his penis. As she ran her tongue across the tip of his erect member, he ran his fingers through her hair. Her tongue swirled around his penis, up one side and down the other she teased. Opening wide, she took all eight inches insider her warm mouth, relaxing her throat slowly going up and down his shaft. Her mouth felt good, Linz was truly enjoying this good pussy and good head. Tootie was the total package! He'd keep this one for a while, he thought.

Tootie was starting to enjoy giving head, it was something that she rarely did but now she was turned on by the way his dick felt in her mouth. She wanted to taste his cum, but didn't want him to think slutty of her.   Kuan and Kuo told her, "Unless he cums, you ain't doing shit!", and they were experts.   She had to think of a way to allow him to cum in her mouth and still keep her respect.

Linz was ready to explode, but didn't want to offend her by cumming in her mouth without asking.   "Baby, if you keep this up I'm gonna cum early.", he warned.   "Go ahead, as long as you get it back hard!", she replied and continued sucking.   He couldn't hold back no longer, he let out a growl then filled her mouth with his soul.   She began to choke as cum shot down her throat, but she held his dick firmly between her lips, taking every drop.   She then got up to wash her mouth, while Linz lay there dazed, but still hard.

She returned, mouth smelling minty fresh.   "Do you need a minute or two, because I'm ready.", she said, caressing herself.   "Naw, I'm straight.", he said reaching for her butt.   She stopped him saying, "I wanna ride first, you just sit back and relax for a minute."   She straddled him slowly rocking back and forth in a circular motion.   The feeling of him bareback inside her was overwhelming.   Her walls was getting touch with every rotation.   She'd surely have another orgasm.   This would be her third time in her life having an orgasm while have actual intercourse, and all three times was by the same man.

As the night wore on, they went through many position.   He'd fucked her silly and she loved every stroke.   It ended with him filling her with sperm 3 1/2 hours later. Linz couldn't deny the fact that Tootie's pussy was super, and that he was starting to get addicted.   She knew her pussy would be sore in the morning, but it was a soreness that was gladly welcomed by her, as she lay spent and smiling in his arms.

PHASE   2

TODAY'S AGENDA

"LET'$ GET THIS

MONEY!"

CHAPTER TEN

Thursday came fast, today was the meeting day for the crew. The girls were anxious to know who the victims were and how much money they'd get out of the deal. The girls made a pact to send some to their mothers and to take a vacation together. First they would go to Bali, then Milan and last London. They wanted to see the world. A million thoughts went through their minds after getting the call to be at Don Pablo's in Robinson Township at 6:30 pm.

The twins, Kuan and Kuo wanted to send their mother on a trip to her homeland to visit her relatives. Camille, would do something nice for her Aunt Tracey, the woman who raised her. Tracey did all she could for her only niece. Camille never forgot that. After this was over, she'd hopefully be able to get her out of the hood to a better place. Maybe a house of her own somewhere in Bexley. Toychica also planned on buying her mom a home and herself a car. The girls tossed around many different "Imma does", but these were the most important to them. Each of the ladies toyed with the idea of getting their own place, but didn't want to live alone. They'd hoped that the men they were with developed into something serious and stable. They all longed to be loved, to truly belong to someone.

Doug met Mike Blair (a.k.a Half a Mil) through a kid he worked with several years ago named Phil. He told Phil that Mike was a snake, he could see it in the way he talked, always trying to get over. One day, Phil let Mike use his car to go some place with his girl. Phil worked hard for that Honda, but was fooled by Mike's sneaky ass. Mike used the car to make a drug run and left some drugs in the car by accident. Two days after getting his car back, Phil gets pulled over for speeding. A search was done turning up 2 ounces of cocaine. Mike didn't even help with an attorney or bond. He left Phil for dead. He told Phil "I ain't got no money", just straight played the lil dude! Doug swore to his friend that he'd get Mike back. Phil lost his car and his freedom for eight years to the Feds. He has two more years to go. Doug didn't like the way Mike did his friend, and that's why Half a Mil was on the list. Doug would make sure that he suffered like Phil did, but longer. Mike had no clue that in a few short weeks his freedom would be snatched away from him, if not his life.

As the others spent time gathering the needed personal info on Half a Mil to give to the girls, Doug wrote his former co-worker and friend who was locked down in Kentucky. He told him that he hasn't forgot about him and that Half a Mil might come his way soon. He threw in a couple of photos and a $200 dollar money order. He told him to stay safe. He got something for him when he touches down. Doug also promised to go see Phil's mom and baby momma for him. Doug was the friend that most people on lock down wish they had in their corner.

By 6:45pm everyone was at the meeting spot. Diamond and Jade was looking good. They turned every head in the joint. The sisters both wore a gold, backless, silk Asian print jumpsuit with matching Vera Wang pumps. They were going to Chauncey's afterward. The Def Jam Comedy Tour was in town. Cristal and Tootie held their own too, but more casual. The discussion took place after they all ate. "Alright, this is how this one is gonna go down.", Linz said, passing Tootie a photo of Half a Mil and the car he drove. All she had to do was find out where he rested his head. "Tootie, your up first.", he told her. She nodded, OK but the look in her eyes told a different story that everybody caught. "What's up girl? You alright?", Cristal asked. "Yeah, I'm cool", she replied. As they continued, they told the girls that they'll move on to the next victim after this one's complete. Diamond looked at the photo of Half a Mil and stated, "I know him, he's a sucka. Tootie you got an easy one!" They spoke some more about Half a Mil, then the convo switched to how much they was gonna get paid. "How about a 40/60 split?", Tootie suggested. "That's cool, but after the first four it will be a 50/50 split.", Linz said. "How many vics in total?", Jade wanted to know.. "Eight, but it's not an overnight thing. The last four will take time and planning They are sitting on major change. I'm talking a couple million. The first four is just practice. Y'all need to let us know now if y'all down for the long haul. If your not, then bounce now. But, if your down, your gonna get rich.", K.J said. Tootie looked at Linz and said, "I'm trusting you with my life and my girls as well. That goes for all of you! We know the code of the streets, our lips are sealed, just take care of us." They went over the plan again while waiting on dessert. Shortly after they got up to leave. A.P said, "Y'all take care of the tip, I got the bill."

Outside in the parking lot, the crew stood in the brisk September air talking. Jade was asking K.J why he hadn't called her since Tuesday morning and wanted to see him tonight if possible. Cristal and Tootie stood by their car having a private talk. A.P said, "Linz, I think something's wrong with your girl. Did you see the way she looked when you told her she was up first?" Yeah, I peeped that.", he replied. "You need to go see what's up. We don't need no misunderstandings or sudden surprises because once we start, ain't no turning back. You heard me?", Doug stated coldly. The look Doug gave told him he was serious. "Damn Nigga, calm down, I'll holla at her.", Linz said. "Man, this one is personal Bro. I need her to come through.", Doug shot back. As he explained why he picked Half a Mil to be on the list.

A few minutes later, Cristal came over to where the men were standing. "Linz, let me holla at you for a minute.", she said. As the two stepped off to the back of Doug's Acura, Linz said, "What's up?" "I know that you caught the look that my girl gave when you told her she was first right?" Linz nodded. "Well she down to ride til the end, she just don't want to be the one getting played in the end. She really likes you. I'm telling you that bitch is crazy about you! The other thing is, when we first moved here, about eight years ago, she used to fuck Half a Mil on the low-low for a couple of months. He was just broke ass Mike Blair, I guess he done came up. Anyway, she won't have no problem with getting next to him. She ain't seen him since she caught him with some bitch he got pregnant. That was back in 98 or 99. Look, we are counting on this caper too. You don't know how much we want this, but if she ain't comfortable, then we ain't. So Bro, make her feel at ease. If you do that, she'll go all out for you." Linz said, "I feel you". "Promise me you won't play my girl. I don't wanna come holla at you on some other shit.", Cristal stated.

None of the girls knew that Tootie even knew Half a Mil, let alone fucked him. Diamond just knew him from seeing him at all the premier night spots and from hearing his name on the streets. But she never would figure him to have screwed her girl, he wasn't her type. Although he was cute, he was short and pudgy. She went for the tall and slim with a little build to em type of men. Plus he was ignorant as hell. It flipped her wig when Cristal told her and Jade. Tootie felt awkward as Linz came towards her. Looking down at her Manolo Timbs, hands shoved deep in her jacket pockets she asked,

"So, what happens now?" Avoiding her question he asked, "You alright?", with a look of genuine concern. "Yeah I'm cool, I was just shocked when I found out I was first and who the first vic was. But I'm still down to do it though. Did Cristal tell you the rest of what we talked about?" "Yeah she told me.", Linz said while pulling her close to him. "Just promise me you won't play me when this is all done, alright.", she said snuggling into his embrace. "I won't Boo, my word is my bond." Using reverse psychology he continued, "If you don't feel comfortable, you don't have to do it." After a couple seconds Tootie said, "Naw I'm cool, I can handle this. I know how much my girls is counting on this whole thing to fall through. I won't let you down. But, if anything goes wrong please don't leave me hanging out there." Linz kissed her forehead saying "I ain't gonna let nothing happen to my future." Tootie knew it was all just game just to gas her up. She smiled because it felt good to hear that come out of his mouth. Plus, it could happen. If things went her way, it would definitely happen. "What if I gotta fuck him and stuff?", she asked. "Do what you gotta do, I know who this pussy belongs to.", he responded with a smile, tapping her on the ass for added emphasis. More gas, Tootie thought, but she went for it and loved hearing it. "You must think you a pimp huh?", she said smiling. "No, I ain't no pimp, just something like a pimp.", he shot back. She playfully jabbed him in the ribs. Cristal walked over asking, "Is everything 100 with y'all?" Tootie answered, "I'm cool now." Then she turned to Linz and said, "I'll call you when I get in tonight."

CHAPTER ELEVEN

The comedy show was packed, ballers and ballettes were out in full force tonight. Everybody who was anybody was there. The girls were looking good. Tootie had on a scarlet and gray Coogi sweater skirt outfit with scarlet Manolo Timbs and Chloe shades. Cristal looked sexy in a tight fitting, custom, purple crochet bell bottom pants and halter outfit with matching five inch heels and fedora. Her hair and nails were freshly done by Robyn Geer's Hair on the Square, and she topped her look off with a pair of D&G shades.

As Mike Epps took the stage, the crowd went crazy. He didn't waste no time cutting into some of the audience. The place was alive with laughter. That's when Diamond seen him, she recognized him from the photo. That sorry ass, Anthony Anderson look a like known as Half a Mil was four rows to the left of them chilling with one of his boys. She tapped Tootie and pointed in his direction. Her gaze followed Diamond's finger until she had seen him. She couldn't believe it was him, but she knew it was. She told her girls, "I'm going to say hi". Cristal stopped her, "Toot, you cool with this?". Jade chimed in, "Don't lose focus, if you can't do it I'll go." "Naw I'm cool, but thanks though. I got this.", Tootie said. "Plus, I know y'all counting on me to set it off.", with that she got up to go say hello.

Mike Blair a.k.a Half a Mil, was no longer a broke ass nigga, he was now a hood rich nigga. He pushed a customized Black Hummer with 28" chrome rims, and rocked frozen jewels. He always bragged that he could put his hands on $500,000 or more any time of the day or night. So that meant the loot was in a house not a bank.

As he sat laughing with his boy, Tootie tapped him on the shoulder. He turned shocked at who and what he saw. "I thought that was you I seen at the bar earlier.", she said before he opened his mouth. "Damn Boo, its been a minute since I seen you.", he said. Tootie just smiled. "You looking good, damn good. Ya nigga let you out like this?", he teased. Meanwhile, he was checking her out from head to toe. She modeled for him, turning around from him to see all of her. Tootie saw the thirsty look in his eyes. "Don't no nigga tell me what to do!", she said with attitude. Half a Mil laughed and said, "You still feisty as hell, I see. I'm just keeping it real." "I don't have a man and if I did he wouldn't tell me what I can and can't do.", she stated. Mike's mind back pedaled to when he use to crack that. She was only about 18 or 19, with just a pretty face and a beginner's body. Now seven years later, here stood a goddess. He was hoping like hell he'd get a chance to crack it again. "Can a nigga get a hug?", he asked. Thinking about the conversation she had with her soon to be man, Linz, she decided it was all good and let him hug her. She knew it was a ploy to cop a cheap feel. Tootie wasn't slow, her street smarts was razor sharp. If it wasn't for the sake of the team and plan, she would have cussed his stupid pudgy ass out royally. Half a Mil's hands roamed up and down her back, cupping her ass on the sly. She pulled away saying, "Well, I just came to say hello, I gotta get back to my girls.", pointing to her crew. "Have a drink with me before you bounce. I'm sure they won't mind if I steal you away for a few minutes.", he said. Tootie knew that she had him. The sooner she got done with this, the sooner she'd be back in Linz's arms. He did call her his future, so she promised Mike that she'd have a drink with him when the show was over and rejoined her entourage.

As soon as she sat down, the girls fired questions. She answered them all. Diamond said, "I knew you'd handle your b.i, you was just nervous that's all." As they all gave her props, Tootie felt good knowing it was almost over. Linz assured her that he will still fuck with her after all this was over. She was still gassed that he called her his "future", and giggled shyly to herself. She took out her cell, dialed Linz, and told him what went down. Linz was delighted and told her to have Cristal drop her off at his place after they left the club.

Half a Mil sat thinking about Tootie the rest of the show and how he could get some of that. He figured that like the rest of the females she'd be impressed with his money, cars, and other material items. What he didn't know was her eyes was on one man. All the others were just a blur to her. As the show came to a close, the staff began to remove the folding chairs off the dance floor to transform it back into the night club essence. He sent a waitress over to take her girls drink orders and word for Tootie to meet him in his booth in the V.I.P area where he had a bottle of Cristal on ice. Half a

Mil was worth a little over $700,000 so he splurged often.

Tootie told her girls to wait a couple of minutes, and drink up, drinks were on him. Diamond took out her cell, snapped a photo, and sent it to A.P who just walked in with K.J. The men seen them but acted like they didn't know them.

Tootie joined Half a Mil in his booth. He stood as she entered. They exchanged small talk, he asked what she'd been up to lately and the other usual questions. She informed him that she was doing good and a bunch of other b.s before asking about his baby momma. "You still mad, huh!", he asked. "Babe, I ain't even with her no more. Listen, I have changed, I should have never let you go.", he said as he held her hand. "I ain't mad, I been past that, but you did fuck up letting me go though.", she said playing along with him. "Let me make it up to you.", he said. "I don't know Mike, you got all these women, I ain't tryna get caught up in no bullshit! Plus, I'm cool being single right now." He said, "Look, we can just be friends aight, just hang out and shit. Don't worry about them other hoes. You killing them." "I'll think about it.", she said. "Well, it's been nice seeing you again, maybe I'll see you some place else, who knows", she said getting up to leave.

"Here, call me anytime.", he said writing his number down to give to her. She accepted the paper and gave him a kiss on his cheek, letting him feel her up briefly. Half a Mil didn't even know he was getting played, he thought he was game tight. "Well, I'll call you sometime.", she whispered breaking the embrace. Mike grabbed his dick, as he watched her walk away. "I gotta hit that again! Damn, she turned out to be a star!", he said to his boy.

Tootie knew that Mike was watching her, so she switched a little extra for him. She was pretending Mike was Linz watching her backside. As she joined her girls, she saw A.P and K.J shooting a game of pool and flirting at some females. She searched the twin's faces for signs of drama, but the girls were cool. "What's up with them?", Tootie asked pointing to the fellas. "They doing them. We already spoke with them. We're gonna hook up later. Right now we are acting like we don't know them.", Diamond said. "Besides, it ain't like we they girls. I'm mean not yet, anyway!", Jade commented. "You right, but stop frontin, you bitches know y'all heated inside. Those are some cute females hanging on y'all men.", Tootie teased. Cristal busted out laughing as both girls turned their heads in unison, almost breaking their necks, only to find the females who were there had walked off. "you got us good. That's cool, we'll get you back!!",, Jade said. Cristal asked, "So, what's with your thingy with Half a Mil?" "I got him, no worries. All he want is some pussy, feeling all on my butt and shit. I almost cussed his fat ass out, he lucky I got work to do.", Tootie said. "Bitch, that ain't telling us nothing! Can you get next to him or not?", Jade said. Tootie looked at her and spit, "Hoe, didn't I just tell you I got this! I already got the number. Damn, Bitch relax. I'll come through! I can't wait until it's your turn!" then she went to the bar to get a drink. Tootie was hot right now because of the way Jade came at her. She didn't expect nothing like that. Jade came over to apologize to her. " My bad Tootie. You know I love you and didn't mean nothing by what I said. I'm just anxious to start getting paid. Plus, I'm heated with K.J. That nigga hasn't called me since Tuesday. Don't no nigga do me like that. I'm the one that play these niggas that way. Shit, who that nigga think he is anyway, just gonna tear my shit up and not call!" Tootie just laughed, she knew her friend was sprung, just like her. Jade's freaky ass done got herself dick whipped. Tootie just laughed harder as her and Jade walked over to Cristal and Diamond. "Oh, Chrissy, before I forget, Linz told me to tell you to bring me over to his house tonight. You can take me now, then come back.", Tootie informed her friend. "Aight", Cristal said as she took out her cell to call Doug. He answered on the third ring, "Hello". "Hey Boo, you feel like company tonight? I gotta drop Tootie off for your boy and was wondering if I could see you also.", she said. "That's cool", Doug replied while yawning. "You sure? You sound tired." Doug replied, "A little bit, but you can still come over. What time y'all coming?" Cristal turned to Tootie and asked, What time you trying to leave?" Tootie looked at the clock on her phone which read 12:10 am and said," In about 30 minutes". Then she turned went on the dance floor as R. Kelly's "Happy People" began. "She said about a half hour, is that cool with you?", Cristal told Doug. "Yeah that cool, do you remember how to get here, or do you want me to meet you some place?" "No I know how to get there.", she replied and then hung up. Doug was kind of glad that she was coming over. After Tuesday's encounter he wanted more.

The girls were on the floor cutting up to the steppers song. Tootie and Diamond stepped with an older gentleman, who was dressed sharply in a gray suit and matching gators. Tootie was having such a good time she didn't notice Half a Mil watching from a distance. While waiting for a break in the music he thought, maybe he'd get lucky tonight.

Jade was hot as some bitch was keeping K.J company by the fireplace. Her hand was all on his thigh, while she was smiling in his face. The killer part though was that he was loving it! So she danced with the first nigga available. Some ugly cat got real lucky. Cristal went to holla at A.P, they played like they just met. She spoke to him about Diamond, and introduced them to each other. Just then, Half a Mil asked, "Hey beautiful, what's up?" "I'm about to go, I gotta get up early tomorrow.", Tootie said.

The girls decided to take some photos. As the camera snapped, Diamond and Jade said, "Y'all bitches wasn't even gonna include us?" They paid the photographer for four more pictures while posing in various stances. Niggas was trying to get their holla on, the ladies was loving it. Diamond chose A.P outta the crowd asking the female who was talking with him if she could borrow him for a photo.

Before leaving, Tootie told Half a Mil she would call him tomorrow. She then pulled out her cell and called Linz to let him know that they were on their way. Tonight was a good night. They'd soon have some cash to fulfill their plans. As they got into the car, Cristal handed Tootie an American Express card she lifted from some white guy who was too busy watching some blondes breast at the bar. The girls were true to their hustle. Feeling good, they blasted Cameron's "Oh Boy" as loud as the little CD player would go.

CHAPTER TWELVE

Doug and Linz lived in an old two story warehouse. The second story was converted into a three bedroom studio flat. They used the first story as a garage. The Maxima pulled up, beeped, and the door lifted. The darkened space was illuminated by the Nissan's headlights. It casted a beam on a black Benz, Doug's white Avalanche and Acura, and two street bikes. The Rover was missing.

As they climbed the stairs, Doug greeted them in boxers and a wife beater. Cristal kissed him lightly. They stepped in and took off their shoes at the door. Tootie was taken back by how plush the place was. Different hues of baby blue was everywhere. Her feet melted in the super thick carpet. She didn't expect this.

"Linz ain't here but he'll be back in a minute.", Doug told Tootie as she padded over to one of the two cashmere lounge chairs. "How long ago did he leave?", she asked. "About 20 minutes ago, he had to meet somebody.", Doug replied. "Just make yourself comfortable, you want something to drink, it's in the fridge. Here is the remote for the t.v.", he handed her the remote as he got up. Cristal was behind him and headed to what Tootie guessed was his bedroom. "You just gonna leave me out here?", she asked Cristal. "You straight, he'll be back soon, relax.", she answered. Tootie got up and looked around the lavishly furnished living area. She liked what the men did with the place, especially the 3/4 circle leather couch that sat in the middle facing a 61 inch plasma screen. The room was accented with blown glass and teak coffee and end tables. There was velour over sized throw pillows that were piled in front of the gas fireplace. She looked at the photos that were scattered here and there. She touched things hoping to catch his vibe. He did say I was his "future" kept going through her mind.

Meanwhile, Linz was sitting downtown outside McDonalds waiting on Lil mac. Linz didn't recognize the black Lexus LS 430 that floated to the curb on 22 inch blades. He gripped his gun tight and said to himself, "Where dis nigga at?" Lil Mac was 10 minutes late, which wasn't like him, that nigga was always on time. As the limo tinted window lowered and a cigarette was thrown out, then Jeanna emerged from the driver's side. Linz couldn't make out who the woman was that was vastly approaching. He cocked the 40 caliber Desert Eagle, placing it in his lap, as the figure got closer. He recognized it as Jeanna and relaxed as she went to the passenger side. He hit the locks to let her in.

"Lil Mac want you to follow him.", she said. As the black Lexus eased away from the curb and into the street, Linz sighed and followed. "Linz, this is nice, when you get this?", Jeanna asked. "A couple months ago.", he replied. Jeanna was flirting as usual, looking good with her chocolate ass. As he looked at her in a different way for the first time, he realized Jeanna was fine! With flawless skin, this little black sista was sexy as hell. Her Lady Enyce outfit was banging and hugged her in all the right places. But as quickly as that thought came, he dismissed it. He lived by the golden rule, 'don't fuck with your friend's girl'. Lil Mac was his boy, no way he could disrespect him. As they cruised the street, Linz flipped his cell and called Tootie. "Hello", she answered. Surprised that it was quiet in the background he asked, "Where you at?". "I'm at your house. We left early. Where you at?", she stated. "I had to holla at my peeps. I should be home in about 30 minutes.", he replied. "Okay, I like your house", she commented before saying, "Be safe!" and hung up. Tootie really wanted to say "I love you" but didn't want to play herself. Like Usher said she got it bad!!

The Lexus came to a stop in the Strip District. Lil Mac got out and him and Jenna switched places. "Like my whip? I just copped it yesterday.", he asked. "I like that, it's clean as hell. What you want for it?", Linz asked. "Fool, I ain't selling it. I just got a body for it yesterday.", he said. "So what's up?", Linz asked, he had some place to be. "I got the two Chargers you wanted, but they won't be ready until next week some time. Also, some people been checking ya place.", he said. "What they look like?", Linz asked. "Some white dudes.", Mac said. "Look, you and Jeanna can have the stuff in that apartment aight, just make sure you clean it good.", Linz informed him. "Man, I got them guns y'all asked for, but I couldn't get the ammo for the AK 90." Lil Mac went over to the trash bin and retrieved a military duffle bag. Lil Mac could also get guns, along with cars. Linz looked at the goods, seen they were straight, and asked Mac, "how much". "Man just give me nine stacks for everything.", he said. He was cutting them a super deal for two whips and nine guns. "Lil Mac, when you gonna sell your own work? I know you got loot stacked.", Linz asked. "Soon, man my paper funny right now and I don't fuck with everybody like that. I'm cool not being the man. Why you ask?", Lil Mac said. "I might have something for you. Something to get you some real paper. I'll keep you posted.", Linz told him. The two exchanged pounds before going back to their cars. "Nigga, you need to get some license!", Linz joked. Lil Mac drove 1000 cars but had no license.

Tootie sat on the couch waiting for her Boo to get back, wondering what bitch he was with. She actually smiled to herself when she realized she was becoming jealous. Cristal came in, wearing only a t-shirt ,to check on her and show her where the bathroom was. She also wanted to tease Tootie because she was about to get her freak on. Tootie wished this nigga would get here.

Linz arrived about 20 minutes after talking with Tootie. When he got in the door he saw her resting on the couch. He went over and roused her awake. She awakened with a startle. "You finally made it home I see.", she said wiping her eyes. He laughed and said "Awwe, Tootie was all alone." She smiled at him and said, "You lucky I was about to..". "You wasn't about to do nothing but sit here and wait.", he stated. She crawled into his lap and rested her head on his shoulder. "Babe, you tired?", he asked. "A little bit.", she responded. He picked her up and carried her to his room. She was amazed at his strength. He picked her 154 pounds up like she was a feather. Tootie loved being in his arms and knew she'd do anything to stay there. She just hoped he felt the same.

Tootie took in the room as he laid her on the king size platform bed. So this is where the king of her heart slept. His chamber was decorated with two dressers, a cabinet, 42 inch plasma TV with stereo DVD player and surround sound. It also had two night stands, track lighting that hung from the ceiling, an over sized chair in one corner, and a huge walk-in closet. The closet was in disarray with clothes and shoes everywhere.

As Tootie stretched out on the bed, his sheets smelled of Curve Body Oil for Men. She inhaled the smell deeply. Linz went to the stereo and the room came alive with music. David Hollister's "Chicago 85" CD started it off. Tootie began to come out of her skirt and top until she was only wearing a lace bra and boy shorts. "Babe, I'm a little tired. Can we wait a little bit before we do anything?", she asked. Linz stood in his boxers and said, "Babe, we ain't got to do anything if your tired.   I'm cool with that."   "You won't be mad?", she questioned.   "Naw", he said, cutting off the lights and joining her in bed.   She snuggled into his arms and drifted to sleep.

Diamond pulled A.P aside and said, "Boo, I'm tore up, niggas been buying me drinks all night.   Can you please take me home?"   "I got you in about ten minutes.", he answered.   He went to holla at someone he knew while Diamond went and found her sister to let her know she was about to bounce.

A.P had found the hottie he was talking to earlier.   They exchanged numbers,   her name was Mahogany.   She said with a smile, "Don't let your girl find my number.   I just want to borrow you for a couple nights."   She put an emphasis on BORROW.

K.J was loving the attention he was getting from this little bird name Keisha.

This white girl had a phat ass and nice body.   He could tell from the way her dress clung to her hips,   He was also enjoying the way Jade was shooting him mean looks.   Her negative attention just made him act even more of an ass!   He began whispering in Keisha's ear causing her to laugh.   He peeped out the corner of his eye at Jade and see her face get a shade darker.   Truth be told, K.J was gonna make it his business to screw this white chick this weekend.   Baby girl was right!   "What's up Ma?   Looking all fine, sitting over here by yourself.", some playa asked Jade.   "Get the fuck away from me.   I am not in the mood for it!", Jade stated with major attitude.   The young man was offended.   He gave her a once over from head to toe trying to find a flaw, but couldn't.   He said anyway, "Bitch, you ain't all that!"   Heads began to turn to peep the scene.   She came back calmly, "Then get your broke ass out of my grill, Nigga!   Step!   Go find some other bitch to bother!"   She then dismissed him with a wave.   Other playas clowned the young nigga who just got dissed, while hoes wondered who did that bitch think she was.   Diamond came up at the tail end of the verbal assault and told her sister she was about to go.   Diamond asked her if she needed a ride.   Jade said yeah and went to get her coat.   Diamond went to find A.P, who just walked away from the cute older female he exchanged numbers with.   Although he is tired of whoring, he couldn't pass this one up.

CHAPTER THIRTEEN

As the days flew by, Tootie spent more time with Half a Mil and less with Linz, but they kept in contact. Tootie numbly fucked Half a Mil twice in a hotel. The next time would be different, her time line was running short. She was tired of his company and faking like his dick game was '100'. So, when he called she flipped out on him. "Hello", she answered. "What's up Boo. Can I see you today?", he asked. "I don't know Mike, we gotta talk.", she stated dryly. "What's up?", he asked concerned, he wasn't trying to let her get away again. "Us, I'm tired of you playing me like I'm one of your hoes. That's what's up!", she exclaimed. "What you talking about babe?", Mike whined. "All you wanna do is take me to hotels and shit. That shit is played. You go holla at one of your other bitches for that. I ain't the one!", Tootie told him with attitude. "Matter of fact, don't even call me no more, I'm done with you. I knew you hadn't changed." Then she hung up praying that he'd call back. She'd hate herself if she fucked his sorry little dick ass for nothing. But her plan worked because her cell phone was blowing up with his digits. She waited to answer letting the first two calls go to voicemail. Deciding the trap was set, she answered on the third call. "What Mike!" "Babe, I'm sorry if you feel I've been treating you like that. Let me make it up to you, aight.", he pleaded. "I don't know Mike.", she stalled. "Come on Boo, don't be like that!", he said. "Look, I'll come swoop you and we'll talk about it." She could hear his friends in the background so she questioned, "Who's that, your baby momma? Where you at anyway?" "Oh, that's Tee and my niggas. I'm at home, I told you I don't fuck with baby moms no more.", he explained. "Whatever, Nigga, tell me anything.", she replied. "Seriously, you the only one. Now can I make it up to you Boo?" "I don't know Mike, I just wanna stay in and chill tonight. Might rent a movie or something.", she stated. Mike was really feeling Tootie and he let his guard down. This would prove to be a costly mistake, but he wouldn't see it until it was too late. "Listen Boo, why don't we make it a blockbuster night. I'll get rid of these fools, clean up the place and then I'll come get you. So bring an overnight bag.", he said hoping she went for it. Half a Mil been dying to impress her with his crib. He always threw his weight around, clowning his peeps in front of her, but it didn't impress her none. "I don't know Mike, I gotta think about it. I don't like being around all that crazy stuff you do, it's not safe. I could get hurt.", she lied. "Babe, I promise you nothing's gonna happen. Just me and you tonight, aight.", he said almost begging. Tootie would never make Mr. Linz beg, besides he was too much of a player for that. If anything she'd be doing the begging, which she'd gladly do. "Alright, I'm trusting you because if you lie, I'm gone. Where we gonna meet at?", she said. "I'll come get you in about two hours. Meet me downtown on the Square.", he told her and then hung up.

Tootie quickly called Linz to let him know tonight was gonna be the night. After some small talk he hung up and informed the boys. Doug checked the weapons, while K.J and A.P got the two black Dodges ready. They changed into black sweats and boots to match the masks and hoodies. Then they headed downtown to wait. Meanwhile, Tootie told the girls that tonight was the night and to pray for her.

Doug was amped, he'd waited long enough for this moment. He had something special in store for Half a Mil. As Linz and Doug rode together. Doug said, "Let me do something with him. Let me run this show, okay." "It's your call Bro, he's yours.", said Linz. Then they informed the others.

Five minutes after parking they spotted the black H2. Half a Mil got out hugging Tootie then kissed her passionately. They went to her car to get her overnight bag and movies. Walking back to the Hummer she asked, "What about my girl's car? I just can't leave it, somebody might tow it." "Well just follow me.", he said kissing her again before getting into the truck and easing into the late rush hour traffic headed towards Penn Hills. After an hour of fighting traffic, they stopped in front of a single story bungalow with a two car garage. The Four Kings parked three houses down and began to wait.

Once inside, Tootie asked to use the bathroom. She unlocked the window, flushed the toilet and came back out in the living room. Mike was in the kitchen throwing something together to eat. She made herself comfortable while making light conversation. As the night wore on they watched movies and fondled each other. She couldn't wait for this night to be over. Just a little longer she told herself as he began to put his hands down her jeans rubbing her pussy. She loathed his fat ass, but she played her role and began stroking his rock hard dick.   He was aroused by every stroke.

Meanwhile in the car, the clock read 12:30 am, K.J said, "Damn, He's been in there a couple hours kicking your girls back in."   Then started laughing.   A.P joined in saying, "His little fat ass got your girl in the buck."   Doug even got one in, "She might have sucked it."   While Linz sat with his poker face on, but deep inside he was heated.   He'd clown them when it was the others girls turn.

Tootie grabbed her bag, she needed to go to the bathroom to change, she had something special for him.   His fat ass couldn't wait.   Soon as she locked the door behind her, she pulled out her cell and called Linz.   She told him about the window and to give her 30 minutes then come in.   She ended her call, then changed into one of her dancer outfits and called his name ever so seductively.   Mike was down the hall in his room butt naked.   When she entered she was wearing a fishnet bodysuit with holes in the crotch and nipple area and a pair of black thigh high boots.   His jaw hit the floor as she began to dance for him.   "Turn some music on.", she said.   25 minutes later, she was getting punished from behind, face buried in a pillow.   Mike was putting in work.

The crew crept in through the window silently.   Once inside they slowly cocked their weapons and eased throughout the house checking all rooms until they got to the last one.   They heard music and voices coming from inside.   They paused and listened for a few moments.   "Ooohh Mike, yeah.. Yeah.. It's your pussy.   It's yours!", Tootie was screaming.   Linz kicked the door in as the crew rushed in guns drawn.   "What the fuck!", was all Half a Mil got out before Linz hit him with the barrel of the 40 caliber. "Shut up bitch, where's the shit at?", A.P said.   POP,   Doug hit him, "Nigga, I'm gonna ask you one more time, then if I can't spend it you can't!   Now, where's the shit at!"   Tootie tried to cove up, but Linz snatched the sheet from her.   She was terrified looking at the masked men, trying to hide her nakedness behind Mike.   Doug pulled her away putting the gun to her head.   Mike watched in horror.   "Nigga start talking!", Linz said.   Tootie began to cry.   WHAP! "Shut up bitch!", K.J said, being a certified hoe beater he quickly tapped her skull with the 44 mag.   She wasn't expecting this, but she stayed in character but her head was throbbing.   K.J smiled underneath his mask. Mike said, "Aight!   Look, don't hurt her.   It's in the closet in the ceiling.   Man, don't kill us!"   A.P went and checked on the loot.   After some searching, he found it stuffed inside with several card board boxes, all fifties and hundred dollar bills.   A.P came out carrying several boxes and K.J went to help.   They dumped the loot in a trash bag.   "Now, where the coke at Nigga!", Doug asked kicking him in the nuts.   "In the kitchen, top shelf next to the fridge.", he cried.   K.J went to the kitchen and came back two minutes later with 14 kilos soft and 3 hard.   "Damn nigga, you really could touch a half a million 24/7.", Linz said.   Doug said, Y'all get out of here, I got this."   He began pistol whipping Half a Mil saying, "This is for my boy from way back."   As Linz turned to leave he went over and smacked Tootie in the mouth.   "That's for fucking with a bitch nigga!"   Then he kicked her in the ass.   Tootie's mind was racing, this wasn't part of the plan.   They done whipped her ass!   "Bitch, get to stepping, consider yourself lucky hoe!"   As she scrambled to get her things, the three men left leaving Doug with Half a Mil.   Doug took one kilo of crack cocaine and one of powder cocaine and scattered it around the living room and kitchen table.   He took the other fifteen birds with him.   Half a Mil was out cold when Doug called 911 and left the phone off the hook after screaming for the operator to help him.   He then slammed the phone to the floor and ran out the door into the awaiting Charger that the three men left running.   Tootie was balled up in the back seat crying.   She took one for the team.

When the police came, they found Half a Mil laying out on the bedroom floor, barely conscious, bleeding from a skull wound.   He was taken to the Medical Center, then later booked and charged with possession with intent to distribute cocaine, in excess of the bulk amount to wit: one kilogram of powder and the same charge but this one was crack cocaine.   Crack carried a possible life sentence for the feds, which who would be handling it.   He might get lucky and get 25-30 years on a plea.   Either way, he was through.   When he called on his homies, they remembered all the times he clowned them in front of people.   All the money he had on the streets that people owed him was forgotten.   No one was going to do shit for him, just like he did Phil, someone did it to him.   KARMA BABY KARMA!!

Tootie spent the next five days at home recovering from the unplanned ass whooping she took at Half a Mil's residence.   Her girls nursed her back to health.   Her lip had went down, but her skull was still a little tender.   Most of all her pride was hurt because she suspected Linz to be the one who smacked and kicked her.   How could he do me like that she wondered.   Each of the other girls sat thinking about how it was gonna be when it was their turn.   Doubt started to creep in, but it was Cristal who got their minds right.   "Listen, what happened to Tootie could have happened to any of us.   That's the chance we chose to take.   The fact is she's alive.   We all knew the risks, so what we get our asses whipped, we about to get paid!   Plus, them niggas ain't gonna hurt us or let no one else hurt us.   Shit, y'all bitches around here tripping."

The girls realized that what Cristal said was 100% true.   It was just the motivation they needed to hear.   That brought Tootie out of her somber mood.   She took a long hot bubble bath before calling Linz.   It had been five days since she heard his voice.   Every time she called him she got his voicemail.   But, all the other girls had seen their men or spoken with them.   Diamond came into the bathroom while Tootie was relaxing in the tub with her eyes closed singing a Mariah Carey tune.   "Tootie, you gonna be alright?", she asked as she began to paint her toenails.   "Yeah, I guess, he could have at least called.", she said almost in tears.   "Don't worry girl, we got your back!   You really like him, huh?"   With tears streaming down her face, she shook her head yes, and sank deeper into the tub.   Diamond felt for her girl, she could understand Tootie's pain.   The women hated to see each other in pain.   Diamond told herself that she'd have a talk with Mr. Linz.   Ten minutes later, Jade knocked on the door.   "Tootie, you have a call." she was hoping it was Linz, but it wasn't, it was Mike Blair (Half a Mil).   He called collect asking to see her.   She told him she would visit on Saturday.   He was happy.   Tootie felt sorry for Mike, the least she could do was visit him once and maybe put something on his books.   After all it was his money.   She decided that she'd get him some books to read also.   During their conversation, the line beeped.   She told Mike to hold on while she clicked over.   "Hello", she said.   Then she heard his voice, "Can I speak with Tootie?"   Before she could catch her self she blurted out, "Why haven't you called me!   Fuck you!   You just like the rest!"   Linz waited before he spoke, "Calm down, you though talking stupid?   If so, we need to see y'all tonight, 8 pm.   Oh yeah, leave the attitude at home!"   Then he hung up.   She sat there dumbfounded.   Then she remembered Mike on the other line.   She clicked back over, "I'm sorry, but I'll be there on Saturday.   What time can I come?   Can I bring you anything?", she said.   "Come about 6pm, bring size 48 boxers, 4x tshirts, some socks and a couple of magazines.

Thanks Boo", he said. "Alright, look gotta go, but I'll be there tomorrow. Then she ended the call

"What did Linz say?", Diamond asked. "He need to see us at 8 pm tonight, then he hung up!", Tootie said. Then she washed her tear stained face, stood up, and drained the tub to shower. Even though she was mad, she was happy to see him tonight. But she would definitely let him know how she felt.

CHAPTER FOURTEEN

Linz took a few days to get away after the robbery. He went to Ohio to holla at his peeps. He had a boy there named Chuck. Chuck was a good hustler but couldn't get that one shot. All that was about to change, Linz was gonna give Chuck that shot with three of those bricks courtesy of Half a Mil. "What up C.H?", Linz said catching Chuck off guard. "Awe man, my boy!", Chuck said eyeing the black CLS 600 Benz that encased his friend. "Get in, take a ride with me.", Linz said. Chuck told his peeps that he'd get up with them later and entered the vehicle. As the Benz pulled away, T.I could be heard drifting outta the slightly opened window. "My boy Linz.", Chuck said as he admired the rich insides of the luxury car. "What's good wit you C.H?", Linz asked. "Man, staying sucka free! Its hard out here Linz, Niggas ain't the same no more.", Chuck stated. "But you still the same right?", Linz asked. "No doubt, I'm always gonna be me. I ain't fake. It's ridiculous out here.", Chuck said. "How's your paper looking?", Linz inquired. "Man, I'mma keep it real, I'm just getting by.", Chuck confessed. They drove for a few minutes in silence, then Linz said, "I got something for you. Can you handle it?" Chuck said, "Nigga, I hustle, that's what I do... Bring it!" Linz took chuck back to his car and told him to go home. Ten minutes later, Linz walked in Chuck's house with three bricks. Chuck's eyes got big as all the possibilities of gaining hood rich status flooded his mind. "Just give me 25 back and do you with the rest.", Linz said as he left. Chuck couldn't believe his good fortune, his boy just blessed him. Linz then went to see his father where he chilled for the next four days. Catching up on lost times help took his mind off Tootie and what he saw at Half a Mil's house. He had to admit, he was pissed even thought he told her to do it. It was something he felt better hearing about and not seeing. He was secretly placing her as a permanent fixture in his future.

Tonight was payday for everyone. The robbery netted $780,000 stacks in cash and 15 birds. Only the cash would be split with the women. The coke would be given out at the crew's discretion. Each member had someone in mind who would love to be put on. The fellas took $450,000 stacks leaving the women with $330,000 to split.

As the girls got ready, Tootie called Linz and apologized for her attitude. He accepted and told her to wear something sexy. They could make it up to each other tonight. Diamond and Jade asked her why she was smiling, she ended up telling them everything. Then she called her mom to tell her she'd be down to visit on Sunday and that she had a surprise for her. She debated if she should tell her mom about the man in her life but decided against it. They spent a hour on the phone before hanging up, it was almost 7pm and she had to get dressed. She wore a pair of skin tight Vanson leather motor cross pants and jacket with stiletto heeled riding boots. The girls clowned her for looking like a superhero. The rest of the girls were dressed to kill as well. It was surprisingly warm night for October in this region.

"Man, we got twelve bricks left, what y'all want to do with them?", K.J asked. "I don't care, do what y'all want to do with em.", Doug stated, "I got what I wanted, I ain't trying to catch no drug beef." K.J and A.P both said, "I feel you!" Both of them had plans for those bricks. While Linz said nothing because he already gave three bricks to his friend Chuck. He didn't want to charge Chuck, but he had to put some kind of price on it. He thought about Lil Mac, but he mostly dealt in weed. "Linz, what you wanna do with em?", A.P asked. "Y'all call it.", Linz replied. They each took four. "You get the most since it was your girl's hit.", K.J stated. Now it was time for the money to be split. As the trash bag hit the table with a thud, money spilled out the side. Half a Mil had the loot in bundles of $10,000 which made counting and dividing easier. None of them wanted to be here all day, even if it was counting money. The total came to just a little over $780,000. $450,000 was their take, $112,000 each. The girls would get $330,000 to split, giving each $82,500. It wasn't bad for giving up a couple shots of pussy.

"Linz, how did it feel watching your girl get hit from the back?", asked K.J the joker, causing the others to laugh. "It's cool, she did what she had to do.", Linz said. "Nigga, I know you was hot, keep it 100 with ya boy. Don't worry, I got her for you. I know she felt the weight of that 44 mag. She looked like she was enjoying it a little too much. Either that or the hoe deserves an Oscar." They all clowned Linz. He tried to act like it was all good, but he was flaming inside. "Nigga, I'm glad there ain't no pistol around cause you would have been shot me, huh?", K.J said while cracking up

laughing.   "Yeah, yeah, get yours off now, it will be Jade's turn soon.", Linz shot back.
""Until then the joke's on you!", K.J returned.   The boys engaged in small talk for about
a hour, then Linz stated, "Come on, I need $2,500 from each of y'all for Lil Mac's
payment."   They each handed over the loot.   K.J needed to holla at Lil Mac anyway, so
he opted to take the money to him.   They exchanged hugs and pounds and agreed to
meet up at K.J and A.P's crib at 7:30pm.   The girls would be there at 8.   A.P took the
girls loot with them since he was going past the house anyway.

K.J gave his loot to A.P to drop off.   He only kept the ten stacks owed to Lil Mac.
He flipped his cell and hit Lil Mac on the direct connect.   "What's up Fool?", Lil Mac
answered.   "Nothing much Nigga.   I got something for you, meet me in East Liberty at
David's Shoes.", K.J said.   Lil Mac replied, "Aight, give me 20 minutes."   K.J then
called Kiesha, his little   white freak he'd met a couple weeks ago.   "Hello.", she sang
answering on the first ring.   "What's up with you Baby Girl?   You busy?", K.J said.
"Not really, I was just about to lay down for a minute.   I gotta work tonight.", she told
him.   Keisha was the white girl with a sista's body.   She was a Neuro-surgeon at
Children's Hospital in Oakland.   "Oh, I was just wondering if I could stop by to see you
for a few, that's all.", he said.   It was only 2:30 pm so he had some time to kill before
he'd see Jade.   He had screwed Keisha for the first time last week, but since then it
became a game of phone tag.   Keisha was good in bed plus her stuff was good, not as
good as Jade's, but good enough to come back for seconds.   He got a kick outta fucking
her doggy style.   She couldn't take no dick from the back like a sista could.   It turned
him on hearing her scream and suck her teeth every time he rammed it in.   He took
pleasure in giving her pain.   As thoughts of their first encounter came to her mind she
said, "When you talking about coming?"   Looking at the dash clock he said, "In about a
half hour, is that cool?"   He spotted Lil Mac standing beside a shiny black Lexus.
"Yeah, I'm gonna jump in the shower so I'll be fresh when you get here.", she said.
"Oh, and get some condoms too!"   They spoke for a minute more and then hung up.

"What's up Fool!", Lil Mac said.   "Who's whip is that?", K.J asked.   "Mine, Linz
ain't tell you?", Mac said.   "Naw, that thing is clean.   What you want for it?", K.J said.
"Like I told Linz, it ain't for sale.", he said.   A couple of broads walked past smiling and
waving.   Both men watch them as they looked back.   K.J being the whore, waved them

back.   Both women were dimes, no doubt.   The women introduced themselves as Meeka and Renee.   "This is a nice Lexus, is it yours?", Renee, the short one asked K.J. "It's my man's whip.", he said pointed at Lil Mac.   Meeka, the tall shy one asked K.J, " What you just riding, huh?"   "Naw pretty, not today, that's me right there.", K.J answered, pointing at the Excursion sitting on chrome across the street.   "Oh, you doing it big?", she asked.   "I'm just getting by, Boo.   But look, I gotta handle something, let's hook up sometime.", he said while putting her number into his phone with her photo. He always added the photo so he wouldn't forget, it has happened before.

K.J interrupted Lil Mac and pulled him to the side to slide him his loot.   He told him he would get with him later, got into his truck and bounced off playing Juvenile's "Slow Motion".   Yeah, he would definitely get back with Meeka, but for now it was Keisha who would cool his fire.   Realizing he was gonna be late, he bypassed the store. He had some rubbers in the truck somewhere.   Keisha came to the door in just a robe. Her body smelled of Jasmine and honey.   She let the robe open loosely, giving him a glimpse of her finely structured body.   Keisha kept her body tight due to trips to the gym three days a week for two hours a day and weekly handball matches.   Keisha was a true California girl, she has only been in Pittsburgh for one year.   They spent the next two hours speaking to each others bodies..   Ironically, K.J like chilling with Keisha, she was down to earth.   When she dozed off, K.J let himself out, leaving a thank you note beside her pillow.   Which happened to be the same thing she did to him at the Ameri-Suites Hotel.

CHAPTER FIFTEEN

A.P got home and showered before cleaning up after his romp with his older chick Mahogany. She was 43 years old with two teenage girls, and an abusive cheating husband. He couldn't figure out why a nigga would step out on this woman. She could pass for 23 or 24 with no problem, her face and body was banging. She was also a corporate attorney, and a very prosperous one at that. The sex was also BOMB! She had never betrayed her husband in the fifteen years they have been married, however, that Thursday at Chauncey's when she met A.P, the alcohol gave her the courage to step out on her husband. She was flattered that the young man took interest in her. She was beginning to think something was wrong with her and that's why her husband cheated on her. But now she knows it isn't her that made him cheat, he was just plain stupid. Revenge is a dish best served between someone else sheets, sexual revenge that is.

A.P had a few hours to spare before everyone came over. It had been six days since he seen his new thang, Diamond. He found himself missing her. Her body fit his perfectly like a glove. He could see himself staying with her. He hoped she wasn't caught like Tootie was when it is her turn to go. He thought about her as he slept.

Linz felt kinda bad for not calling Tootie and for slapping the shit outta her. He was getting attached to her, it was like he wanted her but at the same time he didn't. All because of a bad relationship he had with this other female, who he fell in love with but she toyed with his heart. So, he vowed to never catch feelings for no female, but this Tootie chick was like a leach. Linz couldn't shake her from his thoughts. Deep inside, he prayed that she'd turn out to be his diamond in the rough.

He went to his closet to get dressed, and was amazed at how organized it was. For the first time he didn't have to search for two matching shoes, they were paired up in front of him. All his clothes hung on hangers, thanks to Tootie, she straightened up his closet and drawers about two weeks ago . It has only been a little over a month since the incident at the Red Devil Bar, but from that moment they have been inseparable. He screwed other women, but always made time for Ms. Tootie.

After selecting his gear, he called his boy Big Rob . Rob didn't answer his cell, so Linz called Tonya, Rob's lady friend. Tonya was cool as a fan, and treated Linz like a brother. Tonya has a cousin that used to play hard to get with Linz. Tonya took good care of Rob. She'd proven herself worth by staying true when Rob went through some difficult times.

"Hello", Tonya answered Rob's phone after four rings. "Hey Tonya, is Rob around?", Linz asked. "He just left. I'll have him call you when he gets back. He only went to the store.", she said. "Does he have his cell on him?", Linz questioned. "No, it's charging.", she said. "Aight, tell him get at me when he gets in. How y'all doing?', he inquired. "We just chillin.", she responded in her country accent. "Jennifer's here, wanna talk to her?", she asked. "Yeah let me holla at her." He and Jen talked for a couple minutes, while making plans to hook up in the near future. Rob came back before they hung up. "Rob's back, make sure you call me.", Jen said handing the phone to Rob. "What's up!", he said. "Man, I'm cool, but I need to holla at you.", Linz replied. Rob did a little investing in his spare time. He'd got the crew set up with off shore accounts through one of his frat brother's firm at a small charge of 10%, and every thing is legit. His frat brother knew that Rob was a dope man at heart and was smart, also good for revenue. He didn't want to know where the money came from, or the names of who it came from. All he wanted is his cut that he charge the fellas. He never dealt with them directly only through Big Rob, who was always present. That way he stayed outta risk of getting indicted, which was good for both parties. This way, no one could testify as to ever doing any business together, if it ever got to that point, which in three years never happened.

"When can you make it up here?", Linz asked. "Look man, Tonya and I was just talking about doing something because she got the week off. We could shoot up there. You don't mind if I bring Tonya, do you?", he said. "Naw, that's cool. Oh Bro, you still get down? I know your little vending route ain't all that gravy." "I haven't in a minute.", Rob said, "Why what's up?" "I got something for you, just get here asap, and bring Jen too.", Linz said. "Nigga, let me ask her, hold on.", then he went to ask Tonya. "She cool, we leaving tomorrow." They chatted for a minute more then terminated the call.

Linz decided that since it was so warm out in October, he'd get on his bike tonight. He selected heavy denim jeans and jacket, Polo riding boots, and Vanson motorcycle jacket.   Now all he had to do was figure out a way to kick it with Jen without Tootie throwing a fit.   He decided to call Tootie to see what she had planned for the weekend. She told him that she and the girls were going to visit their mothers out of state.   That took care of his would be problem.   Linz told Tootie that he'd see her at 8pm and thanks for hooking up the closet.   He had an hour to kill, so he called his little brother Jason, who lived in Columbus, Ohio.

CHAPTER SIXTEEN

The girls arrived on time as every one sat gathered in the living area of A.P and K.J's place. The discussion of money was brought up by Diamond. "So how much was our take?" She asked the question they all wanted to know. It was quickly answered by Doug dropping a bag in Tootie's lap. The trash bag was heavy. Tootie gave it to her girls to feel and hold as she asked Linz, "Can I speak to you for a minute outside?" Linz knew this was coming sooner or later so he shook his head yes and got up to leave as everyone watched.

Once outside Tootie paced before speaking. Linz watched her walk back and forth with her arms folded across her chest. "Why'd you do me like that? You didn't even call to see if I was alright. You said I was your future!", she vented through her tears. He did not say anything, there was nothing for him to say. She had a right to be angry, she'd put her life in jeopardy for him. The least he could have done was called and checked on her. She sat on the little stoop and let it all out, tears fell like rain drops in April. Tootie was in love with a man she barely knew. "Do you even have any feelings for me?", she asked as the tears continued to fall. "Or am I just a piece of ass to you? At least be real with me! I deserve that." Linz went over to her and helped her stand. He embraced her tightly as she cried, her body shook in his arms. All he could say was "I'm sorry babe." Tootie cried for several minutes. Once she calmed he spoke, "Babe, I do like you. I know I was wrong for not calling or coming by, but if you can find it in your heart to forgive me I will make it up to you. Babe, you are my future. I know you think it was just a game but I'm being real." Linz was good, he lifted her face and began to kiss her tears away. Tootie had to admit he was smooth with his cause, she fell for it again. She took a moment to regain her composure before going back inside he stopped her saying, "I like that outfit Ma. You look sexy as hell!", as he tapped her ass. "Let me see it jiggle.", he asked. "Later I'll dance for you." He hugged her again, kissing her deeply and cupping her ass in his hands. "You never did answer my question, am I just a piece of ass or what?" "We will talk about that later, seriously.", he replied. Her heart sank a little, but it told her don't give up just yet. "Alright, but I want you to know I am a good woman!", she said then they rejoined the rest of the gang.

Cristal noticing Tootie's tear stained face, pulled her into the restroom along with Jade and asked her what the deal was.   While she told them, Diamond was in the living room with the guys.   "Linz, what's up with you and my girl?   Tootie really likes you, don't hurt her.   If you ain't really feeling her, be real and just tell her.   If you just want to fuck her, tell her.   Just don't play games with her heart.   She'll do anything for you." A.P then said, "Why you in their business, that's between them!   Shut the fuck up!" "Fuck that, she's my girl.   Just like you got his back, I have hers.", stated Diamond. "Look, Me and Tootie cool.   I ain't gonna lie, I like her and I told her that, I just don't want to rush into nothing, that's all.", Linz said looking at his boys, who surprisingly didn't laugh.   Hell, deep down inside they all felt the same way.

When the girls came out, they opened the trash bag and dumped out the loot.   The girls eye's got real big, they'd never seen so much money in their lives.   "How much is that?", Tootie asked.   330 stacks Doug stated.   "How much do we get?", Cristal asked. "It's all yours, y'all split that.", Doug answered.   The girls went nuts!   They seen their dreams on the way to coming true.   Cristal suddenly asked, "Who's next and when? Who's the next vic?"   It got quiet for a minute as the girls thought about what happened to Tootie.   K.J broke the silence and said, "We'll get with y'all next week and give all the details of the next vic. Diamond your next up."   Diamond shrugged her shoulders and said, "Whatever, let's get this money!   If it pays like this, I don't mind."   She was amped.   Tootie said, "Y'all serious, this is ours."   She couldn't believe it.   "Yeah boo, so are these.", Linz said, coming up behind her with a little box with the 3 carat yellow diamond earrings in it from the jewelry store heist from a month ago.   Her face lit up as the girls gathered around to examine the stones.   "These real?", Tootie asked. Diamond answered for her saying, "Hell yeah!!"   Diamond knew her stones.   Each of the men planned on giving the girls a piece of jewelry that they held back.   Tootie took out the cheap hoops and immediately put in the more expensive ones.   They looked good in her ears.   She kissed Linz after thanking him.   "You ready to go?", he asked. "Yeah, where are we going.   I didn't see the truck outside."   He said, "I know, I am on my bike tonight.   The weather is good for it."   "Do I need a purse or ID?"   "Grab your ID, just in case.", he told her.   She gave her purse to Cristal , hugged the girls and instructed them to take care of the loot.   All the girls trusted each other, she knew the loot would be there tomorrow.   Linz gave her the helmet he'd brought with him, then turned the key bringing the big Honda 959RR to life.   As Tootie climbed aboard she held him tightly.   "Don't be driving all crazy and fast."   "Just hold tight.", he replied as they rode off into the night.   Back in the house, the rest of both crews decided to hang out together.   The girls were ecstatic about the money still.

Meanwhile across town back at the old meeting place, three dudes were ransacking what was left of the old apartment.   Lil Mack and Jeanna only took the TV and furniture in the living room.   They shredded all paper that was left behind.   The three men were sent by the Mob to collect what was owed by Spider and Abs.   Since the crew killed them, the Mob felt that they should pick up the $150,000 tab.   The true total was only $75,000 but it was doubled because the club was shut down resulting in loss of revenue.

CHAPTER SEVENTEEN

Linz and Tootie parked the Honda at the bottom of the Station Square and rode the incline to the top of Mt. Washington.   Gazing out at the city as the cart ascended, the city of Pittsburgh had a beautiful skyline.   Once at the top, they sat in the court yard that overlooked downtown providing a breathtaking view.   Linz took out his digital camera and snapped a few photos as Tootie struck various poses.   She then took some of him. Later, asking an older black couple to take a photo of them together.   The older couple smiled at seeing love radiate from two young people.

"I know this might sound crazy, but I think I am falling in love with you.", Tootie said while standing in front of him.   He didn't say nothing, but he too felt the same way. He was desperately trying to fight it, but was losing the fight everyday he spent with her.

Linz was still sitting when she asked, "Can we talk now?", easing into his lap, running her hand over his waves.   "About what?", Linz answered playing dumb.   "You know about us.", she said.   This is the conversation he tried to avoid having.   "What about us?"   "What are we?", she responded.   "We cool, I mean I like you alot.", he answered trying to stall and find the right words.   Tootie wasn't in the mood for it tonight.   Her heart was tired of wondering, she wanted to know where this was headed and if it was worth pursuing.   "That ain't telling me nothing.   I know you enjoy having sex with me.   I ain't slow or dumb.   But I want the man behind the dick too.", she said calmly but firmly.   Then as he was about to speak she said, "Please don't give me no bullshit line, be real with me."   he looked away carefully, choosing his words, "Tootie, I like you I really dig you.   Your everything a Nigga could ask for."   "So what's the problem?", she asked.   "I'm afraid of getting hurt.   I've been through it before and I don't want to do it again.", he said.   "I am not her, ok.   Don't punish me for what some other girl did.", she pleaded.   He knew what she was saying was correct.   "Let's just let things happen, alright.   I wanna take my time to get to know your heart and soul.", he said.   "I can accept that, but I just don't like sharing you with other women, that's all. In my eyes I'm looking at you as my man.   I want you to see me as your woman."   He hugged her saying, "I told you, you was my future."   That caused her to smile, she had fallen for it again.   She hoped he meant it.

As she turned in his arms, facing the city, she began to sing Lauryn Hill's "Sweetest Thing". Linz loved when she sang to him, it made him feel important. She turned around smiling and for the first time he noticed her dimples. "So, now that you are $80,000 dollars richer, what are you gonna do with it?", Linz asked. "Spend it on you!!", she replied smiling. "I'm just joking, but I would if I thought it would make you mine. Your worth it. But seriously, I'm going to do something for my mom. I wanna buy her a house and myself a car. Then I would like to travel." Tootie was telling him her dreams. "I told you I'm going to see my Mama this weekend, didn't I?", she asked. He shook his head yes. "Can you help us get a car? Our car might not make it. We'll pay you.", she said. "I'll see, when you trying to leave, Saturday or Sunday?", he asked. "If I can get one before 4pm tomorrow, we will bounce at 6. Oh, I forgot to tell you, Mike called me collect today." Linz looked at her, "What he'd want?" "He asked if I was ok and if I'd come visit him tomorrow, I told him I would. Are you mad?" He replied, "No, that's on you. If you want to visit, go ahead." She then stated, "I just wanted to tell you first, but if you don't want me to go, I won't. I'm going to take him a few things. After all, it's his money." That brought a smile to Linz's face, she had a sense of humor "If you went to jail, I'd visit you, no matter where I'd be there at least two weekends a month and keep the phone on for you to call. I'd hold you down. I'd also bust your head if you got out and played me for another bitch.", she said with a slick threat behind it.

"How long you'll be gone?", he asked changing the subject. "Why, you gonna miss me?", she teased, feeling his johnson. "I might.", he said. "Stop fronting, I know you like me, you just scared your boys will clown you. They probably feeling the same way about my girls. I'm gonna give my Mama half my money, then keep the other half. I want to get my credit right." As Linz kissed her and caressed her phatty. He asked again, "How long?" Between kisses she said, "Until Wednesday, if I leave tomorrow. Is that cool with you Boo?" He just laughed. "That will give you enough time to let your other hoes know that their time is running short!", she added to be smart.

Tootie was determined to get her man. Linz liked that in her, she wasn't no quitter. "Babe, what's your real name?", he asked her. "All this time we been messing around, you don't know it?" he had a blank look on his face. So she told him, "Toychica

Nichelle Williams and I'm 26 years old." He stored that info into his mental rolodex.

The two had been atop of Mr. Washington talking for about two and a half hours. He was getting hungry as the smell from the authentic Italian pizzeria assaulted his senses. They indulged in a couple of slices with a serving of pasta. Tootie was enjoying the night, kept touching her ears and stealing a glance at her reflection at every opportunity she could. Linz just sat back and admired her. He felt good inside knowing that he was the reason for her joy. Her eyes sparkled even behind tinted glasses. He was developing deep feelings for the multi-talented ride or die siren sitting across from him. They ate and took the incline down to the bike. "Can we ride for awhile?", she asked, enjoying the feel of the warm October breeze. "Sure." As they cruised through the boro of Oakland, on to East Liberty, and then headed to Robinson. Linz was glad that she didn't speak of the beating he gave to her, but the night was not over with yet. He decided to let her use the Rover to visit her mother for a couple days. That gesture would show that he cared. Once back at his flat, she stripped for him. Underneath her leather she wore a fish net bra and panty set, which she took off very slowly. They made love several times to the sounds of "Glenn Lewis and Gerald Levert". He finally experience Tootie's nasty grind. The next morning, Tootie dressed minus the underclothes, which she purposely left at his home for the next bitch to find. She could only imagine the females facial expression who would be filling in until she got back when she found them. She laughed out loud as she maneuvered the Range Rover down the expressway. Wait until the girls see this, she thought, bobbing her head to "Beyonce's Crazy In Love, as it blasted through the speakers. Go home, shower, get items for Mike and visit, then hit the highway to Columbus. I love that Nigga, she said out loud to herself. Tootie looked good in the cockpit of the Rose tinted, white Rover. God was truly smiling on her, plus she got 80 grand to herself.

CHAPTER EIGHTEEN

The girls were up early still geeked about how much loot they had last night. After Tootie left, they chilled out at A.P and K.J's crib, watched "Paid in Full" and ordered out. Then they split the money, each got $82,500, they held on to Tootie's portion. A.P surprised Diamond with the diamond encrusted ladies Rolex. K.J did the same with Jade, as did Doug with Cristal. Cristal cried because no man ever did anything for her, except her pop's and he died when she was ten. The girls wore their ice proudly.

They didn't get in until about 5:00 am but it was 10:00 am and they were up and hype! They all had mad energy because no screwing was done, except for Jade, who managed to give K.J a ten minute quickie. Jade was gonna get her some dick, fuck the dumb.... Diamond gave up a blow job when they went to pick up the food they ordered. He got head in the whip without crashing it! Cristal did not do quickies, she liked to take her time when getting banged. Some may call her old fashioned, but when it came to fucking, she had to have slow so she could feel every stroke and go through many positions. Even thought Doug was horny as hell, he didn't force it. It will be sweeter in the long run he reasoned. They all ran to the window as they heard the bass from the Rover truck. They wanted to show off their jewels the men gave them. They loved the Four Kings, hooking up with them was definitely a come-up move for them and would later prove to be very prosperous.

They were shocked and happy to witness Tootie emerge from the driver's side, all by herself. They gave each other high fives, all lined up at the door. Waiting on Tootie to enter so they could all sang "Go, Go, Go Tootie, it's your birthday, were gonna party like it's your birthday!", borrowing a line from 50 Cents. "I see you put the poo poo on him,driving the whip all by your lonely and shit!", Cristal said. Tootie smiled and said, "You know me, I handles mines!", bragging by jangling the keys in front of their faces. "That ain't the whole, I got it to get us to Columbus for the next five days! I know my pussy's good! Can I get an amen!" The girls all said "Amen". She told them that she told him about her visiting Mike today and he was cool with it. She also told them she left her panties in his room. They shared a laugh. Diamond called her a scandalous but vicious bitch. Then Jade hit her with her take of the heist. $82,500 felt heavy in her lap, she couldn't believe it.   Then she noticed Diamond's wrist blinging like crazy! "Wait a minute, Rewind!   Come here Bitch!   Let me see your wrist!",   she stated while grabbing Diamond's arm.   "when and where did you get this?"   "Two letters A.P!   Oh, you ain't the only bitch around here with some goody OK!", Diamond said, flashing her wrist and giving dap to Jade and Cristal.   Then Tootie caught the glare on their wrist as well.   They all had iced out ladies watches, along with earrings in various cuts of stone.   She really liked Cristal's three diamond strand earrings.   They hung down about 2 1/2 inches, they were truly shining.

They talked for a moment more, then Tootie said, "Y'all get ready, we out when I come back from the visitation."   Tootie told them she was gonna take 45 stacks, $40,000 for her Mom, $5,000 for her to spend and put $1500 on Mike's books.   The girls agreed to travel after the next hit, which was Diamond's turn.   She welcomed the challenge seeing how much this one paid off.   She'd never expect that on her turn it would be double the amount of the last hit and that she'd take a man's life protecting her man.

It was only 11:30 am, the three girls decided to get a couple hours of sleep since they got very little the night before.   So while Tootie showered, got dressed and ran downtown to see Mike at the County Jail, they all crashed.   Tootie had to visit early because she planned on being in Columbus by 7:30 pm.   She was gonna check on some old friends and hang out.   Studio 69 was gonna be jumping tonight.   She called and left a message for her mom that she'd be there this evening around 7:30.   Then she called the jail to get the visiting hours.   They told her 8:30am - 3:30 pm and 6:00 pm - 9:30 pm.   Good, she had time.   She hoped there wasn't a line waiting at the County.

Once downtown, she picked up a couple books, Dutch I & II, Let that be the Reason, Road Dawgs, Flipside of the Game I & II, and Against All Odds.   She figured Mike would enjoy them along with some magazines.   While in line the clerk tried to holla at her.   Tootie had to admit she was cute, but Tootie didn't swing that way, but if she did she'd surely give Ms. Thang some holla.   As she checked out, homegirl introduced her self as Stephani, wrote her number down, and offered it to her.   She started to reject it, then thought Linz would like her.   Tootie had never been with a woman but she can't say the idea hasn't crossed her mind a time or two.   Then the idea of having a threesome with Linz crossed her mind.   That would be a nice birthday present for him, it would be like killing two birds with one stone.   She took the number and said she'd call her sometime.   Before exiting the store, Tootie called her over to see what she was working with.   Stephani walked over and her ass was jiggling in her khakis.   Tootie reached over and gripped her ass to test the softness.   It felt like butter. She flashed a smile and wink to Stephani and said, "I will be calling you Boo".   Stephani followed her out the door with her eyes.   Tootie knew she was watching, so she stopped and bounced her cheeks for her.   The Champion sweatsuit did nothing to conceal Tootie's well shaped backside.   She hopped in the Rover and smashed out, leaving Niggas and Bitches gawking.

Tootie parked the truck in the visitors area, gathered her bags and strode toward the entrance.   The jail visitors lounge wasn't full, which was a good thing.   She signed in and waited to be called.   Some dude came over trying to holla.   She recognized him as one of those broke ass niggas who used to come watch her shake her ass at the Red Devil. He always tried to entice her to trick with him and cop cheap feels.   She looked at him with a frowned up face and with much attitude said, "What you want?   I hope you ain't come over here to holla cause it ain't happening!"   The young dude just slid off. "Williams" the guard yelled.   She stepped forward with her bags and went through the detector.   She gave the bags to the woman at the desk and counted out $1500 for Mike's books.   The lady gave her a receipt and said, "I've seen you somewhere before.   Didn't you sing at Avi's?"   Tootie said, "yes, a while ago."   "I thought you had a great voice.", she said, and then sent Tootie on the elevator up to the 8th floor.

Tootie picked up the telephone and put her palms on the glass to match his.   She felt sorry for what happened to Mike, but what's done is done.   He shouldn't have let her go. Linz had her heart and soul now.   "Hey Boo, I thought you was coming at 6:00 pm.", he said.   "I was but I got to go see my Momma today."   Mike's mind began to fill with memories of the sex they had.   "So how you holding up?   When do you go to court?", she asked.   "I'm cool, I don't know my court date yet but I will let you know as soon as I know."   "I brought you some books and stuff, plus, i left you some money for you to get commissary with."   "Thanks babe, I appreciate it.   So what's going on with you?", he asked.   "Shit, just trying to get past what happened, that's all, but I ain't gonna trouble you with that.   You got enough problems as it is.", she responded.   "Stand up

Boo, let me see you.", he said.   She stood and took a step back.   All she had on was a plain sweatsuit and Airmax, but it was a nice look for her.   Her hair was pulled back in a ponytail.   He motioned for her to turn around, she knew he wanted to see her ass. Niggas in jail was so predictable.   Being a dancer, she learned how to control her ass cheeks, so she bounced them for him, made them clap, and then dipped low.   No doubt he was hard, as was the other niggas who crowded Mike's little glass booth to watch. Some of them left their visits just to watch, or asked their visitors to do the same thing Tootie was doing.   She got some nasty looks but she didn't care.   These bitches didn't know her.   She picked up the phone and said, "I know that's what you wanted to see." "Damn, I miss that, my dick is hard!", he said.   "Oh well, just don't drop the soap.", she commented with a smile.   "Look I done what i could, now I gotta go.   You be safe.", she said.   "You coming back to visit when you get back?", he asked sounding real desperate.   "I don't know, if I ain't busy.", she answered then got up to leave.   Mike knew that as long as he was on lock down, he'd never see her again.   Just as she was leaving Mike's baby momma come in.   The officer also brought him his package of reading material, clothes, and money slip from Tootie.   He smiled at the amount.   At least she kept her word, he didn't expect this much from her because of what went down. Tootie was a memory he'd always hold on to.

Outside Tootie called Stephanie's cell and told her that she didn't mean to mislead her.   She wasn't into girls but thought about it a few times.   The only way she probably would do it was if her man could join.   She told her that she was attracted to her true enough, but her man meant the world to her.   Stephanie understood and agreed to do the threesome it that's what it took to taste her goodies.   Tootie told her she'd call her later with the particulars, Linz's birthday was less than a month away.   Then she called home and told the girls to get ready because it was time to roll out.

She went home, packed a few outfits and stuffed the loot in her bag.   They all piled in the Rover, gassed it up and was out.   Diamond went through the CD's and settled on Fabulous' CD, followed by DMX.   The girls were headed back home for the first time in eight years.

CHAPTER NINETEEN

Big Rob called at 8:00 am to say he was on his way and was in Knoxville area right now. Nine hours later he, Tonya, and Jen met Linz in Robinson at the mall. Rob was going to be in Pittsburgh until Tuesday. Linz had three birds for him, all Linz wanted was 25 stacks back, same as he did for Chuck. He'd take them to Millennium tonight and Donzi's on Sunday. Then handle business on Monday and send him off on Tuesday. He knew Sullivan would do his thing, he was a stingy bastard, didn't do alot of stunting. He still drove a raggedy ass 1991 Lexus LS 400. He loved that piece of garbage, maybe now he could get a newer model. Linz would talk to Lil Mac about that.

Linz called and hollered at his little bro. They were tight, in fact, Linz was tight with all his family, but most of them lived in Ohio. Bigger cities and more jobs had caused that movement to take place. He and his little brother talked for about 30 minutes. He told him he'd be down soon.

"Hello.", K.J said, answering his phone but not looking at his screen. "Hello, is this K.J?", came the reply. "Yeah, who is this?", he said, looking as his phone at Meeka's picture. "Meeka, we met yesterday in East Lib, remember?", she said. "Yeah, what's up with you pretty?" "I'm good, how about you?", she asked. "Shit, I just got up, about to shower and get dressed, then it's whatever. Why?" She told him to hold on for a minute, he heard voices in the background. "Me and my girl Renee trying to see you and your boy if possible.", she stated. K.J rubbed himself, as he thought of this thick, little, young thang. He guessed her to be about 19 - 21. "Look, I'll hit you back in a few, let me call him.", he said then hung up. He immediately called Lil Mac. "What's up fool?", Lil Mac said. "Nigga, can you get free for a few?", K.J asked. "Yeah, what's up? I'm about to drop Jeanna off at her sister's house." "Remember those two youngins we met yesterday? They tryna hook up.", K.J responded. Lil Mac said, "Hell yeah, I'm wit that." K.J placed him on hold and called Meeka. They arranged to meet at the same place. K.J showered and dressed then told A.P he'd holler at him later, jumped in the Excursion and bounced.

Meeka and Renee watched as the platinum Excursion pulled to the curb, followed by a black Lexus.   The window dropped on the truck, grooves from the Isley Brothers flowed out and K.J said, "Get in."

CHAPTER TWENTY

Orlando Black, a.k.a Rich Money was a smooth player, who was game sharp. Also known through out the area as the Branson of PA, the top weed man. If you got any fire weed it came from him. He only sold the best and his prices reflected that. Now, Dee had good trees too, but not like Rich. Just smelling it you got a serious contact, hell, you might get dirty urine sniffing the bag. Plenty of niggas violated parole and probation by being around someone blowing his product. He charged $700 per ounce, 600 if you are a regular customer. As high as the price was, he sold it like chicken and fish dinners at an African American family reunion. His only business hours were from 12pm to 3pm, if you didn't catch him then, too bad. This is what made him so exclusive. It wasn't nothing to sell fifty to a hundred ounces a day. They came from all over to holla at Rich. You had to be an out of towner to get a pound or more from him. He did away with the competition because he had the best weed, period. Even his average was better than most hustlers best and it went for $500 per ounce. He had it all, dro, tye stik, and sess. It came in all colors and was all buds, no seeds or stems. He had the illest Colombian connect this side of the Midwest. He only paid $8,500 per 200 pound bale, but the catch was he had to buy 50 bales at a time. They kept each other paid. Only way out for Rich was death, and that was soon to happen.

Before Rich sold weed, he was a petty hustler. A few years ago, he dropped his work by another hustler just as the task force jumped out on them. Rich avoided jail, but the other dude wasn't so fortunate. Rich though for sure that he'd never see this nigga again, so fuck him! Rich dropped an ounce and a half of crack at the youngins feet. The dude's lawyer was a rookie in the game, but sharp and hungry. The lawyer did something no one expected, he got the dope fingerprinted. His client's fingerprints wasn't on the dope or the baggie, so the district attorney made a plea of three years. The young man that took the wrap for another nigga's coke was A.P. He told himself for two and a half years he was on lock down that he would never forget that grimey niggas face. He heard about Rich's extreme come up while in jail. That only fueled his anger even more and placed Rich's name on the hit list.

Rich was 6'5" and 230 pounds with basketball skills out of this world. He broke plenty of ankles on the courts.   Rich also had a weakness for foreign women.   He favored Asian and Hispanic females and occasionally African.   He drove a Porsche Cayenne turbo on 24's and wore gators from Barbados.   He wore gold, not platinum, sprinkled with high quality rocks.   He also was good with the pistol.   But A.P knew his weakness.   Diamond was the perfect combination of Japanese and Cuban, beautiful but deadly, plus she was down to ride.   A.P has been grooming her for this score.   The streets were talking about this Tyrese look a like was sitting on some change, about 2.1 million.   Rich would throw parties and set out five pounds of different kinds of weed and you could smoke your heart out.   These underground parties was held in a different spot each time to dodge the ATF.   His game was tight, but his love for foreign pussy would be his demise.

CHAPTER TWENTY-ONE

The girls stopped to get something to eat in Cambridge, a small town right outside of Columbus, at a McDonalds directly off the interstate. It was only 5:45 pm, they made good time. Tootie's phone rang, "Hello", she answered, it was Linz. "What's up Babe, everything alright?", he asked. "Awww, you miss me already?", she said teasing him. He smiled at her little humor. "Naw, just checking on my truck.", he replied. "Whatever Nigga, I know the real! But I was thinking about you. Is it cool if I let one of them drive for a little bit?", she asked. "I left you in charge.", he stated. "I just wanted to ask first because some people be tripping about stuff like that." He laughed and said, "Well, I just called to see how your doing. Call me when you get where you're going." "Aight, I love you.", she said before hanging up. The crew looked at her. "What? I can't tell my man I love him?", she said blushing. Cristal said, "Damn, my girl done got herself sprung!" They finished their food and packed back into the SUV. Tootie tossed the keys to Diamond and said, "You drive, I'm tired." She got in the passenger seat, took off her shoes, reclined the seat, propped her feet up on the dash, and continued watching the DVD the girls started.

An hour later, the girls were in Columbus cruising down Morse Rd. The Twins were dropped off first, then Cristal. Tootie came to a stop in front of her old crib. The hood looked the same, just a couple of new faces here and there. She was happy to be home. She grabbed her bag and hit the alarm, causing the Rover to chirp. She climbed the steps in a hurry to see her mother. She paused on the porch, dug into one of the cracked bricks, and took out her old house key. She smiled, remembering what her mother said to her before she left home eight years ago. "Baby, you can always come back home. I'll leave your key in our "secret spot." A tear eased from her eye. She loved her mother, that was her best friend. Tootie took a moment before letting herself in. Her mother was in the kitchen, making her little girl's favorite meal, shells, smothered in spicy tomato sauce and deep fried chicken. Ajia was an older version of Tootie, 50 and still turning heads.

"Momma", she yelled, "I'm home. Where you at?" Then she heard the dishes rattling. "I'm in here Baby.", her mother said. Ajia always called her Baby, unless

Toychica's friends were around, then she called her Tootie.   Tootie dropped her bags at the bottom of the stairs and headed for the kitchen to embrace her Momma.   They both shed a few tears, it had been eight years too long.   Ajia stepped back to look at her beautiful daughter.   Tootie wasted no time helping her Mom prepare the food.

After they ate and cleared the table, they sat in the room to catch up.   Ajia noticed the jewelry that her daughter wore, especially the earrings.   "Baby, them some nice earrings.   They look expensive."   Tootie touched her ears and smiled.   Her mother knew there was a story behind them, but she wouldn't pry.   If Tootie wanted to tell her, she would.   She admired how beautiful her daughter had become.   Her mind thought back, it seemed like just the other day when she was skinny as a string.   Now a full grown goddess sat before her, with a figure like she used to have.

After a hour of talking, Tootie said, "Momma, I love you.   You know that, right."
"Baby, I know you do.", Ajia replied with a concerned look on her face.   "Momma, I want you to move out of this area.   I don't like you being here by yourself.   It's getting crazy out here.", she stated.   "Baby, if I could afford it, I would.   But, I'm alright, Baby.   Momma will be just fine, God watches over me.", Ajia responded.   "I'm going to be here for a couple of days.", Tootie said getting up to fetch her bag.   Ajia just sat with a confused look as her child returned saying, "I want you to find a house in a better neighborhood.   Someplace like Worthington or Reynoldsburg."   "Hell, I'm barely making it as it is, those places out there start at $150,000.   I don't have that kind of money.", Ajia stated.   Tootie dug into her bag and handed her Mom a manila envelope. "This should be enough for a down payment.", she said.   Her mom dumped the contents out in her lap and seen four bundles of money.   Ajia exclaimed, " How much is this and where did you get all this money?"   Tootie took her mother's hand in her's and said, "It's $40,000 Momma, it's mine.   I want you to have it.   I've been saving it for a while."   Her mother began to protest by shaking her head, but Tootie said, " Momma, I want you to have it.   I have plenty more, okay."   Shoving it back into her mother's lap. Tootie kissed her mother's forehead and said, "Momma, I got something else to tell you."   Her mother began to brace herself.   "I'm in love Momma.", Tootie said with sparkling eyes and a big smile.   She began to tell her about the keeper of her heart.   The other three girls were doing the same thing in their homes with their mothers and Cristal with

her Aunt Tracey.

Tootie went up to her old room to nap, then shower. The girls planned to hit the clubs tonight to celebrate with what little friends they had in Columbus. While Tootie napped, her mother sat watching TV, glad that her child was home for a couple of days. Her hands caressed the bills that her baby placed in her lap and mouthed a silent THANK YOU.

11:30 pm... Tootie was dressed and ready to hit the streets. Her Roc-A-Wear denim skirt and jacket was on point with denim ankle length Manolo Timbs paired with a dusty yellow, sleeveless turtleneck shirt, to match the rocks in her ears. Cristal came by to say hello to Ms. Williams, who was just as happy to see Camile. The little albino was always at her house. They chatted for a few minutes, then the girls were out the door to pick up the twins. Once all four were in the Range it was clubbing time. First stop was the Red Zone. They spent an hour there, then chilled in the parking lot of Purple Haze , Cameron's club, it was packed to capacity. So they went to Studio 69 on St. Clair Rd. The line was around the corner. Jade recognized a dude she used to see back in high school. He was working the door, so she worked her magic and they were let in with the V.I.P patrons.

D.J. Kay Slay was spinning a Jada Kiss blend mixed with T.I., the crowd was crazy hyped! Ballers were everywhere, you could tell that by the cars outside. There were 20's or better on all the cars, gators and ice in abundance. Studio 69 was off da hezzy for sheezy! The crowd responded to the D.J's every spin. The drinks were flowing like the Nile, they were truly enjoying the night. The women was on their way to the next plateau. They were looking good in their outfits with iced out watches, all but Tootie. Jealous and insecure hoes threw shade, while real bitches showed love with compliments like, "That fit is banging" or " Girl, you gotta tell me where you got that:. Meanwhile, the haters ice grilled, sucked teeth, and mumbled to themselves "She ain't all that" or "Bitch". But it was all good because the love outweighed the hate.

2:45AM... The staff opened the emergency doors to let air in. People started filling up the main parking lot and others just cruised through getting they shine on. It was the usual scene, niggas posted up on whips trying to entice the females strolling or riding by. While the women strolled and profiled to catch a nigga's eyes with their goodies on display.

As the crew filed out into the parking lot to get their shine on, niggas pulled up on them a little, making comments like, "Damn, Shorty" and "Let me holla at you Mama!". As the girls approached the Rover, they saw some yellow nigga relaxing on the hood. Tootie kept her cool because she knew how hood niggas can act, especially with liquor in their system. "Excuse me, could you get off my shit?", she said politely. Paul, who happened to be one of Linz's boys just looked at her. Diamond said, "Um, we was talking to you. Are you deaf or something?" By now a little crowd was gathering. "If y'all bitches don't get out of my face." Diamond cut him off saying, "Who you calling a bitch?" Paul responded, "I'm talking to you!" Realizing this could get out of hand, Cristal said, "Look man, we just trying to leave, that's all." "Man, this is my nigga's shit!", Paul said. Tootie looked at her girls and said, "This nigga's trippin or drunk." By that time two brown skinned dudes came over and started whispering to Paul. Cristal thought, "Yeah Nigga, say something now." She was instantly disappointed when they also started lounging on the truck. Tootie said, "Y'all trippin, get off my shit!" They laughed at her, the stocky brown skinned one stood and said, "It's cool, this my brother's truck." Tootie said," No it's not, this is my man's truck." The man she was talking to pulled out his cell and dialed a number. Linz answered after four rings. "Man, where you at?", Jason asked. "Why?", Linz said. "I'm at your truck right now, some broad tripping talking about this her shit." "What she look like?", Linz asked. As Jason described Tootie Linz said, "Give her the phone." Tootie said, "Hello, who the hell is this?" Then her face froze when she heard his voice, "Who the hell you think it is? What are you doing in Columbus?" She replied, "I told you I was going to see my Momma, she lives in Columbus, Ohio! How you know this dude?" "That's my brother Jason, my cousin, and my boy Paul. I got fam in Columbus.", he said. Tootie looked a little closer and seen the resemblance. "Wow, I didn't know.", she said and gave Jason his phone back. She then turned to her girls and explained the deal. They were as shocked as she was. Jason gave her his phone again and asked to see the keys to get a CD out the back. He was always stealing his brother's CDs. She gave him the keys and the girls relaxed a little knowing who Jason was. "My brother keep a dime, he must really like you to let you push the Rover down here without him."

Tootie smiled and said, "I guess so." She never thought of it like that. She and Jason talked for a minute, then he gave her his cell number to call if she needed anything. The girls left to go home, Tootie promised her mom that she'd go to church with her tomorrow.

Earlier that day, Big Rob arrived at the Mall of Robinson a hour after he spoke with Linz. He called and told him that he was at the spot. Linz told him he'd be there in twenty minutes, he had something to take care of. Tonya wanted to see the mall, so her and Jen left Rob in the car to wait for his friend. Linz showed up exactly twenty minutes later. He called and told Rob to drive around the front, he'd be in a black '05 Charger with the hazard lights on. Linz dropped his window saying, "follow me", and they found parking spots next to each other in front of the mall.

"What's up Linz?", Rob said. "Nothing much man.", Linz replied exchanging pounds. "So what was you talking about you got something for me?", Big Rob asked. "I got a little something for you if you want them.", Linz told him as they entered the mall to join Tonya and Jen. The men found them in the Gap, "Hey Tonya.", Linz said giving her a hug. He turned and then hugged Jen, but with a little more affection. "See anything y'all like?", he asked. "Not yet, we only been in three stores so far.", Jen said. "I hope y'all brought something to go out in, I plan on kicking it hard.", Linz said. They all said that they didn't bring anything but could find something. Club Millennium didn't have a dress code for women, but at this time of year they did have one for men, no sneakers or jerseys. Big Rob was cool though he didn't get down like that anyway. He was a casual dressed dude.

Linz gave Big Rob three stacks and told him and Tonya to get right for four days. He and jen stepped off in another direction to shop. They agreed to meet in the Food Court at 8 pm. They had almost two hours to browse and shop.

Rob's mind was reeling because he wondered what his boy had in store for him. Most likely it was something he couldn't tell Tonya, at least not yet. They went in and out of different stores picking up things here and there. Big Rob was a phone freak, he had to have the latest cell phone. He and Linz always clowned around with each other when they got together. It was a complete laugh fest. But when it came to hustling they were top notch, down to get loot anywhere. Turning nothing into something was no biggie to these two.   True paper chasers who would set your block on fire!

Tonya was amazed at the stores this mall had to offer and it's size, her head was spinning.   She damn near went in every store, while Jen and Linz just hit a couple.   He picked out a couple of outfits for her.   The one she'd wear tonight was a cute little number by Enyce and footwear by Michelle .   It was tight as hell.   It had been some years since Jen and Linz linked up, she'd grown a little since then.   She was thicker in all the right places.   He loved her country accent.   They hoped the sex was as they remembered it to be.   Jen remembered Linz had stamina, she counted on him still having it or even more.   This was a break from her current lover, who's performance was getting old to her.

8 pm came, they met up then headed out to get something to eat at Don Pablo's before going to Linz's and Doug's flat.   Jen rode with Linz, while Rob and Tonya followed.   Doug, K.J, and A.P were at the flat when he got there.   They'd only met Rob twice in a span of three years they been doing business with his frat brother's investment company.   He'd secured their money $750,000 a piece in accounts in the Grand Cayman Islands, which after this would swell to about 5-8 million for each. The Crew liked Rob because he was down to earth and silly as hell.

The garage doors parted when Linz pulled up to his abode.   The first thing Big Rob saw was the Black CLS 600 Benz.   "Is that the Benz you was talking about?"   He'd heard about it but never seen it.   He liked what he saw and showed it.

They stepped off the service lift onto the second floor of the warehouse that had been converted into a luxury three bedroom studio flat or a very big bachelor's pad.   It was agreed that Tonya and Rob would sleep in the extra bedroom and Jen would stay with Linz.   After meeting everyone and getting settled in the men went downstairs to talk business, leaving Tonya and Jen upstairs.   "This is tight!", Tonya said, truly digging the set up.   "I know.", Jen added.   As the women planted themselves on the baby blue Lambskin circular sofa and mentally assessed the room.

Meanwhile, the men told Rob they had 56 stacks and some change apiece to give his boy.   They always kept half of the loot in an easy to get to spot at all times.   The other half went into their accounts.   Rob knew that if he ever needed anything he could get it from them, no questions asked, that's how tight they were.   But what he didn't know was that he was getting a couple bricks to take back with him and one of the Chargers that Lil Mac sold them a few weeks ago.   They heard and saw his old ass Lexus, so it was agreed that he'd get one of those Chargers.   The other would go to Tootie and her crew.   The men named the chicks the Four Queens.   It was only right for a king to have a queen by his side.

While Big Rob and his woman were in town his money was no good.   The Four Kings took care of all expenses, returning the love for hooking them up with his boy for the low-low.   Linz would take care of Jen.   They all agreed to hook up at Club Millennium tonight.

The weekend flew by fast, Linz showed them a good time in the city and Jen was shown a good time in bed as well.   She got her back kicked in Saturday through Monday night and Tuesday morning.   Rob handled the business for the boys with his Que bro.   On Monday, he gave them the receipts, minus the 10% his boy charged, and the transaction numbers.   All proved legit after the boys confirmed it through a call to the bank in the Islands.   It's not that the crew didn't trust Big Rob or his boy, but business is business and the love of money is a dangerous game.   Tuesday, Linz sent Big Rob off in the black Charger and three kilos on one condition, he had to leave the Lexus, which he did quickly.   Rob wasn't no dummy.   Shit, he could get another Lexus with what he had hidden in the grill of the Dodge.   Plus, the Dodge was what people were riding these days.   The hemi floated down I-75.   Big Rob came up in a major way.

Sunday morning Tootie sat in Donner Baptist Church with her mother as Reverend Jones preached a sermon on Psalms 100.   As he stepped down, the Spirit rested upon her.   She stood in the aisle and began to sing an old Shirley Caesar hymn, one that she always heard her mother playing and singing.   The congregation looked on in awe as her voice resounded throughout the church.   An older member softly hummed along as she blew an acapella version from the depths of her soul.

JESUS!   (JESUS)

MY LORD JESUS   (JESUS)

OH HOW I LOVE...   (TO CALL YOUR NAME)

I MEAN JESUS   (JESUS)

MIGHTY JESUS   (JESUS)

EVERYDAY... (YOU NAME IS THE SAME)

Tears strolled down her mother's face as she watched her daughter sing a song of praise.   She also prayed that God would protect her only child.   Before leaving, Tootie kneeled at the alter and prayed for herself, her girls, and the four kings.   After church, she and her mother went house shopping.   They were riding through various neighborhoods until they found a little Tudor home in a cul-de-sac in German Village for $175,000.   Ajia made the call.

Tuesday came fast.   The girls enjoyed the time spent with their parents and the parents love seeing their children.   They parted with promises to be back soon.   Just as Linz put Big Rob on the road, Tootie, Jade, Diamond, and Cristal were on I-75 headed home to put in work.   Their appetite for loot was growing, as was their appetite for love.

Back in Pittsburgh, the Four Kings gathered and discussed how to execute the hit and how to get Diamond invited to one of the Rich's parties.   Diamond had to be in the right place at the right time to catch Rich's eye.   A.P had confidence that once she caught his eye, it was over.   Diamond was just that fine.   True to her name, she shined in any situation.   A.P made a bet with the crew, well Linz and K.J, because Doug was riding with A.P, that it would only take two weeks after she got Rich to have the job done and over.   Linz and K.J disagreed and bet $25,000 a piece.

Linz called Lil Mac and told him he needed to see him.   They never discussed any type of business over the phone.   Thirty minutes later, the two sat in Pizza Hut talking. "Man, I need a tuner car.", Linz said.   "A what!", Lil Mac asked with a confused look on his face.   "You know, a Fast & Furious type care and I need it like yesterday.", Linz stated.   "Oh, I got you.   I got one already.   A Mazda RX8, lemon yellow, tricked out, and fast as hell.", Lil Mac bragged.   "When you get this?", Linz asked.   "In Cleveland a couple months ago.   My nigga let me use the tow truck.   I got this when I got the Lexus.", Lil Mac stated.   "So when can I get it?"   "Fool, I gotta get a body.   We can go look for one today after I do something.   We can hook up about 1:30.   I'll call some places.", Lil Mac said.   "Bet, what's the price?", Linz asked.   "I need 15 stacks!   It's worth 70.", Mac said.   "Damn Nigga!   We only need it for about a month, then you can get it back!", Linz reasoned.   Lil Mac thought about it for a minute then said, "Ten stacks, and I need it back.   I got somebody who wants the engine.   He's willing to give

15 for it." Linz wasn't one to knock no one's hustle, plus Mac always showed them love, so it was about time they took a beating on a flipped car. Plus, Lil Mac's work was top notch. He was so good he took a couple of flipped cars back to the dealership and got them fixed under warranty. "Deal", Linz said. He knew Lil Mac's services was vital in this plan. He also talked to A.P about screwing Jeanna, it had to stop. They didn't need any animosity with Mac over a female. A.P had plenty of bitches and now Diamond, he didn't need Jeanna, that was Mac's broad. She was vital to Lil Mac, she sold most of the weed he handled for Dee. With the car issue taken care of, they rapped about some other shit, then parted ways. Hopefully the car would be ready by next week.

CHAPTER TWENTY-TWO

Tootie and the Girls were about thirty minutes from their house, Cristal drove as the others slept. She couldn't wait to see Doug, it has been four days since she felt his embrace. She'd missed him badly. She called his cell, but got his voice mail. She tried again, still go the machine. She hoped he wasn't a whore like the rest. She called again, this time he answered, "Hello". She paused, "We almost home, I missed you." Doug replied, "Me too, if you ain't too tired come through." The men planned to meet with the women tomorrow and let them know the vitals. They had moves to make, they planned on retiring and relocating after the last hit. Cristal and Doug spoke for about twenty minutes. As they passed Burgettstown Tootie woke up. Her and Cristal talked about the men currently residing in their hearts. Every time Linz's name was mentioned she smiled. "Where do you think your relationship is going?", Cristal said. Tootie looked out her window before answering, "I'll be honest, I don't know, but I think it's moving towards something serious. I could be wrong, but pray I'm not. I think I love him." Cristal grabbed her hand and said, "Girl, you gonna be alright." Tootie smiled, "I hope so, I'm tired of searching and holding back for these knuckle heads out here. I want someone I can come home to every night or he comes home to me, ya know." Cristal agreed. Tootie asked, "So, what's the deal with you and Doug? I know something's going on, your ass is just as open as mine. So is those two hoes in the back.", pointing to Jade and Diamond. Tootie wanted to call Linz but didn't want him to think she was bugging him. In the end, she couldn't resist the urge to call the man who gave her butterflies. She gave in and called surprised that he was fiending for her as well.

Jade and Diamond woke as the Rover stopped in front of their duplex. They stretched and filed out of the truck. The Girls unloaded their bags and talked for a moment. Tootie and Cristal packed a couple of things into an overnight bag for their sleepover. "Where y'all hookers going?", Diamond asked. "I'm spending the night over my man's.", Tootie said. "You couldn't wait to get back and get some dick.", Diamond said. They paid her no attention. "Like you ain't trying to do the same.", Jade teased pulling out her cell to phone K.J. Diamond played coy acting like she wasn't trying to see A.P, but they seen through her little front. She waited until they left before doing her calling. She just wanted to be held. She couldn't do anything else except give up some head, it was that time of the month for her.

Tootie showered and changed into some old tattered jeans. They had rips and tears everywhere. She called them her most comfortable jeans. She pulled on her Ohio State Jersey, slid into some clogs, and kissed the girls bye as she and Cristal bolted out the door.

Jade and K.J converse for a few moments before she asked, "Hey Baby, can I come chill with you tonight? Tootie and Cristal went over your boys for the night and I don't want to be here by myself." K.J was eager to see Jade. In the time that she was away, he endured having sex with this "Little Sluts" as he called them. Now that he had a taste for some goody and at this moment only Jade satisfied that craving. "Shit Boo, that's cool. Gimme a hour, I should be home by then.", he said. "Where you at now?", she asked. "With Lil Mac about to get some green, then I'm in for the night.", he responded. Him and Mac just got through creeping with Meka and Renee. "What, you in early? It's only 7:30, you alright?", Jade said being sarcastic. "Babe, I had a long day.", he said. "Mmmhum, you probably just got through fucking.", she said. "What you talking about, you tripping.", he said laughing. "It ain't funny Nigga, you better get your nasty ass in the shower. I don't wanna smell no other bitch's pussy, let alone taste it!", she commented with attitude. She was hot and K.J loved it. He knew how to bring out the fiestiness in her. "You jealous!" "Whatever Nigga, you heard what I said, I'll be there in a hour, make sure you're there. BYE!" She said then hung up. K.J and Little Mac both laughed as they sat in Mac's Lexus smoking a dutch, they rode behind tints. K.J had been riding with Mac since 2:30 pm after he found a body for the RX8. "Want me to drop you off fool?", Mac asked. "Yeah, take me home.", K.J answered, as Mac headed towards the West End.

Diamond drew a hot bubble bath, so she could soak she was beginning to get cramps. She grabbed the cordless phone, took off he clothes and dialed A.P's number. He answered on the first ring, "Hello". "Hey Baby, I'm home.", she said. "So, how was your trip?", he said. "It was good, I missed you.", she cooed. "I missed you too Babe.", he responded. "Umm. I got the house all to myself, you wanna come over?", she asked.   A.P said, "Yeah, want me to stop and get something to eat on the way?"   "I don't care, just don't get nothing too spicy."   "What about Boston Market?   That's cool?", he asked.   "That's cool, get some mac&cheese and some cobbler and cheese rolls, if you don't mind."   Diamond decided to tell him about her period when he got there, and hopefully he would be a sweetheart and stay.   She really liked A.P, she wondered if a love and relationship between them could flourish and survive, even with the odds against them because of the lifestyle and lure of the street.   All the girls tossed this question around in their hearts and mind.

Early the next morning, Linz and A.P hit the gym.   They worked out almost every morning to stay in shape.   When they weren't in the gym, they met up to run.   Doug and K.J were not with working out, you could find them hooping on Saturdays at the "Y".   Tootie stretched out on the big bed savoring the warmth of the covers.   As she looked around for her man, she called his name a couple times but no response.   She put on one of his long t-shirts and went out into the front room.   Instead she found Doug and Cristal having coffee and watching the morning news.   "What y'all doing up so early?", she asked.   "I'm always up this early.", Doug replied.   "Where is Linz at?", she asked.   "He went to work out.   He and A.P go almost every morning."   She then strode to the kitchen, "Any more coffee left?"   "There should be.   You hungry Toot?", Cristal asked.   "A little bit", Tootie replied.   "I'm gonna throw something together in a little while.", Cristal informed her.   "Wake me up when it's done.", Tootie said turning towards Linz's room.   "My boy must be wearing that ass out.", Doug teased.   "Whatever!", she said, waving him off and continuing on her way to lay down.   She had to admit, Linz was wearing her ass out, but she loved it.   When they were together she felt more alive than ever and more beautiful.   She cherished the time they spent together and the way he made her feel.

That afternoon after all the women were dropped off with notice that they'd hook up later today to go over plans for the next hit.   The men got together to discuss strategy.   Linz had taken care of the car.   K. J had found a way to get Diamond into the party, Lil Mac's girl Jeanna had a invitation.   She didn't plan on using it and was willing to give it up for a small fee plus introduce Diamond to Rich, if the price was right.   The crew agreed to pay.   With the profile, photos, car, and Diamond taken care of, there was only one other issue left to tackle, A.P and Jeanna. Linz was the first to speak up, "A.P dog, you gotta stop fucking Jeanna! Bro, it's bad for business. We don't need any beef with Mac over her. You don't need it or her, you feel me." A.P just nodded. "I ain't trying to tell you who to fuck, but Lil Mac love that girl, no telling what he'll do about her.", K.J said "Plus you got a dime in Diamond and the old broad is fine as hell. Jeanna is cute and sexy, but she ain't worth the hassle and Lil Mac is like fam to us. It just ain't cool.", Doug stated. "I hear y'all , don't worry, I'll take your advice. I won't fuck with her no more.", A.P said. A.P always recognized the truth. He knew that he had to stop fucking Mac's girl a couple weeks ago. He along with the rest knew that Mac was essential to the plan. He will call her today and fill her in, after they get the invitation. A.P was no dummy. With that said, they parted and set a meeting time for 8 pm at "Damon's Ribs & Steak House".

CHAPTER TWENTY-THREE

The sounds of AZ's "Sugar Hill" banged out of the speakers in the black Charger, as the girls grooved to the beat. Tootie sang the hook, while Diamond rapped.   The girls were happy the men gave them the Charger because the Nissan was on it's last leg. Even though the rain made the day dreary, the ladies were feeling good as they raced to make their hair appointments at Robin Gear's.   Tootie wanted red highlights and braids, the twins wanted a wash and wrap, and Cristal just wanted her do touched up and dyed platinum blond.   After getting their hair done, the ladies darted in and out of several stores, picking up items here and there using stolen credit cards.

"I still can't believe we made that much money!", Tootie said as they sat in rush hour traffic.   "I know 330 stacks!, Diamond exclaimed.   "All for a shot of pussy.", Jade said. Tootie rubbed herself and said, "I knew you'd come through."   They all busted out laughing.   "Power to the pussy!", Cristal stated as the women lifted their fists in unison. Tootie held out her wrist for all to see, "I know my stuff is good, Okay!", showing off the rose gold and diamond bezeled ladies Cartier watch with a mother of pearl face and crocodile band.   All the women sported nice timepieces, gifts from their men.   "Ayo! We coming up for real and this is only the beginning.:, Jade said.   "I wonder how much the next ones worth?", Tootie said.   "Don't matter, I'm gonna put my thang down anyway, who ever it is!", Diamond stated while switching lanes to catch the off ramp to McKees Rocks.   "One thing I peeped, them niggas ain't stupid, these victims are hand picked.   I'm willing to bet that this one is worth more than the last.", Cristal said.   The rest of the ride was done in silence, except for the sounds of Foxxy Brown's latest CD rifting throughout the Charger.

The girls were dressed in jeans, sorta bohemian chic, which was the latest fashion craze.   They sat in the parking lot listening to Tank's first CD "Forces of Nature" while waiting for the men who was a few minutes late.

Once the men arrived it was all business.   They chose a table in the rear and ordered their food.   When the waitress left, K.J spoke, "Alright Diamond, you ready?   Here's your vic.".   He passed her the photo of Rich Money.   She in turn passed it off to the other ladies, who all had the same blank facial expression.   It was clear none of the women knew this kid, which was even better.   K.J continued laying down the plan. There was only a few questions asked as each member understood his or her position. "Babe, you think you can handle this?", A.P asked.   "I got this, don't worry I won't disappoint you guys.", Diamond said with confidence.   A.P was sure he'd win the side bet he had with Linz and K.J.   "Out of curiosity, how much is this one worth?", Cristal asked.   A.P answered, "I don't know for sure, but, word on the street is about 1.5 million.   But that's just a rumor."   Diamond looked at A.P and said in a matter of fact tone, "We shall soon find out.   That I promise."   All the while, Cristal was doing the math in her head.   Tootie knew what she was doing and asked, "What you come up with?"   "A little over 675,000 if it's 1.5 million."   Diamond's eye's lit up at that amount.   "What y'all gonna do with that much bread?", Linz asked.   "Oh, we got a plan already for this loot.", Jade answered.   The food came but no one was in the mood to eat.   The thought of money had replaced their hunger.

As the crew disbanded, Tootie asked Linz, "Hey Boo, what's wrong with you?" Linz was quiet throughout most of the meeting, which wasn't like him.   "I'm cool.", he replied.   "You like my hair?   I got it done after I left you this morning.   Ain't it cute.", she said turning around to let him see the back.   "It's cute.   I like it.   It showcases your face more."   After several moments she asked, "You wanna see me tonight?". She prayed he did, all she wanted was to be close to him.   Linz paused before answering, "Probably" as he looked off.   "Baby, what's on your mind?   Did I do something?", she asked with a concerned look on his face.   "Naw Boo, it ain't you.", he said getting into his car.   Tootie decided not to push the issue, "Well if you want some company, just call.   I love you."   She then turned and joined the rest of her friends who were engaged in conversation with the other men.   She watched as the raggedy ass Lexus with Tennessee plates that Linz drove blended into traffic.   In the back seat, she silently prayed that he'd call her tonight.   She didn't wanna be alone on this rainy October night.   She actually thought of hooking up with one of her ex creeps, Derek.   It had been about four months since she last seen Derek, that was before Linz walked into her life.   Since then, she'd cut all her creeps loose.   Linz became her only creep move. He calmed her whole being like no other.   Just as quick as the thought came of creeping, her heart pushed it out of her mind.   She was frustrated because she couldn't figure this nigga out. Linz didn't move or act like other niggas in the street. He wasn't no Denzel, but he wasn't ugly, that's for sure. His persona leaked confidence. He was the poster boy for the smooth operator.

When the ladies loaded in the car, they noticed Tootie's somber mood. "What's up with you Toot?", Cristal turned and asked her friend. Tootie just stared out the window. "Bitch, I know you ain't back there crying over that nigga!", Jade exclaimed as she started the car. "Shut up Jade! Your slutty ass would do the same thing if you was feeling like she feels about a nigga.", Diamond said coming to Tootie's defense. "Look, all I'm saying is this, don't stress yourself over him. That nigga like you but you gotta let him do him. I'm feeling the shit outta K.J, but I don't cry because he ain't in my ass 24/7. You tripping! The dick got you so gone, this ain't like you Tootie. Ok listen, I'm gonna tell you what to do." The crew was all ears waiting to hear some stupid shit that Jade is famous for. "you need to go over that nigga's house tonight, don't talk, just fuck. No lovey dovey type shit, just straight fucking. Don't show no emotions at all, and right before he is about to come you get up and leave. Bet that nigga act right then. Shit, Charlie Baltimore taught me that one." Even though it sounded silly, the girls had to admit it could work, as they pictured themselves doing exactly that. "Only your dumb ass is stupid enough to try some shit like that.", Diamond said. "Well it worked on Chris' ass. Y'all remember how he use to play me.", Jade stated. The crew remembered that all to well. Chris used to dog her out, but one day that shit changed. Whatever she did it got Chris acting right. The nigga stalked her for like six months. "I did what Charlie said and his ass was over. K. J next if his ass don't quit playing with a bitch like me." They all laughed, as the car blended in with the flow of traffic. Tootie asked, "What did you say do again?" Cristal looked at her and said, "Girl, are you serious!" Tootie responded, "At this point, I'm ready to try anything. Y'all just don't know how he makes me feel, even when we ain't doing it." Cristal had jokes as she began to sing Usher's "You Got It Bad". They clowned her, but she didn't care, these girls were like family to her. The laughter lifted Tootie's somber mood, but she had stored Jade's suggestion in her mental rolodex for future use.

CHAPTER TWENTY-FOUR

Rich Money's party was Saturday, three days away, A.P called Jeanna to check on the invitation and see if she'd introduce Diamond to Orlando (Rich Money). He also told her that he couldn't fuck with her like that anymore. She understood and told him that she had wanted to tell him the exact same thing. Jeanna believed that Lil Mac knew about her unfaithfulness and that he might have another chic on the side. He was spending too much time with K.J and she knew K.J was a certified whore in all 50 states and across seas. She was afraid some of that behavior would rub off on Mac. She even thought K.J told Lil Mac. She didn't want to lose Lil Mac. He was the only someone who loved her and treated her with respect. Jeanna couldn't and wouldn't risk her position in Lil Mac's life

They arranged for Jeanna to hook up with Diamond on Saturday morning then they would attend the party together. Jeanna decided to go and bring Diamond as her guest to make sure that Rich seen and spoke to her and to watch Diamond's back. Although jeanna had loose ways, she was a true ride or die bitch, her gangsta was pure. She wasn't afraid to fight or let loose with the chrome .380 she toted. That's one of the reasons why Lil Mac kept her around.

After A.P hung up with Jeanna, he called the other members of the crew to inform them of the plan and to rub it in their faces. Then he called Diamond to tell her show time was Saturday and that he'd holla at her later, which was good because the girls decided to make this a girls night out. They decided to go to Ladies Night at Sweet Georgia Brown to cheer up their girl Tootie. The drinks were half price until midnight, plus the crowd would be nice. The brothers would be out too. Even though they had so called men, it didn't hurt to look.

Saturday came fast. Jeanna and Diamond spent the day getting to know one another while shopping for something to wear at Ross Park Mall. The two ladies clicked almost at once.

It had been three days since Tootie seen or heard from Linz, so she decided to pay him a visit this morning and give Jade's suggestion a try. After she dressed in a black sweatsuit with a pair of black Nikes, she grabbed the keys to the Nissan and hit the streets.   Tootie had to work herself up to pull this off.   She called Cristal, who was at Doug and Linz's place, to find out if he was home and so she could let her in.

Linz was in bed asleep when Tootie came in his room at 8:30 am, took off her clothes and crawled into bed with him.   He was laying on his back so that made her job a lot easier.   Now all she had to do was get his boxers off.   Peeling the covers back two things: 1. He wasn't wearing boxers and 2. Like most men, he had an early morning erection.   She couldn't figure out why that happens to men, but luck was on her side, all she had to do was straddle him and ride.   The hardest feat would be showing no emotion during the episode.   She grabbed his dick and lined it up with her opening, gently lowering herself onto him, stretching her walls to accommodate him dry.

Linz thought he was dreaming as he felt the warmth surrounding his penis.   He dared to open his eyes, but when he did he came face to face with Tootie.   She stared at him with an expressionless face as she bounced up and down on him.   He began caressing her breasts with his hands.   Tootie fought hard with her body to ignore reacting to his skilled touch.   'Just one more minute then I'll be coming.   As soon as I'm done, I'm out!', she told herself.   She focused on the anger she felt to block out the pleasure he brought her.   "AAAuuughhh" she cried as she came hard.   Leaking juices all over his groin, she jumped up, grabbed her clothes, and ran for the bathroom leaving Linz hard and surprised.   As he lay on the bed waiting for her to return, Tootie dressed quickly and bolted out the front door.   Linz ran after her but it was too late, Tootie had made it to the car.   He just watched her drive off.

An hour later, Linz called K.J and told him what just happened.   K.J fell out laughing.   Linz told him that he needed to see him to take a ride with him.   K.J said he'd be over in a half hour so Linz showered and dressed.

Linz wanted K.J to come with him to Danore, PA to look at an old school car that he seen in the Auto Trader.   It was a '68 Olds 442 convertible with only 75,000 miles. The owner wanted $9,500 or best offer.   Linz was getting ready for flossing season. The draft started in April, that's when all the ballers and playas got their whips in the paint shop so they would be ready for opening day, May 1st.   Linz wanted to go in the first round, which was the whole month of May.   The streets talked and told whose ride was the cleanest.

Linz heard K.J before he saw the Excursion.   He grabbed his keys and some money and went out to meet K.J.   "What the business is Playa?", K.J asked laughing.   "Man, I need you to go look at this car with me.", Linz replied.   "Where at?   What kind of car is it?", K.J asked.   "A '68 Olds 442 convertible in Danore."   "Shit, I thought you didn't like old school whips.", K.J teased as Linz got in the Excursion.

Once in Danore, Linz called and got directions to the spot.   An old white lady was the owner.   The car was in her storage shed behind her house along with four other classics.   The Olds was white with black guts and top.   It was in good condition except it needed two tires and a muffler.   Ms. Barksdale had her son start the car.   Although the car had been sitting for 15 years it started on the first try.   She didn't want to sell it but needed the money.   Linz talked her down to $7,500 and the title was exchanged. Linz called the tow truck to tow it back home.

K.J looked around at the other classics and set his eyes upon a blue Caddy Deville convertible with white interior.   "How much for this right now?", he asked.   The elderly woman hesitated then said, "$10,000".   K.J looked at the car, trying to find a way to jew her down.   Her son turned the key and the big engine came to life instantly. This Caddy was in pristine condition.   K.J knew a steal when he saw one and this was ONE.   The Lac' had 45,000 miles with all original equipment.   "Shit, if you could follow me home I'll give you that, all I have is $7,300 on me."   The woman thought about it and said, "You boys seem like nice young men, if your friend will give you $2,000, I'll let you have it for $9,000."   Linz quickly gave K.J the loot, he didn't even have to ask.

The tow truck driver agreed to tow the car to Robinson for the $500 that Linz had left.   K.J drove the Caddy while Linz pushed the truck back to the city.   While the tow truck followed.

Linz had plans for the Olds.   Later today, he'd get K.J's boy Motorhead and his partners Spray and Drip to bring his vision to reality.   Motorhead was called that because he could do anything to a motor in his sleep.   Spray was the illest unknown painter, airbrusher, and pinstriper in the tri-state.   While Drip was a master tailor of car interiors.   Their work was something straight out of a Lowrider Magazine.   Linz visioned the Olds an emerald green with canary yellow Gucci guts and top sitting on 22" chrome daytons. Draft Day he would definitely be ready.

CHAPTER TWENTY FIVE

The Oasis was packed as Jeanna and Diamond pulled up to the valet. Niggas was trying to get in without an invitation as always. Jeanna presented hers and she and Diamond were allowed into the packed building. People were everywhere! Niggas and Bitches showed up and went all out for a Rich Money party. Everyone was dressed to impress, even though Rich wasn't among the top 20 biggest ballers in the greater Pittsburgh area, he without a doubt threw the livest parties. Niggas was guaranteed dime bitches in over abundance and the females were guaranteed balling niggas in abundance.

Jeanne and Diamond mingled with the crowd for a hour before spotting Rich who was talking with a group of guys and girls. Jeanna sent him a drink, which he accepted once he realized who it came from. That's when Diamond caught his eye. He excused himself and walked towards them. "Jeanna, long time no see! Who's ya friend?" he wasted no time cutting into Diamond. "Oh this is my girl Kim Lee.", Jeanna said giving him a fake name. He kissed Diamond's hand and said, "Pleasure to meet you". She smiled and said, "Likewise". Rich was entranced by her beauty. As he openly admired her checking her from head to toe calling her a vision of love.

Diamond looked good in her Michael Kor's outfit and Prada heels. She and Jeanna were turning heads. "I don't mean to be rude, but, what nationality are you mixed with?", Rich asked. "My mother's 100% Japanese and my Pops is Cuban and Black.", she said. This fulfilled Rich's taste for foreign women. He had to have her at whatever cost.

Jeanna stepped off and let them talk. They went to his VIP booth for about two hours. During that time, friends of Rich stopped by to show respect and complimented him on the party and the weed that was available in each of the three back rooms. Club Oasis was privately owned by some Mafia oldies who had a couple of uniforms on the payroll. So the club getting raided was never a threat.

Diamond sat taking the whole scene in, puffing on some of the best weed in North America. Her eyes became even more slanted, making her even sexier. Yeah, Rich had to have her. "You having a good time Baby?", he asked. "Yeah, I'm feeling good. How about you?", she responded. "In your presence, one can't help but to feel good.", he flirted.   They talked for a few minutes more before she rose to find Jeanna.   She was ready to leave, the weed was starting to get to her.   She wrote her number in his palm before leaving.

Once outside, they gave the valet their ticket and waited for him to bring the Mazda around.   Rich went out to thank Jeanna.   "make sure your girl get at me.   I'll owe you.", he whispered to Jeanna as Diamond got behind the wheel.   Rich liked the Mazda she pushed.   The engine whined as they sped away.

Diamond couldn't wait to get home and to sleep.   She dropped Jeanna off with promise to call tomorrow.   She went home and got straight in the bed.   She'd call A.P in the morning, but A.P called her instead.   He said that he was on his way over. "Damn, can't a bitch get some sleep!!", she screamed.   She was too tired to talk, let alone fuck!.   It was her first day off her period and she knew A.P wanted some.   Hell, so did she but she was just too tired.   What was she gonna do?

A.P came and they talked about the night's events.   He told her about the bet he had with Linz and K.J and agreed to split it with her if she could pull it off.   Her eyes felt heavy as he continued to talk with her.   She was too damn tired, sleep overcame her . A.P undressed her and tucked her in before he left to holla at one of his other broads.

Diamond was up and ready early the next morning.   She and Tootie put in a yoga tape and followed.   It was something they started doing a few days ago.   It helped them relax and stay flexible since they didn't dance no more.   Her and Tootie talked about last night's events.   "Man, the weed was bomb!   I mean true one hitter quitter.", Diamond said, while relaxing in the Lotus position.   "You ain't stash some?", Tootie asked.   Diamond shook her head no.   Rich called just as the taped ended.   "Hey Baby, what's up with you?", he asked.   "Nothing, just got finished exercising.", she answered. They talked for twenty minutes resulting in a dinner date at the Sushi Bar at 8 pm.

Rich lived on the outskirts of the city, but kept an apartment in the city.   His money was stored in the basement of his home and the weed in an insulated storage shelter behind the house in the field.   Rich owned five acres in Carlise, he believed in seclusion. He just picked up his shipment of one hundred 200 pound bales of super high grade Colombian weed, which he got every three months.   Rich was presently worth 2.9 million, without the value of the weed he had stored.   Rich had no enemies that he knew of because he was a fair guy and known to bust guns quickly.   He never would have believed that a female would do him in.

Over the next ten days, he and Diamond spent almost every waking moment together.   She even pushed the Porsche SUV a few times.   She was seen on his arm at all the functions looking fabulous.   In the bed, she was doing her thing.   She sucked him dry every morning.   He woke up to the best head in the USA.   Rich had no time to grasp what was going on and to realize that he was slipping bad... REAL BAD!   They talked about everything even personal business, but Rich didn't disclose the location of his money or product.   No matter how strong her jaws were, she couldn't extract that info.   She also had never been to his home, only his apartment.

Diamond knew that Rich didn't live at his apartment because it didn't possess that "lived in" vibe.   One day when they traded cars she called her twin to meet her at the salon.   There she gave Jade the keys she had to the truck with three other keys on the ring.   She told Jade to get copies made at the key place around the corner.   Jade got three copies made of the extra keys on the ring.   She couldn't get a copy to the truck made though.   Twenty minutes later, Diamond had the keys in her hand.

Jade called K.J and told him about the keys, now all they had to do is follow Rich and watch his every move.   Doug, Cristal, and Tootie took turns watching this nigga 24/7.   It seem like they'd be doing this forever.   Rich always took a long alternate way home, but lately he ain't been home, he been staying in the city.   After two weeks of surveillance, the crew got a break, it came on Cristal's watch.   She followed behind in the Lexus as he took her on a two hour joy ride before turning down a non marked driveway in the country part of Carlise.   She marked it in her little hand held GPS navigator compass.   She pulled off the road a few yards from the drive and settled to watch.   About six hours later, she spotted his SUV coming up the driveway, which was about 1/4 mile.   Cristal took a chance and stayed behind.   As soon as the truck was out of sight, she got out and ran down the drive, going straight for the mailbox.   She took three bills addressed to Orlando Black, 4429 Stirrup Rd.   She then stuffed the bills in her pocket and ran back towards the car.   Once safely inside the Lexus, she phoned A.P and told him where she was and what she found.   A.P confirmed that it was Rich Money's home and told her to come on back.   They got what they needed.   Now they'd have to wait for an opportunity to present itself.

A.P realized that he'd lost the bet with Linz and K.J, he was hot.   He'd take it out on Rich, A.P hated to lose.   Linz and K.J called and asked, "Can we get our bread in small bills please?", followed by sounds of laughter.   "Nigga, you'll get it how I give it to you.   Keep laughing and I'll give it to you in pennies.", A.P said mad as hell.   Rich cost him fifty stacks.   That was a nice chunk of change to anyone.   A.P then called Diamond informing her about the latest news and told her to get that nigga alone tonight.

Jade was out at Rich's apartment seeing if any of the keys fit this lock, one did.   She just opened the door and peeped in, not knowing if it had an alarm system or not.   She waited by the steps for a couple of minutes, nothing happened and no one came.   She went in careful not to touch anything.   She just looked then left.   She called Linz to tell him about the key and which one it was that opened the apartment door.   She also described the layout of the place.

CHAPTER TWENTY SIX

Rich and Diamond spent a wonderful evening together and was on their way back to the apartment when she called Jeanna to tell her where she was, who in turn relayed the message to the Four Kings. Jeanna liked hanging with Diamond, they became good friends in the last few weeks. Jeanna gave Diamond a little .380 to protect herself with. She had an inkling things could get sticky. Diamond tucked the two shot derringer in her purse at all times, not thinking she would use it tonight. Her and Rich got in about 11:30 pm. She went straight to the shower to freshen up, while he rolled a blunt. They engaged in sex for a few hours which was abruptly interrupted at 2:30 am by Rich hearing a noise. "SHHHH...", he said while reaching for his weapon and chambering a round. Diamond tried to cover up but instead grabbed her purse.

The Four Kings crept through the apartment unaware that Rich was alert and armed, ready to give it to them. He motioned for Diamond to get down and keep quiet. He then eased through the hall one step at a time. As he made his way to the living room entrance, he caught the shadows of two people. He squeezed off three quick shots hitting one of the masked men in the shoulder causing him to drop his gun, while the other man scrambled for cover.

Linz and K.J were at the back door when they heard the shots. They kicked in the door, but was greeted by gunfire causing them to duck out the door. A.P laid on the ground bleeding from the bullet he took in the shoulder. The bullet from the 9mm went straight through and out the back. He screamed in pain.

Rich let off two more shots, catching Doug in the thigh and ass and sending him toppling over the dining room table. Diamond came running out of the bedroom just as Rich stood over a maskless A.P. "Where I now your bitch ass from?", he asked pointing the gun at A.P's head. A.P's face was adorned with terror, it all seemed to be happening in slow motion. A.P saw Diamond raise her gun and pump two shots into Rich's skull at point blank range, dropping him like the World Trade Center. He couldn't even hear her voice or the gun blasts. Everything sped up as the weight of Rich's body came down on him.

Diamond ran to A.P's aid as Linz and K.J came charging through the back door.

Doug groaned as he struggled to get up.   Diamond cried as she held A.P.   "Babe, get dressed we gotta bounce.", Linz said pushing her away from A.P.   K.J helped Doug get to his feet.   Diamond returned dressed and ready to go.   She couldn't believe that she just took a man's life protecting the man she had fell in love with.   She gathered up the guns off the floor.   Linz told her to get Doug and A.P out of there.   The boys in blue would be there soon.   Linz and K.J cleaned up the apartment.   Diamond and the two men piled into the Lexus and smashed out, while Linz and K.J collected the shell casings and bolted out the back door.   In the distance they began to hear the sirens approaching.

Linz called Tootie and told her, Jade, and Cristal what went down and to meet them at Rich's place in Carlise ASAP.   Diamond assured them she'd take care of A.P and Doug.   They were on their way to a hospital in Youngstown, Ohio which was an hour away.

Linz and K.J arrived after Tootie and the girls.   The five of them went to the front door and used one of the three copied keys, it worked.   They split up and searched the house from top to bottom.   At 3:30 am, they converged on he basement.   It was empty except for a pool table.   "Shit, it's gotta be here somewhere.   I know it is!", K.J said frustrated.   "We looked everywhere.", Tootie said.   "Check the ceiling pipes or something like that.   Hell, he might have hid it in the walls.', commented Jade.   K.J looked around then noticed the basement had two hot water heaters but only one had a lit pilot and hummed.   "I think I know where it is!", K.J said inspecting the units.   He noticed some loose screws.   He found a screwdriver and removed the screws.   Once the top was removed, money fell by the bundles at their feet.   "Go find some bags or something to put this in!", Linz said to Tootie.   They found a couple suitcases and duffle bags to put the money in.   They loaded the loot into the Nissan's trunk.   Linz told Tootie to go to his house and gave her the keys.   "Go straight there and wait for me to get there, O.K.", he said.   She nodded as she eased down the driveway.

Back in the city, Homicide detectives was going through Rich's apartment searching for clues to the cities 59th homicide this year.   The weed heads would surely miss Rich Money's product.   Everyone will put one in the air tomorrow for a street legend in the game and on the courts.   Damn Rich, you had a good run but that's the price you pay when you do some foul shit. KARMA BABY KARMA!

CHAPTER TWENTY SEVEN

Tootie and Jade sat at the kitchen table drinking coffee and talking. "I did what you said to do a couple weeks ago.", Tootie said. "What are you talking about Girl?", Jade replied. "You know... I went over his house one morning, fucked and left before he could get his off!", she revealed. Jade smiled then asked, "Did it work?" Tootie blushed then confessed, "Yeah, I think. I've been getting it on the regular now. I even got some space in his closet." Tootie was happy that for the past few weeks she'd spent alot of time with her man. Linz was also enjoying her company. They did alot of things together. It wasn't just about sex, they had became close friends also, doing things that lovers do. They looked good together.

"So, I take it the relationship is progressing in the direction you wanted right?", Jade asked. "Yes", Tootie replied smiling. She always smiled when his name was mentioned. "So how about you and K.J?", Tootie inquired. "Girl, he's a piece of work, but I can handle him.", Jade said. The girls talked for a few minutes about Linz and K.J before switching the subject to their mothers. Tootie made a mental note that she needed to call her mother. "Speaking of calls, I need to call and check on my Sissy.", Jade said getting her cell out. While Jade phoned her sister, Tootie called Linz. He told her that the boys were cool and would be released sometime tomorrow afternoon. He also assured her Diamond was okay, just a little shaken up. He told her he'd be home soon and to stay until he got there. Tootie asked if it was alright for Jade to lay in the guest room. He quickly said yes. The call ended with her saying "I love you."

Diamond couldn't get the events of the night out of her mind. Now she knew what it felt like to kill a man. Every time she closed her eyes it played like a picture in her head. She told her heart that she did it for a good reason, but murder is murder, no matter how you slice it. However, now wasn't the time to break down. She stared at A.P as he laid on the bed dozing from the meds they gave him. His gun shot wound was clean and didn't do any damage but he would be in some pain and discomfort for a while. She squeezed his hand to assure him of her support.

Cristal, K.J, and Linz clowned Doug for getting shot in the ass. The thigh wound was just a graze. He'd be okay, just couldn't sit for a while. His woman was going to nurse him back to health.   Linz thanked the Lord that his boys were okay.   He'd wait until later to tell them of the spoils the night brought.

CHAPTER TWENTY EIGHT

Lil Mac and Jeanna learned of the death of Rich Money by way of the street. Everyone was talking about it, speculating that it was his Colombian connect that did it to him. Some even said it was the Mafia. No one thought Rich had any enemies, but none knew of the one blemish he had on his street cred record. All over the Burgh, people were sparking up in memory of Rich and mourning the death of the best bud in the Midwest.

Lil Mac puffed a blunt as he cruised down Pennsylvania Avenue. 'This is some good ass weed.', he thought to himself. Then it hit him, only one man had trees this fire... Rich! He'd put the two events together, Rich's death and the Four Kings had a shit load of marijuana. "No they didn't!", he said out loud to himself. Then thought back to the night that he'd met Linz downtown at McDonalds. It was about two months ago when Linz told him that he might have something for him.

Mac took a monster hit, holding it in for a few seconds, before exhaling and saying, "Well Rich your downfall is my come up. You done crossed the wrong niggas. I don't know what you did, but it cost you." As he piloted the Lexus through the city of Pittsburgh, blowing some of the good stuff. His mind spinning from the thought of what his future would be like now that he had bales and bales of the finest grass. Yep, He and Jeanna were about to do a "George and Weezy Jefferson moving on up routine".

Doug and A.P had been home for two days before the incident of that fatal night would be discussed. During the days that followed, Diamond had trouble sleeping. She woke in cold sweats triggered by nightmares of the scene replaying in her head. None of the other girls knew that she was the one who actually killed Rich or that she did it to save A.P until today when they all met to split the loot. The woman's take was $1.2 millions, netting them 300,000 each. The men's amount was $1.7 million, which was $425,000 each in cash and a few millions more in weed. The money put Diamond a little at ease. A pound or two of the dro erased those nightmares, along with the comfort of A.P's embrace.

The only dilemma the boys were facing is how they were going to get rid of and store all that weed. At this time they couldn't flood the city with it because then everyone would know that it was them who took out Rich and they didn't need that kind of heat.   Lil Mac had kept them up on what the streets was saying.   He would be one of the outlets for them to move the green.   Also, Linz would go holla at his little brother this weekend.   Columbus was a good market for weed.   None of the men regretted what happened with Rich, neither did the ladies.   They all agreed to continue with the plan, but they'd chill until A.P and Doug was back to 100% or at least able to perform.

"What you gonna do with your share?", Linz asked Tootie as they soaked in the tub. "I'm buying my mom a house.   I already gave her $40,000 the last time I went home.   I want to go home this weekend for a couple of days.   Why don't you come with me so you can meet my Momma.   I already told her about you."   Linz tossed it around his mind before agreeing to meet her mother.   "Then me and the girls want to do a little traveling.   Why?   What are you going to do with yours?", she asked turning to face him.   "Stack it and invest.", Linz answered as he reached for a towel.   "No, don't get out yet.   Sit with me for a while.   I take showers with you when you want me to, don't I?", Tootie stated.   "Babe, the water is getting cold!"   "So, just for a couple more minutes.   It ain't gonna kill you.", she shot back.   Linz settled back into the water, allowing her to relax against his chest once again.   The tub in the girls house was one of those vintage claw footed tubs that you could really relax and soak in.   Out of the blue, Linz whispered, "I love you." into her ear causing her to turn around.   These were the words she'd been longing to hear for the last couple of months.   "About time I get to hear it from you.   Next time don't take so long!", she playfully stated.   "Whatever", he replied.   "Alright whatever, I was about to do a Mariah Carey and shake your ass off.", she said and began to sing Mariah's new single.   Linz loved to hear her sing.   Tootie had a voice.   After they dried off, they took turns massaging each other down with lotion.   Tootie wanted to call her mom before it got too late.   He searched for a movie to watch while she made her call.

"Hello", Ajia said in a sleepy voice after several rings.   "Hey Momma."   "Hey Baby.", Ajia said happy to hear from her child.   "What's wrong with your voice Momma?   Are you sick?"   "Chile, I think I'm getting a cold, but I'm alright don't you worry about me .", her mother replied.   "So, what they say about the house?", Tootie asked.   "Girl, you late.   I've moved in two weeks ago.   If you would have called like you was supposed to you would have known that.", her mother said in a playful tone. "Momma, I'm sorry. I have been so busy, but guess what! I'm coming down this weekend and I'm bringing my boyfriend to meet you.", Tootie exclaimed. "Well how long you staying? Y'all can help me move the rest of this stuff. I've been working so much lately.", Ajia rambled. Tootie asked Linz how long they were going to stay. He told her at least a week. Her mom was delighted at the time period. "Momma, how much is the payments?" Ajia said, "$750.00 a month for fifteen years, but, since I'm buying directly from the owner I could probably work out something cheaper." Tootie responded, "Momma, I'm going to give you some more money to put on the house. See if you can pay it off early." Ajia grew silent for a minute then asked, "Baby where are you getting all this money from?" "Momma, stop worrying. I told you I got enough. Now are you going to let me do something nice for you or not?" "Baby I just...", was all that Ajia got out before Tootie cut her off saying, "Momma, I told you, stop worrying. You worry too much. Sit back and let me do something for you. I'm alright." It is only natural for a mother to be concerned about her only child. "Well I just called to tell you I'd be home this weekend and to say I love you. I'll talk to you soon.", Tootie said hanging up before her mother got a chance to get started. Tootie and Linz watched "All about the Benjamins", then made love slowly before falling victim to sleep in each others arms.

CHAPTER TWENTY NINE

It was about 10 am when the phone rang, Tootie answered, it was K.J calling for Linz.   Linz looked puzzled as she handed him the phone.   He wondered who could be calling him at her house.   "Hello", he said.   "Nigga, you forgot what we was supposed to do today?"   Today they were taking the cars to Motorhead's shop.   "Awe man, I did forget.   I'll be at the house in about thirty minutes.", Linz stated.   "We waiting on you.", K.J said.   "I'm leaving now."

Linz turned to Tootie and tried to kiss her.   She playfully resisted and said, "No boy your breath stank!"   He kissed her anyway as he got out of bed to put his clothes on. He'd have to shower later.

"So, am I going to see you later or will it be later tonight?", Tootie asked.   "In a couple of hours.", he replied.   "Yeah whatever, I guess I'll see you tonight.", she said with sarcasm.   He just looked at her.   She threw a pillow at him as he laced up his Timbs.   "We are going to Columbus right?", he asked grabbing his coat.   "We're leaving today?", she asked obviously shocked.   Today was only Wednesday and they weren't supposed to leave until the weekend.   "Be ready by 4:30.", he said before descending the stairs.

Linz pulled up to see K.J, Motorhead & Spray waiting outside.   They loaded the Olds onto the wrecker and he followed them to the shop.   Once there Drip and Spray went to work while Linz and K.J voiced their visions to Motorhead.

Linz wanted an emerald green bowling ball with green-pearl, platinum, and emerald flakes, canary yellow Gucci guts with white piping and a Gucci top with interlocking G's done in yellow and green, burl wood dash, steering and console.   He wanted it sitting on 22 inch chrome rims.   Oh yeah, and a white rally stripe with yellow tribal pin stripes through it.   The price Motorhead gave was $27,000 which included all body and motor work plus a chroming, suspension, brake upgrade.   Best believe that when it was done it would be a one of a kind work of art.   Linz told him to go to work and to call when it was done.   Linz then turned and gave K.J some dap, said peace to the rest and bounced. He had somethings to take care of before he left.   Plus, he wanted to check on Doug and A.P to see how they were doing and to tell them where he was headed just in case they needed him.

K.J was going on a road trip also.   He and Jade had a little getaway of their own planned.   They were headed north to Canada to check out the World Mall.   Ever since Jade returned from seeing her peeps, K.J was doing a lot less whoring.

Linz went home, showered, and changed into a pair of jeans and an Ohio State throwback Archie Griffin jersey with some red Timbs.   He packed a few things , not much because he knew he'd do some shopping down there.   He then grabbed a stack of loot and went downstairs to the garage area to retrieve one of the compressed bales of high grade hydro which he placed inside the spare tire compartment.   He threw his suitcase in the trunk of the Mercedes Benz CLS 600 and called Tootie to tell her he was on his way to get her.   Tootie was pissed because she just got in and didn't have time to really pack nothing.   She just got out of the tub, so she threw on an Adidas classic track suit and a pair of Adidas tennis shoes.   She went to her closet and just hastily put things into a small suitcase.   She thought, 'Fuck it, I'll just buy something down there."   Putting a $100,000 dollars under her clothes, she planned on giving her mother $50,000 towards the house and using the rest to get her mom new furnishings for her home.   Value City would get most of their business.   Tootie and her mother never forgot the times when they didn't have much.   Ajia still shopped in discount stores, rarely splurging.   Tootie grew out of that phase, but never forgot it.   She knew that is where her Momma would go to buy furniture, besides they had good quality stuff.   She hoped to get her mother better transportation.   Ajia still drove a '91 Audi.   She figured about $35,000 would do the trick, the rest she'd use on herself.

Tootie had just got off the phone with her mother when Linz arrived.   Her Mom was glad that she was coming early, hopefully she'd be fully moved in before they left.   Even though she had the house, she still spent the night at her old house.   Linz didn't bother getting out the car when he got there, he just hit the horn.   She came to the door with suitcase in hand.   As she approached the Black Benz, Linz popped the trunk for her.   After her bags were in place, she joined him in the cockpit of the luxury sedan.   Tootie had seen the Benz, but never rode in it.   She was taken back by the black leather and mahogany wood interior.   "this is banging, you gonna let me drive?", she asked adjusting her seat to comfort.   "Yeah, you driving half the way", he replied.   Tootie wasted no time settling in. She took her shoes off and went through the CD collection. These past few weeks she has became real relaxed around him. She came across a few white pop artist like Phil Collins and Hootie & the Blowfish. She began to question him about the groups, she didn't think he listened to groups like that, but he did. Music had no color to him. She loaded the changer with Donell Jones, Musiq, Monica, Luther, Carl Thomas and R. Kelly.

"Lately you just been doing what you wanna do, huh?", he said pulling into the B.P to get gas. Tootie just smiled as he got out of the car to pump the petro. She dropped the window and asked him to get her a juice and pack of gum. Tootie reclined back in the seat as they cruised down 279 into Weirton, WV, through Steubenville, Ohio and onto Wheeling, West Virginia, each of them lost in their own thoughts.

"We gonna stay with my Mom or get a room?", Tootie asked breaking the silence. "Whatever you wanna do is cool.", he answered. She turned in her seat to face him putting her feet in his lap. "Baby, my Mom is gonna try to get you to go to church with her on Sunday. I'm just warning you before hand. OK?" She knew Linz was a Christian and that he read his Bible and prayed but she didn't know his church going habits. "That's cool with me, I don't mind going." She smiled and said, "My Momma is going to love you."

Just as Carl Thomas began to play the volume muted and a ringing sound replaced it. The Benz was equipped with blue tooth technology. His cell was plugged into the system "Hello", Linz said. "I got your message, what's poppin?", his brother Jason asked. "Man, I'm on my way now, I'll be there in about two hours. I'll hit you when I get closer. Oh yeah, I got Tootie with me.", Linz told his little bro. They rapped for a few minutes more then hung up. Carl Thomas resumed playing. The two shared an intimate conversation mainly about where their relationship was going. He absent mindly massaged her feet while she voiced her goals for this love affair. She wanted to see a marriage come out of it, along with a child or two. He was thinking along the same lines but said nothing. He'd just let things happen. A wall was still around his heart. "Who knows Boo, it could happen.", he said. "Do I need to start wearing condoms again?" It's been about a month since they used protection. "No, Boy I'm on birth control. I would not do that to you, I'm trying to keep you not lose you." The subject was changed.   Tootie began looking through the center console and found his drivers license.   "Your name is Lionel?", she said laughing.   "Boy, your 29... your old! Wait, your about to be 30 in three days!   Why didn't you tell me?"   he looked at her and said, "you ain't ask."   "What do you want for your birthday? And don't say nothing because I want to get you something.", she stated.   She began thinking about the threesome with him, her and Stephanie.   "I got something for you when we get back home, but think of something you want.", she told him.   Linz pulled over outside of Cambridge to let her drive, he was tired.   He told her about the stuff in the trunk and to do the speed limit.   He also wanted her to wake him when they got to Columbus.

Tootie slid in behind the wheel and adjusted the seat, storing the settings into her memory.   As she merged back into the flow of traffic, Linz began to relax, watching her as she drove.   Tootie was beautiful, a true natural beauty, she looked good behind the wheel.   He pondered what she told him in their earlier conversation.   Inside he hoped like hell that Tootie meant what she said.   Like her, he was also tired of searching for true love.   In his heart he didn't want to be a player no more, but for now he had an image to uphold.

Linz was sleeping when Tootie looked over at him.   She smiled to herself and mouthed a silent thank you to God for blessing her with Mr. Lindsey.   He was everything she wanted in a man.   She admired the way he dressed and how he carried himself.   He was very handsome and he treated her with respect.   She was truly happy with him.   There was no way she was going to let him go, and to top it off, he was not a broke ass nigga.   What more could she ask for.

Tootie began to get hungry and realized she didn't eat nothing all day, so she stopped in Zanesville at Wendy's.   She didn't want to wake him, so she got him something she thought he would like.   Linz was awakened by a kiss and the smell of chicken.   "Baby, I got you something to eat.", she told him placing a bag into this lap.   "Thanks Boo." He wasted no time tearing into the food.   "Damn Boy, slow down, ain't nobody going to take it from you.", she joked as she started the car.

It was 6 pm when they arrived in Columbus.   Linz phone his brother and told him he'd be at his crib in about twenty minutes.   Tootie called her mom to let her know they were there safe and would be over after they see his little brother.   Ajia was happy to know Tootie was on her way.   She couldn't wait to meet the man who stole her little girl's heart.

Jason was outside with Paul and Sha'Hien when the tinted out Benz on chrome stopped in front of him.   Like Tootie, Jason knew of the Benz, but never seen it.   The window lowered revealing its passengers.   "Y'all all spooked!", Linz said as the men relaxed.   "Shit, i ain't know who you was.", Jason said, giving his brother some love. Linz exchanged the same with Paul and Sha'.   They wasted little time talking as Linz told Tootie to hit the trunk so he could get the dro.

"Jason, can I use your bathroom?", Tootie asked as she cut the engine and exited the vehicle.   Once in the house, Tootie was shown the bathroom and the men hit the basement.   They couldn't believe how much dro was compressed before them.   "How much is this?", Jason asked.   "200 pizzy's", Linz replied as he tore a chunk off to let them sample.   Paul took one look and said, "That look like that goody!"   He inhaled real deep and said, "Smell like goody too!   I know you gonna let us blaze one!" "Nigga, this true one hitter quitter.   How much does an ounce go for?   What about a pound?", Linz asked.   He really didn't care, he was giving this one to his brother to advertise and come up.   "It depends, the cheapest I've seen is $600 and ounce and $3,800 a pound, and that's rare.   On average $750 - 800 an ounce and $5,000 a pound.", Jason said.   "What, you charging?", Sha asked.   "I don't know, I'm just trying to move it.   I'll let it go for $500 an ounce and $3,600 a pound", Linz said.   "Shit, I know some people who'll get a couple right now for that price.", Jason said reaching for his cell.

"Y'all need to break it up.   It's been compressed and we need a scale.", Linz said. "I got that, I'll be right back.", said Paul as he went to go get the scale.   Jason got off the phone with his people.   Jason said, "If it is what he said it was and the price was also he'd get five now, but he wanted to sample it first."   Linz gave his bro a chunk to let him sample.   Tootie stayed upstairs talking with Jason's woman.   Sha' had some people he needed to holla at.

Paul came back with the scale before Jason did.   Linz, Paul, and Sha' weighed out a couple pounds.   They looked like big,lime green boulders.   Each rock was a pound or more.   Linz didn't care, they had so much back in the Burgh.   Sha' rolled a blunt and sparked up.   He took two tokes and choked.   He then passed the spliff to Paul who did the same. "Man, this is that shit!", Sha' said. Linz already knew it was the real deal. It took Jason 30 minutes to get back. He had his boy Broc with him. Jason and Broc had been boys since '99. When Jason moved to Columbus, Broc went all out for Jason. Trust wasn't an issue with them. Since Linz didn't know Broc like that, he let Jason deal with him.

"My boy said it's on point, he wants five pizzys now.", Jason stated introducing Broc to his brother. Sha' and Paul knew Broc, they passed the dutch to him, then Jason took a toke. "Can I get em at this price all day?", Broc asked. Jason said, "I'll talk to my bro, he'll work with you." Jason counted $18,000 and handed it to his brother. Linz, in turn, weighed out five and a half pounds and gave them to Broc. "How long will it take you to get rid of these?", Linz asked. Broc sold weed all over the Bus, but he never had enough supply to meet the demand. "Shit, a day or two.", Broc replied.

Linz's mind began to churn, a plan was formulating. He called his brother to the side and told him what he was thinking. Jason was with it. He was sure that Paul and Sha' would be also. If Jason wanted to bring Broc in on it he could. Linz got a good vibe about Broc. Jason took a few moments to holla at the others about the plan. They were in agreement. Linz wanted his little brother to come up, him and his crew. Unlike Linz, they held down regular 9-5 jobs.

"Look, since y'all super cool with me and we fam, y'all just bring me $2,500 off each pound.", Linz said cutting them a super deal.. He stood to profit half a mil off of each bale. Jason and his peeps knew a super deal when it presented itself. They talked for a few minutes, then Linz told them he'd get back at them tomorrow after work. He and Tootie left. He felt relieved to get that dro out the car. That with the money was at least ten years in a state prison and about 15 - 20 in the Feds.

CHAPTER THIRTY

Ajia was watching TV when Tootie came in calling, "Momma, where you at?" "Girl stop yelling, I'm in here!", Ajia said as she laid on the couch watching CSI: NY. Ajia was anxious to see this man her daughter brought home with her.   She hoped he wasn't white, short, or ugly.   Tootie dropped her bags at the door, like she always did, and made her way into the living room followed closely by Linz.   He was nervous because he didn't know what to expect from his girl's mom or what Tootie has told her about him.   What he saw when he entered the room was an older version of Tootie, a splitting image.   It gave him an idea of what his woman would look like in twenty years, still beautiful.   When she stood up to greet him, he saw she still had a young girl's body. Now he knew where Tootie got her goods from.

"Hello, I'm Ajia, Tootie's mother and you are?", she said extending her hand.   As Linz began to speak, Tootie cut in saying, "I told you Mom that's my man!"   "Girl, I asked him not you!"   Linz introduced himself, Ajia was exceptionally pleased with her daughter's taste in men.   She felt a good vibe from him and prayed he wouldn't break her little girl's heart.

After they got settled in, the women talked while Linz just listened.   Ajia was silly as hell, just like her child.   Linz enjoyed being around her, not once did she ask what he did for a living or how they met.   She reasoned that it would all reveal itself in time. Tootie learned that her mom was off tomorrow and Linz learned that he'd be helping them move over the next few days.   He was cool with that, he liked what Tootie and the girls did with their money by spreading the love to their peeps.

Before going to bed, Tootie gave her mother $50,000 to use for house payments. She also told her that she was taking her to get new furniture tomorrow and before she left she was going to get her some dependable wheels.   Ajia started to protest, but Tootie stopped her before she started.   Linz watched as his woman took control of the situation, she had leadership skills.

Tootie packed $100,000 and planned on spending it all on her momma, along with majority of her time except for the weekend.   She planned to shake her ass, see and be seen at the clubs with her man, and old friends.   She kissed her momma good night and went up to shower for bed.   Linz stayed behind and spoke with Ajia for a few minutes before joining Tootie upstairs

The next morning, Linz awoke to the smell of breakfast.   Tootie and her mom were in the kitchen talking and cooking.   The chemistry between the two was golden, almost unreal.   They woke up early to go shopping for furniture and to do work at the new house.   The women were in mid conversation when Linz appeared dressed in sweats and a wife beater.

"Bout time you got up!", Tootie said kissing him.   "Sit down, let me get you a plate.", Ajia said motioning for him to sit.   Tootie came up behind his chair and placed her arms around his neck whispering "I love you".   Ajia just stared, a feeling of joy washed over her knowing her daughter was happy.   Her mind reeled back to a time when she was young, happy, and tipsy in love with a certain fellow who didn't share the same feelings as she did, leaving her alone and pregnant.   She hoped that her love child had more success with Linz then she did with Dontello.   As past hurts began to well up within her, she took a deep breath and pushed those thoughts aside.   No way she was going to let old hurts ruin her day.

It was about 10 am when they left the house.   As Ajia stepped outside, she looked around for the truck her daughter drove the last time she visited.   "Baby, where's that cute little truck you drove last time?"   "At home", Tootie answered as she unlocked the Benz.   Ajia instantly fell in love with the car.   "Baby, whose is this?"   Tootie just pointed to Linz, who let Ajia ride shotgun.   Her breath was stolen when she examined the soft leather and wood interior, and felt the softness of the cushions.   The essence of luxury assaulted her senses.   She pictured herself owning something like this for herself

The next four and a half hours were spent going in and out of two Value City stores and a Furniture Outlet.   They accumulated a kitchenette, two bedroom sets, a dinette set, a leather living room set, and a couple odds and ends to be delivered in the next two days. Everything came to a grand total of $12,937.56.   Next, they hit the mall where Tootie treated her mom to a new wardrobe and brought herself a few outfits to wear to the club this weekend.   She came across a Stacey Adams ad that she thought would look nice on Linz, so she had him sized for the outfit.   She wanted for herself the same dress the woman wore in the ad.   I know it sounds corny but she liked it.   Linz did a little shopping.   He bought something for each of his crew members.   While in the Food Court, Tootie asked her mom what kind of car she wanted.   Ajia jokingly said, "One like the one you are driving."   Tootie did not speak for a minute, then said, "Momma, I can't get you that right now, but in a year or two, I can.   I promise I will, ok.",   Tootie wanted to give her mom the world because Ajia did all that she could to try and give it to her only child.   The sacrifices she made and things she did was unmentionable.   If asked she would do it again for her little girl.   No matter how old Tootie got, she would always be her little girl.

Ajia sensed Tootie's mood change, she didn't mean to hurt her baby's feelings.   She grabbed her hand and said, "Baby, I was just joking.   You've done enough for me already.   I'm cool with the car I got in my driveway."   Linz was touched by Tootie's dedication and love for her mother.   It reminded him of the bond he shared with his parents.   There was nothing he wouldn't do for them..   "Momma, I'm gonna get you something nice.   I don't want you breaking down somewhere.   That car got almost 270,000 miles on it.   Plus the heat don't work.   No Momma, I won't have that, not if I can help it."   She was relieved her mom was only playing about the Benz.

Tootie spotted one of her old friends and went to holla at her, leaving Linz and Ajia to talk.   "I don't care what you do to afford this lifestyle, just don't hurt my baby, or you will have to deal with me.", she said with a stern face.   Linz was both shocked and amused that she came out of her mouth sideways at him like that.   Mom Ajia wasn't going for no bullshit, she maybe old, but her gangsta still remained.   "Chill Annie Oakley, your daughter is in good hands.   I promise I won't let no harm come to her.   She's my future.   I don't mean any disrespect, but somebody is gonna beat your old ass if you keep wolfing like you a killer.", he said with a smile on his face.   Ajia laughed and said, "Nigga, I ain't old and I still look good, better than half these women out here that are half my age.   I still got it, you better ask somebody.   As for somebody whooping me, please run up and get done up."   Linz fell out laughing.   He like Ajia, his soon to be mother-in-law.   They both tripped off each other.

When Tootie returned her mother and man was both laughing.   "What's so funny?", Tootie asked.   "I like him, he's silly as hell.", Ajia said, getting up to use the restroom.   "Your mom is cool as hell and fine with her old ass, she thinks she's 30 again."   "Don't be trying to holla at my momma.", Tootie replied.   When Ajia returned they left.

On the way out to the new house, they stopped at a used car lot.   Tootie set her hazel eyes on a 02' Grand Cherokee 4x4 for $19,500.   This would get her mom around in the winter time.   "Momma, come here, look at this."   Hoping her mom liked it as much as she did.   Linz inspected the Jeep, it was in excellent shape.   It came with chrome crash bars and side steps, all it needed was some rims.   He could see her old ass now, balling down the street, thinking she is 30.   Getting looks from young and old heads, truth be told, Ajia could pass for 30 easy.   Her face and body were right.

"Momma, what you think about this?" Tootie climbed into the drivers seat and her mother in the passenger seat.   "It's nice, but don't these things eat gas?", she asked.   Tootie said nothing.   "I'd put some other wheels on it though.", Ajia teased.   "Momma, do you like it?"   Her mom was getting on her last nerve.   They spoke to the dealer and reached a deal of $17,000 even plus the Audi.   They could pick up the truck today about 7 pm.

At the house, they hung photos and little things like that.   There was no use unpacking until the new stuff arrived, so they cleaned.   Ajia gave her daughter a copy of the house keys.   Linz changed light bulbs, fuses, and did other odds and ends.   Tootie and Ajia left Linz to go get the Audi and $7,000 to put down on the truck.   The owner of the car lot agreed to let her buy here, pay here because they agreed to pay it off within 90 days.   Hell, he was happy to move the truck with the car market being like it was these days, especially with SUV's.

While Linz waited for the two sirens to return, he called his brother and talked to him for a while.   Then, he called his sister Sherry to check on her and her two little girls.   Next, he called his Pops.   After building with his Dad, he called to see how Doug and A.P were doing.   K.J wouldn't answer the phone.   Linz guessed he was busy or knee deep in some good shit, so he left a message.   The rest of the day was uneventful.   He relaxed and chilled with his Boo Boo and her Moms.

K.J's phone rang several times as he stood staring out the glass balcony doors of the Windsor Montreal Couples Resort in Montreal, Canada as Jade massaged his penis with her throat.   His body was momentarily paralyzed by Jade's oral skills, he couldn't answer the phone if he tried.   K.J and Jade had grown very close in the last few weeks.

They showed more affection towards each other and spent alot of time together. Jade knew that the key to keeping a man like K.J wasn't through sex, that was just a bonus. The key was letting him be him, not trying to change him, but being strong in herself and supportive, yet able to stand her ground. Jade was determined to keep her man. She didn't want to be a playette no more. She was the free spirited, aggressive, and live life for the moment of the two. While Diamond was more relaxed and laid back type, but lately Jade was morphing into that kind of woman. She began to think and plan for her future, a future she hoped included the nigga she has been gradually changing for. Make no mistake, her gangsta and hustle was on point, just her ways with men changed. K.J was the force behind this change.

While in Canada, the couple spent plenty of time really getting to know one another, not just sexually, but mentally and spiritually. She told him of her childhood dream of being a most celebrated Geisha and explained what a true Geisha is and does. She corrected the American stereotype of the art of Geisha. They spoke of her culture. She even told him her full birth name, Kuo Ziyi Iko, with promise that he didn't laugh and keep it between them. Not even Tootie and Cristal knew her middle name. He also revealed things about himself to her and how he felt about her. This was new ground for both of them, neither one ever felt this deep about someone else before.

Jade was shocked to find a store catering to the Asian culture in the World Mall. There she purchased several clothes that where only sold in her mother's homeland. The Japanese had their own style. She bought several kimonos for her and her sister. She splurged on the "Bathing Apes" brand of clothes. K.J was introduced to a whole new style and many brands of clothes from all around the world. This mall was something the boys had to experience. No doubt he'd return here, and the females were off the chain. Jade caught his eyes wandering a few times. Men will be men as long as he didn't react and disrespect her to her face, she was cool with it, but if he crossed that line she'd act a donkey. Besides, her eye's roamed a few times also. The two spent a wonderful week together, it was a break they both needed, something to refresh the soul.

CHAPTER THIRTY ONE

"The weekend is here, Columbus!", the radio DJ yelled. "Don't forget the party at Club Temptation! It's on and poppin tonight. It's a can't miss event! DJ Caramel will be on the 1's and 2's, keeping your body moving. She along with special guest Ebony Eyez and Brooke Valentine. Fellas you don't wanna miss these two ladies." Tootie and her friends, Sade and Mika, sat in the nail salon waiting to be called. It seemed like every hair and nail salon in the city was full.

Later that night as Tootie got dressed she wondered what the other girls were doing. She was looking stunning in a orange leather skirt and jacket by Dollhouse, with matching heels and clutch. While Linz sported a black Aviso Jean hookup with matching Timbs. They took a photo for Tootie's mom before they left. Linz would be meeting his brother and his crew there and Tootie was hooking up with her peeps.

The night was going smooth until Tootie's friend Sade seen Linz touching and feeling on this little Somalian chick in tight pants. Once she told Tootie and she seen it with her own two eyes, it was over, she was about to act an ass. She stormed over to the bar where Linz and his peeps was parlaying. The Somalian chick was still there smiling and shit, little did she know a hurricane was coming towards her. Linz saw it too late, he knew he was busted, so he decided to just accept whatever came. Tootie pushed past the broad and stood right in his grill, "Motherfucker, I know you ain't trying to play me? All the shit I do for you! Fuck naw, you got me twisted!" Then she turned to the female, "Bitch get somewhere before I stomp you out." The chick got the hint and bounced, leaving them to fight. A crowd gathered as the screaming got louder. She was up in his grill now, he'd never seen this side of Tootie. Before he could react, she slapped him. Even she was shocked that she hit him. Everyone just knew it was about to be some shit, but Linz took the slap like a champ. He considered it payback for when he slapped her. When he didn't react, she got bolder. She became madder when he refused to argue with her. Face it, he got caught trying to holla at some strange tail, what could he say. Linz didn't like all the attention they were drawing, so he reached for her saying "Can I holla at you for a minute?". Tootie wasn't going for it she said through clenched teeth, "Fuck you nigga, you done fucked up. Go holla at that bitch you was touching on!"   As Linz tried to walk past her, she grabbed his arm and when he turned around, she threw a drink in his face and said, "And take that with your dumb ass!"   Niggas began clowning Linz, even his brother was clowning him.   When the bouncers came and asked if there was a problem, he said "Naw" and stepped off to clean his face.

DJ Caramel got the ladies on the floor stepping in unison to Gwen Stefani's "Holla Back Girl".   Everyone was moving to the five minute mix and the crowd was crazy hype.   It was so many women in the house, a nigga couldn't help but come up.   Tootie shook her ass with any playa in arm's reach, trying to get back at Linz.   Her feelings were hurt but she wasn't gonna let that stop her from having a good time with her friends. They hit the dance floor damn near every song.   The DJ began to slow it down with Bow Wow's "Let Me Hold You", Tootie looked around for Linz, but he was no where to be found.   She knew he didn't leave because she had the keys and his boys were still there.

Ebony Eyez took the stage about midnight, followed by Brook Valentine.   The rest of the night went smooth.   Linz found the jump off that he got caught with, her name was Narobi.   He got the number, but she didn't want no parts of Tootie so she slid the digits to him via the waiter.

As the club started to close, the parking lot filled up, parking lot pimpin was in full effect.   Linz was leaning on his whip waiting on Tootie to get his keys.   He didn't want to argue, all he wanted was his keys.   He had to play the passive role because Tootie and her crew was vital to the plan.   But best believe he was going to get her back.   She walked up with her friends and told him she got a ride home and gave him his keys and walked on.   Deep in her heart, she wanted to stay and talk with her man.   Despite what happened tonight, he was still her man.   She wanted to go and apologize for her actions, but it's too late for that.   What's done is done, tomorrow she'd talk to him.   "Girl, I see you handled your B.I!   Who he think he is trying to play you?", Mika said, throwing gas on the fire.   "Fuck that nigga, you can do better then him anyway!", Sade added. Tootie didn't feel like hearing that bullshit.   It was bad enough she had to see that shit, now she gotta hear about it all night.

Outside niggas did what they do best, trying to holla at the women and vice versa.

Tootie stood by as Mika and Sade got their holla on.   Niggas tried to holla at her but her mind and heart were across the parking lot on Linz.   He was not stunting the events of earlier, the player in him was back.

Shorty Narobi would most definitely get a call tonight.   He peeped Tootie watching him across the lot, he said to himself, "She ain't going no where."   He climbed in the Benz and smashed out called Narobi's digits.   She was getting in her car when her cell rung.   "Hello", she said.   "What's poppin Baby Girl?"   "Your girl was trippin!", she answered.   "I know, but anyway, I'm trying to see you tonight if possible.", he said getting straight to the point.   "As long as your girl don't show up.   I don't have time for that mess."   They set up a meeting at the Comfort Inn in Whitehall.   He was bout to punish Narobi.

Ajia woke up the next morning and found Tootie balled up on the couch, tear stains decorated her face.   She knew something was wrong.   She held her daughter in her arms, fresh tears fell from Tootie's eyes.   "What happened Baby?"   She began to recall to her mom the events of last night.   "Well Baby, where is he at?", Ajia asked.   "I don't know, probably with some bitch!", Tootie answered.   Her mom didn't want to take sides, she liked Linz, but Tootie was her daughter.   After listening to her daughter vent her feelings she gave her opinion.   "Baby, don't you think you was a little hard on him?   All you did was catch him flirting.   It ain't like you caught him kissing on her or in bed with the wench.   Baby, men are gonna be men.   That boy is crazy about you, he ain't gotta say it, I can tell.   Don't let a good thing pass by pushing him into another girl's arms.   Make her take him from you   Now you stop all that crying and call him.   Besides, he is going to church with me on Sunday."   Tootie thought about what her mom said and decided to call after she showered.

Ajia didn't want to see her daughter go through heartache and pain like she did.   This was the only man that her daughter brought home for her to meet, so she knew he was special.   She prayed that they'd settle their differences.

The delivery trucks were due to arrive at noon.   Linz was supposed to help them get settled in.   Ajia pressed her daughter to call Linz.   Tootie dialed the number and gave her mom the phone.   He and Ajia talked for a few minutes.   He told her he would meet them at the new house.

Linz got there a little after noon because he had some business to take care of with his brother, who was selling the dro like hotcakes.   He and Tootie barely spoke the whole time.   Finally Ajia made them talk.   "Look, y'all need to cut this b.s out.   Both of y'all tripping.   Now y'all go talk about whatever it is y'all are arguing about."   Linz had to admit that Tootie was looking good.   "Boo, I admit I was wrong for slapping you and tossing a drink in your face, but I was mad.   You shouldn't have done what you did. That was not right and you know it.   I don't do stuff like that to you, I love you.   That was disrespectful on your part.", she said.   All he could do was agree.   He apologized for his stupidity and she accepted.   They kissed and made up.   That night they had the best makeup sex.   The next couple of days went by fast, they had been in Columbus for a week.   It was time to head home, they had work to do.

Jason and his peeps had moved 73 pounds of dro in a week.   Columbus was going to be a gold mine for weed.   The last night in Columbus they spent with Ajia.   They went out to eat and just talked.   Ajia hoped to see Linz again.   Before Tootie left she told her, "Remember what I said.   Don't let a good thing pass you by."   She thanked Linz for helping her move and reminded him of their conversation they had in the mall. Linz just laughed even though he knew that Mom Toot was serious.

CHAPTER THIRTY TWO

Back in Pittsburgh, the Four Kings sat together discussing the plans for the next hit. It would be Cristal's turn to perform.   This one was leading them to Atlanta to holla at some nigga named Cedric Taylor a.k.a Expressway.   He got the name because he lived on the expressways, dropping coke off here and there.   No matter where you were, he'd get it to you.   He didn't use workers, that way no one could turn states evidence on him.   He was worth 5.5 million.

He was a true street nigga.   He stayed in the hood, kept his loot at home, tricked off in strip clubs, had five different baby mommas, and owed a bunch of child support. There is no telling why he was on the list.   Since the crew needed to chill for a minute because of the heat from Rich Money's death, they spent the next 90 days focusing on the out of state victims.   After Atlanta, they chilled for a week then hit Memphis.   Jade stepped up to the plate, knocked it out within three weeks.   Nigga didn't know what hit him.   He was some old head who K.J knew named Tray Ray.   Tray was an old head who had been in the game for quite some time.   He been pimping and hustling since the early 70's.   He had old bills and kept a low profile, but loved some sweet young pussy. He couldn't resist it, ages 18 -24 was his preference.   Old bastard popped Viagra by the box.   Tray Ray was know to thrash a young bitch in the bed.   His downfall would be his old ways, too stubborn to change.   He kept his loot at home in a floor safe.   A mistake that cost him 4.9 million.   It wasn't a total loss for him though, they let him keep his coke and his life.

Tootie was the next batter up, her task took her to Detroit to holla at Motown.   This was a nigga who had wronged Linz while doing time with him in Manchester, KY. Dude pulled a shank out during a fight and threatened Linz.   Linz let it pass but didn't forget, now it was payback time.   Motown would lose everything, 6.7 million dollars, 130 kilos of cocaine, and his life, which Linz had the pleasure of taking.   They tied him up, poured antifreeze down his throat, and taped his mouth shut.   He was found two weeks later by his ten year old son when his mom dropped him off   to spend the week with his dad.

The total amount of loot for the three scores came to $17.1 million.   The money was divided as planned. The take from Expressway and Tray Ray combined netted the women $ 3.4 million to split at 40%, giving them $850,000 each. Then they added the 50% they got from the 6.7 million from Motown gave them a grand total of 1.69 million each. Damn good for a few months work, the ladies could retire now. The Four Kings take came to $2.6 million each. Swelling their rainy day money to a little over 2.5 each. That's not counting the cash they kept on hand. The Four Kings had a king's ransom tucked away. There were only three more names on the list, then they could retire. It had been six months ago when the two crews linked up. Neither one ever imagined that they would be sitting on this much change.

CHAPTER THIRTY THREE

Tootie awoke early on this cold February morning, it was Valentine's Day. She had thought long and hard about what to get her man, she finally decided on the threesome. Stephanie had kept in touch, constantly trying to taste the goodies and to let Tootie know she was still down for the threesome. Today was the day it would take place. She phoned Steph with the details of when and where it was gonna go down. Steph was excited and more than ready. Tootie told her she'd stop down at the bookstore later today to see if she was still holding like she was a few months ago. She also planned to get a few books for Half a Mil. He called her a couple days ago to ask how she was and to inform her of his upcoming court date. She thought she'd give him a surprise visit to make his day. She heard that his baby momma was out sack chasing and was too busy hoeing to visit. She also heard he was doing bad up there. Tootie had a heart, and now she had money. She decided to put 3,000 on his books and get him some new reading material, underclothes, and some court clothes. She had to be sneaky about it because if Linz found out he'd stomp her or worse, leave her and she didn't want either one.

Tootie returned to the bed and shook her man awake. He woke up groaning and grumbling about how cold it was, she paid him no attention as she kissed his face. "Happy Valentine's Day Boo!", she said between kisses. They wrestled around awhile, the softness of her body was comforting to Linz. He had grown accustom to sleeping with her every night. Whether it was at his place or hers, 90% of the time they were together. "Baby, clear your schedule today, I got something for you, ok.", she said. He just moaned. "I'm serious boy!", she said getting out of bed. "Where you going?", he asked. He wasn't ready to give up his comfort zone just yet. "Baby, I got a couple things I need to do this morning.", she said as she walked towards the shower leaving him hard. "Come on, I'll take care of you while I shower.", she called back to him after making sure Jade and Diamond's doors were closed so they wouldn't see her man's nakedness. Linz was happy that his woman was attentive to his morning needs. That's what he admired about Tootie, she always did whatever to please him. She wasn't self centered when it came to him, she put him before herself.

They shared a shower and a quickie, satisfying both of their sexual cravings. Linz dressed and spoke to Diamond before he left.   She was helping him with Tootie's gift. He as getting her pair of Michael Kors leather sherling boots and a lace corset and boy short set.

Tootie dressed and left, headed downtown to take care of business.   It was about 10:30 when she strolled into the bookstore.   Sure enough, Steph was still fine and all that ass was still jiggling.   They spoke for a moment, then Steph took her into the back room where they could be alone.   Once in the back, she stripped for Tootie letting her see what she was working with.   Tootie was thrilled with what she saw, Steph was banging.   After she dressed, she kissed Tootie full on the lips.   This time Steph tapped Tootie on her ass and said, "Mmm, I will see you later, believe that!", and flashed Tootie a smile.   The whole thing caught Tootie off guard.   Her mind was in disarray and she realized that she was wet.   After gaining her composure back, Tootie told her to wear something sexy.   As she gave Stephanie a once over, she noted that Steph had style and flavor.   Tootie had to get out of there before temptation took over.   She paid for her books and bounced.   Tootie's mind was still on Stephanie as she pulled up in the jail's parking lot.   She went through the usual with the visiting process, left the money and books and went up the elevator.

Mike was happy to get a visit, it had been about three months since he'd seen anyone.   He had lost weight and looked stressed.   Tootie was glad she could brighten his day, she felt for Mike.   When he seen who was at the visit for him, he smiled and said, "Hey Boo, it's nice to see you again.   You look good."   "It's nice seeing you too. Just thought I'd stop through and holla at you.", she said.   They chatted for a while before Tootie told him about Linz.   "Mike, I gotta tell you something.   I'm in love with this guy, we've been together about six months and I'm happy with him.   Me and you can only be friends.   I don't mind if you call every so often and I will do what I can for you.   He knows about you, but just respect that I got a man now."   Mike nodded.   "I left you some money and more books, okay."   Mike knew that Tootie was gone from his life.   He was happy to have her as a friend.   He wished her well.   She promised to write and send photos.   They talked for a few minutes more then said their goodbyes. She read the look in his eyes, the look of defeat.   "Hey, don't look so sad, I'll be back to visit.   I'll always be your friend.   Plus, my man ain't tripping off stuff like this visit, he knows who I belong to." Mike smiled and said, "He's a lucky dude." The guard came and announced visitation was over. Tootie went and reserved a suite at the Hyatt for the little rendezvous tonight she planned for Linz. She just hoped it didn't backfire on her.

Linz was with K.J in Motorhead's shop. The Olds was almost ready, the engine and paint was complete. They were now waiting on the wood dash, console, and some of the sounds to come in. The guts were complete, just needed to be installed. Motorhead had put his thing down on the Olds. When they started it up, it purred. Dual chrome pipes serenaded a brother. Linz couldn't wait until May 1st.

Linz and K.J stayed awhile and rapped with Motorhead and his crew about a business venture. They'd supply they money for Motorhead and his crew to get a bigger place. The little two car garage that he called a shop wasn't doing it. There was mad money to be made in the custom car market. The possibilities was endless. They decided to call the shop "2 Major Automotive Works". Linz and K.J would put up $50,000 a piece to get the shop open, in turn they became equal partners in the venture.

Diamond and A.P were inseparable, he never forgot that she saved his life a few months ago. A.P cut all his other women loose and decided to be exclusive with Diamond. The hardest one to let go was Mahogany, his older chick. That woman was something special, she treated A.P like a true king. Recently her husband began to step up and be a man. He caught her out with A.P at a play that stopped in the city. He begged her for another chance, she gave in, after all he was her husband and father of her children. Plus, they had been married for about 15 years. A.P understood so he let her go with the promise that if she ever needed him to just call.

Mahogany said goodbye by dedicating a song to him on the local radio station FM 106 W.A.M.O's quiet storm show. She dedicated Shirley Murdock "As We Lay", A.P was touched when he heard it.

A.P promised Diamond that when this was over he'd take her on a 21 day cruise. She was delighted and told him that she'd hold him to that promise. She told him of the girl's plan to travel for a while, also the plans that she had for the two of them. They talked about getting a spot together, she was tired of running from house to house, and so was he.

On this Valentine's Day, Cristal and Doug were in Columbus, Ohio visiting her Aunt

Tracy.   Like Tootie, she also copped her peeps a house and car.   Tracy was ecstatic, she just had another baby and needed the extra space.   She already had two teenage boys, ages 13 and 15 and now she has a 7 month old girl.

Cristal wasn't tight with her loot when it came to her Aunt Tracy.   She was the only family that she knew of or cared to know of.   Cristal and Doug moved as one.   They brought his and hers motorcycles, went in on some stocks together, and when this was over they were moving to California together.   The two had secretly been checking into real estate out there.   They came across a cozy little bungalow in Palo Alto for $780,000.   It was originally listed for 1.3 million but since it has been on the market for five years, the owner decided to let it go for the best offer he could get.   The only thing the house needed was a new roof, and a loving family to occupy it.

Doug had been taking the Carlton Sheets real estate course during his recovery from the gunshot wounds he suffered from the robbery of Rich Money.   He and Cristal both wanted to cash in on the real estate market.   They purchased several fixer upper houses in the Pittsburgh area.   Doug gave most of them to his mother so she'd have a steady income.   Cristal purchased six homes in Columbus and the surrounding areas.   The construction company that Tracy's new husband worked for was contracted to renovate them, that guaranteed quality work.   The homes were then HUD approved.   She signed them over to her aunt.   Cristal never forgot how Tracy opened her doors to her as a child and raised her as one of her own.   Tracy gave her a place to call home, and now she gave Tracy several places to call home.

Cristal's two little cousins loved her to death.   Ever since she got paid she kept them in the latest fashions, as long as they kept their grades above a B average.   The boys loved Doug too.   When he was in Columbus he let them shine in the malls and stunt in the truck.   He got them both 14kt white gold link chains and bracelets for Christmas with promises to get them ice if they made the principal's list.

Diamond and Jade was dressed in kimono's, traditional Geisha wear, when the men came to get them for their dinner date.   The two looked like something out of an old Japanese karate flick.   Jade wore a jade green silk kimono with a fishnet body suite underneath.   She had on matching slippers and her hair was in a single french braid.   She had on jade green eye shadow and lipstick.   Diamond's silk kimono was silver, with matching heels.   Her hair was pinned up in a traditional bun and she wore silver eye shadow and lipstick.   These two were stunning, they caught looks of admiration from every one they encountered.   Further playing the role by speaking in their mother's native tongue to each other, pretending to speak no English.   That is until "Bitch, don't make me fuck you up!", came out of Diamond's mouth in perfect English when the hostess tried to holla at A.P thinking that the ladies did not understand English.   The men received many props from the other players with comments like, "I see you playa" and "play on playa", or "Damn nigga! You doing it like that!"   K.J and A.P felt and looked like international players running the game worldwide, cool as Clyde with two bunny rabbits by their side.

Meanwhile, Tootie was dressed to thrill in a hip hugging, rose hued velvet suit, with a white corseted blouse with the top two buttons open, with matching pumps.   To top the outfit off, she had a rose colored fedora cocked to the side and a pearl choker around her neck.   She looked like a true gangstress from the 1920's.   She checked herself once more before leaving to pick up Stephanie in the Range Rover.

Tootie was visually paralyzed when Steph answered the door.   The red backless jumpsuit hugged her curves like Goodyear do asphalt.   "Don't just stand there, come in.", Stephanie said.   Tootie stepped into the little apartment, while Steph finished dressing.   Tootie looked around and noted that Steph had good taste in home decor.   "Girl, you working that outfit!", Steph said, raping Tootie with her eyes.   "Naw, you the one hurting them.", Tootie replied, staring her down when her back was turned.   Steph caught her and said, "You see something you like?", with a seductive smile on her face as she got all up in Tootie's grill.   Tootie got bold and kissed Steph deep and long, caressing her body in the process.   Steph was enjoying this, it was something to see, two dime bitches kissing each other.

Linz was dressed in a pair of mustard colored Gucci slacks and silk shirt with black square toe Gucci slip on's.   Wooded rimless Cartier's graced his face and his hair was cut fresh and crisp, waved up and tapered.   Nigga looked like he just stepped out of the Savoy and GQ magazines.   He was sharp as a razor and cool as a fan.

CHAPTER THIRTY FOUR

Tootie pulled in front of Linz's crib and got out, leaving Steph in the truck. When Tootie returned followed by Linz, Steph couldn't place the face at first, but when he got in she recognized him immediately. "Hey stranger! I ain't seen you in a long time.", she said smiling. Tootie shot both of them a glance before speaking. "Y'all know each other?" "Yeah, this used to be my girl at Mo'Gear. She stayed hooking me up with deals.", Linz said. "How long ago was this?", Tootie asked. "About three years ago, he used to come in every week, always crying broke with a pocket full of money. I didn't know that this was your man!", Steph said. "Anything else I should know about?", Tootie said pulling into traffic. "Naw, but she's gay, so the question is what are y'all doing together?", Linz said. The ladies exchanged a look, then Steph said, "You wanna tell him or you want me to?" "You can if you want to." Steph began by saying, "I seen your girl one day last year and I was attracted to her so I went and pushed up on her. She told me that she wasn't into women but I continued to press her. Finally she said she thought about it before but never acted on it and that I was cute with a fat ass. So she finally ended the conversation by saying that if she ever tried it she'd holla at me, but only if her man could join. She made it very clear though that without you ain't nothing happening. So here we are, a one time deal, you game or not?" Tootie waited anxiously for his answer. "Is you silly? Hell yeah I'm game! How many times does an offer like this come along?", Linz said smiling and thinking about the punishing he was going to give out to these two dime pieces. Tootie and Steph were both relieved that he was game for this little rendezvous, but for different reasons. For Tootie it was so she wouldn't look stupid and so she could have her first experience. But for Steph, it was so she could finally taste Tootie's goodies. She been trying to do so for almost a year now. Tootie was one of the baddest woman she'd ever laid eyes on. It was a win-win situation for all three of them.

Avi's was packed as Linz strolled in with two dimes in tow, one on each arm. He was not only looking like a pimp but feeling like one also. Horace gave him his props as he got seated.

The three enjoyed a nice dinner before moving to the bar/club area to watch Syleena

Johnson perform.   After she sang two songs off he new album, the M.C gave an open mic call.   Tootie surprised Linz by standing up, taking the mic, and reciting a poem she wrote for Linz titled, "He Is"

He is....

The symbol of strength

The essence of love

My personal angel

God's gift to me

Sent from above.

He is...

My backbone splitter

No mater what

My money getter,

Kiss craver

Love maker,

The jaw breaker,

100% real,

Not a faker!

ALSO,

A knucklehead,

Bad boy,

Thug N tha'

Streetz

But a true king

Between tha'

Sheetz!

He is...

Tha' wind in my

Sails,

My source of motivation

#1 fan when I succeed,

My comfort,

When I fail.

He is...

My fix when I

Get a love jones,

Tha' reason I spend

Alot of tyme at home.

He is...

My light in

This darkness

My partner,

My friend,

My lover,

The window to my

Soul!

He is...

The crowd liked Tootie, Linz was amazed at her words. He didn't think that she had it in her, but little did he know, she has been brushing up on her poetry skills lately. They chilled for a few minutes to listen to others recite bars of wisdom, love, anger, heartache, joy, and passion woven into an intense jazz score, painting a picture of life through spoken words. Inviting those with ears into their world, to feel what they feel, see what they see, and go where they've gone.

The evening was going great, some female even sent a dozen red roses over to Stephanie with a note for her to call her later, along with her contact numbers. The roses came from this cute little female who was selling roses and taking photos in one corner of the cafe. Steph went over to thank the woman for the roses and to peep what she looked like. When she came back she had copped us some free photos and a dozen long stem roses. Steph had game that you couldn't deny.

The three left a little before 11 pm. Linz was feeling nice off the Moet he had been sipping on, so were the ladies. They were mellow when they reached the lover's suite at the Hyatt in 1 PPG Plaza. Once inside, Steph and Tootie undressed each other while

Linz watched. They then started to slowly undress him. Steph began to slowly kiss and caress Tootie, touching her in away that only a woman knew how and sent her soaring to new heights. Tootie lost all control when Steph began to eat her. Steph was skilled at what she did, this is more than Tootie could ever imagine in her wildest dreams. Tootie enjoyed every bit of it. She ground her pussy into Steph's face with fury. Linz loved the site that was before him, two beautiful women pleasing each other. "Baby, come here.", Tootie said waving him over. Once there she grabbed his dick and began to suck while he played with Steph's pussy. She was soaking wet and moaned into Tootie's pussy as he fingered her.

Linz pulled out of Tootie's mouth and was set to enter Steph from behind. He slowly teased her opening with his penis, easing into her inch by inch, her pussy felt so damn good that within seconds he began to pound her with force. Steph cried out, "Yeesss, Ooohh Yeesss! That's it Baby! Tear this pussy up!" Linz responded by thrusting into her harder. Tootie slid from under Steph and came up behind Linz, her hands gently massaged his balls while she whispered sweet nasty things in his ear. As he got ready to cum, Tootie changed positions with Steph before he could explode lessening the chance of an accidental pregnancy. He plowed into her luscious body with the same force as he did Steph. Linz was feeling sheer pleasure, he loved the way Tootie's ass jiggled as he hit it from the back, it was a pretty sight.

Linz secretly committed the sight of Steph's body to memory, hoping that he'd get another stab at it all by himself. Meanwhile, Steph was scheming on getting Tootie alone so she could really unleash the freak inside that Tootie held back. Steph knew women, she rolled up under Tootie in the 69 position, licking her pussy as Linz stroked in and out slowly, occasionally sliding her tongue up and down his shaft as he pushed deep inside of Tootie's warm vagina. Tootie was caught up in the rapture and buried her face in Steph's box, parting her lips and gently sucking her clitoris like she liked her to be sucked. Only a woman knew how another woman wanted to really be touched. It was a language that they rarely relayed to the men in their lives.

Tootie found that the taste of pussy turned her on. It was taboo for her, but she also knew in her heart that this would probably be the only experience that she would have with another woman, she was strictly dickly. Then she thought, well maybe one more time with Steph wouldn't be bad, to get the full effect.

Linz came with force, as he poured his soul into Tootie's womb, filling her with his spirit.   Steph caught little drops that managed to leak out as he pulled out.   He let the two women go at it and enjoy one another.   He watched for a while, but the combination of Moet, sex, and sleep got the best of him.   When he awoke the next morning he found Steph and Tootie in the midst of a shower together.   He did what any other man would do, he joined them.   He got his last fill before this once in a lifetime event came to a close.   This was a night he would remember.

PHASE 3

"WHAT'S BEEF"

CHAPTER THIRTY FIVE

In the past 120 day's, Jason and his crew got rid of eight bales of grade "A" dro, which is about 1600 pounds. They worked at a pace that satisfied themselves and kept them off the police radar. Columbus was a big city with a population of about 800,000, so the noise they made was low. All of the crew kept their legal jobs, and kept their profiles low, but stacked paper in a major way. The men gave Linz over 3.5 million already, business in the Bus was booming.

In return for their help, the Four Kings had Lil Mac get them all trucks. Mac provided the men with four Dodge Ram SRT's, the ones with the V-10 Viper engine. Jason and his crew were shocked when they received them. They came up to holla at the Four Kings for the weekend. They left the '85 Regal they came in with Mac. Linz's brother and his crew were on the come up in Columbus. It was spreading that they had the best dro in the five surrounding states, along with the lowest price outside of Texas. The stash of weed the Kings had was steadily decreasing thanks to Lil Mac and Jason and his crew. The stash went from 88 bales down to 51 bales, generating money by the ton.

Lil Mac was a smart hustler, he paid attention to how Linz and K.J moved. His hustle game was sharp. Mac stored the 20 bales of dro and tye-sticks that was given to him a few months ago when he and Jeanna helped move it from Rich's house. Mac put it up for a rainy day or when all the weed the Four Kings had was gone, that way he would still be in business for himself. He sold the dro that they fronted him first, stacking tall paper for him and his girl, they were one hell of a team. After the money came in like water, the two moved into a condo in Monroeville.

The streets were ready to appoint him heir to Rich Money's throne, the only thing that stood in the way was his former supplier Dee. Dee had began to hate on Mac and toss death threats at him and Jeanna. Mac just brushed it off at first but, once he found out Jeanna was three months pregnant he began to take it serious. He swore not to let no harm come to his girl or seed.

Mac had been playing the role of the middle man in the streets, casting the illusion that he had to go get it from his peeps, when in fact he had it all the time. He further strengthened this phantom by being seen with his cousin from Cali at all the major club events.   Darren, Lil Mac's cousin, came to Pittsburgh once a month to transport cars that they sold out west, but the streets thought otherwise.   This kept the jackers and robbers off his ass, plus he never sold more than a few zones to any one person at a time unless he truly knew you or was one of his out of town customers, then you could get up to four pounds.   His product was fire and his prices were reasonable.   He charged $600 for an ounce of dro or tye stick and $400 an ounce for sess, no matter the color.   Mac had undercut Dee's prices and converted over half of his customers, plus Lil Mac would bring it to you if you didn't have a ride.   He put his customers first just like any legitimate business would.

Mac held another ace up his sleeve that Dee didn't think to capitalize on, he sold already rolled blunts.   The dro went for $15 a pop and the sess for $10.   The college crowd loved him, so did the project dwellers.   Mac had love in the streets, he made sure that everyone cold afford a taste of something good.   One could easily see why the streets were ready to crown him king.   Dee was the only one who threw shade and stood in his way.   Sooner or later they'd bump heads.   The only advantage that Dee had was that he had a crew of about eight other nigga's that he fronted.   They relied on him to eat and feed their families.   They also lost money because of Lil Mac's hustle game.   With Mac out of the way they could eat hearty once again, but as of right now they were on a forced diet.

All that Lil Mac had riding with him was his trusty side kick and woman, Jeanna and a friendship with the Four Kings, but he wasn't sure if they would ride with him or not.   They never talked about issues like that but they'd rode for him before.   Little did Mac know, the Kings had much love for him and some low key killers in the wing who would do their own momma if the price was right.   K.J knew two brothers who were young and trigger happy and loyal to him.   He'd got their mother out of a bad situation about two years ago, while they were upstate on parole violation charges.   These two white boys handle business.   They are not to be fucked with unless you were as crazy as they were.   Armando and Aaron are no joke!

It was after a dice game that Linz and K.J learned of the beef brewing between Lil Mac and Dee.   "Man, I need to holla at y'all about something.", Mac said.   "What's the business?", K.J said.   Linz was busy chopping it up with his boy Rello about something. Rell and Linz went way back, before his crack peddling days.   Rello was like family, lately he had came up moving them thangs out of state in a spot he had.   He had linked up with Chuck and the two of them locked down a small city in Ohio.   Now the two was getting major bread and riding real big.   Linz was happy for the two young hustlers that they were getting their just due.   He told Rello that he had that white for the low low and to come holla at him.   Rello said, "Bet, I'll get up with you this weekend."   The two gave each other a pound then Rello bounced in his S600 Benz, while Linz walked to join Lil Mac and K.J in Mac's Lexus LS430.

Mac waited until Linz got in the car before speaking. "I know y'all heard about me and Dee beefing right.", he stated more than asked.   "Naw, when this happen?", K.J replied.   "Every since I started getting weed from y'all and my own paper.", he said. "So, what he talking about?", K.J asked.   "Shit, nigga talking about he gonna kill me and me and Jeanna better cut him in or cut it out.   Then he said if we ain't selling his weed then ain't shit moving.   He told us to watch our backs.", Mac said.   "For real, he doing it like that?", Linz asked.   K.J never liked Dee anyway, he thought he was bitch made.   "Man, look Jeanna is pregnant, about to have my son.   I can't have that.   I'm not scared but he got a crew, I only have Jeanna.   I know she gonna ride, but I don't want her in this in her condition.   One of his people threw some bullets at my whip yesterday while Jeanna was driving.   Man, that shit had me hot.", he said.   K.J said, "So what you saying is you want us to ride with you."   "Something like that or if y'all know anybody who wants to make a quick 50 stacks.", Mac replied.   "Shit Nigga, you like fam, fuck with you he fucking with us, plain and simple.   Let me holla at Dee first, see where his head was at, if he just wolfing or not.", Linz said.   Mac sold about twenty bales for the crew, he made them and himself a couple million in four months.   It was only right.   No way they'd turn their backs on him now.

As they made a left on Buckeye Street, they caught a glimpse of Royce's Phantom
rolling through the intersection.   "Your time is coming soon.   So have fun now Baby.",
K.J thought to himself.   Linz's phone chirped, he looked at the screen and seen it was
Tootie.   He didn't want to answer it because he was supposed to be home a hour ago,
but if he didn't answer it she'd swear he was out creeping.   Ever since the threesome
Tootie has became insecure about her place in his life.   "Hello", Linz said.   "Where
you at?   You said you'd be here an hour ago.   What's up?", she asked.   "I got caught
up with K.J and Mac, something came up.   I'll be there in a few.", he responded.
"Whatever .. I hope she's worth it!", Tootie said and slammed the phone down.   "Damn
Nigga, you having trouble?", K.J said laughing.   "I got 99 problems but a bitch ain't
one!", Linz said borrowing a line from Jay-Z.   "Look my nigga, I'll get at you later, I'm
gonna call two of my peeps, just have the 50 stacks ready.", K.J said as Mac pulled
beside his vehicle.

After Mac dropped the boys off, he went and had Jeanna count out $50,000 and find
three clean weapons.   He was relieved that the weight of going at Dee alone was off his
shoulders.   To take his mind off things, he went to the garage to work on the Lexus SC
430 he lifted a week ago, it was time to switch cars.   He wasn't taking no chances, the
LS 430 had served it's purpose, now it's time to let it go.

K.J called Armando and Aaron as soon as he got in the truck.   The boys answered
pronto.   "Speak Dude!", Armando aka Doe said.   They were hardcore bikers.   "I need
to see you ASAP.", K.J said.   "Why, trouble brewing?", Doe asked.   "You know it, I
got 50 if you solve it.", K.J answered.   "Consider it solved.   Meet me tonight at Banana
Joe's.", Doe said.   The hit was in motion, Lil Mac's problem would be taken care of
soon.

Linz took his ass home to deal with Tootie.   It started soon as he walked in the door.
"Bout time you come home.", she said.   "Look don't start, I ain't in the mood for it,
aight!", he responded walking back to his room.   She followed behind him cussing and
fussing.   Doug and Cristal came out just as he snatched Tootie up and slammed her
against the wall yelling, "Bitch, didn't I tell you I wasn't in the mood for your shit
tonight, huh!   What the fuck is wrong with you!"   Tootie didn't open her mouth.

Doug grabbed Linz saying, "Calm down bro,"   As he held Tootie pinned against the wall, Cristal just looked trying to figure out what happened.   Linz relaxed his grip and told Tootie, "Sit your ass down or get the fuck out!   Don't ever cross my path again!" She went and sat down looking stupid and embarrassed.   Cristal went to console her friend while Doug went to talk to Linz.   Cristal came in the room as Linz began to tell Doug how Tootie been acting after the threesome.   Cristal was shocked, as was Doug. "My girl wouldn't do that!", Cristal said..   Linz just looked at her, his look told it all. Cristal got up and called Tootie into the room and asked her if what Linz said was true. With her head down she confirmed it saying, "It only happened once that's it."   Linz got up and apologized to Tootie, but warned her, "Babe, if you keep accusing me of being with other bitches, you are gonna find yourself by yourself.   I don't got time to be arguing with you about that.   I told you, you're my future, so stop tripping.   Trust me like I do you."   Then he told them about the thing with Lil Mac and Dee.

CHAPTER THIRTY SIX

James Smith aka Abdula Muta, was to be the sixth victim. He was one who talked all that pro black shit about build the community up instead of tearing it down. He parades the blocks selling bean pies and newspapers, but sells more cocaine than a little bit. He and his friend Habib, who owned chain of jewelry stores downtown and a couple clothing stores. Those were fronts for storing his coke and laundering his loot. He was on the list for being a fake ass Muslim.

This would be Cristal's job. She was to get a job at the main store, act like she was interested in their way of life, wear the clothes and veils, the whole nine. She needed to study and know when and where they stored the loot at. Cristal got the job and pretended to be interested in the religion. She wore the traditional garb including the head wrap. She earned their trust, Habib place great duties in her hands while he tended to the traffic that ran in and out of the backroom. Nothing but ballers on every level of the game came to the backroom, from the ounce buyers to the kilo boys. They served them all. While closing up one day, she found an AK with a 30 round clip in the cabinet. She took the bullets out and replaced them with blanks and did the same with the two extra clips that were in the bottom drawer. She had been working for about a month when she overheard Muta talking about a shipment coming in. Then later one day she ease dropped on Habib's long distance call to New York, talking about the money needs to be picked up soon. He felt uncomfortable with that much sitting around the store. On her lunch break, she relayed the message to the Kings, whom decided to strike after closing today. All she had to do was cut the VCR to the cameras off and play along when they came in.

It was about 6:30 pm, Cristal and another female were taking inventory while Habib and Muta tended to some business in the back room with several men in suits. The Four Kings strapped on Kevlar jackets, Uzis with silencers, and holloween masks covered their faces. On the count of three, they rushed the store front catching the woman off guard. Fatima, the other female clerk, reached for her weapon, yelling something in Arabic, but was quickly cut short as A.P fired a short burst into her torso, sending her crashing into the jewelry cases. Linz, Doug, and K.J hopped the counter and stormed the back. Linz took the office, where he found Habib and three men talking.   Habib was so engrossed in conversation when Linz appeared wearing a President Nixon Mask.   "You know what it is!", he said.   The men turned to face him with a look of disdain on their faces.   After a barrage of bullets riddled the man closest to Linz, the look turned to fear.   Habib dove behind the desk trying to get to the file cabinet with the AK inside.   Linz let him get it because he knew of the blanks in the clip.   Habib cocked it and came up firing, but Linz just stood there with a grin on his face.   When Habib realized what was up, he threw the gun at Linz and charged him.   Linz aimed and let loose, ripping his chest cavity wide. The other two men just looked in horror and begged for their lives.   Doug and K.J stormed the loading areas as two men loaded boxes into a van.   "Get em up Nigga!", Doug said.   The men dropped the boxes they had, money littered the floor.   All the men saw before dying was the faces of President Clinton and Reagan.   K.J threw the box in the van and smashed out.   Doug joined Linz as he tied the two gentlemen up. Realizing that Muta wasn't around, Linz said, "Muta said thanks.", to the bound men as he left.   He signaled for Cristal to call the cops, as she shed her gown and veil joining Doug and Linz in the awaiting car.   Leaving behind 300 kilos of cocaine and stolen diamonds for the police to find.   Muta may have gotten away from them but the word would be out that he set it all up.   The Arabs would be at him.

Meanwhile across town in Homewood, Dee's girl Shay-Shay stood in the kitchen fixing dinner for their two kids when the two mohawked white boys appeared with guns drawn.   She froze when she saw them.   The kids began to scream.   Shay-Shay pleaded, "Don't hurt my babies.   Please! Take what you want, just don't hurt us!"   But her cries fell on deaf ears.   Aaron grabbed her five year old daughter and sliced her throat from ear to ear with the blade he kept in his boots.   He did the same with the three year old boy and said, "Tell Dee he got 24 hours to leave or I'm killing his whole family. So bitch make sure he gets the message."   They left her holding her two lifeless children.   Not only did Dee's kids get touched, three members of his crew also lost children too.

The first person Dee thought about doing this was Lil Mac, but his woman told him and the police that the culprits were white.   Her description matched the same as three other separate incidents with the same M.O.   The streets were bloody with the blood of nine children.   Dee didn't know what to do, he didn't know he had white enemies.   His decision was made for him when his mother phoned him saying that two white guys had just left her house after delivering a disturbing message, 'You have 20 hours now!'. Dee folded, he packed his girl and his loot and headed south to North Carolina where Shay-Shay is from.   Mac's problem was solved.

CHAPTER THIRTY SEVEN

Tootie sat on the couch talking on the phone with her mom.   The jeep was paid off and she'd given her the total amount left on the house.   Ajia told her about a guy she met while on her shift three days ago.   He was an engineer who broke his arm in a work related accident.   Tootie was happy that her Mom was dating again, but got silent when the talk turned to her and Linz.   "Baby, what's wrong now?", Ajia asked.   Tootie couldn't bring herself to tell her Mom the truth about what really happened so she said, "Nothing, we just had a disagreement, that's all".   Tootie ain't seen Linz in a week, he ain't called either or accepted her calls.   She knew about the robbery and murder of Habib and his friends.   She also just got wind of the killing of Dee and his worker's children.   Tootie felt embarrassed around Cristal now that she knew about her little secret.   It didn't matter because Cristal loved Tootie all the same, what and who she did was her business.

"Well Momma, I gotta go.   I'll try and come down soon.", she said before hanging up.   She changed into a pair of boxers that Linz had left along with a t-shirt that still held his scent.   She settled in to watch 'Girlfriends' and 'All of Us' on TV, since she wasn't going anywhere.   Just as she got comfortable, there was a knock at the door. "Who is it now?", she grunted because she had to get up.   All that went away when she opened the door finding her man standing there.   He was the last person she expected to see at her door.   "Can I come in?", he asked.   She couldn't speak, but nodded and stepped aside to let him pass.   After shutting the door, she threw her arms around him and began to apologize, "Baby, I'm sorry for acting stupid and accusing you of being unfaithful.   I was just insecure.   I don't wanna lose you.   I love you."   Linz embraced her and said, "Didn't I tell you that you're my future and that you're my girl?"   She nodded.   "Then believe me when I tell you that.", he continued.   They kissed and went to watch t.v together.   During the commercial Tootie asked, "You gonna stay and let me make it up to you tonight?", as she eased into his lap.   "Babe, you want me to stay?", he teased caressing her silky thighs.   He knew that he was gonna stay before she asked. "Yes", she moaned as he ran his hands up her shorts.   "I love you.", she said.   He ran his hands up her shirt across her stomach.   "Boo, you gaining weight, you pregnant?", he asked.   Since Tootie stopped dancing, she'd put on a few pounds, mainly in her butt and thighs and a little in the belly area.   It still looked good.   "I know I'm getting fat, I'm going to start working out again."   No, I ain't pregnant yet!", she said brushing his hands away, embarrassed by a few pounds she gained.   They spent the next couple of hours watching UPN's Tuesday night line up.   "I heard about Habib and them on the news.   I ain't seen Cristal yet, is she with Doug?", Tootie asked.   "Yeah, she's with Doug, they're   counting the loot now.", he said.   His stomach growled because he didn't eat all day.   "Babe, you hungry?   I'll fix you something to eat.", she said getting up to go into the kitchen.   Linz got up to follow. "What you want?"   He just hunched his shoulders.   "Want some chicken tenders and fries?   I don't really feel like cooking all night."   He came behind her, placed his arms around her after tapping her bottom. She smiled to herself because she'd be sleeping with her man tonight.   Plus, she knew how much Linz admired her ass.   He whispered something in her ear making her explode with laughter.

After eating, the two went upstairs to her room, where they spent the rest of the night showing each other how much they missed one another, making love over and over again.   She kept him hard even when he didn't want to get hard.   Tootie wore him out! As they were basking in the afterglow of sex, he asked her, "When this is over, will you have my baby?"   She thought she was hearing things.   "What did you just ask me?" "If you'd have my baby when this is done.", he repeated.   She immediately said, "Yes, Yes, we can start tomorrow, if you want!"   Jumping up dancing around the room, Linz loved her joyful and bubbly spirit.   She dove on the bed showering him with kisses.

CHAPTER THIRTY EIGHT

The total take from the Habib job was $8.3 million. Most of it was in small bills, tens and twenties. There was only two million in fifties and hundreds. It took three days to count it all and to top it off, there was over 500,000 in five dollar bills. Nobody felt like counting that. Each person got $1,370,500, life was getting better with each sting. The group celebrated by going out to eat. The fella's later took a handful of fives and went to the strip club. The Red Devil was back open for business under new management. It was now ran by some Asian dudes who renamed it "Club Akari". Most of the dancers were Asian. The women went to Club Passion for the all male review. The place was packed with wall to wall bitches. The ladies only event lasted from 9 to 12, then it would be open to all people.

The ladies sat in a corner booth with two bottles of Moet reflecting on the past seven months and how their lives have drastically changed for the better since meeting the four men. They spoke of their plans to travel like they said they would. They were able to now bless family members and also their own individual plans. It was clear that each wanted to live with their man. Tootie told them about Linz asking her to carry his child after this was over. Cristal told them about her and Doug purchasing a home in Cali together and after the last job they were gone. She promised them she'd stay in touch. Diamond and Jade had plans to open a high end clothing store downtown and in Ross Park Mall, so they weren't going anywhere. Tootie just said, "Wherever he goes, I'm going" They all started laughing. It was then that Jeanna joined them. They congratulated her on her pregnancy. The five of them just sat back and had a good time acting silly until some broads walked past their booth and one of them called Tootie a trick bitch and kept walking. "Toot, you know her?", Cristal asked. At first she said no because she couldn't see her face, but when she turned around, she recognized Natalie. "Hell yeah I know that bitch. I had to check her about Linz once but now I'm about to beat her ass!", she said while getting up to go holla at Nat. The crew followed behind her trying to stop her but Tootie was determined to fight.

Natalie had her back turned, her and her friends were flirting with some men. Tootie tapped her on the shoulder and when Natalie turned around, Tootie punched her square in the face.   She followed with three quick rights screaming, "Bitch, I told you about fucking with me, didn't I!   I warned you.   I bet now you wished you listened!" Tootie continued to punch and kick her as Natalie crumbled to the floor yelling for help. The men just watched it happen.   The bouncers came over snatched Tootie up.   She swung at him screaming "Get your fucking hands off me!"   The other bouncer tried to restrain her, but ended up tearing her shirt, exposing her breast.

When the ruckus was over, Tootie and her titties were barred and Natalie's face was swollen.   Tootie was so amped that she finally got hers off, she didn't even care that she broke the heel of her favorite pumps.   Once outside, she called Linz to see if he would pick her up and explain what happened.   He said he would be there in 15 minutes. While she waited one of the male strippers came outside to chat with her.   She tipped him $500.00 because he kept dangling his dick in her face.   They exchanged numbers. She almost found out what 10 1/2 inches felt like if it wasn't for the fight.   Curiosity was getting the best of her, her mind kept traveling back to when he danced for her.   Just the thought was making her wet.   She never fucked around on Linz, except to carry out the plan, but Dexter was so enticing.

Dex knew that the young lady was interest by the way she looked at him and the big tip she stuffed in his briefs.   "Let's hook up tonight, I'll give you a private showing.", he said with a smile.   He'd seen her kind before, young, fine, and horny with a little bit of money.   They were all fascinated by the size of his manhood, only to set themselves up to be ruined.   Tootie nervously said, "Not tonight, I'll call you tomorrow, okay."   Then walked to the curb to check for her ride.   Dex watched Tootie's ass jiggle in the satin capris she wore as she walked away.   "Damn that bitch got a phat ass.   I'm gonna fuck the hell out of her.", he said to himself rubbing his thang.

Linz pulled up laughing.   "You got your ass whipped, huh?"   She replied, "I beat that bitch's ass!   Ask anybody up in there.   Bet she won't fuck with me no more."   He gave her some dap while teasing her.   "I'm horny, you gonna give me some when we get home?", she asked.   Dexter had her juices flowing.   "I'll think about it.", Linz answered smiling.   "Oh, you must be mad cause I beat down one of your ex hoes.", she said.   Linz had no idea who she was talking about, so he simply said, "I don't know what or who you are talking about.", getting into the far left lane to enter the Fort Pitt

Tunnels. "That bitch Natalie that you use to fuck with. I beat her ass, so don't be shocked if she call you. Now is you gonna give me some or not?", Tootie asked. Linz could tell that she was a little tipsy, so he paid her no mind.

When they got to his house, he told her, "Get your drunk ass out!", and opened the door for her. "I ain't drunk, I'm just nice right now.", she replied. As soon as they entered the house, she got naked and went to shower off that smokey club smell. He took his time undressing, letting her shower by herself. When he got through showering, he found Tootie sprawled out on a sheet in the living room in front of the fireplace with two glasses and a bottle of Moet. The setting was perfect for a love scene. Tootie was beautiful. Linz joined her on the floor, they began to caress each others bodies softly. She moaned as his skilled hands roamed all over her and his tongue explored her mouth. She fondled his penis, wishing it was him that was packing ten and a half inches, but his eight inches will do. That was enough for her because for the past seven months he has been rocking her world with it. The boy had skills in the sheets, but her body still wanted to know what ten and a half inches felt like just once.

"I love you.", she whispered spreading her legs and arching her back as he entered her. She moaned as he began to build a slow circular stroke. "Damn baby, this pussy feels so good.", he said staring into her hazel eyes. She wrapped her legs around his waist, allowing him to go deeper into her womb. She flexed her vaginal muscles to match his rhythm. He began to thrust deeper and harder as he neared climax. "It's your pussy. Tear it up Baby, tear it up!", she cooed while running her nails lightly up and down his back and across his buttocks. "Aauugh" he cried as his body bucked, filling her pussy with his sperm. The hot liquid coated her walls as she screamed, "I'm coming baby! Don't stop! Don't stop!" Her body shook with force as she released her juices. The post orgasm trembles lasted for several minutes. When she calmed down, she turned onto her side with her back to him as he stretched out beside her wrapping his arm around her. "I love you Lionel.", she said, calling him by his first name and snuggling back against him. He playfully ran his finger along her hips and thighs up between her breast, tracing the outline of her jaw, onto her lips. She closed her eyes and got lost in his touch.

Linz was in love with Tootie, she was everything he searched for in a woman. He finally found his soul mate.   When he told her that he loved her, he really meant it.   He admired her body in the glow of the flames, as it casted a golden hue to her skin damp with sweat.   As he stroked her body, his dick got hard again.   He gently rolled Tootie onto her stomach and got on top of her.   He eased her legs apart and entered her from behind..

Tootie rose up on her elbows allowing him to massage her hardened nipples.   Her head fell forward as he brushed her long wavy hair to one side and placed wet kisses at the nape of her neck.   She began to moan quietly.   She cherished the song their bodies sung together.   As she felt a wave of pleasure come over her, he took her past the stage of euphoria.   She felt his manhood jerk inside of her filling her with his soul, once again.

CHAPTER THIRTY NINE

Yusef Star sat on the steps outside in the crisp March air in a leather parka, smoking a spliff with two of his lieutenants from the Shower Posse. The crew he oversaw, ten rude bwoys, looked forward to gun play. They were called the Shower Posse because every time that they were on the scene, it rained bullets.

Star was a hot headed, knotty, dread locked rude bwoy from Kingston, Jamaica. A true gun toten, head busting don-dada, who lived for the moment to engage in gun play with his next opponent, backed by a vicious crew. Star sold and supplied the city with exstacy, double and triple stacks. He had the college campuses on lock. He threw the biggest and livest raves every weekend. If you scored any X, nine times out of ten, it came from him. He managed to manufacture, distribute, and sell his own, fuck the middle man.

Star had been doing this since '98' with no hassle from the police and only one attempt from robbers, who quickly were made examples of. If you come for him, you better come correct and ready to die because Yusef Star damn sure was. His favorite line was 'Who won' come test me? Speak now!'. He always played Biggie Small's "Somebody's got to die." and Bounty Killa's "Dem No Murda."

Star was on this list because three yeas ago, he waved a Tek Nine at the Four Kings one night while he was drunk tripping over this little Jamaican trick. She smelled like blunts and musk, plus the bitch looked like a dude, but she had a bad ass body. Didn't no one want her stanking ass but him. She gassed him to think one of them was trying to hit on her. A move that would soon cost him his life and empire.

Taking out Star would take some serious planning because he was a true head busta, rude bwoy was no joke. He showed no weakness or signs of fear. Bad bitches didn't amaze him, so the boys couldn't use that angle. He was a hustla's hustler. Money is all that mattered to him.

Star was 32 years old, he drove an 06' 760IL BMW, white with gold grill and 23" rims. His top two lutenients pushed five series Beemers. The rest of the team whipped around in M3 Beemers. Altogether Star was holding $16.7 million. He lived in the tenant building that he owned. He took the top floor apartment, while his lutenients took up residence in two of the remaining 13 apartments. While Yusef Star was out politicing with his yutes, K.J sat across the street studying him. Even though Star wasn't amazed by beautiful women, his top two were. They were some ugly dudes. Without Star and his loot, they got no play. K.J found a weakness in Star's armor.

Tootie woke up alone in the bed, Linz had gone with A.P to work out. She dragged her ass to the shower before calling Jade to come swoop her up. Next she call Dex, she wanted to hook up with him ASAP. Her pussy got wet just thinking about it.

"Hello", Dex answered. "May I speak to Dex?", she said. "This is he." "This is the girl from the club, we spoke outside.", she reminded him. "Oh yeah, what's up with you?", he asked. "Nothing, I called to see what's up with you. Can I get my private dance now?", she said getting right to the point. Dex smiled at her forwardness. "Yeah, when you trying to get it?" "Now!" They arranged to hook up in an hour at the Comfort Inn by the airport.

An hour later, Dex watched as Tootie parked the Charger and entered the lobby. He had already paid for the room. She spotted him by the elevators and he waved her over. They spoke very little on the ride up, but once in the room, it was on. She sat on the bed as he did his thing. The dancing didn't really turn her on, but when he stood naked in front of her she began to get second thoughts. He helped her undress, licking his lips in want. He admired her tear dropped shaped ass as he caressed it. He began stroking himself to his full hardness. Her breath caught in her throat, it was too late to change her mind. "Put it in slow, ok." he smiled a devilish grin knowing he was about to ruin this bitch. She laid back on the bed as he reached for a condom. She watched as he put it on and prepared to enter her. Tootie closed her eyes and winced in pain as he stretched her pussy to the max. This nigga lived up to his stage name 'Big Dick Dexter' and he planned to bury every inch inside his present victim. She began to wonder what she had gotten herself into as she tried to scoot away. Dex had a firm grip on her waist as he slowly inserted inch by inch until their pubic hairs mixed. Tears flowed from her eyes as he paused a minute to let her feel the wrath, before pulling out only to impale her once again. "Oouuchh!", she cried as he built up a rhythm. Her insides felt full. Tootie realized that taking all this dick ain't fun, it is painful, a pain she never wanted to feel again. It made her appreciate Linz's eight inches. She lay numb as Dex pumped in and out of her.   She prayed her walls wasn't permanently damaged and stretched. Tootie was relieved when Dex came, but horrified when he pulled out a bloody condom. Her body ached pain shot through her midsection as she tried to get up.   Dex just sat back and watched as she dressed slowly and in pain.   She just pulled on her sweats, didn't even bother with her panties.   It hurt with each step she took, and when she sat down to drive, it was no better.

When Tootie arrived at the duplex the girls were all sitting in the living room when she entered.   Jade was the first one to notice her walk, "Damn Toot, Linz must be laying the pipe, got you walking all funny."   They all laughed except Tootie.   Then Diamond said, "Wait, ain't Linz and A.P together and when you left here earlier you was walking just fine and now this.   What's up, Linz is still with A.P, so come clean."   Tootie responded, "Y'all help me upstairs first and I'll tell you everything."   They helped her to her room, laid her on her bed.   She pulled her sweats off with Jade's help.   Blood stains were left in her sweats and her coochie lips were swollen.   The girls sat around the bed waiting to hear what happened.   Tootie began crying as she told them what went down. She shed tears for two reasons, she was afraid she was going to lose her man and because she was in pain.   "Bitch, ain't no use for crying now.   Your dumb ass shouldn't have done it.   That's just plain stupid.   You have it made, a man who is good to you and shit and you wanna go fuck around on him with a broke ass male stripper with a big dick who don't give a fuck about you!   Bitch please, I don't even wanna hear no more.   If it wasn't for them niggas, we'd still be just some petty ass thieves shaking our asses for tips.   I don't know about you, but I ain't trying to go back down that road.", Diamond said.   She was furious that her girl had been so stupid.   "Bitch, you lucky I don't slap you!", she added before going to run Tootie a hot bath for her to soak in.   Hopefully her stuff would go back to normal.   If Linz ever found out, he'd beat her ass good and then leave her.

"Get your slutty ass in this tub right now!   I don't know what you gonna do, but you better get it back tight.   Believe me, a nigga can tell when their bitch been fucking, especially a nigga bigger than them.   How could you be so stupid, Tootie!", Diamond asked as they helped her into the tub.   The other girls said nothing during the encounter. They left Tootie alone with her thoughts.   She just sat soaking and crying.   Jade and

Cristal felt sorry for Tootie, so did Diamond, but somebody had to tell her the truth about how foolish that move was.   Lucky for Tootie, her shit was not permanently stretched, but the pain still lingered.   Now all she had to do was hope her man didn't notice that she wasn't as snug as she used to be.

Phase Four

"I Dun Came Up.....

Put my Life on the Line"

CHAPTER FOURTY

Royce sat in Nettie's Cafe with both his trusty soldiers, Rick and Roc, two twins brothers also from Detroit. The men recently got through counting and stashing this months figures. The total was only a mere 1.7 million, it was a slow month for Royce. He usually took in about 3.5 to 4 million monthly. Man, I don't know what's going on this month.", Roc said. "I know, it seems like people don't want to get high no more.", his brother Rick said with a laugh. Royce just shook his head, "Man, I've been feeling lately like retiring from this bullshit. It just ain't thrilling to me anymore. Maybe I just need a vacation.", He continued, " I have fucked some of the baddest bitches, I'm sitting on fifty mil plus in cash, and been all over the U.S and abroad. I push some of the hottest whips, there ain't too much that I haven't done. I know y'all banked at least 15 - 20 mil each right?" The twins just nodded in agreement, never letting the envy they felt show. "Yo, I'm feeling you on that vacation shit.", Roc said. "Me too", his brother chimed in. "Let's catch a couple birds and skate to Hawaii or the Bahamas, or some place like that for a week so we can clear our heads.", Roc proposed. It was evident that the brothers weren't planning on retiring any time soon. "Aight, let's do it, we out tomorrow.", Royce replied.

The three was set to go. "Don't bring none of them loud ass trifling nothing ass bitches that you be with.', Ric said clowning his brother. Royce busted out laughing. "Whatever Nigga, just make sure I don't take none of your bitches!", Roc shot back. Royce just laughed harder. "Y'all keep playing, I might take both y'all bitches!", Royce said popping his collar. "Nigga please, don't none of my hoes want your trick ass!", Roc

said, giving his brother a pound. "It ain't tricking if you got it.",
Royce replied digging in his pockets pulling a knot of big face
hundreds. It was nothing but love between the three men.

The crew sat for a minute more bullshitting and flirting with
this cute little waitress named Eryca. Roc bagged her with his
smooth demeanor. When he went off to get her info, Ric and
Royce watched as people walking by gawked at the cars the men
drove. Royce's triple black Phantom on 26 inch chrome rims
always got second and third looks.

Across town, Linz sat clothed in a Johnny Handsome
sweatsuit in the new office of 2 Major Automotive, talking to
Motorhead. The Olds was done and ready to roll.
"Motorhead, you da muthafucking man! You got me sitting
right.", Linz said complimenting his business partner on his
handy work. "I told you dudes I'm the illest out here, fuck with
your boy, we'll get rich in this car game.", Motorhead said.
"Oh, I applied for the dealer license to sell rims too. I want to
have a complete one stop shop where you can get it all right here.
I got some stuff in the works with some stereo and speaker
companies. I also got a deal worked out with this fabric supply
depot so I can get it below wholesale costs.", Motorhead said.
Linz had faith that this investment venture would prosper. "Did
you check on the brokerage license too?", Linz asked. He
wanted to sell high end cars as well as customize them. The city
had three sports teams and that meant money. Plus, Cleveland,
Columbus, and Cincinnati are not far away, the potential was
endless. "Yeah, I'm waiting on the paper work to come in
now.", Motorhead responded.

The new shop was a 25,000 square feet warehouse that held
two state of the art paint bays, three detail and install bins, a three
car show room floor to show off their work, and a few rooms to

display the rims and other products they intended to sell. The building also provided two nice sized offices and a plush customer lounge with the furniture made out of the seats of various luxury automobiles. The table and end tables were fashioned out of different styles of rims, car grills, and hoods. Motorhead had done wonders with the place. Linz and K.J trusted his vision, that's why they gave him the green light on everything. The men were legitimate business men now. The only thing left to do was find a receptionist to handle the calls and things like that. Motorhead left that up to the boys to handle.

While Linz talked with Motorhead, Drip detailed the Benz for him. "Man, I'm thinking about getting some new shoes for the Benz. You think 22's would be a good look for me?", Linz asked Motorhead. "Yeah, I got the perfect look for you, some 22 inch platinum T-928's, just came out. Holla at me next week, I should be able to get you some, but they run $3,500 without rubber.", Motorhead said before answering the phone. The shop would be officially opened on Monday. While he was on the phone, Linz looked over some of the fliers and cards that they designed and printed up. "Like I was saying, y'all got to find us somebody because I'm not trying to answer phones all day. Now back to the rims, these new shits is the hottest things out. Trust me on this, it'll push the Benz to some next level type of shit." Linz just smiled and said peace to the crew while heading out the door.

Linz navigated through the streets of East Liberty banging Black Rob's 'Star in the Hood'. It subliminally put him back in the hustling mode. That old urge was starting to surface once again. With about 85 kilos and 38 bales of that fire green at their disposal, it was hard not to slip into that old nature. The stage where cash ruled everything around me. The Four Kings combined only had a handful of friends to thank for helping to keep that side of them buried. Lil Mac, Jason and his friends, Rello, Chuck, and Big Rob, these are the ones that choose to get their hands dirty so that the Four Kings didn't have to indulge in that side of the game. The set up made sure everybody ate. You were guaranteed to get rich if your hustle game was up to par because the crew damn near gave the stuff away at the super low price they offered. To be honest, they could care less about the dope, that was just an added bonus. They had stepped their game up and robbed for the cash. They hit the big players that most nigga's only talked or dreamed about robbing. The killer part was that they got away with it so far, and was not afraid to let them hammers ring. If lady luck rode with them these last two hits they'd all walk away with a little over 10 million each in tax free cash.

As Linz turned right on Washington, he spotted the last victim on the list. Royce's black Rolls Royce Phantom was two cars up on his right, waiting for the light to change. He eased up beside the car sitting on 26's, chrome shining like diamonds. One could not help but to bow down to it's elegance and beauty, including Linz. That Rolls Royce was a sight to behold.

Royce relaxed behind the protection of the tinted bullet proof glass of the armored beast. Deep in his heart, he knew someone would eventually try him one day, so he took precautions early, but arrogance over shadowed his reasonable thinking process. He honestly siked himself to think it couldn't happen to him. He would soon learn.

Linz sat in his Benz saying to himself, 'Soon and very soon, your time is coming'. When the light changed Linz made another right on to Holcomb and cruised with the flow of traffic,

completely forgetting were he was supposed to be going.   He
turned into a KFC to turn around, as he did he spotted a female
he knew.   She was a cute little bird that he never got to screw,
but they became tight like glue.   The two referred to each other
as sister and brother.   Matter of fact, the whole crew re-guarded
her as that.   They all looked out for her from time to time
because they felt bad for her.   Both her parents were deceased
along with the father of her six year old daughter.   Society had
dealt her a fucked up hand, but she hung tough and never let
life's set backs cause her to fold.

Eryca was strapping her little girl in when Linz rolled up on
her.   He hit the horn startling her and causing her to bump her
head.   She was embarrassed and heated.   Linz just sat behind
the wheel laughing.   She gave him the finger.   "Nigga, that shit
ain't funny!", she said rubbing her head.   "Get in for a minute.",
he said through the open window.   "I just got her little bad ass
strapped in.", she complained while undoing her daughter,
Ka'tier.

"Uncle!", Ka'tier screamed with a big smile on her face
when she saw Linz.   The little girl called all four of the men
Uncle.   "Where we going?   I got homework to do, plus I gotta
find a sitter for her for a couple of days.", Eryca asked as they
pulled off.   Eryca was a single mother, working hard to finish
school, hold down a crappy job, and raise her child without
losing her self respect or getting played by men.   She hated to
ask anyone for anything, especially men, because they always
wanted something in return, mainly sex.   Don't get it twisted,
she was fucking, but it was on her terms.   Every once in a while,
she'd set something out to some lucky brother who had
something going for himself.   Her tuition at Pitt was kicking her
ass, but, she only had one year to go before she received her BA

in business management.

"How's life treating you?', Linz asked while hitting the parkway to Monroeville Mall.   "Fine, just broke as hell, as always.   Other than that, these classes are kicking my ass.   She is getting on my nerves, but other than that I'm cool.   "Uncle, where are we going?", Ka'tier asked.   "To the mall babe.", he answered.   Her little brown dimpled face lit up as she cheered and bounced up and down in the back seat.   "Girl stop, before you tear something up.   You know Mommy can't pay for it!", Eryca told her daughter who paid her no attention at all.

"She's cool, let her have fun.", Linz said pulling into the mall parking lot.   Eryca looked at Linz for the millionth time and repeated to herself once again, I wish he was her father. Linz patted her thigh and said, "It's gonna be alright, you know if you need us we all are here for you."   She smiled and said thanks.   Before entering the mall, he gave her $3,500 and told her to take care of her bills and get something nice for herself. He and Ka'tier strolled off in the direction of the toy store.

They spent an hour and a half in the mall.   He spoiled Ka'tier.   All the kings did, and she loved it.   When they reached the car, Eryca asked if he would mind keeping her for a couple days.   She prayed he would.   She really wanted to go on this much needed vacation with the pretty boy she'd met today at work named Roc.   She wouldn't tell the boys that she was about to set something out to a nigga she just met, they'd surely cuss her out.   Little did she know, Roc's time on earth was limited, as so was his brothers and boss.

Linz called Tootie, Diamond told him that she was sleep. He left a message that he was on his way over.   When he hung up Linz told Eryca that he would keep Ka'tier for a few days. "Who was that?", Eryca asked.   "My woman."   "What, you got a woman? When did this happen and why haven't I met her yet!", Eryca asked sarcastically. Linz smile and said, "You'll meet her soon. I've been kicking it with her for a minute now. I'm really feeling her too, I think she's the one." Eryca was surprised to hear that come out of his mouth.

They rode in silence until they reached her car. "Do you ever wonder how things would have turned out if we would have hooked up?", she asked. "All the time, babe.", he responded, then hugged her. This was the queen that got away. They held the embrace a little longer than friends should. Eryca kissed his cheek and said, "Take care of my baby.", then got out of the car. He watched the '89 Escort as she pulled away.

A.P's truck was parked across the street when Linz arrived at Tootie's place. "Uncle, who lives here?", Ka'tier asked. He paid her no mind as he opened the door for her. Cristal answered the door when he knocked. Ka'tier was hiding behind him when he entered. "Tootie's upstairs sleeping.", she told him. Linz told Ka'tier to go sit down until he came back. "Who's little girl is this, she is so pretty.", Cristal stated. Cristal loved kids, one day she hoped to have some of her own. She took Ka'tier into the kitchen to get some candy. Linz dashed up the steps to holla at A.P and Tootie. He knocked on Diamond's door before entering. "Y'all dressed?" "Come on in.", Diamond replied. He stuck his head in and spotted the two laying on the bed watching TV. "What's up?", A.P asked. "Nothing, about to holla at my girl, but somebody wants you downstairs.", Linz said. "Who?", A.P asked getting off the bed to go see who wanted him.

Tootie was fake sleeping when Linz entered. He jumped on the bed, disrupting her so called sleep. "Get up girl.", he said. "Stop boy! I'm tired! Plus it's that time of the month, I'm cramping.   I don't feel good and I'm not in the mood to be playing.", she said, lying to cover her ass so he wouldn't ask her for any pussy.   This gave her three days to heal from the bashing she took for creeping with Dex.   Linz continued to mess with her.   "Stop boy!!", she cried, as he climbed on top of her.   He tried to kiss her, which she gladly accepted.   "Babe, I need a favor.", he asked.   "What is it now."   "I need you to babysit somebody for me.", he said.   "When and who.", she inquired. He kissed her lips and said, "Come on, I'll show you.", and pulled the covers off her revealing her nakedness.   Linz was still amazed that every time he seen her naked it was like the first time all over again.   "Move so I can put something on.", she said getting up and going to her dresser to get her granny panties to enhance the lie she told a few minutes ago.   "Damn Boo, why you gotta start today?", he asked salty because he couldn't get none.   As she threw on a t-shirt and shorts she said, "Baby, I can still take care of you in other ways."   Tootie had grown to love giving oral sex to him.

Ka'tier was having a ball with A.P, Diamond, and Cristal when Linz and Tootie entered the living room.   Ka'tier ran across the room to Linz when he came in.   "Uncle, look what I got.", she said showing him some candy.   Then she ran back to A.P.   "Who's little girl is that", Tootie asked.   "Our peeps.", Linz replied, "Can you help me babysit?"   Tootie agreed, like Cristal, she loved and wanted kids.   "When you see Eryca?", A.P asked.   "When I as coming from the shop.", he said   Linz then told him about seeing Royce.   "Don't she gotta go to school?", Tootie asked.   Linz completely forgot to ask Eryca about that, so he called her to find out.   Eryca had forgot too, but she told him she'd call the school and notify them that her little girl will be absent for a few days.   She also told Linz how

long she planned to be away and her return date. Before
hanging up she asked to speak to her child who was busy playing
with the ladies. A.P took the phone and spoke to Eryca for a
few minutes before making Ka'tier get on the phone to talk to her
mother. Eryca knew that her child was in good hands with the
men, each one of them treated her as if they were Ka'tier's
biological father.

"Babe, are you staying here tonight or do you got other
plans?", Tootie asked. She felt guilty about not being able to
screw her man because of the lie that she told, but she was eager
to please him in other ways. "I got a couple things to do then
I'll be back. I can leave her here right?", he stated. She
nodded, she could use the company since the others were going
to the movies and out clubbing at Frankie's for reggae night.
Ka'tier would do just fine until her man returned.

It would be later that the crew would get together and discuss
plans to take out Mr. Yusef Star, one of the deadliest men on the
list. +

CHAPTER FOURTY ONE

Star sat in Montiego's with this light skinned girl enjoying a plate of jerk chicken, ox-tails, and spicy rice.   The sounds of Bob Marley's "No Woman, No Cry" caressed their ears. Montiego's was the cities premier island eatery.   Star was feeling good sitting with his long time girl, Senica.   She too was from the islands, a rising dancehall star, presently burning up the charts in Jamaica and the U.K with her hit single "Long Tyme Bwoy".   When she was state side, Star spent time with her point blank.   Sometimes she was here for a few days, other times it was for a few weeks.   During these times he turned control of things over to his top two yutes.

The couple finished their meal and bounced.   Star admired Senica's backside as she sashayed to the 760IL Beemer that sat glistening in the March sun.   "You drive.", he said in his strong island accent, and tossed her the keys.

Senica resembled one of those girls you see in all the reggae videos, beautiful, banging body that's barely covered, hair in twists.   To the naked eye she was just another hot gal out to have fun, but like Star, she was a true rude girl who always carried a straight razor and never thought twice about using it. There were plenty of females back in Kingston Jamaica wearing make up to cover up the infamous telephone cut that she placed on their once beautiful faces for many different reasons.   Senica put on her shades and slid behind the wheel of the big BMW, adjusted the seat, plugged in her I-POD, and smashed out.   Star relaxed and rolled a spliff.   "Where to Dada?", she asked. "Anywhere ya want.", he replied, blowing out a cloud of smoke passing the spliff.   She maneuvered the big sedan across the Fort Pitt Bridge, toward the notorious North Side and Hill District.

Pounding beats pulsated out the Bose speakers relaxing Star as his woman drove him to an unsuspecting murder that lay across the bridge. As they made a right on 5th Avenue, you could hear the sounds of dancehall coming out of Frankie II's, a well established night spot frequented by NFL and local ghetto stars. It was quickly becoming the next hot spot to be seen at.

"Whoa now!", Star exclaimed, as he sat upright in the leather seat with a look of disbelief. "What the bloodclot, fuck dis bwoy doing? Go back around!", he commanded. "Me can't be-lee dis pussy clot bwoy.", he yelled. With a look of confusion on her face, Senica quickly recognized the point of her man's anger, an out of town hustler named Perry Frazier, who went by Young Perry". He was a transplant from Dyersburgh, Tennessee, a little town known for narcotics and robbery. Perry, though mild mannered, had been the ring leader in several robberies from Tennessee to Texas. A southern bandit you could say, yet with the tag came a lot of enemies. Perry had only been in Pittsburgh for a short time when he realized two things. First money, like time, flies when your having fun. Second, old habits die hard. A few months after Perry moved to the area he got close to a couple ballers and woman, which is how Perry came to know Star as a friend and later as an enemy.

As the story goes, Perry had a southern drawl along with a good hustle hand, which caught the attention of Star, who scooped him up and made him a part of his murderous Shower Posse. Young Perry had earned the trust of Star. He was given the task of driving for Star. He was trusted with many things, including his most prized possession, his girl Senica.

Perry, in a matter of months, went from drive to third lieutenant . This move was made after Star discovered the youngins willingness to air anybody out for any reason at the drop of a dime.   This yute would clap at your soul without fail if you crossed him the wrong way.   He brought a new meaning to the term 'get down or lay down' and he meant just that.   That's the part that Star loved about this dude, and it was that attitude that saved Star's life one day.   Bamba, one of Star's closest lutenients was plotting to kill Star.   The plot was exposed to both Star and Perry.   Before any questions could be asked or answered, Bamba was taken care of by Perry.   After that incident Perry climbed the ranks very quickly.   The other members complained but could do nothing about it.

After a few months of the Posse life, Star asked Perry to watch over Senica while he was away on business.   Star had dealings in London, Miami, and Texas.   These were his most profitable spots outside of Pittsburgh, so he had to make sure that they stayed stocked with X pills.

At first being paired with Senica was difficult for Perry because she stayed in revealing clothes and her mouth was foul as hell.   It was a battle to not be attracted to her and not be offended at the same time.   Perry lived by the code, never mix business with pleasure, but it was getting harder each time that he had to be with her.   Senica was starting to see this little country boy in a new light.   It began as the two just smoking a blunt together, then it gradually escalated to something more.   Since Star was away alot during the fall months handling business, Perry had to guard Senica.   It was then that he gave into her flirtatious ways.   They were coming from Donzi's Nightclub one night she was dressed in a sizzling outfit that complimented and highlighted every curve of her body.   The memories of her winding on the dance floor left him hot and bothered.   He tried to shake the urges he was having for her but she kept on pushing him.   It started with little touching here, to rubbing there, and then her saying little things like she needed some bad and how wet her stuff was. Tempting him by saying, "If I put this wind on you, it's ova, ya can't handle dis ere' poon-poon." Dude tried his best to resist but the combination of Henny and Hypnotic, mixed with the weed they were blowing on was too much for him to take. He gave in to her advances, but the thought of crossing Star was in the back of his mind. "Sen, we shouldn't do this, your Star's girl!", he said. "So what! Star ain't here and I need some. Your job is to take care of me while he's gone, so do ya job and take care of me!", she stated while running her hands up his thigh, blowing in his ear. "Babe, I don't thing he meant me fucking you.", he pleaded with her. She was determined to get some of him tonight. "What's a matter? Star got you scared too? Huh! Speak up bwoy!", she said playing him like a fiddle. Senica was a dime no doubt, Perry couldn't deny that. The way she moved her body on the dance floor, one could only imagine how she moved in bed. He took another toke of the spliff, and inhaled real deep.

While he drove contemplating his next move, Senica climbed in the back seat and began to undress. Every time he looking in the rear view mirror he got a birds eye view of her shaved pussy. This broad wouldn't give up. Senica then took her middle finger and dipped it into her own pussy, swirling it around and then placed her juices in her mouth. "Ya sure you don't want none?". She asked while she began masturbating, rubbing her clit in circles. That last stunt did it for him, he took the bait. "Your place or mine?", he asked. Then before she could answer, he changed his mind. "Better yet, let's get a room that way it's on the low." She nodded in agreement as they hit the express way toward the Hilton by the airport.

Once inside the room, they wasted no time getting busy.

Her body was amazing from head to feet, this bitch was bad. Senica moved her body like a snake in bed, while on top of him, her movements were effortless and almost fluid. "Damn Sen, this shit is the bomb!", Perry said as she continued to put it on him. "I told ya it was good, you never had it like this before, huh.", she teased while riding him. The sex lasted for three hours, it was late in the afternoon when he returned Senica to her home. "We must do it again sometime soon.", she said before getting out the car.

Over the next couple of months, Senica and Perry got very close and were screwing on the regular when ever Star wasn't in town. They were hooked on each other and were almost caught a few times by Star and one of his other workers.

Perry had began to see how much Senica was becoming attached to him, so he tried his hand by asking for things. First, it was jewelry, then it was money. His leverage was that he threatened to tell Star, which Senica didn't want but wasn't falling for because he had as much to lose as she did. But then he threatened to stop fucking her, which she rally didn't want. She was willing to do anything to keep her affair going, including staging a robbery so Perry could get on his feet. He strengthened the plan by telling her that he'd take her with him and that she could come kick it with him once he got a place of his own. She bought it.

As time went on, the plan was perfected. The take was 1.4 million. That was the money from one of his pick ups. The plan was for Senica and Perry to be tied up and beat by Perry's cousin, Big Dub and then tell Star they didn't know who did it. The plan went down but the only one who got an ass whipping was Senica. Perry fucked her, tied her up, and left her for dead in an abandoned house. She was found by one of Star's yutes.

Star was furious, not about the money, but what they did to his heart. He swore death to who ever was responsible for this.

Senica played her part well thinking that Perry was coming to get her soon, but as time passed without even one call she realized that she'd been played. As anger welled up inside of her, she couldn't do shit about it because that meant telling Star that she helped set it up. She swore to herself that if she ever saw Perry again, she'd kill him herself.

Perry and Dub were on their way back down south to Dyersburg, not thinking about Senica or Star because they never thought to return to Pittsburgh ever. The two parlayed their lick into a couple prosperous businesses. They opened a rim shop called 'Sitting Lovely' and a cellphone and pager shop, and they were still slanging them thangs. There were now regarded as big ballers in the little town of D-burg, doing whatever and whenever. He took on an attitude that he was untouchable. Well that was three years ago, but now he was back in Pittsburgh like it was all good between him and Star.

Perry walked slowly to his Chrysler 300C with his date for the night. Perry was rarely seen without a woman. He was a little tipsy and feeling good, thinking he was about to punish this broad, but as fate would have it this spring night would be his last.

Senica drove slowly behind the two walking through the parking garage, her heart burned with anger and rage. Perry didn't even notice the white Beemer crawling at a turtles pace behind them with only the parking lights on. He tossed the key's to the broad that was with him, he was too bent to drive. He finally turned and saw the sedan behind him. It all seemed to happen in slow motion, the doors of the BMW opened and a cloud of ganja smoke escaped along with the sound of Berrington

Levy's voice. Before Perry could react, Star appeared with twin Desert Eagles pointing at his face. He glanced over to his right and saw Senica arise out of the smoke, straight razor twirling in her hand. The blade gleeming under the dim light of the garage. Senica was just as Perry remembered, beautiful. He was also about to find out how deadly she was. "Ya won test me now huh pussy bwoy?", Star said, then let out a grueling laugh. With lightening speed, Star popped two shots to Perry's knees, sending him to the ground. "No man steal from me! Ya broke rule number 1, Don't bite the hand that feed ya!" Perry knew that death was certain so he knew there was no use in asking for mercy. "Fuck you Star, you and your bitch Senica! By the way the pussy wasn't all that good, but the head was!". That was all he could do to save face. Star was heated at the remark made towards his girl. Star knew of the affair that the two had but never said anything to Senica about it. Senica was hot about the way Perry talked about her sex. She kicked him in the face and spit on him. To think she actually fell in love with this creep! Perry just laughed and said, " Babe, it is what it is, but I had fun Bi...." That's all he was able to get out before Senica had grabbed him from behind and slit his throat, leaving him to choke on his own blood. As Perry laid choking, Star pissed on him. The date that was with Perry had passed out from the scene that took place. Senica slapped her awake and told her, "Keep quiet whore or your next!" Placing the blade up to her face. "Now get in the car and go!", but before she let her go she sliced her face, leaving a hook from ear to mouth for emphasis that she meant business. The broad was too drunk to recall the faces of the assailants.

Star and Senica returned to the car leaving Perry's piss and blood soaked body on the pavement. As they drove past the

now lifeless body, Senica fought to hold back the tears.   The
two went directly to the airport to hop the next flight to London.

Two weeks later, Perry's remains were claimed by his cousin
Big Dub and other relatives from Tennessee.   It was then that
Dub promised that he'd get whoever killed his cousin, it was bad
enough that they slit his throat, but they didn't have to piss on
him, that was down right cold blooded.

A few days after Dub claim the body, he received a call from
one of his old friends Screwface, the only one in Star's Shower
Posse that like him.   He told him that Star was responsible for
the killing of Perry.   Even though Dub knew that Star was
behind the killing of Perry, he knew that he could not go at Star
sideways because Star was walking death.   He decided to be
patient but little did he know that the chance to get revenge
would come so soon by the way of another friend he'd met
through Perry.

CHAPTER FOURTY-TWO

The girls enjoyed watching Ka'tier, they all pitched in and bought her a bunch of clothes and things because Linz had forgot to go get her things before her mother left.   Eryca at this present time was on an island beach getting dicked down and sipping daquari's with some nigga she just met.

Ka'tier started calling the four women her aunties, they spoiled her rotten.   Tootie noted how Linz acted with Ka'tier and wondered if he was her real father on the low.   She finally concluded that he'd be a good father to her children when they had them.   That made her smile knowing that her kids wouldn't be fatherless like her.

The ladies took Ka'tier out for walks around the hood because the weather was unusually warm.   Tootie had used this as an exercise that she added to her daily routine to get into shape.   She started working out again to her sexy back on track and lose the few pounds she'd put on after she stopped dancing. Even thought Linz was cool with the extra weight, she wasn't so she decided to tone up.

Eryca returned on Tuesday after a lovely week on the beach getting her back blown out.   She got to know Roc well but decided that she didn't want nothing to do with a man in the streets.   The thought of messing with someone in that lifestyle brought back painful memories of her babies father.   He lived and lost his life in the streets hustling.   The flight home was grueling and turbulent, once she touched down in Pitt International she phone Linz to check on her baby.   She found out that all was well and let him know she would be picking her up in about an hour or so.   He told her that he'd be home waiting and Ka'tier was at Chuck E. Cheese's with Tootie. Eryca would soon meet the object of her play brothers affection.

Roc dropped Eryca off at home, she rested for a minute, showered, changed clothes, and checked her messages. She returned a few phone calls, one to her girlfriend Danni and gossiped about the trip and the sex. Then she went through the mail which was nothing but bills. She was sick of this shit. Her car was on the verge of breaking down, her job didn't pay shit, but she was happy for the trip. Her and Danni were supposed to get together later on to go over some of the homework that she missed for the past week. Eryca bounced out the door happy as hell on her way to get her child. She decided she would ask Linz for a loan until she got her taxes back so she could get caught up on her bills and hopefully put something down on this car she seen for the low. She knew the Four Kings would buy her a car if she asked, but her pride wouldn't let her ask.

Tootie answered the door when Eryca arrived, the two hit it off instantly. Ka'tier ran to her mother's side with her arms open wide yelling "Mommy! Mommy!". The two embraced. Ka'tier began telling her mom everything that went on. Linz came and introduced Tootie and Eryca to each other. The three of them sat down to talk for a few moments. Linz offered Eryca a job at the shop, which she gladly accepted and asked if her girl Danni could get a job also. Linz was cool with Danni working too as long as they were willing to work, then he told her what the job required.

After Eryca picked up Ka'tier, Linz, Tootie, Diamond, and A.P went to the movies to see 'Gospel'. Afterwards they went to Outback's for something to eat. K.J and Jade, along with Doug and Cristal joined them. They began to formulate the plan to dead Mr. Yusef Star.

K.J had his ears to the street, he'd recently found out about the killing of Young Perry. He also knew that Perry had a cousin who was seeking revenge on Star for doing his peeps and would jump at the chance to get it. K.J relayed this to the crew. K.J planned to use his two white boys, Armando and Aaron, Lil Mac, Big Dub and his crew to help them pull this off. The only ones they had to pay was Dub and his three man crew, they would get six kilos for their help, and the two white boys would get $100,000 each for their help. Lil Mac took it as a favor for a favor. This made the Four Kings ten men strong to go at it with Star. Then to everyone's surprise Diamond's appetite for death rose again, she wanted in after she heard about Senica. Jade, Tootie, and Cristal followed suit with Diamond and also wanted in. The team increased to 14, now all they had to do was call Dub.

Dub sat on the porch getting his hair braided when his cell phone went off. He glanced at the caller ID, which read unknown. He thought before answering, "Hello", he said sounding country as hell. He was greeted with a strange voice, "Dub, just listen, I'm a friend of Perry's, we met twice, I think you and I both share the same feeling about Mr. Star, so let's help each other, you interested?" Dub said, "Hell yeah, what's up?" "Just get here and bring three of your peeps that you can trust, then call me at this number.", the voice said rattling off the phone number. Dub wrote it down, "We'll be there day after tomorrow." and hung up. He rounded up his crew, gassed up the Suburban and hit the highway back to PA.

Next, K.J placed a call to his white boys. After six rings, Aaron answered, "This better be good". He was in the middle of fucking his girl when K.J called. "I need to see you, troubles brewing. 100 G's help us solve it.", K.J said. "11:30 tonight, usual spot.", Aaron said then hung up so he could get back to his business at hand. The thought of taking a life excited him even more. Aaron and Doe kept alot of funeral parlors in business.

Now all they had to do is holla at Lil Mac. Linz called Mac and let him know he needed to see him. Mac already knew the business when calls come through like that. A minute later, Jeanna called and asked where Tootie was. This is the code for where he wanted Mac to meet him. Linz told them and they were on the way. Once Mac showed up the five women excused themselves to let the men talk. They told Mac the plan and what they needed for him to do.

The plan was to take Star's soldiers at the club and at the same time take him at his apartment, hit him quick and hard. Mac had two days to be ready because Friday it was on and popping. They'd meet back up Friday morning, everybody would see who was on their side.

The crew said their goodbyes and broke out in different directions. K.J went to holla at Doe and Aaron. A.P, Diamond, and Jade headed back to his place. Mac and Jeanna rolled out. Linz and Tootie bounced to his place, it had been a week since he had her brown legs wrapped around him. She too was itching to feel him pushing deep inside of her. She was getting tired of sucking him two and three times a day, her jaws were starting to hurt. Tonight she was getting some dick.

Doug and Cristal went to Frankie's to see if Star had returned from his trip with Senica. Sure enough, he was there mashing it up with his yutes. Senica was no where in sight. She must have stayed behind because there was another hot gal latched on to Star's side, Dominga, one of the regular DJ's at the club. The crowd was crazy open when Senica's underground hit 'Long

Tyme Bwoy' was played. Star and his crew rushed the dance floor winding with any cutie willing to log on. Frankie's was Star's stomping ground and on Tuesday night he was the brightest star.

During K.J's stalking of Star, he learned that Star and his top two lutenients never went out on Friday. They strangely spent that time mediating and smoking. They put their own twist on the Rastafarian faith. For them, Friday was a day to relax the mind, body, and soul. The rest of the soldiers were thugs from the city, Friday was club night for them. They liked to be seen and this would be their downfall. This would be the last Friday for many of their young lives.

Thursday morning, the grey Suburban with the smoke tint eased through the Fort Pitt Tunnels carrying four brothers with gold grills and two sistas, Jayla and Monique. The Suburban stopped in front of the Vista Hotel, downtown Pittsburgh. Once the entourage was checked in, Dub called the number he'd been given. K.J answered instantly, "Hello". Dub said, "I'm here at the Vista." "I'm on my way now, meet me in 30 minutes in the lobby.", K.J instructed before disconnecting the call. Dub wondered who the voice belonged to and if it was a trap of some sort. The voice sounded so familiar. "Oh well", he thought, "I'm up here now. If it's a trap, then I'm going out blazing."

A.P and Doug were with Mac checking and cleaning the weapons once again. Jeanna's peeps came through major this time supplying them with enough guns for a small army. Three SKS's, four mac-11's with silencers, a couple AK-47's, a couple Calicos, two Desert Eagle 9mm, clips, ammo, and stage 3 kevlar body armor. The price wasn't cheap, but neither were the buyers. Jeanna's peep didn't even want to know who or what it was for, they decided to wait and watch it on the t.v. With this much artillery some bodies were sure to be left around.

Meanwhile, the ladies were plundering the airport parking garages collecting license plates for the stolen cars Mac had put away.   Most of them were small imports except for the '86 Grand National and SS Trailblazer..

K.J and Linz entered the lobby from the 3rd Street entrance. They spotted Dub and the two females posted on a sofa reading The Pittsburgh Press.   They strolled over towards him, "What's up Big Pimp.   Long time no see.", KJ said, extending his hand to show love.   "Shit, I been chilling, staying low.", Dub replied. "Yeah, I know you remember me, we used to always see each other at Donzi's.", Linz said.   As Big Dub searched his memory Linz said, "You used to mess with my home girl Eva, she worked at the gold store on Wood Street."   "I sure do remember you, you had that Range Rover. Linz right?", the big man said as thoughts of his ex Eva came to mind.   "Yeah, that's me.", Linz answered.   "So what's the business with Star?   I'm gone get that nigga, fo sure, I promise that.", Dub said as wrath and pain showed on his face.   "Y'all got a room because I need a sit down.", K.J said.   Dub shook his head yeah and lead them to the elevator.   Linz noticed three men following a few steps behind them.   He reached for his heater for security, but Jayla stopped him whispering in her southern accent, "Relax, they with us.", as she placed her hand over his.   It wasn't until K.J gave the ok that he relaxed.

Upstairs K.J and Linz laid the plan down to Dub and his boys.   After that Dub asked, "What Star do to y'all?"   The Four Kings reasons for getting Star wasn't as strong as Dubs, but it was reason enough.   While he waited on an answer, K.J and Linz searched their minds to come up with an acceptable answer that wouldn't expose their true motive as to why Star was in their sights. "He violated.", was all Linz said, leaving everyone in wonder of how he violated.

Linz and K.J rose to leave and Jayla asked, "What y'all getting fixin to do?" The two looked at Dub and his peeps before answering. Dub said, "Man, if y'all wanna holla go ahead, them my cousins." With that being said, the player in both men showed it's face once again. "Shit, run around for a minute, why what's up?", K.J asked. "Because he gonna be here for a few days, I ain't tryna stay couped up in no room the whole time.", Jayla replied. "I feel you ma, I'll come swoop you in about an hour.", Linz said. Monique said, "What about me?" "Chill Ma, you coming too.", K.J said scoping her frame. Both chicks were short and stacked, about 5'4", 120 -135 pounds and sexy as hell. Before Linz got to the door Dub asked about Eva. Linz told him where she worked at. Dub was on his way as soon as he got out of the shower. Dub loved him some Eva.

Linz had K.J swing by the shop to pick up his Benz. He also had Tootie meet him there. He told her about Dub's two cousins. She was cool about him showing them the city for a few hours. She just warned him saying, "Don't do nothing I wouldn't do." Although Tootie felt a little insecure inside, she never let him know.

Once K.J and Linz picked up the two girls, the day flew by. They arranged for Jayla and Monique to enjoy the night life with Tootie and the other girls. Chauncy's was the jump off on Thursday night.

CHAPTER FORTY-THREE

It was about 8:30 am when everyone came together to see who was on sides and to go over the plans once more because 1:30am tonight was showtime.   It seemed that no one had any questions, everyone was in their own zone preparing for the night.   Everyone fully understood their position and the risked involved.   They all knew off top that Star and his crew were killers who would take no thought in blasting first.   Bottom line it was kill or be killed.

Aaron and Armando, the true psycho killers came up with the plan to divert the police to one area for awhile by staging a bomb threat in the Strip District by using a stolen car and a few boxes of TNT.   That would give them enough time to blaze Star's crew and escape without a police chase.   Hopefully the other team would be hitting Star at the same time.

The team assigned to hitting up the Shower Posse consisted of Mac, Doug, A.P, Dub's three men, Diamond, and Cristal. The team assigned to attack Star and his two top yutes were Linz, K.J, Doe Aaron, Dub, Tootie, and Jade.   The teams split up to get food and rest at 11 pm.   They would meet back up to suit up with Kevlar and receive weapons and stolen whips.   There would be three people to each car.   Most of the fully auto guns would be used for the spraying of the Shower Posse, while the smaller one's for Star.

1:00 am rolled around rather slow, everyone had been on edge.   All the parties were accounted for except for Dub's two cousins but they weren't part of the plan.   The weapons were loaded and handed out.   Everybody had on black sweats or military style cargo pants.   Murder was in the air, everybody had their game face on.   They gathered in a circle, gloved hands held as Linz said a prayer for each of them, tonight they would surely need it.   As they broke the huddle Tootie grabbed Linz and whispered, "Be careful."   He hugged her and said, "Thanks", then disappeared into his vehicle with Dub inside. K.J, Doe, and Aaron, the three loose cannons, rode together. Tootie and Jade followed in one of the Acura Legends Mac provided.   Mac and A.P jumped in the Grand National as two of Dub's boys packed the '05 Nissan Max.   Doug, Diamond, and the last of Dub's peeps rode in the Honda.

While the other cars rode in silence, Diamond bucked and put in 50 Cent's "Many Men" to set the mood for her.   Everyone in her car seemed to zone out as they got closer to Club Aurora. The club was just starting to let out and there was alot of parking lot pimping going on.   By the time they got there it would be in full swing.   When the three cars carrying team one passed, Star's soldiers were posted up on the hoods of their M3 Beemers. All eight of them sitting like the world was theirs with several hoodrats hanging off of them.   They were enjoying the life of a hustlers never thinking that tonight their clocks would expire and their lives would be lost or changed forever.

At the same time Mac was turning left on Hudson to make the second pass of the club, a fleet of Pittsburgh Police cars and EMS trucks flew by responding to the APB of a confirmed bomb threat in the center of the Strip District.   All surrounding precincts responded.   This provided the window the men needed to carry out the plan.

It seemed like something out of a movie, the three cars pulled up and stopped in front of the Shower Posse, who was too busy engaging in the shine they were getting from the rats. They never saw the hit until it was far too late.

When Mac stopped, A.P popped up through the t-top with

the AK letting loose,, spitting armor piercing shells as flame erupted from the barrel.   As he was emptying the 100 round clip in seconds, the other cars started releasing hot steel as well.   A.P reloaded and emptied another 100 rounds into the targets in front of him sending 7.2 mm shells through flesh, bones, and metal. The result was mind blowing, bodies lay twisted on the pavement or slumped across the bullet riddled cars.

Blood stained the concrete like oil in a body shop.   When the paramedics and coroners finally arrived, the death toll was at 38.   Thirty of the casualties were innocent bystanders in the wrong place at the wrong time.   The final sound of this night, similar to war, would ring in the surviving patron's ears for months, maybe even years to come.

The adrenalin rush that Diamond felt was intense as she gripped the steering wheel of the Maxima, jumping in and out of lanes, taking corners at high rates of speed trying to keep up with Lil Mac and A.P.   They were three car lengths ahead, leaving the other two cars to follow it's tail lights.   Cristal's heart raced as Diamond ran the light at the corner of 8th and Smith Street barely avoiding a collision with a taxi.   "Shit, slow the fuck down!", she said aloud.   As the two cars continued to pull away Diamond said, "Hold on!", as she made a hard left onto Davidson Ave racing towards the North Side.   The plan was to abandon the cars on the streets in the notorious Earl E. Plaza Housing Complex, one of the largest in the city.   Some asshole would more than likely take the cars with the guns inside, along with the murder charges on the weapons.   These North Side niggas was crazy, but Lil Mac was raised in this area, he had Ike's over here, so they were straight.

Meanwhile, Tootie and Jade waited outside, guns cocked and ready as the crew of men crept through the halls of Star's building.   Star lived on the fourth floor, he'd taken two apartments and converted them into one.   He used another apartment on that floor for storing his loot.

As the men got closer to his floor the pulsating sound of Tenor Saw's classic hit 'Ring the Alarm' got louder.   The booming bass line vibrated through the halls, rattling the bones of anyone within reach.   The pungent odor of ganja could be smelled two floors down.   One could catch a contact just walking through the halls.

When they reached Star's door, the sounds of reggae was deafening.   The men lined up on either side of the door, using hand signals, counted to three then charged the door, the steel door withheld, but the frame gave a little.   This caused the men to repeat crashing the door again which gave Tuffy, one of Stars top yutes, a heads up allowing him time to grab a weapon.   He tried yelling to warn Star and Screwface, who were in the back rooms screwing a few of the female tenants who lived in the building.   However, the volume was too loud and they couldn't hear the commotion.

When the door swung open, Dub and the others rushed the smoke filled apartment with guns drawn.   It took a few seconds for their eyes to adjust to the smoke.   When they did they found Tuffy crawling on the floor with a tech-nine in his grip.   Before he could raise it to fire, the spittle from the silenced Uzi cut him down.   The half naked cutie that was with him began begging for her life saying," Please don't hurt me, please I got three kids. I won't say nothing, I promise.   Please!"   Her cries fell on deaf ears as Aaron went to slice her throat.   Linz, the soft hearted one, saved her.   He said, "She ain't got nothing to do with it, let her live."   The Christian in him wanted no parts of innocent blood shed, plus the fact that she had three little ones to look after.   He refused to take their mother from them.   He motioned for her to keep quiet.   She balled up in a corner trying to cover her breasts, which Doe stared at with lustful eyes.   In his twisted mind he wanted to fuck her then kill her.   It aroused him to watch her cower with fear.

"Where Star at?", Linz asked.   She pointed a trembling finger towards the back of the apartment.   "Who's all back there?"   "Star, Screw, and two other girls.", she replied.   "What they doing?", he asked.   "Fucking I guess.   They just went back there a few minutes ago.   Their clothes are over there.", she said.   The crew began to ease towards the back rooms, leaving Doe to watch the frightened mother of three.

The men split up searching rooms.   Dub was the first one to find Star, who was in mid stroke when Dub placed the barrel of the calico inches from his skull.   The girl who lay under him seen Dub, but Star kept stroking.   It wasn't until he looked in her face and caught Dub's reflection in her eyes that he reached under the pillow to grab the Ruger he always kept there.   The pillow muffled the sound of him cocking it.

"Bitch, you killed my cousin!", Dub yelled.   Just then the music stopped and Linz and Aaron appeared in the doorway with Screwface and the naked chick who was sucking him off when Linz and K.J found them.   The two women began begging for their lives, which was no surprise because that is what is expected in a situation like this.   Star silenced the women by yelling in his strong island voice, "Stop ya blood clot crying whores, die with some dignity."   Then he spat in the female's face who lay underneath him.   "You da reason for all dis here confusion!" He slowly rolled off of her and revealed Senica, his long time gal. The other female was Dominga, the club DJ.

Star still had his hand under the pillow when he rolled over,

"Ya can't kill me fat boy! Ya pussy like ya batty bwoy cousin!",
Star said breaking out in a wicked laugh. Dub was enraged, he
pumped six rounds into Senica's torso. Star continued to laugh,
"Tanks Fat Bwoy, fa da favor!" He then brought his hand from
under the pillow clutching the 9 mm Ruger. Dub was a half a
second quicker and pumped the remaining twelve shots into
Star's body and face, completely removing his head. Dub
finally got some peace and avenged Perry's death.

Screwface's eyes bulged at the end result, while Dominga
fainted. Blood and brain matter painted the teak headboard.
As much blood as Screwface and his deadly Shower Posse
spilled, he couldn't stand the ghastly site before him. He knew
that death was imminent for him, but he still thought of a way to
get out of it. He searched the masked men's eyes looking for
answers but found none. The only face he recognized was
Dub's, who wore no mask because he wanted Star to know who
shot him. "Big Man, no kill me. We go way back no?", Screw
said begging Dub to save his life. "I da one tol ya about Star
killing ya cousin no? And I look out many times right? Take
what ya want, don't kill me man." Dub's mind reeled back to
the times that Screw did look out for him. Even when Star
killed Perry, Screwface called him. He often helped Dub out in
the past, hoping to bring him into his own little side hustle with
the extra's he kept. Dub never seemed to stay on his feet, he
was always to busy chasing women. Dub took all of this into
consideration and made his call. "Let him live, I got who I
wanted.", walking down to wait in the truck and sending Tootie
and Jade upstairs.

Once Dub was gone, Linz put the Uzi to Screwface's head,
"Where the loot at?" Even though Big Dub had given him a
pass, he wasn't too sure that the men who held him at gun point

would.   He valued his life more than a dead man's money.   He took them to the adjacent apartment.   They kept him butt naked because Jamaicans were sneaky bastards.   Aaron and Doe kept watch over Dominga and the other female, while the other four followed Screwface to the safe.

The safe was cleverly disguised as the entire wall of a walk in closet.   Star was good at hiding his shit.   When the safe opened, they found burlap sacks full of money plus a couple money and adding machines.   In total, there was seven sacks equaling 21.5 million and a shoe box that held personal papers such as Star's I.D, green card, and title to his 760 IL BMW which was in a fictious name.   Also there was a brown duffle bag and briefcase with about one million double stacks of Ecstasy and three pounds of Ganja.   They took all the drugs but left the box of personal papers.

Linz stayed with Screwface while K.J and the girls took turns loading the money.   If he would have left K.J to watch him, Screwface would have been dead.   While they were loading the money, Linz took four bundles out to give to the two frightened women in the next apartment with the two psychos.

"Man, I no say nutt'n, my word is my bond!", Screwface said to the masked man with the Uzi.   When the others returned Linz said to the now defenseless gun toting rude boy, "You wanted Star's spot for the longest, now you've got it, all of them, just don't let me see you in Pennsylvania no more or I'll kill you myself.   That's a promise.   Now get the fuck out of here and take that bitch Dominga with ya!"   Screwface offered a thank you, before he was let go, he went in the box with the personal papers and got the title to the BMW.   He handed it to the masked man and said, "Here man, give this to the Big Man Dub, tell him tanks."   Then he got the extra keys for him.

Once back at the other apartment, Linz gave the frightened mother of three the money he'd held back and told her get dressed and bounce.   He also gave her a warning that if she said anything, she'd be next.   Then both of the masked women walked her downstairs while the men talked to Screwface.   They released him with Dominga.

Outside, Linz tossed Dub the keys to the Beemer and told him what Screwface said.   They gave Aaron and Doe the briefcase, the bag of pills, and the keys to the Honda Accord they were in, with instructions to ditch it pronto and call tomorrow for their loot.   They told K.J, "Take ya time, we trust you.   Your word is gold with us."   Tootie and Jade followed Linz and K.J in the Trailblazer, followed by Dub in Star's Beemer.

The girls went home with the loot, while Linz and K.J took Dub to the old shop to hide the Beemer until he was ready to bounce.

After the girls unloaded the loot, they ditched the Acura Legend at the airport entrance.   They left the flashers on in a tow zone.   Tootie drove the Legend, while Jade followed in the Charger.   The guns were thrown in the river and the Trailblazer was wiped clean and left in an alley.   They caught a jittney to their places of rest.   Dub met up with his peeps back at the hotel. The Four Kings went to the girl's home.   They'd hookup with Dub in the next few days, in the meantime, it was time to lay low.

PHASE

FIVE

"If It Isn't

Love...."

CHAPTER FOURTY- FOUR

The massacre of the Shower Posse in front of the Aurora Club was plastered all over the news stations for two weeks. It was billed as the most heinous crime the city has ever seen. The police still had no clues or suspects. Also making headlines was the murder of Senica, the rising reggae sensation made national headlines. BET, MTV, and VH1 ran stories about it for a week. Rastas everywhere mourned her untimely death. Record company executives profited off her death, her follow up single to 'Long Tyme Bwoy', was called 'Sweet Fyah'. It was getting heavy spins, setting her soon to be released CD entitled 'Street Sexy' up for platinum status. Her underground stuff that she recorded was coveted. "Lighter's in da air" was the chant that was heard whenever her songs were played. Frankie's held an all night jam session in remembrance of her and Star, the true Don Dada. The turn out was massive, yutes were everywhere. People lined the streets, packed the parking lots, and the club beats pulsated throughout the night. Doug and Cristal were in attendance.

The heat from the Yusef Star incident was more than the crew anticipated, causing them to freeze all plans and be real still. This forced them to extend the time limit on Royce's life, but on the other side, it gave each of them more time to spend with their mates. Tootie damn near lived with Linz, most of her things were at this place. She spent five out of seven nights there. Meanwhile, Doug and Cristal had taken over her old room, it was a glimpse of their futures together. Tootie enjoyed living with her man she became accustomed to all his moods and habits, and he knew hers.

Linz knew in his heart what Tootie was the one, he felt

blessed to fall asleep and wake up with her everyday and night, and he told her so every morning. She was hopelessly in love with him, in her eyes he could do no wrong. She even gave him her take from the robbery, which was 2.38 million to hold or invest for her. After the seven capers, each of the women were worth over five million and the men were over seven million. Together, Tootie and Linz were holding about 12 million, damn good for a couple of nobodies from the hood. Tootie would give her last dime to become Mrs. Lindsey. She even added him on to her savings account. Little did she know, that if all went well on her birthday, June 2nd, Linz had intentions of asking her to become Mrs. Lindsey. She already had a set of keys to his crib, both of his cars were at her disposal to use whenever she wanted. Only rule was she had to put gas in them when she used them.

As she sat in Robin's waiting to get her hair and nails done, her mind drifted to her mother and her mother's new boyfriend who was coming to spend a few days with her. If the weather permitted, they'd have a picnic in the park. April weather was always tricky, one day it would rain and the next it would be cool and clear.

"Tootie, you ready?", Kendra, her hairstylist asked. Kendra has been doing her and the other girl's hair for the past four years. She kept them looking fly. Tootie spoke to all the women doing hair or getting their hair done as she walked to Kendra's chair. "What do you want done?", Kendra asked. Tootie picked up a magazine to show her the style that she wanted. "I want it cut like this, but my man will kill me if I do." The cut she liked was a short layered style that she seen in last month's Essence. Tootie didn't know if her man would like it, so she just decided to get it washed and relaxed. "Just relax it, then I'll ask him before I get it cut that way. If he doesn't mind, then I will be back here next week to get it done. I know he likes it this way, and y'all know I gotta keep my man happy.", she stated blushing. Tootie's hair was down to the middle of her back and it was all hers, no weave. Kendra laughed and said, "Girl, you something else. Linz must really be doing you right." All heads turned and focused on Tootie waiting for an answer. Tootie felt embarrassed but said, "girl, he handling his business. I'm so gone, y'all just don't know." The shop erupted in laughter. Most of the women in the shop knew Linz and that Tootie was his boo thang. Hell, a couple of them were in the club a few months ago when she beat Natalie down about him.

Two and a half hours and several laughs later, Tootie emerged from the shop with her hair and nails done. She was ready to go meet her man for a bite to eat. Doug and Cristal were out Cali preparing their home. The twins, Diamond and Jade, were in Vegas attending the Fashion Expo with A.P and K.J, getting things lined up for their clothing store. Tootie had to spend lunches with her man or Jeanna and sometimes Eryca. Eryca had grown close to all the women lately.

2 Major Automotive was buzzing with people when Tootie pulled up. The shop had been open for about three weeks and business was booming already. Several NFL and MLB stars were on the waiting list as client's as well as several major street hustlers. Linz's Old's 442 convertible and K.J's convertible Cadillac were on display at the shop on the show room floor as well as the shops other three cars which were driven everyday to boost advertising.

"Hey Toot, looking for Linz?", Eryca asked from behind the counter. "Yeah, he in the back?", Tootie replied. "No, he stepped out for a minute, he told me to tell you to wait here though." K.J and Linz had hired Eryca and Danni, this banging white chick, to keep up with the secretarial duties and things of that nature.

Tootie sat in the lounge area with the other customers watching videos on one of the 41" plasma screens that hung between the displays of Lexani and Giavonna rims. A video by Pherrell was playing when her phone rang. Looking at the screen before she took the call, she seen it was her mother. "Hello Mother", she joked. "Hello to you too Daughter", she joked back. Tootie and Ajia acted more like sisters than mother and daughter. "Momma, where are you? Did you leave yet?' "Child, I been left. I am almost in Pittsburgh. We at the tunnels now, how do I get to where you are?", Ajia asked. "Just come through the tunnels in the far left lane and take the downtown exit. Pull over at Wendy's on the corner. I'm coming to meet you, I'm only ten minutes away.", Tootie instructed getting up off the couch. She told Eryca to tell Linz she had to go meet her mom and she would be right back.

Ajia and Devon sat parked in front of the news stand on Penn Ave. It wasn't long before Tootie pulled beside her and said "Follow me". Back at the shop, Tootie met Devon. "Where is Linz? What is that boys name anyway?", Ajia asked, she didn't like calling him Linz. "His name is Lionel.", Tootie said laughing. "But don't tell him I told you, he will kill me. He went to run some errands, he'll be back soon." Tootie gave her mother a tour of the shop. She began to take them back to wait in his office, but Ajia went to look at the wheels instead, leaving Tootie and Devon to talk.

"So you feeling my momma, huh?", she asked. Devon was taken back by her forwardness. "If that means do I like her , then yes."

"How old are you? You look too young to be messing with my mom. She's over 50, you know." He replied, "I'm 47 and well aware of Ajia's age and her beauty." The two made small talk for a few minutes. Tootie found out a lot about Mr. Devon Smith. "Is this interview over with?", he asked jokingly. She shook her head yes and began to laugh. Just then her mom came in to get her to show her some wheels she liked. Devon followed behind the ladies.

Just as they were asking Drip about the wheels, Linz came in. Ajia spotted him first, "Lionel, come here!", she called. Tootie shot her mom a look. Linz turned to see who called him, that's when he seen Ajia talking to Tootie, Drip and Devon. Tootie and her moms were laughing when he reached them. "Lionel, can you hook a sista up with some of these?", Ajia said pointing to the rims. "Mom, I told you he don't like to be called Lionel.", Tootie said laughing. Drip was laughing also. 'Child, his mom and daddy named him Lionel, that's what I'm gonna call him. If he don't like it , tell him to whip my ass!", Ajia said, ice grilling Linz. Everyone within earshot started laughing, the joke was on Linz. "I told you somebody is gonna mop your old ass one day if you keep bumping your gums like you some certified killer.", Linz said. "Well we know one thing, it won't be your weak ass, Lionel." "Keep playing with me!", he said. "Like I told you last time, run up and get done up!", Ajia responded shaking her fist. Linz bused out laughing, "Give me a hug with your old fine ass.", he said embracing her. "Whew, I thought we was gonna have to beat that ass up in here.", Tootie said to Linz. "Boy, I'm serious, hook me up with them wheels.", Ajia said as they followed him back to his office. He had Drip check to see if they had a set of the KMC Evolution's in stock. They did, but they wouldn't be able to service her until Monday, they were booked solid Friday and Saturday. Ajia was cool with that. Linz then spoke to Devon, whom was interested in getting some work done on his Escalade and restoring his '69 GTO.

Meanwhile out in Vegas, K.J and A.P checked out the SEMA Aftermarket Show. Some of the hottest and newest automotive products were displayed there. K.J's mind was blown away by all the rims and stuff coming out. He manage to secure a few deals and distribution rights from several companies. Once everything was 100, he called the shop, Danni answered the phone. "Hey Danni, is Motorhead or Linz around?" "Just a sec, I'll transfer you", she said and transferred the called. "Hello", Motorhead growled. He was mad because his shipment was late. "Damn, whatever it is, I didn't do it.", K.J replied laughing. Motorhead relaxed, "What's up K? How you liking Vegas?" "Man, it's all that! I need you and Spray to hop the next flight out here." "Why, what's up?", Motorhead inquired. "Man, I was at the SEMA Show and I talked to several company spokesmen and got us some deals, but they need the tax id numbers and licensing numbers which I don't have. Plus, I want you to check out all this shit. Linz and I are ready to drop another half a million into the shop. Nigga, we want to be top flight, ya dig!", K.J said. Motor just listened, his mind was spinning. His dream was really happening, owning the best custom auto shop in the tri-state. When he didn't respond, K.J said hello into the phone jolting Motorhead out of the clouds. "I'm here, does Linz know about this?", he asked. He still couldn't believe his ears. "Not yet, I'm about to tell him, but you and Drip get out here tonight. I'll pick y'all up at the airport and charge it to the store's credit card.", K.J said before being transferred to Linz. Linz was in the middle of a conversation with Tootie and her peeps. They were getting ready to leave when he call came through. "Linz speaking." "Dig dat, my nigga sounding all professional and shit!", K.J teased. They both laughed as Linz sat back down. "What's poppin?", Linz asked. K.J ran the business down to him, Linz smiled ear to ear. They all shared the same vision for the shop.. "You and Spray gotta hold the shop down until we get back or do you gotta ask your girl first?", K.J joked. "Nigga, I'm grown!" "Oh yeah, I seen Grench, he gave me that paper, it was 185 stacks.", K.J informed him before hanging up.

Just as Linz got off the phone, Motorhead stepped in his office. "K.J tell you the deal?" "Yeah man, what you waiting on, y'all got a plane to catch.", Linz replied with a grin. "You gonna be straight here at the shop?", Motorhead asked, worried because Linz really didn't know nothing about cars, except how to drive them. "I'm cool, I got Spray and the others with me. I'm sure Spray can handle the install and shit, I got the clients.", Linz stated. Motor head had a team of about seven including himself, Spray, Drip, Diesel, Loco, Ya-ya, and Flood. They were all hand picked for the radical custom talents they possessed. Loco and Diesel were sick with the body work and fabrications, while Ya-ya and Flood did their thing with the sounds.

Linz was about to leave when his cell went off, "Hello". "What's up Little Ruby!", Chuck screamed through the phone. Linz could hear them laughing. "What's up Chuck!", he asked.. "Nothing, me and Rell just chilling. We up your way trying to holla at you.", Chuck said. "Well swing by the shop, I heard about the Durango.", Linz commented. "Aight, we on our way. Oh, I need a deal on some rims and system nigga! It's ya boy!", Chuck said. Linz heard Rell said me too in the background.

Rell stacked his loot, he didn't spend it on foolish things. However, Chuck was a stunner, he loved to floss. These were Linz's friend from way back, his true friends outside of the Four Kings and Big Rob.

"Tell that cheap handkerchief head bastard to spend some money.", Linz said to Chuck. Chuck relayed the message and Rell grabbed the phone. "Tell Ruby to take off that flip flop wig looking like Steve Harvey.", he said laughing. These three always played dozens. "What about when you mom got caught screwing Lester!", Linz asked laughing. "I'll see y'all in a few.", Linz said hanging up.

Tootie and Ajia was outside when Linz emerged from his office. "Boo, we still on for our lunch date or what?", Tootie asked. He had totally forgot about it. "Damn Boo, I forgot about it, I'm sorry. Let me make it up to you at dinner tonight." She nodded and said, "I'll just take my Mom and Devon." It was clear that she was a little pissed. Not only because he canceled on her, but he didn't even say anything about her hair. She kissed him quick and tried to walk off, but he picked up on her attitude and bear hugged her whispering, "Boo, I'm sorry, I really am. I promise I'll make it up to you, ok?" She nodded saying, "Whatever.", trying to free herself but his grip was too tight. "Babe, I like the outfit and hair, you're beautiful.", he whispered causing her to smile. "You thought I didn't notice? You lucky I don't tap that ass real quick in my office.", he continued grinding up against her backside. "Y'all nasty!", Ajia said eyeing her child. This caused the two to break their embrace.

CHAPTER FORTY-FIVE

Chuck and Rell arrived as Tootie and her peeps were leaving. "What's up Linz!", Rell said giving Linz a pound. "Chillin man.", Linz replied, giving Chuck a pound also. "this is a good look for you, especially after we put some 24's on it.", Linz commented to Chuck on his SUV. "How much you gonna charge me?", Chuck said. "I got you!", Linz replied. "Linz, w-w-what you got for my Tahoe?", Rell said as they went inside the shop. "Damn Linz, she is ridiculous!", Chuck said pointed at Danni. "She work here?" Linz nodded

After picking out rims, he showed them on the computer what they would actually look like on their trucks. While Linz looked for Ya-Ya or Flood, Chuck saw a customer's truck in the install bay and was amazed. "That's sick Linz." "Yeah, that's Ya-Ya's work.", Linz stated feeling proud of his team of installers. "I want mine done like that. Linz I need a vision.", Chuck exclaimed. Since Linz knew Chuck was a stunner, he suggested a smurf blue candy paint job with matching velour guts, and a cherry wood kit. For Rell, a burnt orange paint, with white MCM guts, and orange piping. The men stood transfixed while visualizing the images that Linz painted for them.

"What's the ticket?", Rell asked. Linz thought for a minute, then called Spray over. They spoke for a minute, then came up with the low price of $18,500.00. "That includes everything, paint, sounds, wheels, guts and tint. You can't beat that.", Spray stated. Both men knew they couldn't, so they jumped on it. He had Danni mark them down for next week, it would probably take a week or two to do both trucks. A deposit of half would be needed when the vehicles were dropped off. With all that out of the way, the three men went to Linz's office to talk business. "Linz, what's the ticket on 10 of them thangs?", Rell asked while Chuck went to get his backpack out of the truck. Since Rell and Chuck were his peoples and looked out for him when he went to jail, he quoted them a super low price of $120,000. Rell and Chuck expected to pay 15 for each. When Chuck came back in the office Rell told him the price, Chuck was amped. "Shit, what will you give us for the 150?", Chuck asked. "Don't worry, I'll hook you up. Let me see your keys." Linz told them to wait in the lounge until he came back.

Linz jumped in the shop's cherry red Dodge Magnum, followed by Danni in Chuck's Durango. Linz felt it was better move to have the coke a in a plain car. Danni waited in the parking lot of the Giant Eagle waiting for her boss to come back. She knew Linz and K.J were hustlers, vets in the coke game. She could tell by their swagger and vibe they exhibited. She knew Eryca since her first year at Pitt. They had grown very close over the past three years. Although Danni was a typical Arizona white chick, she possessed a transitional soul. She was able to vibe and blend in with both the black and white crowds. One minute it was Nelly Furtado and Lincoln Park, the next it was Floetry and Young Jeezy. She also had transitional looks, from the waist up she was a typical white chick, pretty face, blond hair, blue eyes. She had big breast, flat stomach, 5'7" with a serious tan. But from the waist down, she was built like a sista. Danni packed a nice sized ass that held it's shape when viewed without the help of jeans. Unlike most white woman, Danni didn't care how plump or how jiggly her ass got, she loved being a white woman with ass. To top it off, she had a nice pair of legs. She loved her job. She didn't have to dress a certain way, had mad fun, met cool people, and got a serious discount for herself. She was also allowed to drive one of the shop's cool cars and made $9.00 an hour.   She sat listening to the radio while waiting for Linz to return, she knew ten minutes to Linz really meant twenty.

Meanwhile, Linz was inside Motorhead's old spot pulling on overalls preparing to crawl into the crawlspace behind the locker. That's where he kept the coke stored, only him, K.J, and A.P knew this.

After about half an hour, Linz returned to the parking lot to rejoin Danni with 13 bricks secured in a case that used to contain Valvoline Oil.   He placed the case in the back of the SUV, explained to Danni what was in the truck.   He told her to drive safe and that he'd meet her back at the shop.   Danni was no stranger to riding dirty, she'd done it before back in Arizona.

Linz had reached the shop first.   When he got there, the shop was packed with potential customers.   Rell and Chuck sat watching ESPN's Sports Center.   He called them into his office, where they waited until Danni showed up twenty minutes later with McDonald's for her and Eryca.   Linz looked at her. "Sorry, I'm late, I didn't have lunch yet.   I'm starving.", she said handing the keys to Linz.   Once she was gone, Linz told them where the coke was at and how many, Chuck and Rell were happy.   On the way out, Chuck asked Linz again if he was going to hook him up with Danni.   "I got you.", he said calling her over interrupting her lunch.   "What's good?", she said.   "You think you cool, huh?", Linz said jokingly.   "Think, I know. I'm ice.", she stated confidently showing her pearly whites. "Anyway, my boy Chuck wants to holla at you."   he said leaving the two to talk while he showed Rell the Magnum.

"What's up with you?", Chuck asked.   "Nothing, just chillin.   What's up with you?'   "Shit, I'm trying to see you sometime when you're free, if possible.", he said giving her the once over as she stood dressed in a G-Unit tank top, army fatigues, and crisp white Air Force Ones. She did the same thing, peeped him from head to toe, as he stood dipped in Rocawear jeans and button down, with white and yellow Air Force Ones. "I don't know, I might could work with you.", she said smiling. Chuck laughed saying, "Come on with all that bull, like you Pamela Anderson or somebody. Cut that out!" "Aw, so you got jokes, huh?", she said. Danni was feeling Chuck's sense of humor. "Naw, I'm just keeping it real, you banging but you ain't all that.", he replied starting to walk away. "So, you ain't tryna holla now Mr. I Keep it Real?", she teased. Chuck turned and said, "I ain't got time for all the games." "Look, call me later after I get off if you still interested.", Danni said. Chuck nodded and took the number. When he joined Rell and Linz he said, "Damn, she got a phat ass." "I know, that white girl got cheeks for days.", Rell said. "Linz, where you find her at?", Chuck said. "That's one of Eryca's friends."

After the men left, Linz called Danni into his office and gave her three stacks. "What's this for?", she asked. "For driving." "Oh, you don't have to pay me for that.", she said. He act like he didn't hear her. "Danni, keep this between us, aight.", he stated. "Yeah, most def.", she responded before turning to leave.

After his office was clear, Linz leaned back in his chair, kicked his feet up, and relaxed for a minute before calling his boo. Then he remembered, before doing that he called his boy Grench in Vegas.

"Starko & Sons Jewelers", the receptionist said. "May I speak with Mr. Starko please?" "May I tell him who's calling?", she asked. "Tell him Mr. Lindsey." "Alright, please hold.", she said as she placed the call on hold to relay the message. "Linz what's happening?", Grench bellowed. "Not much, how life with you?", Linz said. "So so, can't complain, what's on your mind?", Grench asked. Grench was an old mobster with family ties to the Petera and Delucia Syndicates. His roots were deep and his arms stretched wide, in other words, he was not to be fucked with.

"Man, I need a personal favor from you.", Linz said. The Sicilian's face tightened and said, "Sure anything for you." His mind began to wonder what that favor could be. Grench had much love and respect for the Four Kings, as they did for him. They were part of a dying breed, stand up guys. He was hoping it was not a favor that would jeopardize that.

"You know that girl I told you about? The one I've been seeing for the last eight months or so. Well, I think she's the one for me and I need you to craft me something special. I need it by June 2nd, I'm gonna make it official on her birthday." Grench's face relaxed. "Sure, just give me her ring size and yours too, I'll get started. And hey the price, forget about it!", he said laughing. Grench had a jolly spirit. "I got to get her size, but mine is 9 1/4. I'll get hers to you in a few days.", Linz stated.

"So how's that car thing going for you guys?", Grench asked. "So far so good. We are building a solid customer base.", Linz said. They spoke for a few more minutes about life in general then ended the call. Next he called his Boo. "Hello", she answered. "What's up Babe? Where you at?", he asked. "We out in Monroeville at TGI Fridays. Why?", she asked. "I'll be done here in a minute, I wanted to kick it with you and your peeps." "We will be done in about ten minutes then I was planning on swinging by the mall for a second. You can just meet us there.", she said. He thought for a second, then agreed. "Let me speak to your mom for a minute.", he asked. "What boy!", she exclaimed. Ajia liked Linz alot, that's why she always messed with him. "Look, I need a favor, you got me?", he asked. "It depends on what it is. You got me on those rims?" Mom Toot was trying to out hustle the hustler, Linz admired her attempts. "Yeah, I got you. Now listen close, you can't let Tootie know.", he said. "Alright, now what it is?", she was eager to know. "You know that I love your daughter and I got a soft spot for your old ass too." that made Ajia smile. "I plan asking Tootie to be my wife on her birthday, but I need her ring size. Can you get it for me because I need it ASAP.", he said. Ajia smiled ear to ear. Her heart fluttered with joy, just knowing her daughter had found a good man and she would become something she wasn't, a wife. "Baby, I'll take care of that for you, just don't forget about me, you hear.", Ajia said.

Linz could hear Tootie in the background asking her mom what she was so happy for. Ajia said, "Stay out of grown folks business!" Tootie grabbed the phone, "What you and my momma talking about?" I know it has something to do with me." "Ain't nobody talking about you. I'll see you in a few.", he said and hung up.

It took Linz twenty minutes to get to the mall. He met Tootie in front of Foot Locker. He greeted his Boo with a kiss. Tootie noticed that over the last three months, Linz began to show more affection towards her in public. When they were out together, he was always touching on her in an affectionate manner. He was either holding her hand or placing his arms around her, whatever it was he let his feeling for her be known.

She placed her arms around him, returning his kiss. "I love you", she said. "I love you too." She then grabbed his hand

and pulled him into the store. "Come on, I have something I want to show you.", she whined. She pulled him to a old throwback Green Bay Packers Jersey from 1946 that she wanted to get. Diamond and Jade could make it into a summer dress for her to wear on May Day. The colors matched his old school Olds at the shop. She picked out a custom pair of Air Max's to match the jersey. For him, she thought about the white Green Bay jersey with matching Adidas shell toes. Linz liked her idea, they ordered and paid for their stuff.

After leaving Foot Locker, the four browsed through the mall. Ajia pulled Tootie into Zale's Jewelry Store, while the men went into Style Gate. Ajia and Tootie looked at and tried on several bridal sets, that's how Ajia got her daughter's ring size Tootie was too caught up in her little daydream to catch on to what was going on around her. She like the look of a rock on her finger and imagined the day she'd look at her hand and see a ring there given by the one she was hopelessly in love with. It was her mother's voice that snapped her back to reality. "Come on girl, I'm tired from all this walking, I'm ready to lay down for a while." They left the store and found the men outside in conversation about cars.

The two women approached the men and asked if they were ready. The men nodded and got up still engrossed in their conversation. "Babe, where you parked at?", Tootie asked. "In front of Kaufmann's ." Tootie parked on the other side in front of Burlington's. "Well, we will just meet you back at the house okay.", Tootie said. Linz nodded. "Devon, ride with me. We can stop by the shop and get the bags out of the Jeep.", he said kissing his Boo and soon to be mother in law. As the two women walked away, the two men watched and admired their backsides. "Damn, both of them is bad!", Devon said.

Linz looked at him. "What Nigga, I ain't that old!", he
reasoned. Linz just laughed, he liked this Devon cat. "Nigga,
you a fool.", Linz said. "Shit, I've been trying to knock holes in
Ajia's ass. She is fifty something and still fine.", Devon said
Once inside the Benz, the conversation changed and went back to
cars, then sports. They hit the shop, then headed to Linz's
place.

CHAPTER FOURTY-SIX

The April sun beat down on the Vegas strip as A.P and Diamond cruised the boulevard in the rental drop top 360 Ferrari Modena.   K.J and Jade trailed loosely behind in a silver topless Dodge Viper.   The four had been in Vegas for three days and this was the first leisure day they had.   The other days were spent conducting business for their own individual investments.

Motorhead and Drip sat lounging by the poolside of the MGM Grand, basking in the Vegas sun in the company of some of the finest and wealthiest young women that Las Vegas had to offer.   "Man, this is the life.", Drip exclaimed.   He was thrilled by the Vegas life style, to him it seemed as if gorgeous women, fast cars, and big money flowed like the Nile.   Both he and Motorhead were thankful for this little business trip.   This was the first time that either of the men had been outside of the tri-state area, let alone Las Vegas.   "We gotta come back here soon dude.", Motorhead said, giving Drip a pound as a trio of brunette's swam over and began talking to them.

A.P was truly feeling and enjoying the Vegas scene.   It had been about two years or so since he had been out here.   The last visit was only a few hours to handle some business for their friend Grench.   Grench had a problem with one of his main competitors in the jewelry business.   Since he couldn't do it himself he called the crew in to do it for him.

A.P was truly digging this little getaway as he cruised down the strip in an exotic car with an exotic broad in the seat next to him.   Both of them was nodding to Young Jeezy and Akon's "Soul Survivor".   "Damn Babe, I'm really feeling Vegas.", he said as they headed toward the Circus Circus Mall.   Diamond turned in her seat and said, "Me too Boo."   It was Diamonds first time being out west. "I could see us living out here, what you think?", he asked with a smile. She thought before answering, "I think that we could do this, I just don't wanna have to kill none of these bitches out here over you.", she said with a look that backed her words. A.P knew in his heart that she would do just that.

Diamond knew that A.P was a player, in fact she lightweight expected him to play. As long as she never had to hear about it in the streets or see it in her face, it was cool. If she ever saw him with one of his little freaks or jump offs, that would be the end for her and the beginning of a long night for him. She hoped that his game was as smooth as he claimed it to be so she would never have to be faced with that dilemma. So far A.P was game sharp, swinging like Tiger Woods on the back nine at the Master's. His performance for the last eight months had him wearing the green jacket.

A.P knew what he had in Diamond was a true ride or die chick that was down to ride to the very end. Not many niggas could say that about their girl. He felt good knowing he was among an elite few. No matter how much pussy came his way or how fine the other females were, he wouldn't do anything to jeopardize his relationship with the beauty that sat next to him.

"What's on your mind Boo?", he asked rubbing her thigh. "Nothing", she answered, eyes hidden behind shades. "Come on Boo, penny for your thoughts.", he persisted. She looked at him before speaking, "I was thinking that.. I mean I know that we came out here for business and all and I know your digging this and want to run wild, but I was hoping that we could get away tomorrow, just the two of us. We could go to the lake, rent a boat, or something. Spend the whole day together, you know what I'm saying?" A.P felt where she was coming from, it had been some time since the two spent a solid day alone. "Alright Babe, we can do that.", he said making a left on S. America Blvd. He opened his cell and called Grench at his store. If anybody could get him a boat for a day on lake Havasu, it was Grench.

"Starko & Son's", Grench said. It was rare that he answered his own phone. "Grench, I need a solid.", A.P said. "I'm listening." A.P then proceeded to tell him what he needed. After he was done Grench said, "What you guys going soft on me now? First Linz, now you! You guys must have got a hold of some really good pussy!" He began laughing and said, "Look, swing by let me look at her, ok. I gotta see these dames that got my peeps thinking about giving up the player status, not that anythings wrong with it, I just gotta seem em." A.P promised to swing by with Diamond, then hung up. After about thirty minutes of stop and go traffic, they pulled in front of the Ventian. The valet parked the sports car for them.

Grench greeted the men with a hug and handshake, and the two twins with a gentleman like kiss on the hand. It had been about eight months since he last saw the boys. He stood back and admired the women, it was evident that he liked and approved of what he saw. He told the ladies to look around, while he spoke to the men in the back office for a few minutes. If they found something they liked let the clerk know it's on the house. Both ladies beemed, they never seen so many diamond pieces in one store in their entire lives. Diamond and Jade started to realize that the men in their lives had a lot of connections. They couldn't wait to get home and tell the other girls. The twins spent time browsing over the various pieces while the men were in the back doing whatever.

Once back in the office Grench made a few calls for A.P to set up his request through a friend down at the lake. After the he made arrangements for K.J and his female companion to view the lovely city of Las Vegas via helicopter Sunday night.   The men thanked him for the last minutes hook ups and for getting them the two rental sports cars.   Vega was the city of high rollers and when in Rome, do as the Romans do.

Diamond chose a three carat tennis bracelet for their mother, while Jade picked a matching three carat cluster dinner ring, also for their mother.   Grench had the clerk gift wrap it for the ladies and told them, "If you have any trouble outta these two bums, let me know.   I'll handle em for you!"   He then turned to the men and said, "You guys better take good care of these two ladies."

As the day went on, the couples toured the mall, stopping at every store,   The men hated it but the women loved it.   They got a bite to eat at one of the restaurants on the strip.   The weather was too damn good to be eating inside, they wanted to be seen out and about.

Diamond was excited about her alone time with her man tomorrow.   After she tried on the Gucci two piece bikini with the sheer wrap skirt, she showered and went to sleep.   She knew that she would probably do all the driving on the three hour trip to the lake in the morning at 6:00am while he slept.

Jade, on the other hand, talked on the phone with Cristal and Tootie.   She told them all about her trip so far and how she fraudulently obtained shipments of designer clothes from several high end companies by having the clothes shipped to a fake address by next day air freight.   She asked if Tootie could possibly pick them up for her.   Tootie agreed only because she knew that the twins were good at defrauding people and businesses.   With them two bitches around, nobody's shit was safe.

Jade gave Tootie the address to the place the stuff was going to be dropped off and the time schedule for each shipment, along with what names to sign under.   The building that the clothes were to be delivered was an old store front that the girls thought about leasing for their boutique.   The building was nice and roomy, but the location of it was not good for them.   The owner left them the keys to look at the place because he didn't have time to show it to them due to a family emergency.   After the girls caught up with each other about the past couple day's events, they said their goodbyes and hung up.   Jade went to sleep shortly after.

A.P and K.J linked up with Motorhead and Drip at Club Rain.   The four of them had a blast!   Motorhead was invited to have drinks and later spend the night with one of the brunettes he'd met earlier by the pool.   Her name was Trisha Daniels, she was 34, 5'6" and a casting agent on vacation with her girlfriends. She was really digging Motorhead.   He was amused that this older woman was attracted to him, he was only 24.   The others teased him because Motorhead possessed no game what so ever! "Remember, what goes on in Vegas, stays in Vegas!", Drip said, happy to see his friend get lucky.   "Ok, you up next!", K.J said patting Drip on the shoulder.   The men really was enjoying themselves tonight because Tuesday morning they'd be on a plane back to Pittsburgh, so tonight they let loose in Sin City.

It was about 1:00 am when the club really started jumping thanks in part to the arrival of Dennis Rodman, Kid Rock, and Paris Hilton.   Droves of people flocked to the spot, the whole party was kicked up about three notches and well past capacity. The drinks were flowing and the music was blasting.   Just then, two blondes surrounded Drip and began dancing and grinding up against him pulling him away from the bar and onto the dance floor.

K.J and A.P just laughed and wished him well, they knew that Drip couldn't dance worth shit. It was hilarious watching him make a fool of himself with two bad white bitches. Drip shot them a look that said 'I'm the motherfucking man!'. The two blondes were bombshell, and you could tell they were offspring of the rich by their attire.

The scene was a little too much for A.P and K.J, so they headed over to the Ghost Bar, when DJ Envy and Slim Thug was holding court. The place was packed with wall to wall dimes. There was white, black, Mexican, and any other race you can think of, but these two Brazilian chicks stole their attention. "Damn, did you see those two bitches over there?", A.P asked K.J. "Nigga, you think I didn't! They some bad bitches!", K.J replied running his hand over his face. "I gotta have one of them kinda bitches on my reserve team.", A.P said. "Me too, Nigga! I ain't gave up my player card yet, especially outta town.", K.J said. The men decided to send the women drinks hoping to break the ice. It worked, the women sent word for the men to join them at their table in the VIP lounge.

Octavia Diaz, an international fashion model, stood to greet them as they came toward the couch the women were seated on. The other female, Mesa San-Perez, was the host of a popular South American talk show, the Latin version of the Oprah show in the states.

"Oyi Papi.", Octavia said to K.J as he took a seat next to Mesa. His spanish was terrible so he just smiled and licked his lips. The ladies giggled because it was apparent the men spoke no spanish at all. A.P flashed his award winning smile, the ladies started whispering to each other before speaking in spanish to one another.

"Tanks for da drinks fellas.", Mesa said. The men

mouthed, "Our pleasure", then Octavia got to the point. "Ju fellas come here alone?" She crossed her legs causing the hem on her already short skirt to raise even higher up her thighs. A.P heard nothing that she said, he was too busy staring at her big brown nipples which you could see through her top. "We with some friends, but they at another party.", K.J said.

Three bottles of Dom Perrigion later, Mesa grabbed K.J's dick and whispered, "Is it true what they say about black men?", in her sexy accent. "I don't know, look and see", he responded. She then stuck her petite hands in his pants, fondling his manhood, bringing it to life. The smile on her lovely face confirmed her satisfaction. Mesa turned and said something in spanish to her girl then pulled K.J to his feet. She waved at her friend as the two headed upstairs to the girl's penthouse suite.

Ten minutes later, A.P and Octavia joined K.J and Mesa upstairs. When they got there, they were greeted by the sight and sounds of K.J and Mesa having sex on the back of the sofa. Octavia wasted no time stepping out of he skirt and halter. Her coco brown nipples danced as she strode across the floor to the bedroom, with A.P close behind. It wasn't long after they entered the room that she began massaging his penis with her throat. Her mouth did wonders to a dick! Although her head was the bomb, A.P wanted to see if she sounded like her friend in the next room. He laid her on the bed, threw her legs over his shoulders, and long stroked her. Octavia's face twisted with pleasure as her body bucked in rhythm to match his strokes.

""Oyi Papi!", Octavia screamed as A.P continued to pound his penis into her slippery vagina. That went on for about half hour before Mesa entered saying something in spanish and smiling. Mesa began rubbing A.P's back placing kisses on his spine. Octavia slid from underneath him while Mesa stroked his penis.   A.P couldn't believe his good fortune, he was about to fuck the other one!   Two bad bitches at the same time in the same night!   Octavia said, "Tener buen tiempo" to her friend as she exited the bedroom going into the living room.   K.J was sitting on the couch smoking an imported cigarette and drinking a miniature bottle of Grey Goose.   Octavia stood in front of him with a devious smile on her pouty lips.   In one motion she dropped down to her knees and began giving him head.   K.J threw his head back and enjoyed the brain he was receiving.

Back in the bedroom, A.P was laying the smack down on Mesa from behind.   Her moans only encouraged him.   "Deeper Papi!   Deeper!", she said between moans.   She placed her hands on the headboard to stop her head from banging on it.   He gripped her hips and plunged deep into her womb with the aggressiveness of a drowning man grasping for a life jacket. Mesa's body bucked wildly as her eye's rolled and mind spun from the pleasure that this mandingo warrior brought to her. Fulfilling her fantasy, she also got the answer to her question about the black man with every stroke.   Mesa began to cry out, releasing pent up frustration that had been building up for the last four months.   Mesa was experiencing multiple organisms even after her body went limp.   A.p continued to glide in and out of her pussy until he pulled out and shot cum all over her lower back and ass cheeks.   As she lay there in sexual bliss, A.P showered because he knew that he couldn't return to his room with the scent of sex on him.   While K.J waited to use the shower, he spoke with the two females keeping them company. When they were about to leave, Mesa wrote down all her numbers and those for Octavia also in hopes of hooking up with the two fellas again.   A.P and K.J promised to keep in touch. Mesa and Octavia was something they were both looking forward to screwing again.

CHAPTER FOURTY-SEVEN

The sound of the waves and the sight of the California sunset provided a lovely setting as Doug and Cristal strolled along the beach hand in hand.   The two spent the last10 days painting and re-carpeting their new home.   It was during this time that they grew alot closer and really got a chance to dig deep into each other's souls.

California was a new experience to the both of them.   Back in Pittsburgh they had family and friends close by to lean on when times get rough, but out here it was just the two of them.

Cristal fell in love with the weather, palm trees, beaches, and the whole Cali vibe amused her.   "Baby, let's go half on a nice little convertible.", she stated,   Doug was also feeling the Cali scene, "We can do that, what kind you got in mind?"   "I don't know, something sporty.", she replied jumping on his back.   The two acted like teenagers new to love as he carried her down the beach on his back tossing around names of different types of convertibles.   When they reached the concession stand where their rented Volvo was parked, she spotted a bright yellow Boxster speed past.   "Man, I like that!", she exclaimed, pointing at the car.   "What kind of car is that?"   Doug followed her finger, then responded, "A Porsche Boxster."   "Babe, can we get one of those?", she asked still watching as the Porsche's tail lights got smaller and smaller.   "We'll see.", he said.   Doug was not really a big fan of Porsche, especially the tiny Boxster. He'd rather have a Corvette, they were roomier and faster, plus they had more power than the Porsche.   If it's left up to him, he was campaigning for a Corvette.

Cristal caught the dislike in his voice, "Well, what did you have in mind?' "A Vette", he said quickly. "Those things are too big for me, plus I won't get to drive it as much.', she whined. "No they ain't!", he said, defending his choice. She put her arms around his waist and pleaded, "Please Baby, can we get a Boxster, please Boo?" When he didn't respond she added, "Can we at least go look at one tomorrow? PLEASE?", standing on her tip toes placing a kiss on his lips. He waited before answering, "Aight, I guess we can go look at one tomorrow, but I still gotta think about us buying one."

The next morning, Cristal was up with the sun, stretching for her morning run. She'd taken to running every morning about a month ago. While out here in Palo Alto, she mapped a route in her neighborhood to run. She quietly gathered her Sony micro MP-3 player, tied up her Nike's, and slipped out the door into the California sun, leaving her man to sleep a little longer since he'd be taking her to the dealership this afternoon.

Doug woke up as Cristal was opening the door. "Hey Boo, did I wake you?", she asked, kicking off her shoes. "Na, it was time for me to get up anyway." He began wiping the sleep from his eyes and got up to go to the bathroom. The couple had spent the night on the living room floor because there wasn't any furniture in the house yet. They were going shopping for that today also.

The two wanted everything to be new to symbolize a new beginning of life together for them. The only thing that they were bringing with them from back east was Doug's two cars, which they planned to drive the 3,200 miles back out to Cali, filled with their clothes. Whatever wouldn't fit they would either have shipped or leave behind. The his and her bikes were most definitely coming. The move would be final as soon as the hit on Royce was complete.

Cristal was just about to get into the shower when Doug came up behind her placing his arms around her, cupping her sweaty breasts, caressing her nipples, and whispering his intentions in her ear. "Baby, not right now, I'm all sweaty and stinky.", she said trying to pull away. "So what, I still want some.", he said turning her around and crouching to kiss her nipples. "We gonna get sweaty anyway, Boo.", he stated between kisses, enjoying the salty taste of her skin, running his hands over her butt. She reasoned that it would be a waste of time to shower, then get all sweaty and have to shower again. She gave into his advances but not before warning him again that she was a little tart and sweaty from her morning run. She was still feeling a little uncomfortable about her little smell around Doug, even though he was her man. Those feelings quickly dissolved once he began giving it to her just how she liked it right on the bathroom floor.

Three hours later, they were both smelling fresh and clean, browsing through Mallories Furniture Emporium & Import Gallery. They were picking out things for their new home. After they left there, it was Pier 1, where they purchased the bedroom furnishings they seen. It was a wicker platform bed set with matching night stands. Cristal just had to have it, but Doug was equally fascinated with it. They finally reached Prescott's Porsche of Palo Alto around 4:00 pm. There were Porsche in every model and color. "Gavin Winters, what can I help you with today?", the salesman said, extending his hand. Doug shook his hand, introducing himself. "We wanna see the Boxster, right Honey?", Cristal said casting a sideways glance. "Yeah, she'd, I mean, we'd like to see a Boxster.", Doug said. It was clear that he still wasn't feeling the little Boxster.

"Not a Porsche man, huh?", Gavin asked. "No, he wants a Vette. A car that's too damn big for me.", Cristal said pouting. Gavin looked at Doug and said," I used to be the same way, until I drove a Porsche." This was just a sales ploy Doug thought, until he laid eye's on this ocean blue 2006 Gambella GT-2 Twin Turbo Cabrio. "Can I test drive this?", he asked looking at the price. "Baby, we're here for the Boxster remember!", Cristal reminded him.

Gavin wasn't one to let a potential sale pass by. So he called another sales woman over to take Cristal out for a ride in the Boxster S, while he took Doug out in the 996 GT-2. They could kill two birds with one stone and possibly get a sale or maybe even two.

After the test drive, Doug was convinced driving a Porsche was exhilarating. Now the only problem he had was convincing her to like the 996. That would be hard because she loved that little Boxster. Gavin waited as they talked. Her mind was made up, she wanted the Boxster, end of story. "Babe please, I don't ever ask you for anything. Just this once do it for me!", she pleaded. When he didn't give in she said, "Never mind, I'll buy it myself!", then turned to Gavin and said, "I'll take it." Gavin looked at Doug who said, "Give us a few minutes please." He then turned to his woman, "Look, you drive this one and I'll drive that one, just to see how you like it ok." She agreed and they were off.

Cristal raced through the gears as Stacy, the saleswoman, guided her down the coastal highway, leaving the Boxster far behind. The symphonic hum of the Porsche's twin turbos was hypnotizing, enticing her to apply more pressure to the gas pedal as the brute hugged curve after curve.

"Damn this thing is fast!", Cristal said applying more gas as soon as she reached the straight a way, pushing the needle past the 150 mph mark. Stacy sat pinned to her seat, as the wind whipped her hair into a frenzy. Only one thought ran through Stacy's mind, 'This bitch is crazy!'. The speed freak in Cristal was rearing it's ugly head again, she felt the adrenaline rushing through her veins just like when the massacre of the Shower Posse took place. Doug and Gavin had turned back ten miles ago, when the 996 became a spec in front of them. Even though the Boxster S was equipped with turbo, they both knew that it was no way they'd catch the 996 GT-2. "Well, I hope she likes it.", Gavin said as they pulled back into the dealership lot.

"Maam, please slow down!!", Stacy screamed over the wind. Cristal nodded and eased up on the throttle bringing the car down to 70. They turned around and just cruised back to the dealership enjoying the California sun in a drop top Porsche.

"I love it! I love it!", she screamed as soon as the engine was cut. Stacy was happy to be standing still. Gavin approached the car with a smile asking, "So how did you like it?" Cristal was just bubbling with excitement, "I love it!". Doug smiled real big, he knew he was getting the 996 for sure now. "How much", Doug asked Gavin. "Let's step into my office, get the paperwork started, then we'll talk price." Gavin showed them the way to his office,parading them in front of all the other sales personnel letting them know that he's the man and was about to close the deal. His coworkers were green with envy, but it wasn't his fault, they shouldn't have just assumed the black couple couldn't afford a Porsche or was just a waste of time. Well the jokes on them.

"Now, let's get down to business.", Gavin said handing them forms to fill out. While Doug filled out the paperwork, Cristal asked once again what's the price of the car. Gavin was afraid that he'd lose them when he stated the price, so he wrote it on a post it note and slide it across to them. When Doug and Cristal saw the asking price of $125,000, they raised their eyebrows and looked at each other, but they both wanted the car so bad. They whispered to each other then she wrote $105,000 on the post it and slid it back over to Gavin. He looked at the price, let out a whistle and said, "Let me go talk to my boss first." Doug and Cristal grew tired of waiting in his office so they toured the showroom floor. This dealer had every kind of Porsche available, but the crown jewel of all Porsche was the coveted twin turbo all wheel drive 959 Porsche. This car was only made from 1986 to 1989 and was never legally certified in the U.S. Only five are know to be in the states but many replicas exist at a cost of $200,000 or more. An authentic 959 with all the papers and matching documentation, sales for well north of 1.7 million. This was a serious Porsche collectors dream care and here one sate in front of them with a price tag of $2.3 million.

"She's a beauty isn't she?", Alford Prescott asked shaking Doug's hand. "Gavin tells me that your interested in the 996." "Yes, if the price is right.", Doug stated. Gavin just looked hoping that his boss didn't blow this sale, it would be his fourth sale in two months that he'd been working at Prescott.

In the time that Doug and Cristal were waiting, a credit check was done on them to see if they could afford anything on the lot. The credit score came back as 750, along with a list of several accounts in many prestigious off shore and U.S banks. Gavin knew that they were serious about purchasing the car.

"So, can you do it for $105,000 or not? I don't have all day to debate this price.", Doug stated. Doug knew that no dealer in his right mind would let $105,000 walk out the door. "$110,000 is the lowest I can go on this.", Alford said, hoping they would bite.   Doug stuck to his offer, "$105,000 that's it, take it or leave it."   When Alford didn't respond Doug and Cristal thanked Gavin for his time and headed towards the door.   The couple was just about to start the car when Gavin came running out to stop them.   "Alright you win, he'll do it for $105, just don't leave.   I really need this sale you guys."   Gavin threw in two matching Porsche jogging suits and key rings as a bonus, things that he got for free as an employee at the dealership.

Two days before they hopped a flight back to Pittsburgh, the couple took possession of the 996.   They were now the proud owners of a brand new Porsche.   Life was good!

CHAPTER FORTY-EIGHT

Linz stood in the mirror brushing his waves when Tootie walked in to use the bathroom. "How long you been up?", she asked, sitting to relieve her bladder. "I went and worked out already.", he said, looking at his reflection. Tootie loved her man's body and the fact that he took care of it. "Did you shower yet, Boo?", she asked, wiggling into his arms and running her hands over his bare chest. "I just got out.", he answered, enjoying his woman's touch. "Get back in with me.", she said fondling his penis. "I'll make it worth your time, I promise.", she said kissing his chest. Linz couldn't resist.

As they dressed in the outfits she picked out to wear for Draft Day, she said, "You think you all that don't you?" She had a big smile on her face, taking in the sight of her man looking so fresh and clean. She was proud to be his woman. "Babe, I don't think, I know and so do you.", he stated playfully, while brushing his waves once again. He stole a glance at Tootie dressed in a yellow thong, pulling her jersey dress down over her head. He had to give Toot her props, she was a quarter piece and she belonged to him. It made him feel good knowing that someone like her was by his side, down to ride to the very end. Tootie was truly a blessing in his life, a blessing that he truly appreciated.

"What?", she asked when she caught him staring at her. "Nothing." "Then why was you staring at me? You don't like it do you?", she asked, turning around modeling the jersey dress for him. "Babe, your beautiful.", he said, bringing a smile to her face while he pulled her into his lap. She loved the affection that he showed her. He always complimented her making her feel like the most beautiful girl in the world. Tootie knew that she was pretty because niggas told her all the time, but it only mattered when it came from her man's lips, everyone else's compliments was just game.

"Boo, I love you,", she said, running her fingers over his hair. "How much?" She giggled and said her usual reply, "I love you so much that I'd walk downtown butt naked and barefoot for you." They always said something silly like that to each other. He tapped her on her bottom as she got up to finish getting dressed. "Stop Boy, I'm trying to get dressed!", she screamed, pulling her hair back into a ponytail. "Soon as I put my shoes on, we can leave.", she said, applying her lip gloss to her lips then going to the closet to get her shoes, baseball hat, and her tinted yellow shades. Babygirl looked like she was in a video shoot for Nelly, P.Diddy, or Paul Wall. "I'm ready Boo.", she said grabbing her cell off the charger.

The couple was looking lovely in the Olds 442, that turned heads on every block. They cruised Forbes Avenue down to Penn Avenue into Point Park at a slow pimps pace. They joined a long line of others flossing in their cars as they waited to enter the park.

Tootie stood in her seat and looked out over the windshield at all the other cars and said, "Damn Boo, we gonna be here for days because it's packed. It's almost 100 cars in front of us." She then turned and looked behind them, it was a line behind them as well. They sat for about forty-five minutes before the line began to move again at a steady pace. After waiting for a little over an hour, they finally entered the park. Now it was time to find a spot to post up, which would probably be impossible.

"Linz, Linz", someone was calling his name. Tootie looked around puzzled until she spotted K.J waving his hands, sitting on the hood of his Lac. "Boo, K.J calling you. He's over there.", she said, pointing at him. Linz drove over to where K.J had his Lac stretched out to reserve a space for his boy.

"About time you showed up!", K.J said, giving Linz some dap. "Awww, that's so cute! Look at y'all dressed alike!", K.J said clowning Linz and Tootie. "Fuck you K.J!", Tootie said, giving him the finger. Tootie and Jade went to get a soda from one of the vendors, while the men kicked it with the other niggas posted up close by.

The show stopper was when this female name Jazmine came though in a fuchsia and pink '67 Impala on 22's with Chanel leather guts. She was followed by a pack of females on bikes. Her crew came doing it real big, everyone gave her props with no fuss. "She's killing them.", Tootie said, posting back up on the hood of the Olds. Jade nodded her head agreeing with Tootie. Jade sat on the passenger side of the Caddy, turning up the Franchise Boys on the system. It seemed to turn the little space where they were posted up into a block party, everyone popped the trunks at once, beats blaring out of every car.

The girls spent most of the afternoon walking around the park taking pictures of all the different cars, bikes, themselves, and the men in their lives. It wasn't until 6:00 pm that people started clearing out of the park, taking the car show on tour through the streets of Pittsburgh. As Linz, Doug, A.P, and K.J jumped in their cars to join in with this rolling car show, a familiar vehicle stood out as it passed. Royce's drop top Phantom demanded respect, platinum with blood red guts sitting on 26's. "That shit is ridiculous!", Tootie said, pointing at the Phantom. "I gotta get a picture of that, pull up closer." Linz made a sour face. "Nigga, I know you ain't hating?" Linz said nothing, but continued to drive. "Boo, that ain't like you to not give props where props are due. What's the deal?", she asked. He just looked at her and continued to drive. It wasn't until they were out of the park that he spoke again. "Do you know who that is?", he asked in a calm voice. "No, should I?" "Are you serious, you really don't know who that is?", he asked again. "I said no! Why, who is he?", she stated with a slight attitude. While they waited for the light to change Linz said, "His name is Conrad Jenkins, but everyone knows him as Royce. A real bitch nigga, but also a real rich nigga, sitting on major change." He let her think on that for a minute. "What does that got to do with me?", she asked. "Alot, that's the last mark on the list!", he said with a smirk on his face. Tootie sat speechless as the entourage of cars paraded down Forbes Avenue in Oakland. They stopped at the popular hang out spot Originals which was already packed, it was like part two of the park.

Linz parked, flipped his cell and called K.J. "Man, you see Royce?", he asked. "Yeah, I seen that sucka!", K.J said. "Where y'all at?", Linz asked. "Shit standing in front of Miami Subs, where are you?", K.J asked. "Down by the museum, we about to walk up your way.", Linz replied putting the top up on the Olds. "Alright, I'll see you in a few.", K.J said ending the call.

As Linz and Tootie crossed Madison onto Forbes, a cranberry color Lexus SC430 pulled up driven by a very pregnant Jeanna with Lil Mac relaxing in the passenger seat. "What up with you fool!", Mac asked, reaching over giving Linz some dap. "Hey Tootie." Jeanna said, "Look at y'all two in matching outfits, that is so cute." Lil Mac busted out laughing. "I see y'all took it back to '88." Linz was tired of getting clowned, he couldn't wait until this night was over. "Don't hate Mac, you know we fresh!", Tootie said snuggling up to her man. "Where

y'all going?", Mac asked. "Up there to holla at K.J and them.",
Linz answered pointing up the street. "Boo, ain't that one of the
shop's cars?", Tootie said pointing at a car smoking the tires,
beating heavy in the middle of the block. "Sure is.", Linz said
as the car drove passed with Danni behind the wheel. "Alright,
I'll get up with y'all later.", Mac said as they pulled away from
the curb. As Linz and Tootie strolled up the street she asked,
"Boo, are we staying long?". "I don't know, why?" "Because
really don't feel like hanging out all night, it gets boring after
awhile.", she said. "I know, I feel you. We'll just chill for a
couple hours, then bounce.", he replied.

A.P's Nova stood tall on 22's parked in front of Miami Subs
under the joint's neon lights. Since Doug wasn't into old cars
yet, he borrowed K.J's Chevelle for the night. "Bout time my
nigga showed up.", Doug said giving Linz a pound. After that,
they clowned him for the matching outfits, but it was cool, as
long as his girl was happy it was worth it. "Man, did you see
Royce? That Nigga shitted on them today.", A.P said. "You
ain't lying, that Nigga did it big.", Doug replied. The two gave
each other pound. "No doubt, he fucking somebody tonight!",
Linz said. "Shit, he fucking a couple hoes tonight. Did you
see how many bitches' necks that Nigga snapped when he came
through?", A.P asked. "Shit, I'm looking for my bitch now,
where she at?", K.J said, looking around for Jade. She walked off
with the other women while the Four Kings posted up on their
cars kicking it. "Nigga already stole one of my bitches! Shit,
think I'm gonna let him steal another one. What you think this
is an R.Kelly and Mr. Biggs video or something? Hell naw, that
nigga got me fucked up. I'll shoot that pistol at his ass, tell him
steal that!", K.J said laughing, being the joker that he was. "Dat
Nigga balling out of control.", someone in the crowd next to

them said.   The four men turned to see who they were referring to and sure enough Royce sat behind the wheel of the topless Phantom singing the hook of a Pretty Ricky song to a flock of smiling females standing on the curb waiting to cross the street. Some of the chicks paraded in front of the car letting him see what they were working with.   All he had to do was say the word and any of them birds would have hopped in.   You could tell by the look in their eyes they were hoping he'd holla at them.

Just then, Tootie and the girls approached the corner wondering what all the fuss was about.   As they got closer it became clear that Royce was holding court.   The ladies were curbside when Jade said, "that nigga killed em today.   He shut shit down!", joining in conversation with some other females about the events of the day.

Once Royce made his selections from the jumpoffs itching to ride he pulled off, but not before telling Jade, "Next time Boo, next time!".   She just shot him a whatever look.   Once Tootie and the crew were away from the crowd, she asked them all, "Do y'all know who that is?"   Not one of them had a clue.   "I don't know him, but I do know he balling like a motherfucker!", Diamond said.   "And he cute too.   If only I wasn't in love with a psycho, I would have been right there along side them other bitches.   But I would have just went and got it his shit, fuck waiting to be picked.", Jade added.   "You a scandalous bitch with ambition, I see.", Cristal replied.   They all laughed. "Bitch, don't hate!", Jade shot back, while giving her sister a high five.   Tootie said, "Well you might just have to do that.   I just found out that he is our next vic, he's the last on the list."   The three women's faces turned to stone for a brief moment.   "Get the fuck outta here!   Who told you that?", Diamond asked. "Linz, who else.", Tootie answered.   "When he tell you this?",

Diamond asked. "About an hour ago as we were driving down here. I was flipping over his car and he got heated because I asked him to get closer so I could get a picture. Then he asked if I knew who he was, I told him no and asked why, then he told me."

Each of the women pondered on their own thoughts as the Grand Finale drew near. "Ain't no use in us being sad. I'm happy this shit is gonna be over soon so I can take my ass out to Cali for good!" After this we can all just relax.", Cristal said, trying to get them amped. "Did he say when?", Diamond asked. "No, all he said was who he was and that he was caked up. I mean really caked up!", Tootie said, crossing the street. Her thoughts were on the baby that he asked her to have when this was over.

As Linz and the crew sat chillin, Natalie's friend, Reka, came up to him and asked if she could holla at him for a second. She said it was important, so they stepped off to the side. "What's up.", Linz asked. She hesitated for a few seconds before saying, "Well, Natalie is the one who really wants to holla at you about some real shit. She really needs your help." He looked around for Natalie but couldn't spot her. "Where she at?", he asked. "Down there by the pay phone in front of 7-11." Linz and Reka started to walk towards the 7-11 when Tootie called out to him. He told Reka to tell Nat he'd be down in a minute and went to holla at Tootie.

"Where you going?", Tootie asked. "Just gonna go holla at somebody.", he replied. "Can I come?", she teased. "Naw, this is about some business." "Excuse me, I was just playing, I didn't want to come anyway!", she said with a little attitude. "Look, go get the car, aight,", he stated tossing her the keys and trotting off down the street.

Natalie was sitting in Reka's car when Linz reached the 7-11. Nat was still fine as hell, but looked stressed like she has been crying. "What's up?", he asked. She ran her fingers over her face, through her hair and took a deep breath before speaking, "I need a favor. I ain't go no one else to turn to. I promise I will pay you back." "Nat, what's wrong?", he asked, concerned about his former lover but still his friend. "Well, first I got fired, then I got evicted. Next, my kids were taken away all over some bullshit, and I can't get them back until I get a new place. I don't start at this new job for another two weeks. All my shit is in storage. Reka's letting me crash on her couch for awhile, but you know I'm a good mother. I miss my kids. I'm fucked up out here.", she said with tears streaming down her face. She began digging in her purse pulling out $17.00. "Nat, it's gonna be alright. Don't worry, I'll help you get your kids back. Holla at me tomorrow at the shop, I got you.", he said, giving her a hug reassuring her that things will be alright. He then gave her $200.00, "Pull yourself together and enjoy the rest of the night on me." She kissed his cheek and said thank you. Before leaving he asked, "Is your girl Reka still fucking with Ric?" "Off and on, on the low, why?" "I need his address and his brother Roc's. Can you get that for me?", he asked. "Yeah, just don't tell nobody you got it from me though.", she replied. Nat knew what Linz did for a living and that if him or any of the Four Kings came after you it was for a reason. "Look Nat, keep this between us. How soon can you get that for me?", he asked. "I could get it for you in a couple days. I know Ric's already, I just gotta get Roc's. Just give me a heads up, so I can try to keep her away that day, aight.", she pleaded. Linz agreed and said, "Get them addresses and we even on the loot I'm gonna give you." "Bet", she replied. "Will seven stacks hold you until things pick back up for you?", he asked. "Hell yeah, thank you Linz. If you ever need some company, a hug, or some loving, come holla at me.", she said, flashing him a sexy smile.

When Linz returned, Tootie had the Olds at the curb with the top down, sounds banging, door open, lounging in the passenger seat nodding to Lil Kim's "Lighter's Up". He sat in her lap. "Fix your face and lose the attitude.", he said, while trying to kiss her. "Naw Nigga, you gonna make me bust your fucking head, keep playing here.", she said after he kissed her. She tried to stay mad, but a smile was slowly making it's way on her face. "You ready Boo?", she asked. "Give me ten minutes, I need to holla at my peeps for a minute.", he responded getting off her lap to go holla at the crew. She playfully punched him in the back as he got up. "Hurry up too because your ten minutes turn into hours. Shit, you could call them Niggas later.", she said reapplying lip gloss and sliding behind the wheel.

Linz told the crew about Natalie and the info that she said she could get for them on Ric and Roc. The men were grateful for the help. "So, when y'all wanna get together and put a plan down?", Doug asked. He wanted to be in California by July 1st. "Shit, we could do something tomorrow or one day this week.", K.J said, since this was his idea to begin with. "Just hold on, be patient, come July Royce will be just a memory and we'll be set for life, if all goes well.", K.J said feeling the crew's impatience. "Just chill, trust me on this."

Linz gave the crew a pound before leaving. They clowned him once again, walking to the car saying, "What Tootie won't let you hang with the fellas?" Doug went to the driver's side and asked, "Damn Toot, what you done to my boy? He on curfew and shit. What's up with that?" She just smiled, pointed at her pussy, and said," This right here is that make a nigga act right coochie.   You see the results."   "Damn Nigga, it's like that?", K.J said.   Before Linz could respond, Tootie balled her fist up and said playfully, "I'll bust your head if you lie!".   Linz just laughed.   "Say it ain't so!", A.P stated.   Linz just threw his hand up and said, "Y'all know the real."   Tootie said peace to her friends and pulled into the street.

After they were about two blocks away she said, "Boo, I was just playing but I will bust your shit open if you try to play me." Linz paid her no attention, his mind was else where.   It was only 8:30 pm, still early, so he flipped his cell and called his sister Sherry.   It had been a minute since he last spoke with her or her two kids.   He got the machine instead and left a message. "Who was that?", Tootie asked.   "My sister, didn't I tell you I have two sisters?", he said.   "No, when can I meet them?"   He thought about it for a moment then said, "Tonight, we gonna go see my oldest sister, Sherry, in Steubenville, Ohio, then go past my mom's and pop's tomorrow."   Tootie took this as a good sign.   For the next thirty minutes they rode listening to Avant, deep in their own thoughts.

Cruising down 7th Street in Steubenville was like a blast from the past for Linz, it brought back plenty of memories.   At the gas station, he ran into one of his best friends, Bookie.   He hardly recognized Bookie because the streets had taken him under causing him to break Rule #1 of the hustlers code, Don't get high on your own supply.

"Linnnzzz!   What's up man?", Bookie said, giving Linz a pound.   "Nothing much, just chillin, about to go see my sister.", Linz said.   "Sherry just went up the hill a few minutes ago." "Alright, I'll get up with you later.", Linz said, getting behind the wheel while waiting for Tootie to pay for her soda.   "Damn

Linz, you keep a bad bitch by your side.", Bookie said as Tootie came out of the store. "Let your boy hold something, I'm broke as hell Linz. Come on, its your boy." Linz and Bookie went way back to kindergarten. "Get your stuff together and I'll do something for you.", Linz said, giving him two hundred dollars. "Bet Linz, I'm through smoking.", Bookie said.

After they pulled off Tootie said, "Why did you give that money, you know he going straight to the dopeman and get high, don't you?' he didn't say nothing, he knew that she was right, but he was hoping that he wouldn't. It saddened Linz to see his boys that were once hustlers now full fledged crackheads.

The Olds pulled up in front of his sister's house, her two girls were on the porch. "Uncle, Uncle!", Shamiah yelled running off the porch to meet him. Qua yelled, "Mommy, Uncle Bobby is here." Sherry was in the kitchen putting away groceries when Linz entered the house with Tootie behind him with his two nieces. He introduced Tootie to his sister and to his nieces. Tootie helped Sherry put away the groceries, while Linz took the girls for a ride to see his mother real quick.

While Linz and the girls were gone, Tootie and Sherry talked. Tootie found out alot about her man from his sister. When he came back the two women were sitting on the porch drinking wine coolers. "Bobby", a name his family called him, "how long you gonna be here?", Sherry asked. "Not sure, probably a day or two, why?" "Just asking because I got Qua until Sunday and I need you to talk to them both.", Sherry said.

About 11:30, his cousin Manard came over so they could hit the streets and bar hop. Tootie didn't feel like going, so she stayed and talked with Sherry until about 2:00 am. Meanwhile, Linz and Manard was out clowning. They linked up with Rell and Chuck and when to The Chateau. It was there that Linz seen his ex, Tanika.   She was first girl he ever loved and she was looking real good.   She was there with her two cousins. "Hello Tanika.", he said standing in front of her.   She smiled, "Hey Linz.", she said in a soft voice.   "Can I get a hug or something?", he asked embracing her.   The warmth of her touch brought back a tidal wave of cherished memories.   He held her for a moment savoring her touch.   When they broke the embrace, they engaged in small talk.   It felt good seeing Tanika, she was still fine as hell.   He almost wanted to take her back, he truly loved her.   He would've given his left arm for her, but when he went to jail she dogged him.   No matter how fine she was, he couldn't shake the acts of betrayal that she inflicted on him and his heart.   "Well Babe, it was nice seeing you, take care of yourself.", he said getting up to join Rell and them at the bar. Before he walked away, Tanika gave him her phone number. Linz pocketed the digits and stepped off.   As he walked away Tanika thought to herself how great things could be if she didn't dog him out.

The next day, Linz took Tootie to meet his parents.   First, they went to his mom's house.   Then they went to the mall to get some clothes to put on .   Finally, they went to holla at his pops.   Tootie like his family, she adored his two nieces.   He left Tootie at his sisters while he jetted back to Pittsburgh to meet Natalie at the shop.   He couldn't let her down.   He was about twenty minutes away when Motorhead called him for Natalie. He told him he was on his way.   He took care of Nat and headed back to Steubenville.   Linz spent the day kicking it with his cousin, Rell, Chuck, and a few others.   Tootie chilled with Sherry and braided the kid's hair.   That night they chilled together, watched a movie and sat on the porch sipping Coronas until 1:00 am.   They decided to get a hotel room and made love like it was their first time all over again.   While basking in the afterglow of sex, he told Tootie of his run in with is ex, Tanika and the thing with Natalie.   She was surprised that he told her and asked, "Why are you telling me this?   You could have kept it to yourself, I would have never known."   He kissed her forehead and said, "Because I love you."

CHAPTER FORTY-NINE

Tootie, Cristal, Diamond, and Jade all sat in McKinnley's Church of God on a divine Sunday morning in May, listening intensively as the pastor delivered the message from Luke 18: 1-14 to a congregation of about 300 or so.   The congregation was made up of men and women of all ages, mostly black.   This was a church that was come as you are, it didn't matter what you wore as long as you came to hear the word,   praise his name, and give God the glory.   This was the girls first time at this church.   It was also the first time they ever attended church services together.   They received and invitation while pumping gas on Thursday.   Tootie thought about it but hadn't made up her mind to go until she returned home later and found her man sprawled across the floor reading his Bible.   She took that as a sign that God was trying to tell her something.   So that Sunday she sat in service, asking for forgiveness for the acts she was about to take part in.

Her soul shook as two kids mimed a song by Donnie McClurkin, 'We Fall Down'.   Tears fell from her eyes as the words tore through her body, penetrating her heart.   The words let her know that we all fall sometimes, but Jesus allows us to get back up again and stand strong, no matter how many times we may fall.   God is always there as long as we humble ourselves to him and repent our sins.

As Tootie stood on shaky legs with her arms out stretched as if she was receiving her blessings, Jade mouthed, "Sit down!", through clenched teeth and pulling at the hem of her skirt. Tootie stood silently pouring her heart out to God.

After the performance was over, Tootie still stood praising God.   Since she was the only one still standing the Pastor asked, "Is there something you want to say young lady?".   The tears flowed as she continued to tap her foot and shake her head, waiting for the words to come.   "It's alright baby, take your time.   God hears you, whatever it is, he hears you.", an elderly woman in the pew behind them said.   That was followed by a thunderous "Amen!".   When she found her voice she said, "I just want to thank the Lord for touching my spirit and for allowing me to be here this morning.   Hallelujah!!"   Tootie squeezed Cristal's hand tighter as the spirit moved her to lift her voice to Jesus.   "Do y'all mind if I sing for a minute?", she asked, with her eyes closed and tears racing down her face. "Sing your song child!", someone from the back of the church said.   With the congregation's approval, she began to sing.   In her mind she wanted to sing Smokey Norful's 'I Need you Now', but instead when she opened her mouth Yolanda Adam's 'Open My Heart' flowed out flawlessly.   After the first verse was out, she regained her confidence and stepped out into the isle walking toward the pulpit, singing with everything in her soul.   She was passing faces she seen every weekend in the clubs and strip joints when she used to dance.

When the service was over, the choir director asked her to join.   She thanked him and let him know she would think about it.   On the way out the Pastor thanked her for her song and asked if she'd be back.   She gave him hug and said, "I hope so.", then ran to catch up with her girls.   Tootie just couldn't wait to get home and call her mother to tell her all about her morning.

Across town at the car wash on Jefferson, the Four Kings washed their cars while mulling over the bombshell that Natalie dropped on them last night about Roc and Eryca, when she came to drop off the addresses for Ric and Roc.   They thought that she was lying until she spoke about the vacation that he took her on a few month ago.   "Damn, why she gotta fall for that nigga!", K.J said heated because this could turn out to be a real problem for the men.   "And she starting to catch feelings for him too!", Linz said while applying Black Magic to his tires.   "I wonder if she even know the type of nigga that she's dealing with?", K.J asked to no one in particular.   "Apparently not.", A.P replied.

Doug was quiet but his mind was in overdrive.   "Doug, what you think about this situation?", Linz asked.   "Well, if you look at it from my view point we got the advantage.   We could use Eryca without her even know it.   Just think about it for a minute, I'm sure you see what I'm talking about.", Doug said letting them ponder on his words.   He continued to school them on how to use Eryca.   He ended his thoughts by saying, "It's just like a game of chess, a pawn can either help or hurt a king." Linz and K.J smiled wickedly because they knew the game of chess well and played it often.   "I knew something was going on up there in your mind, you was too quiet.", A.P said giving his boy props.   "Sometimes, you just gotta sit back and assess the situation from a different angle, then make your move.   You feel me!", Doug said.   The crew nodded in agreement.

The last caper meant a lot to all of them, each one knew how high the stakes were, but none of them ever imagined that it would be worth almost $100 million dollars in cash and several more in high grade heroin. Each man had their own plans for the take on this last robbery, but they all shared the same vision, to walk away breathing and be set financially for the rest of their lives.

As the men sat lost in their own worlds, Lil Mac pulled in to holla at them. "What's up fools.", he asked going around giving each man a pound. "Shit, just cooling, tossing around some ideas.", K.J replied. "I heard that. So what's the business on that fool Royce?", Mac asked. "That's what we politicing about now.", Linz said. "But we haven't came up with nothing solid yet. Any ideas?", K.J asked Mac just hunched his shoulders. They continued conversating for about an hour more then started to spread out in different directions. Before everyone broke out, Mac said, "One of y'all need to get with me because I'm done with that. I don't like holding other people's loot, ya dig." Lil Mac got rid of another eight bales of dro. His customer base was steadily increasing, stretching down the eastern sea board into Atlanta, courtesy of Jeanna's cousin Meeka, who came up to visit a few months ago. "I'll send Cristal over in about an hour.", Doug stated out the window, while merging the Acura into the flow of Sunday traffic.

The crew was now two million richer and down to just 33 bales of dro and tye. After this hit went down, the Four Kings decided to leave the drug game alone completely. Being greedy got a lot of niggas locked up or six feet deep. They vowed to make it out alive, something that most hustlers never do. It was agreed that whatever they had left in their stash, they would give away and let someone else come up.

"My stomach is growling like a mutha!", Cristal said. "Mine too, let's stop and get something to eat, I'm starving.",

Jade said, urging Cristal to pull into the Long John Silver's that was up ahead. "Tootie, what's wrong with you?", Diamond said. Tootie sat in the backseat of the Avalanche lost in her thoughts with a smile on her face. Diamond bumped her again, "Toot, you okay?". "Yeah, I'm cool. I just feel so good inside. Thanks for coming to church with me, I really appreciate it.", she said "you know we got your back girl.", Cristal said. "Yeah, plus you tore that song up! I knew you could sing, but I didn't know you had pipes like that.", Diamond said. "It's cool that you into God and all that stuff. Don't get me wrong, I believe in God, but I just ain't with the church scene, you feel me. Just don't go getting all holier than thou on us ok bitch!", Jade said, grasping her friend's hand. The women busted out laughing. "Seriously y'all, I know that y'all ain't all churchy, but say a prayer tonight for us, because we are going to need it, and thank him for watching over us all those times before.", Tootie said. "Amen to that.", Cristal added, "because after this is over, I'm through with Pittsburgh and the bullshit." "I feel you girl, I'm trying to settle my ass down, have some kids, and get married.", tootie said. The others just laughed. "Shit, y'all think I'm playing, that nigga is gonna wife me, fuck the dumb shit! If I have to propose to his ass, we getting hitched!", Tootie stated. "Girl, you just came from the church not ten minutes ago, and you cussing like a sailor. You need Jesus!", Jade said. Cristal added, "Well we know she ain't gone totally holy ghost on us yet."

After the women ate, Tootie was the first to be dropped off, she couldn't wait to get out of those heels. Her feet were relieved when she opened the door and kicked the shoes half way across the room. The thick carpet felt like heaven, she actually let out a sigh of relief. "Hey Boo!", she called out walking through the living room.   She began undressing as she went looking for her man only to find out that he was not home.   She stood in the middle of the living room in just a bra and thong. "Where is he", she asked herself.   "Oh well, I'll see him when he get here, let me call my momma.", she said, talking to herself. She picked up the phone, plopped down on the couch and prepared to share her blessing with her mother.

"Hello", a man's voice answered.   Tootie recognized Devon's voice.   "Hey Devon, is Momma around?", she asked. "Yes, she just got out of the shower.   I'll get her for you.", he said, calling Ajia to the phone.

"What my child!", Ajia said.   "Excuse me for calling.", Tootie said.   "Girl, I'm in the middle of something and you are interrupting me.", Ajia stated.   "Eww Mom, you nasty!"   She was happy that her Mom was enjoying life once again.   She always thought her Mom was too fine to be single, but the thought of her Momma getting her freak on turned her stomach. "Now, what do you want?", Ajia continued.   "Momma, I called to tell you about my day at church.   Me and the girls went to this service, it was good and I sang.   I felt the Holy Spirit moving. Momma, it was so powerful!   I can't wait to go again.", she said.   Ajia was happy to hear that her child was taking a step towards getting back into the church.   "How did Lionel like it?", she asked.   "He didn't go, he had some stuff to take care of. Maybe next time he will go.", Tootie responded.   She continued to tell her mom about the service and how she felt inside.   She kept what she had been doing for the last year and a half to herself, she would tell her when this was all over.   "So, how's things with you and Devon?", she asked.   "Lovely Baby, I haven't been this happy in a long time.", Ajia said.   "Momma, I'm really happy for you.", Tootie said.   "Baby, I need to talk to you about some things.", Ajia said. "What's going on?", Tootie asked with concern. "Oh, it's really nothing, I was just thinking of retiring next year and, if you won't mind, I want Devon to move in with me." "The reason I asked is because you brought this house for me, so it's yours as well.", she explained. Tootie teased her mom, "Momma you in love, huh!" "Child please!", Ajia responded, trying to down play her feelings. "Yes you are, I can hear it in your voice, Momma he got you whipped!", Tootie said, still messing with her mother. Ajia denied the comment and said, i got him whipped. Shit, you don't know!" Tootie couldn't believe that her mother was 54 years old and sprung. She couldn't wait to tell Linz. "So, how you feel about what I told you?", Ajia asked. "do what you wanna do Momma. If you want him to move in with you, then let him. If you want to retire then do so, I'll take care of you. You stood by my side all these years and took care of me, now it's time for me to take care of you. Sit back and enjoy life. If Devon makes you happy, then I'm happy. Just don't get pregnant on me!", Tootie stated. "Don't be telling Lionel my business either. Shit, I'll never hear the end of it.", Ajia said. "Now Momma, you know I have to tell him, as much as you pick with him I can't hold this in.", Tootie said. "I like Lionel, he's a good man. Remember what i told you, hold on to him, he's worth it.", Ajia said. "Mom, I am." "When y'all gonna give me some grand kids?" Tootie laughed before responding, "Mom, we are working on the babies now, hopefully it will be soon. He already asked me to have his child, but I don't just want his baby, I want him too.", she said. "Girl, that boy ain't going nowhere. You about to be a permanent fixture in his life very soon, trust me.", Ajia said. She wanted to tell her daughter of Linz's plans to marry on her birthday, which was a few weeks away, but she gave Linz her word that she'd keep quiet. No wedding, just the two of them and the judge on June 2nd. "Momma, how do you know? Did he say something to you about it?", Tootie asked. "Just trust me baby, and don't fuck up okay. Now, I've been on this phone for forty-five minutes to long. My man is waiting on me so I have to go. I love you baby.", Ajia said. "I love you too Momma!", Tootie said before hanging up.

Tootie laid on the couch thinking about what her Momma just said. A million things went through her mind. This was truly turning out to be a blessed day. She got up and took some food out to cook later. She took off her bra and put on an old cut off t-shirt because she wasn't planning to go anywhere or have company no time soon. She then turned on the stereo, cued up Mary J. Blige's 'What's the 411' and stretched out on the couch once again. She began to fall asleep letting the music take her mind while waiting on her man to return home.

Cristal just got in the door after dropping Tootie off and running errands with the twins. She had her mind set on relaxing for a minute when the phone rang. "I got it", she yelled and picking up the receiver. "Hello?" It was the twin's mother. "Hi Ms. Iko, how are you?", she said before yelling for Kuan and Kuo to pick up the phone. Ms. Iko still hated the nicknames the girls chose for themselves as teenagers. She said they sounded like harlot names and refused to address them as such. She always used their birth names.

Just as Cristal was about to undress, her cell rang. "Who is it now!", she exclaimed, answering the phone without bothering to look at the caller ID. "What!", she barked. "Whoa, you alright? Calm down.", Doug said. "Oh, I'm sorry, I was just trying to rest for a minute and every time I try, the damn phone rings!", she explained "Well boo, I hate to do this to you but I need a favor from you real quick.   I need you to go over to Jeanna's house and pick up something for me, then meet me over Linz's.", he said.   "Aughh! Alright, let me change first.   Fuck it, I'm leaving now, do they know that I'm coming?", she asked. Yeah, I'm calling them now.   I love you.", Doug said before hanging up the phone.   Cristal just grabbed a pair of sweats, panties, and a pair of Nike's.   She picked up her keys and bounced out the door.   She'd shower and get a shirt from Tootie. She threw the clothes in the backseat and rolled out towards Monroeville.   It would take her about half an hour without traffic.   She prayed that the Sunday traffic was light because she was tired of driving.

Meanwhile, Doug called Lil Mac and let him know that she was on her way.   Then, he called Linz to let him know that he'd be over in about 45 minutes and that Cristal went to get the loot and was bringing it over.   While Linz finished tying up some loose ends and checking on Eryca, Doug headed over to Linz's. Even though he spent most of his days at Cristal's, he still had a key to the place he used to share with Linz.   He put the Acura in the garage and let himself in.   As soon as he opened the door the smooth sounds of Angie Stone greeted his ears, along with the sight of Tootie half naked asleep on the couch with her legs wide open.   He had seen her like this before, but that was the night that they first met at the Red Devil Bar about a year ago.   Now here she was again asleep with her ass and titties hanging out for all to see.   He stood transfixed by her beautiful body and understood why his boy Linz was so hooked on her.

Doug went and shook her awake, this wouldn't be a good look if Linz or Cristal happened to walk in.   Tootie awoke with a groan and a little stretch.   Without opening her eyes she said, "Baby, what time is it?", thinking that Doug was Linz.   When she opened her eyes she seen Doug standing over the back of the couch. "Oh shit!", she exclaimed, as she jumped off the couch and ran to the bedroom to put something on. She felt embarrassed when she returned dressed in an over sized t-shirt and shorts. "Where Linz at?", she asked picking up her clothes that she wore to service, that were scattered about the living room. "He's on his way now and so is Cristal.", he replied. Both of them felt awkward about what just happened. "I'm sorry for just barging in on you like that. I should have knocked.", Doug said apologizing. "It's cool.", Tootie said, and started boiling the water for the spaghetti noodles and put the sauce on to simmer. Doug helped dice the green peppers. The tension was gone, they were back to their normal state of friendship.

"Y'all staying for dinner?", she asked. "I don't know, we could if that's cool with y'all. It looks like you had other plans though.", Doug said. "Shit, I was just being lazy and fell asleep.", she said, opening the fridge for something. The phone rang as she was about to call Linz. "Hello?" It was Linz, she told him that Doug was there and to stop and get some croissants and stuff for the salad from the store. After she hung up, she and Doug talked about life and him and Cristal's future plans. She also told him about what she wanted for her and Linz.

After they ate, Cristal showered and changed while Doug and Linz played NFL Live on the X-Box 360. After Tootie was dressed, the four went out to Holiday Lanes to bowl. When the ladies went to the restroom Doug took the opportunity to tell Linz what happened at his house today with him and Tootie. Linz didn't sweat it because he knew that Doug didn't get down like that, plus he was his boy. The Kings lived by a golden rule, don't fuck with or think about fucking with each other's girl.

That rule was told to the ladies also, just so there would be no misunderstanding. The females enforced that rule among themselves. Respect for each other was evident in the bond that the man and women shared.

The night ended with Doug and Cristal beating Linz and Tootie. On the drive home Linz teased Tootie. "So, my boy seen your cheeks, huh?" Tootie was embarrassed that his boy had seen her like that, she looked out the window most of the time. She did not think that Doug would tell, but he did. "It was an accident, I was waiting on you and fell asleep.", she said looking out the window. Linz picked up on her uneasiness and pulled over so he could put her mind at ease.

Tootie picked her nails as he got out of the car and came around to her side. He opened the door and said, "Step out Babe." She looked puzzled as he helped her out. "Where are we going?", she asked, walking over to this little neighborhood park. "Babe, it's cool, I know that ain't nothing happen. Doug's my boy, he told me what went down and that it was his fault. He apologized to me and you.", he said, pulling her into his arms. "I was going to tell you, but I didn't think it was that big of a deal. I mean he seen my ass before when we first hooked up. I wanted to tell you but I just didn't know how you would react. Baby, I love you and would never break the golden rule.", she said. "Babe, I trust you, now let's go home and you can show me what you had on and what he saw, after you tell me about your day.", he said, then kissed her deeply. That was all Tootie needed to hear to bring a smile to her pretty face. She was eager to tell him all about the service today, hoping that he'd join her next week when she went. She hoped that they could start reading the word and praying together every night before they went to bed. Her grandma used to say that a family that pray's together, stay's together.   She hoped her grandma was right.

CHAPTER FIFTY

Today was June 1ˢᵗ, the grand opening of the twins clothing boutique called 'La Bella Dame'.   The girls had gotten up early, this was their baby.   It was only 7:30am and the twins were already down at the shop getting ready for the 10:00am opening.

"I hope that a lot of people show up.", Diamond said. "Sissy, don't worry, it's only the first day.   We are going to be alright, trust me.   We put to much into this to fail.", Jade said, boosting her sibling's confidence.   La Bella Dame, sold the latest and hottest in women's designer fashion, from all the top names, known and unknown, throughout the world.   Most of the brands that they carried were exclusively sold only in their store, unless you planned on traveling to New York, Chicago, Miami, or LA to get them.   After today's opening the ladies planned on taking the whole staff out to celebrate tonight.

"You know Linz is going to propose to Tootie tonight at midnight.", Jade commented to her sister.   "I know, I can't wait to see her reaction, she's been wanting this for awhile, fell in love as soon as she met the nigga.   That nigga's shit gotta be bomb!", Diamond said.   "Shit her stuff gotta be good too, because that nigga is just as sprung as her.   He just hide it better than she do. I know my girl is putting it down in the bedroom.   But, I am happy for her, now she can quit crying about it.", Jade said, folding a pair of vintage Jordache jeans.   "That's my girl, she hung in there and got her man, knocking bitches out and shit over him.   I am truly happy for her.   I wish that K.J's ass would do something like that."

"What, not you talking about settling down!   When did you decide this Ms. Thang?", Diamond said, teasing her sister. "Shit, I've been doing a lot of thinking lately, it too much shit out there and niggas is passing out AIDS like it's cool. I admit I used to be a little slutty, but since I met K.J I've changed.", Jade said. "Bitch please, keep it 100!", Diamond exclaimed. "Alright, I'm light weight sprung, shit that boy got that fire!", Jade said. The girls laughed as Diamond starting singing, "I'm so sprung, he got me doing things I never do..", then went to turn on the radio to hear the advertisement they paid for a few day's ago.

The boutique's interior was made up of different shades of green and silver. A jade green convertible Corvette with several maniquins in and around it dressed in items that the shop carried took up space in the center of the boutique. Also two Honda motorcycles with rider's dressed in the latest fashions was placed in a corner near the dressing rooms. The shop also sold shoes and handbags from Kate Spade, Fendi, Gucci, Jimmy Choo, and Manolo. There was a room about 1000 sq. ft. on the side to display the various types and brands of shoes and accessories. Leather chaise lounges, benches, and casting couches were scattered throughout the boutique. This old warehouse wasn't so bad after all, and the location was perfect, smack dab in the middle of one of the busiest streets in downtown Pittsburgh.

While the twins were downtown preparing for their grand opening, Tootie was at home, ass naked, getting her back blew out by her man. "Baby, it feel so damn good! Oh yeah work it baby, work it!", Linz moaned as she continued to grind her pussy onto his dick in a circular motion, riding him like no tomorrow. She was working her magic, bringing him pleasure beyond words.

"I love you Boo, I really do.", she whispered, looking him in his eye's. Linz lay captivated, locked in a trance by her gaze and hypnotized by her body's motion as she continued to rock his world. "Boo, did you hear me?", she asked, playfully slapping his face. "Huh?" Giggling she said, "Boy, you didn't hear nothing I said, did you?" Linz hadn't heard nothing she said, he was too caught up in the moment. "Naw, babe, my mind was gone.", he said, grabbing her hips as she leaned back and rocked slow, getting more stimulation for herself at this angle. "Say my name Boo.", she whispered, wanting him to talk dirty to her, she liked it when he did that. "Tootie", he moaned as he got in rhythm with her body. She changed to the reverse cowgirl position and cooed, "Oh baby", as he cupped and spread her cheeks while she bounced up and down on his penis. "That's it babe, ride this dick! Ride it bitch, ride it.", he commanded, making her ride faster and harder. Tootie didn't mind him calling her bitch during sex, but anytime outside of sex was a no-no.

Tootie was fully aroused, her eyes were glossy and lips were little swollen. Every time she got really turned on she would bite down on her bottom lip. "Hit it from the back for a while, please!", she moaned. She loved it this way, face down ass up! Tapping her on her ass he said "Get up!". Before she got into position, she gave his penis a quick sucking. Once behind her, he took the head of his dick and ran it up and down the opening of her slit. "Is this what you want?", he teased. "Yes", she replied. He continued to tease her with the head of his penis. "Please Daddy, stop playing and give it to me!", she whined. Linz granted her wish and commenced to burying all eight inches deep into her womb with forceful strokes. Her titties rocked back and forth as she cried out, "Yes baby, fuck me! I'm your bitch!", hunching her back to meet his strokes. Linz loved the way her ass jiggled every time he pushed inside of her. Tootie closed her eyes and let out a moan from somewhere deep down in her soul when Linz hit her spot. She had completely forgot she as supposed to be downtown helping the twins prepare for the grand opening. This went on for another twenty minutes before the phone rang. "Let the machine get it.", Linz said, plowing into her and pulling her hair. The phone rang several times before the machine finally picked up. After the greeting they heard Diamond say, "Tootie, get your dizzy ass up! You are supposed to be down here helping us open up! I know you didn't forget!" Tootie heard Jade in the background scream, "Bitch, you can get the dick later, get your silly ass down here now!" "Oh shit!", Tootie said, finally remembering that she was supposed to be helping them. She reached for the phone trying to catch it before they hung up. "Hello, Hello", she said. "Bitch, you tripping!", Diamond stated. "I'm sorry, I just woke up.", she lied. "Ho, stop lying! We know the real!", Diamond said. "I'm on my way now, let me hop in the shower first. Thirty minutes, ok.", Tootie promised. She heard Jade scream, "That's fucked up Toot! You played us for some dick!" "I'm on my way now.", Tootie said. "Whatever, just get your ass down here ASAP!", Diamond replied, then hung up. Diamond could tell that Tootie was getting banged by the way her voice kept rising and falling when she was talking. Plus, she could hear Linz in the background talking shit. Linz kept fucking while Tootie was on the phone. He smiled to himself knowing that he gave them something to talk about. "Babe, you ready to cum yet? I'm supposed to be downtown helping the girls.", she asked. He answered by pumping harder and faster, she knew he was about to cum. Suddenly, he moaned really loud as he shot cum deep inside her vagina. Thirty minutes later, Tootie was showered, dressed and on the parkway headed towards downtown.

"So, where we going tonight?", Jade asked. "Some club called Avi's that Tootie been talking about.', Diamond replied between sips of espresso. "I've heard of that joint, they say it's real laid back.", Gia, one of the sales girls, commented. By now most of the staff were there, except for Stephanie, she was on her way. It was only 9:15am, she still had 45 minutes to get there. The twins liked Stephanie, they truly digged her style, humor,and looks. The two agreed with Tootie, Steph was a bad bitch from head to toe. Several times in the last few weeks Jade caught her sister flirting with Stephanie while they were hanging displays and posters. Diamond would touch her ass on the sly, but Jade wasn't mad because she did the same thing when Diamond wasn't looking. Both of them wanted to indulge in a bowl of Steph.

One night while they were working late, Steph whispered to the twins on her way out, "Don't be scared. I won't bite.", then walked off to meet her woman, leaving the twins with their mouths hanging open. Steph knew that the twins wanted her, she could see it in their eyes. She also picked up on the vibe that they have been intimate with each other before. She could tell by the way they touched one another. After Steph left that night, Diamond looked at her sister and asked, "You thinking what I'm thinking?". Jade replied, "You know it." Diamond stated, "We gonna tear her ass up!". They gave each other a high five.

Later that night, after Tootie and Cristal had left, Diamond was in the backroom bent over picking up some boxes when Jade came up behind her and wantingly tapped and palmed her ass. "I ain't had none of this in a while, what's up with that?", she asked, licking her lips. "Same reason that I ain't had none of yours.", Diamond replied, enjoying her sister's touch. "Well, what's up now!", Jade said. "Shit you ain't said nothing, go lock the door and pull the blinds down.", Diamond instructed. When Jade returned Diamond was naked, laying on the casting couch rubbing herself. Jade stripped off her clothes and joined her sister, running her hands up and down Diamond's silky thighs. Jade buried her face in her sister's pussy, Diamond moaned. It had been at least three months since their last encounter. It used to be three times a week, but now that Doug was there all the time, they chilled out.

The twins was so caught up in each other that they didn't hear Steph come in when she came back to get her cell phone. Steph heard the moans coming from the back room and went to investigate. She was taken back and amused at the sight that greeted her. Diamond had Jade bent over the arm of the couch eating her from behind, several sex toys lay on the floor next to the couch. Jade was moaning so loud, "Oh Sissy, right there!" That was enough for Steph, her pussy was starting to get wet, she began to undress. After Steph was naked, she walked over to the couch and placed a kiss on Diamond's ass, causing her to turn around with a startled look on her face. "I know y'all wasn't going to start without me.", Steph asked, touching Jade's breast, while sticking her finder up in Diamond's pussy. The girls just smiled, then began their attack on Stephanie's fine ass. For the next two and a half hours the twins worked Stephanie over.

The next day, the twins asked Tootie if the golden rule applied to Stephanie too. Tootie told them to do them, but to watch out because Steph was addictive. The twins asked Tootie if she wanted to join in for a session. The twins had often plotted to fuck Tootie but never acted on it. Tootie also had thought about it just like she was doing now. The offer was tempting as hell. She told the twins she would think about it, but later declined.   The twins asked her to keep it between them and she told them she would, it was their business.

Tootie arrived about five minutes after Steph, "Ho, I should choke you!", Diamond said.   Tootie started to explain, but was cut short by Jade.   "Whatever Tootie, save it!", offering her a donut.   "I couldn't help it, shoot!", Tootie said in her defense, taking a creamstick.   Jade understood where Tootie was coming from, if it would have been her she would have done the same thing.   "Bitch, you just had a creamstick at home, now you want to take the last one.   You a true ho!", Diamond stated, making all the other girls laugh.   Tootie licked the cream off her top lip and asked, "What, you jealous?", giving Jade and the other girls a high five.   "Whatever", Diamond said waving Tootie off. Tootie got up and gave Diamond a hug, then blew her breath in her face, "Smell that, still got dick on my breath!"   Diamond screamed and stepped back.   "Y'all don't forget, we going out tonight.", Tootie said to everyone, then turned to Jade and said, "I need something to wear for tonight."   she stuffed the rest of the creamstick in her mouth.   Lelia, another sales woman, was the last to show up.   "Sorry I'm late, the sitter had car trouble.", she said, going straight to the stereo to turn up Jagged Edge's 'So Amazing'.   This got the store crunk.

While the women were conducting business at the boutique, Tootie's mother was packing up some things for her trip up to see her daughter and spend her birthday with her.   She also wanted to be there to see Mr. Lindsey propose to her child.   Tootie would be 27 tomorrow and a wife.   Ajia wouldn't miss it for the world.   Everyone else knew that Linz was going to ask Tootie to marry him but Tootie.

K.J spent most of the afternoon laying in bed with his white freak, Keisha, at her apartment watching this Russian mob flick about some hit men.   It was at that time that the solution to get Royce came to him.   He jumped up and grabbed his phone to call the fellas.   He told them to meet him at his house ASAP. "Can I borrow this?", he asked, ejecting the DVD.   "Yeah", she said, disappointed that he was leaving.   It had been weeks since he last broke her off.   "So, I guess I'll see you in a few more weeks huh?", she asked.   K.J responded, "Babe, don't be like that.   I got something I gotta take care of real quick, ok.", putting on his shorts.   "If you gotta go then you gotta go, but I just don't ever get to see you anymore.   I know you got a girl and shit, but I need some time too, at least once a week.   You got a bitch strung out like a junkie.", she said embracing him. "You got that, boo.", he said looking at his and her reflection in the mirror.   Keisha really liked K.J, and he liked her too, but Jade was his woman, his heart belonged to her.   Whenever he was ready to truly settle down with one woman, it would be will be with Jade.   At this point he wasn't ready to do that yet.   He kissed Keisha before leaving, promised her he would be back soon, and bounced. He thought to himself, Keisha was one he'd keep around for a while.

The Four Kings, Lil Mac, Doe, and Aaron sat in the TV room watching the DVD, while he explained his plan to them. After watching the flick and listening to K.J the crew understood a little better.   "It looks doable to me.", Linz said, everyone agreed but Doug.   He wanted to study it more.   "Hold up fellas, this is just a movie, we talking real life here.   Anything is possible in Hollywood, but not in these streets.   Let me study this movie for a couple days, then I'll get back with y'all with a plan.   I see a few things in this flick that you over looked, that we could also do.", he said.   The crew knew that he'd watch this film over and over for hours and take notes.   Doug was the most patient of the Four Kings and that when he went into thinking mode he always came up with an infallible plan. "I gotta bounce.", Doug said, collecting the DVD and giving each man a pound. Doug had to get somethings in the mail before 3:00 today. He had written his boy, Phil and told him about his moving to California. He made sure to give him his info on where and how to reach him and when to start using it. He also sent him a money order for $3,500 for his books and a bunch of photos of the fellas, the girls, him and Cristal, and some sexy shots of the girls that Cristal took in thongs and such, with permission from the crew. Doug kept Phil in the streets. The crew respected Doug for the way he looked out for his peeps on lock down. Phil only had a year left. The twins gave his baby momma a job, and Doug put a million up for him so he'd be straight when he touched down, now that was love.

"So you really going to wife Tootie, huh?", A.P asked, looking at the platinum and rose gold ring adorned with diamonds that Grench created for Linz. "Yep, at midnight I'm going to ask her to be my wife, that's her birthday present. I'll kill two birds at the same time.", he responded. They knew that he was going to propose, but they didn't know that tomorrow he'd say 'I do' in front of a judge. "Listen at this old in love ass nigga!", Lil Mac said, they all laughed. "I wish you the best my nigga, for real.", K.J said, giving his friend a pound. The men talked some more about this and that, then broke out in different directions. K.J went back over to Keisha's place to finish her off, while Linz headed back to the shop to holla at Eryca about some things. He also needed to talk to Motorhead about getting him that Ashton Martin he'd been wanting. Since he was going to be a married man tomorrow, he figured he'd fuck around on Tootie one last time, Danni would be his victim for this. Linz had seen Danni naked last week while she was at Eryca's house. He'd stopped over to holla at Eryca about Roc. Danni was getting out of the shower when he let himself in, she tried to cover up but it was too late, he'd already seen everything he wanted to see. Ever since then, she'd been flirting with him at work, so today he was going to call her bluff. If Danni wasn't the one then he'd go hit off his ex, Tanika, who had some super pussy. Maybe even Natalie, who also had that goody, but one way or another, somebody was gonna get fucked this afternoon. A.P and Lil Mac went scoping for the cars they were going to use.

La Bella Dame was packed with customers, some just browsing, some buying, and some seeking employment. The twins were happy as hell that their grand opening was a success. Things were flying off the shelves and racks. Tootie even purchased an outfit, instead of trying to get it for free. She bought a denim miniskirt, silk halter top, and a pair of beaded sandles. "I know my man is gonna kill me, but I am wearing this tonight.", she said. Tootie wanted to show her legs tonight while she still could.

When the crowd subsided, Tootie slipped off down the street to the tattoo parlor and got "Lionel" above her right ankle and "Lindsey" inked on the other. While she waited to get tatted, she contemplated the best time and way to tell Linz that she was five weeks pregnant. She found out two weeks ago when she went to the doctor because she woke up several mornings feeling light headed.

"Girl, where you been?", Jade asked from behind the counter, after ringing up a customer. "I had to run down the street for a minute, why?", Tootie asked. Cristal came out of the back with a handbag to match the shoes for this dude and his lady and said, "Because your mom will be here in about an hour. She just called ten minutes ago.". Tootie smiled, "For real?". Cristal nodded. After the shop closed for the day, Tootie reminded all the girls to meet her back here at 10:30 so they could go out together, all the ladies agreed.

Ajia showed up at Tootie's around 6:00, they talked for awhile. After Tootie told her about the shop, Ajia said, "Call them girls, tell Platinum and Gold, or whatever their names are, that I need something to put on. I want to shake my Beyonce too!" Tootie busted out laughing and dialed the twins. As soon as Diamond answered Ajia said, "Platinum, Diamond, whatever your name is, let's go open up that shop. I need something to wear!". Diamond responded, "Hold on Mom Toot, I'm about to lay down, tell your daughter to bring you down to the shop about 9:30, you can get dressed there." Ajia thanked her, then gave the phone back to Tootie. Ajia could remember when Diamond and her fast ass twin Jade would come spend the night over her house as kids, now they've blossomed into full fledged women, beautiful women at that. Ajia was proud of them, she treated them like they were her very own. It was her who they came to about sex and when they got their first period. She talked to the girls about everything. When they were afraid to talk to their own parents, they came to her, and she kept it to herself. She was cool with the mothers of all the girls, and in Cristal's case her Aunt Tracey.

"Mom, you like my tattoos?", Tootie asked, showing her mother her ankles. "They're nice, what does he say about them?", Ajia asked. "He hasn't seen them yet.", she said rubbing ointment on them. "He doesn't know that I'm pregnant either.", she said. "What?" "Yes, I'm five weeks pregnant. Your about to be a granny soon.", Tootie said, touching her belly.

Ajia smiled and gave her daughter a hug.   Linz came home and
went straight to bed, he'd had a long day.   As soon as he hit the
sheets, he was out.   Tootie woke Linz at about 9:00 and told him
that she as taking her mom down to the shop to get some clothes
and that she'd meet him at AVI's at about eleven.   The ladies
had a few couches reserved for their celebration.

After Ajia got dressed, she came out of the dressing room
talking cash shit.   "Y'all see me, I still got it!   Now, don't be
hating if I steal the spotlight from y'all.", she stated, then looked
at Diamond and said, "Especially you!".   She then turned to
Jade and said, "I'll take your man!".   The women all laughed as
Jade said, "Ms. Ajia please, I will beat you up over my man.   I
don't mess around when it comes to him, alright."   "I may be
old, but I look damn good for 54.   Shit, you young girls don't
want none.", Ajia said, pointing to all of them, including Tootie.
"And Miss Fast Ass, what am I supposed to be doing while you
beating on me?   I hope you don't think that I'm just gonna stand
there.   I knocked out plenty of young chicks who think they
fly!", Ajia said, putting on her shoes.   "Tootie, your mom is
funny as hell.", Gia said looking for a purse to match her shoes.

CHAPTER FIFTY-ONE

Club AVI's was packed with people when the ladies arrived. "I like this little spot.", Tina said, as they were being ushered to their V.I.P spot. The DJ was spinning all the latest tunes. People were everywhere, dressed to kill. The crowd was made up of people 25 and older. "Hey, that's my song!", Ajia screamed, pulling the girls off the couch when the DJ played Destiny Childs 'Check Up On It'. The women rushed the dance floor shaking their asses in tune with the beat. Just then the men walked into the building.

At midnight, Horace stopped the music and took to the stage. "Ladies and Gentleman, can I have your attention please." The crowd quieted down, "First, I'd like to give a birthday shout out to Tootie from the ladies of La Bella Dame and from your man, my boy Linz." Everybody clapped, "Now her man would like to say a few words to you.", he said then handed the mic over to Linz.

"This goes out to a special person in my life, just to let her know how thankful I am for her and how much I enjoy her company.", he stated. The crowd cheered as Tootie sat blushing. Then Linz called her up on stage. As Tootie walked on stage, Linz said, "She's wearing that outfit, right! Now you see why I'm so thankful.". He kissed her then sat her on a stool that Horace provided. He turned to her and said, "Baby, this is for you. It's called The Letter.", then he began to recite the metaphors of passion.

Hello beautiful!
What's good?
I hope all is well and that
Life is being generous to U...
Me,

I'm maintain'n
Doing my Use-U-Al
But...
At this present moment
Sitting here scan'n
My Vis-U-Al
Reminisee'n...
on how you used to
De-La-my-Soul,
With just your touch....
Caress'n my mind
Verbally
With words of
Sensuality
Spoken fluently
From a seasoned
Lyrical lingual linguist...
Dialogged in a tongue so rare
It had me
Intoxicated!
Relaxed & mello
Like 2 shots of
Henny,
King Louie the 8th
Mixed with
Remy X.O
Inna state of pure
Utopia...
Feeling like
Sade & Alicia
Whispering N my left ear
While
Ms. Badu & Mary j.
Echo'n in my right!
The voices of 4 sirens
With golden harps
&
Platinum pipes
Combined in to 1
Serenading a brotha'
On a cool summer night....
SHHHHH...
Don't speak...
I can hear you...
See Baby girl,
Just the though of U

Got me 3 feet high
&
Rising!!
Those images distinctly familiar,
So vivid & familiar
Your making my dream girl jealous!
(We still here tho' Lisa Raye!)...
Tempting me
Like those caramel apples
At a carnival
Taste like chocolate
But underneath
Is it's
Forbidden fruit!
As I explore
Your secret garden
Tasting your juices
From Halle's Berry
Savoring your flavor
Quenching my thirst
Like a tall glass of
Ice water
On a hot summer day!
Releasing energy from
Our souls
With the force of
Mass times 3 squared
Rounded to that 5th power
Working to solve
Loves mathematical equation
Deep into the midnight
Hour....
Competing in the
Art of the
Karma Sutra
While yelling out
"I JUST DON'T WANNA STOP!!"
Physically borrowing a line from
LUTHER....VANDROSS
We can no longer
Hold off...
We relax & let go
AAAAHHHHHH!
Thanks 4
De-La'n my-Soul!!!

After he was through speaking, the crowd erupted in applause. He then said, "Hold up, I got one more thing to say.". He got down on one knee, retrieved the ring, and said, "Tootie, will you marry me?" Tootie was shocked and excited, she couldn't even speak, all she could do was nod her head yes. Tears of joy flowed from her eyes, also from her mother's eyes as well. Tootie found her voice as he placed the six carat yellow and white princess and baguette diamond ring on her finger. She screamed, " Yes, Yes, I'll marry you!" The crowd clapped for them as he took her into his arms and kissed her passionately. When they were seated, the girls gathered around to peep the rock on her finger.

After all the excitement had passed, Linz sat with Tootie in his lap on one of the couches. She ran her fingers over his waves, her dream almost complete. "Babe, I got something to show you.", she said lifting her legs to show him the tattoo's on her ankles. "You like them?", she asked. He smiled as he traced his name with his finger. "I love them! When did you get these done?", he asked. "Today on my break." "Why", he asked. "Because I love you and I've found my everything in you.", she replied.

As Alicia Key's 'Unbreakable' began to play, Tootie snuggled closer in his lap and sung along with it softly in his ear, tracing his jaw line with her finger. "That's gonna be us, unbreakable, Boo.", she said, as the DJ began to slow the party down with an onslaught of slow grooves. Couples took the floor, slow grinding and just holding each other tight as the DJ spun a nice selection of the latest slow songs. Linz cupped Tootie's bootie, pulling her closer, inhaling her scent, and enjoying the softness of her breast pushed up against his chest. Her arms were limp around his neck, as she planted soft wet kisses on his neck. "I'm trusting you with my heart and soul, don't disappoint me.", he said. "Boo, I won't, I promise you that. I mean it when I say I love you.", she whispered, as they rocked slowly from side to side, in a lover's groove.

Ajia's eyes filled with tears of joy as she watched her daughter and soon to be son-in-law move as one on the dance floor. "I know you ain't crying, Ms Mouth all Mighty!", Jade said. Everyone looked at Ajia. "What y'all looking at? That's my only child out there!", Ajia said. "Besides these are tears of joy.", she finished, taking a sip of the bubbly. "Don't worry Ms. Ajia, you still got us.", Diamond said. "Wait a minute, your Tootie's mom?", K.J asked, looking Ajia up and down in disbelief. He couldn't believe that Tootie's mom was this damn fine. He thought that she was one of the sales girls that worked at the shop. "In the flesh, can't you tell where Tootie get her looks from?", Ajia stated, standing up profiling for the men. "If you don't sit down, I'm telling Devon on you!", Jade said. "Don't hate!", Ajia replied and dipped it low, "Yeah, it's true, I got my groove back!" The girls laughed, they enjoyed being in the company of Tootie's mom. "I told y'all that she was crazy, didn't I?", Cristal asked, pouring another round of bubbley. "Shit, Tootie's mom is cool as hell!", K.J said, while A.P mumbled, "And she got a fat ass!".

It was clear to everyone that Ajia took good care of herself. Jade gave Ajia a hug, "You know you are like a mother to us all. We are happy for Tootie too.", Jade said, with a tear in her eye. The group engaged in small talk as Ajia was introduced to the fellas. "Y'all nigga's better treat my babies right.", pointing at the girls, "because I will bust some heads about them there.", she stated. "Linz said you liked to pop fly Ms. Ajia.", K.J said. "Now that's one nigga whose head I'm gonna split just for the hell of it and about my baby!", Ajia replied. "Don't worry, your daughter is in good hands. Linz is a good dude, my boy won't hurt her.", Doug said, speaking up for his friend.

Linz and Tootie's little groove was broke up, when the DJ switched up on them and put on Nelly's 'Grillz'. Everybody filled the dance floor as the song blasted through the speakers. The two danced to two more songs and decided that they wanted to be alone. They informed the others that they were leaving. "Can my mom stay out with y'all?", Tootie asked. "Yeah, she's cool. We will look after her old ass.", Jade said. The crew planned on hitting up this after hours spot when this closed. "You better hope you look this good when you get my age!", Ajia said. Tootie gave her mother the keys to the Range Rover and said peace to everyone.

Early the next morning, Tootie rose to find Linz kneeling by the bedside praying. She smiled at herself, then looked at her left hand, yes the ring was still there, this was not a dream. Linz finished praying, shook his soon to be wife, and said, "Babe I need you to run downtown with me real quick.", he stated. "When?", she answered looking at the clock, it was 7:10 am. "In a few, I gotta be in court at 9:00, plus we have to find a parking space.", he responded, getting up going to to the closet to pick out something to wear. He selected the white and baby blue Denver Nuggets shooting jersey, a pair of denim shorts, and matching Nike Air Max shoes, then he went to take a shower.

Tootie admired her man, in every sense, his mind, body, and soul. She was glad that her man had a good eye for fashion because not many niggas could dress. Some can't put together a pair of socks, let alone an outfit. She sat staring at her hands, her dream was almost complete. Tootie got her lazy ass out of bed to pick out something to put on. She felt like exposing her legs and tats to the world today, deciding to put on this cute little backless tennis dress, sky blue with matching flip flops. Satisfied with her selection, she joined her man in the shower. They quickly washed each other and rinsed off. Tootie was expecting to get her some like she did most mornings, but today it was just a plain shower. "What's up Boo, you don't want none?", she asked. "I want some, it's just that I gotta be somewhere and I don't have time to give it to you good, the way you and I both like it.", he replied, stepping out of the shower.

Linz was dressed and ready to go before she was. He was looking good, neck and wrist frozen, yeah she was proud of her man. "Girl, come on. I told you I got to be there by 9!", he stated, urging her to hurry. Tootie threw her bracelet, earrings, toe ring, and watch into her clutch purse. There was no way she was going to let him shine by himself. She was looking too damn cute in that outfit, the ice was just the icing on the cake. "Boo, I'm ready. Let me leave my Mom a note.", she hollered. While she was doing that, Linz grabbed a stack of money and stuffed it in his pockets, thinking this should be enough to cover everything.

As they cruise down the parkway towards downtown, Tootie wondered what he was going to court for. She put her feet on the dash and began to put her bracelet around her ankle, and toe ring on. Then, he reached into the center console and got her lip gloss out and applied it to her lips. Damn, you just took over my shit, huh?", he asked. Putting her sades on, leaning back in the seat she said, "You said that I could drive it, and what are you going to court for?", switching subjects.

They found a spot outside of the courthouse, parked and entered. As Tootie climbed the steps ahead of him, he noticed that she was jiggling a little too much, like she didn't have any panties on. "Babe, I know you got some panites on, right?", he asked outside the courtroom. "Yeah, why?", she responded. "Because it don't look like it the way your ass is shaking.", he said. "Boy, I got on a thong. Why you watching my ass anyway? You nasty, you need to be worried about this business of yours in this courtroom instead of my ass.", she teased. "That ass is my business, don't worry about the courtroom, I got that.", he said.

Linz and Tootie entered the courthouse boyfriend and girlfriend, thirty minutes later, they exited officially husband and wife. Her dream had come true, she couldn't wait to tell her mom and the girls. "See, I told you that you was my future, didn't I?", he stated, opening the door for her. "Yeah, you said that, at first I didn't believe you, I thought it was just game so you could string me along until this was all over, and to keep me from fucking somebody else. Now I see that I was wrong, please forgive me for doubting you, Boo, it won't happen again.", she said. "Babe, it's cool, just don't let it happen again or I'll tap that ass!", he joked, pulling into traffic. Thirty minutes later, they were heading east towards Philadelphia. "Where are we going?", she asked. He paid her no mind, "Boo, you forgot that my Mom is here?" "Babe, just relax, I got this.", he said turning up the radio when his song came on. Tootie decided that it was no use in talking to him, so she called her mom to inform her of what was going on. "Momma, guess what, I'm married!", she exclaimed. "Congratulations baby!", Ajia said, happy for her child. "Momma, I don't know where he is taking me, we on our way to Philly, I guess. I'm sorry to be leaving you all by yourself.", she said apologizing. "Girl, I knew all about it two months ago. I'm cool, Cristal is on her way to get me now. I'm going to hang out with them for a few days, then I'll see you later.   Remember I told you that he wasn't going anywhere? Listen, you just relax and enjoy yourself and your husband. Don't forget to put that whip appeal on him, you know good pussy runs in our family!", Ajia said.   Tootie just laughed and replied, "Mom, you know I'm gonna handle that. Your an old freak!".   The two women talked for a while longer before Tootie finally said, "I love you Mom.", then hung up.   Next, she called the shop to inform the girls of her new status.   They were shocked and excited as hell, Linz could hear them screaming through the phone.

Three and a half hours later the newlyweds checked into the rockstar suite at the Ritz Carlton at the Pocono's Resort in Pocono, PA.   As soon as they entered the room, their breath was stolen.   The whole suite was mirrored, including the ceiling, with wall to wall thick purple shag carpeting, white leather over stuffed couches, 60 inch plasma screen tv, a fully stocked bar, and a round king sized bed.   The thing that stood out the most was the spa tub, it was shaped like a giant 8 feet tall champagne glass.

Tootie ran around the room like a kid in a candy store.   She felt like a celebrity.   Linz sat on the bed watching his wife go crazy.   Tootie came and jumped on the bed, bouncing into his arms, "I love you Boo!", she said.   He ran his hands up her dress,cupping her ass.   "This is legally mine now.", he said. That brought a smile to her face, it still hadn't sunk in yet that she was his wife now.   "This is mine, all mine.", she said pointing to his heart then his penis.   "No doubt.", he responded, Linz truly loved Tootie.

"Boo, we didn't bring any clothes, how long are we staying?" she asked, gettingoff the bed and opening the doors to the balcony.   "A few days, I wanted it to be a birthday surprise, so that's why I didn't tell you to pack.   We'll hit the mall in a couple of minutes.", he said, joining her on the balcony.   When this is all over, we'll spend a few weeks in Aruba or Monte Carlo for our honeymoon."   She nodded yes, truth be told, she didn't care if they went on one or not, she'd got what she wanted, him as her husband and father of her child.

The two spent the next five hours at the mall shopping. Linz walked around in and out of stores with her for a little while, then she sent him off so she could do a little shopping by herself. Tootie planned on turning him on with some sexy little outfit every   night that they spent in the Poconos.   She purchased several outfits in Frederick's of Hollywood and Victoria Secret. She knew from her experience as an exotic dancer the things she selected would surely fuck his head up.   She went all out to please her man.   The first outfit she planned on wearing was this fur bra and panties set with matching stillettos.   While there she got him several pairs of silk boxers and a pajama set.   She doubted he's ever wear them, but she bought them anyway.   On the way out of Frederick's, she picked up a tube of tropical flavored body syrup to spice things up a bit.   They was about to get their freak on.

The newlyweds spent the next four days trying to play tennis and golf, they even went on a hot air balloon ride.   Each day it was something different.   They took full advantage of all the resort had to offer.   At night, they took turns exploring each other's bodies like it was the first time all over again.   They did it all over the room, in the bed, on the floor, in the tub, on the balcony, up against the wall.   You name it, they did it.   Both of them loved watching their reflection as they fucked.   Tootie was fasinated at watching Linz's dick disappear in and out of her pussy.   He like looking at hisself stroke Tootie, it turned him on even more.

One night after a love making session, she sang Mary J's 'Be Without You' to him.   Then while laying in his arms just talking about life she decided it was time to give him her news.   "Boo, I have something I want to share with you.   I am pregnant." Linz smiled and said, "Really, how far?"   "Five weeks.", she said.   Linz continued to smile and said, "Thank you.   I can't wait to name him or her.", as he rubbed her belly.

Back in Pittsburgh, Doug was going over the master plan that he'd came up with, along with the other members of the crew. Each of them were schooled on their part and position, they would fill the newlyweds in when they returned.   For three days straight, Doug drilled them on the plan.   Everyone knew that one mistake could be fatal.   They'd come too far to turn back or lose one of their lives.   The gang knew how much loot was at stake, well they had an estimate of fifty to sixty million in cash and a king's ransom in high grade uncut heroin.

Doug went over that DVD about a hundred times during the last few days.   He couldn't wait to get this over and done with so he and Cristal could be on their way to Cali, leaving Pittsburgh behind for good.   The hit was scheduled to go down during the annual June-teenth Celebration.   The clubs would be packed and anybody who was getting money was sure to be out stunting. Also, the Summer's Players Ball would be that weekend, and knowing Royce his ego wouldn't let him miss it.   The pillow talk that Ric engaged in with Natalie's friend confirmed their intentions to be there.   That is when Roc planned on breaking out his new whip, a midnight blue Maybach62' sitting on 26's. The night of the hit rolled around fast but everyone knew their position.

PHASE

SIX

"Game Over...

Checkmate!"

CHAPTER FIFTY-TWO

Ric and Roc paid no attention to the two white boys walking towards them.   Dressed in shorts, boots, long coats, and pulling on a Marlboro, they looked like your typical grunge band members.   The two men proceeded to walk through the parking garage, engrossed in coversation about the Maybach Roc just purchased.   "Yo son, I killed them today.", Roc stated to his brother.   When Doe passed Roc he purposely bumped into him, almost knocking him down.   "Punk ass white boy, you need to watch where you are going!", Roc said, turning to confront the two white boys who kept walking.   "Muthafucka, you hear me talking, bitch!", Roc yelled, walking toward the two white boys who had their backs to the brothers.   Ric and Roc were both killers in their own rights, but they were no match for Armando and Aaron.

At the time that Roc started to confront the two white boys, a red Expedition pulled in to the open space next to the Maybach.

Four black men got out and watched the scene in front of them. "Sorry dude!", Doe said with his back still turned to Roc. "Next time, I will fuck your white ass up!", Roc said. "Dude, we said we're sorry, let it go, alright!", Aaron said. "Who the fuck you talking to, punk!", Roc said, playing right into their hands. When Roc was about three feet away, Doe and Aaron spun around brandishing nickle plated riot pumps. "Dude, fuck you!", Doe said. Roc was caught like a deer in headlights. Ric reached for his weapon, but was stopped by the four men, who pulled out heaters too. "That's not a wise move, playa.", A.P said, pointing an AK47 at Ric's skull. Roc turned and looked at his brother, both men stood with their arms up. "What's going on?", Ric asked. "Give me the fucking keys, you know what this is bitch!", Doe said, digging in his pockets and taking the keys. He then hit him in the face with the pump, Roc screamed like a bitch. He hit him once more in the back of the head knocking him out, then stuffed him in the trunk of the Maybach.

Rick looked in horror as the white boy gun butted his brother then stuffed him the trunk of the car. He felt angry and helpless as he stood with three 45's and an AK pointed at his head. "We can do this the easy way or the hard way, the choice is yours.", Doug said. Ric chose the easy way. He climbed into the awaiting Expedition with two gunmen on both sides of him. They followed the Maybach out to Roc's Squirrel Hill home in a predominately white gated community.

Meanwhile, the girls were trailing closely behind Royce's Phantom in a stolen Escalade. At the deserted intersection of Naple and Corthia, Jade purposely rear ended the Phantom. "No the fuck you didn't!", Royce yelled, jumping out of the Phantom, ready to flip out. He was immediately disarmed by the four beauties who were dressed to kill in revealing but classy outfits. "Oh my gosh, I'm sorry.", Jade said, getting out to view the damage. "Bitch, can't you drive! You tore my shit up and I know you can't afford it. Dumb Ho!", he bellowed. Jade just continued to apologize. "I'm sorry, I really am. My heel got stuck!", she tried to explain. The other ladies got out to survey the damage. Diamond bent over to get a closer look, exposing much clevage to Royce's roaming eyes. While Jade bent over with her ass facing Royce, the hem on her already short skirt rose even higher, stretching tighter across her ample cheeks giving Royce an eyeful.

While Royce was preoccupied with the twins, Cristal slid up beside the female in the passenger's seat, running her mouth on her cell. Tootie positioned herself behind Royce, each of them waiting for Jade's signal. As Royce stood thinking about how he could fuck the two Asian twins, he didn't see Jade reach into her handbag and pull out a chrome .380. By the time it registered in his mind, Diamond upped a glock 45 and pointed at his face. "Damn, its like that? Y'all bitches is tripping!", Royce said, contemplating on whether to call their bluff. Cristal made the decision for him when she placed the gun to the back of the girl's head and pulled the trigger, sending the front of her skull onto the dash and winshield. No one was expecting her to do that, she just wanted to get this shit over with. She was tired of Pittsburgh and in four days, she'd be on her way to Cali.

Royce was so scared he pissed on himself. Cristal walked over to him, placed the Ruger to his head and asked, "What's it gonna be Nigga? I'm short on patience." He thought for a minute, then said in a shaky voice, "Alright, y'all win, what you want? Money? My car? Jewels?" He thought this was just a routine robbery. "Naw bitch nigga, we want it all!", Tootie said, cuffing his hands behind his back, forcing him into the back seat of the SUV.

Lil Mac and Jeanna watched from across the street in an old lot. "That's my girl, pushing wigs back!", Jeanna exclaimed, giving Mac a pound. Mac hopped out of the car and ran across the street, jumped in the Phantom, and sped off raising the top in the process. Mac looked at the lifeless body slumped against the door. The sight of death didn't faze him, he wondered if the blood would come out of the carpet. He knew that he couldn't sell the car here, but his cousin in Cali knew a chop shop that would gladly take it. He drove to his shop with Jeanna in tow, while the ladies headed out to Squirrel Hill to meet the boys at Roc's place.

Royce's mind raced as he sat cuffed between two sirens with pistols. "Look, I got loot, just let me go! Do you know who I am!", he stated trying to compromise. "Nigga, we know who you are, now shut the fuck up!", Cristal said. Royce proceeded to try and reason with the girls. "It ain't gotta be like this!", he said. "Look dude, you just seen what happen to your girl, so if I was you, I'd shut the fuck up because we not trying to hear it.", Tootie said.

Ric seen his life pass before his eyes, praying that it didn't end like this. He or his brother wasn't suppose to get caught slipping or go out like this. They were supposed to die in a blaze of glory and definately not today. Now he was surrounded by killers like himself with no escape. Death burned in the skinny mixed kid's eyes. Ric assumed that although he wasn't the crew leader, he was the deadliest.

K.J parked the Expedition in the garage next to Doe and Aaron in the Maybach. Once the door shut, Roc was let out of the trunk. The crew ushered their captives into the house to the living room. The men were then seated and their hands and feet duct taped. "Fellas, you know what we are here for, so give up the loot. Oh and don't worry, Royce is on his way, now one of y'all can live, I'll let you two decide who that will be.", K.J said. Just then his cell rang, the ladies were outside with Royce. A.P went to let them in. When Royce entered with the armed bandits and seen his two trusy soldiers bound on the floor, he new it was over.

"Hey Royce, glad you could make it. You could have been anywhere in the world, but you chose to be here with me tonight. Thank, appreciate it.", K.J said jokingly. "Oh, you don't remember me do you?", he asked. Royce said, "Naw player, sure don't" "Well let me refresh your memory. About six years ago we were in Chauncey's, you were with these two clowns.", pointing at Ric and Roc. "I was with this broad named Tara, you remember her?" Royce said nothing but listened, trying to place this dude who held the 50 cal in his lap. "Anyway, I was with her and you came over and started talking to her, pulling out big loot, and asked her what she was doing with a sucka. I admit I was fucked up about that Nigga.", K.J said. "Man, all this over a bitch! Come on Nigga, it ain't like that!", Royce said, figuring out why he was in this situation. "Naw, I got over that bitch, but the disrespect i didn't appreciate, feel me. See you tend to do that to a lot of niggas, just gorilla their hoes and clown them because you got these goons riding with you. They scare the piss out of niggas, well I ain't scared and I feel you need to be taught a lesson, and I'm going to teach you and these two assholes today. Well they gotta suffer for your mistakes.", K.J said laughing. "Now that we are all here, let's get down to business. Cough up the dough! You got one chance, then I'm gonna start shooting. Oh, one of y'all can live, the first one to spill it." Then he looked at the two brothers and said, "Why die over this nigga's loot?   It ain't worth it."   He let them think about that for a while as the girls searched the place. Lil Mac and Jeanna showed up half hour later.

The women tore through the house collecting jewelry and other valuables.   Down in the wine cellar they found the personal safe of Roc.   The safe was state of the art, it could only be opened with a scan of Roc's forefinger.   Damn, this nigga went all out to keep his loot safe.", Diamond said.   She was a true high tech and computer geek.   Roc was a ex-felon with convictions for money laundering and drugs on his record, so he didn't use banks or put anything in his name.   He was just like any other hustler, he kept his loot within arm's reach, all three of them did.

The ladies continued to search the cellar, pulling on every bottle, twisting knob, flickering switches, looking for hidden compartments.   They got lucky when Jade tugged on a bottle of 1946 Merlot.   The wall slid back revealing an air tight stock room with boxes of money, a few adding machines, and 1000 kilos of high grade Asian herion.   "Jackpot.", Diamond yelled, sending Cristal to get the men.

"So,have you clowns made a decision on who's gonna live yet?", K.J said, releasing the safety on the .50 cal.   The bound men looked at each other, then Royce, true to his nature, began singing like Whitney Houston.   Everyone knew he was the bitch of the crew.   "Man, the loot is in his   safe downstairs, it's at least twenty million."   Ric and Roc just looked at him in disbelief.   Roc said, "You a real bitch, I always knew you'd snitch.   I hope they kill your sorry ass anyway!" Roc knew that the men would kill them anyway, so he decided to make sure Royce got it also.   "Yeah, it's loot down there, but there is more at his place, about fifty million.   I know y'all

gonna kill me, you'd be fools not to.   I know I'd do y'all
without blinking, so do what you do.   I lived by the gun, I'll die
by the gun.   Just do me one favor, let me watch that bitch nigga
die first.   Then I can truly rest in peace, ya heard."   The men
respected Roc's gangsta, he was going out like a true soldier, if
only he was on their team.

Doe cut Roc's finger off and passed it to A.P to go open the
safe.   They found stacks and stacks of money bundled in
amounts of $100,000 and placed in a large black travel trunk.   It
turned out to be $23.6 million, Roc's personal stash.   They
loaded the money and part of the heroin into the Escalade and
sent Tootie and Jade off.

Roc laughed while Doe was cutting his finger off.   "Man,
y'all might as well get his thumb", nodding at Royce, " because
he got the same kind of safe."   All the while Ric said nothing, he
just sat there watching.   "What you got to say about all this?",
A.P asked.   "I'm with my brother, we came in this world
together, we gonna die together.", Ric said looking at his brother.
"I guess I'll see you on the other side, bro."   The Four Kings
really admired these brother's gansta.   "Damn, I wish i didn't
have to kill y'all.   Y'all two of the realest niggas I've met, last
of a dying breed.", K.J commented.   "No, you don't youngster.
In the game, once you show weakness you are tagged lame and
that could cost you your life.   Just a little bit of wisdom for
you." Ric said.   He then told them where the loot was stashed
and the combination of the safe.   He favored the old fashioned
combination safe in his home out in Greentree.

Linz and A.P followed by Diamond and Cristal in the beat up
service van headed over to Ric's Greentree hideaway to confirm
what he'd told them.   The loot was all there, $19.6 million, also
this month's take of 4.8 million.   The men loaded the money in

the Expedition, while the girls plundered in the house. After everything was packed, Linz sent the ladies off in the Expedition, while the men took the van back over to Roc's house.

Just one more house left to hit, then it was over. "Help me load these fools in the van.", K.J said to the others. He went around duct taping their mouths. The Four Kings had decided to move the bound men to Royce's home just to make sure things were on point. "Grab the rest of the H, bring it too.", Linz said. He planned on making it look like a drug deal gone bad. That's probably what the media would say anyway with all the victims being black. After the captives were placed in the van, Jeanna jumped in the Maybach. While the men piled in the SUV and van. This was about to get ugly. As the entourage made their way out to Royce's mini mansion in Sewickly, the Pittsburgh P.D were responding to a call of a dead body found in the middle of Collinwood Avenue, were Mac dumped Tasha's lifeless body.

Sargent Finley rubbed his bald head, he was stressed because he knew the parents of the female laying in the streeet with the top of her head missing. He thought of the right words to say, as he dialed the number to her father, Chief Harris of the Homestead P.D.

"Yo, go under the speed limit, Sewickley is not the place to be getting stopped.", Linz said to a very amped K.J, who just shook is head in response. He drove past two cop cars sitting in a convenient store parking lot, at 2:30 am, there wasn't much happening in this boro for the affluent. As the convoy made it's way up Royce's driveway, he prayed that his grandmother wasn't home yet. She'd went on a senior's cruise, but was supposed to be in sometime tonight. "God, please protect my Nana.", he silently prayed. As soon as the van stopped, Royce got nervous.

"Alright, here's the business, if the loot ain't here or it's some kind of trick, I'm blasting off top. Now what's up with the alarm system.", K.J asked. He already knew that Royce had one and the code, this was a test to see if he'd lie. Ric mumbled something, A.P removed his gag so he could hear him. Ric gave up the code and told about the two German Mastiff that patrolled the house. Doug screwed on the silencer.

The men entered the house with no problem. The dogs were taken out immediately. They ushered the three men into the kitchen and bound them to the chairs. "Royce, is that you?" It was his grandmother calling, apparently the barking from the dogs had awaken her. Doe followed the sound of her voice and returned a minute later with the old biddy in one arm and the gun aimed at her temple.

"Well, well, well, who do we have here, Royce?", K.J asked. "Look man, take the money, just don't hurt her, okay.", Royce pleaded. His Nana meant the world to him, but to the Four Kings, she was just a bag of bones. "Royce, what's going on? Who are all these men with guns?", she asked. "Nothing Nana, everything is going to be alright, they're leaving soon.", he said, hoping they'd spare his Nana. "Let's go playboy, we ain't got all night.", said Linz, motioning for Royce to get up after Doug untied him.

Doug, Linz, and A.P followed as Royce lead them to his safe and opened it. The safe held eleven plastic tubs filled with money, mostly hundred and fifty dollar bills. There was also several pieces of expensive custom jewelry and watches. "Man, let my Nana live, she ain't got nothing to do with this!", Royce said, hoping they had a soft spot for the elderly. Doe and Aaron watched over the hostages, while the others loaded the money into the van. After they were done, they brought the heroin into the house and scattered it about the home, leaving a mountain of powder on the kitchen table. Next, K.J turned to Royce and said, "Don't worry, she'll go painlessly". He loaded a needle with the grade A, uncut heroin and shoved it into Nana's arm, sending her to her death feeling good.

"Noooo!", Royce screamed as he watched his Nana's body jerk as the drug traveled through her veins, attacking her heart. Nana was a goner. Royce jumped up and charged K.J, even though his hands were bound behind his back. "I'll kill you, bastard!", he yelled. Those were is last words before A.P cut him down with a short burst from the AK. His body lay twisted on the marble floor. Already knowing their fate, Roc yelled, "What you waiting for, let's get this over with!". He was ready to meet his creator. Doe said, "Let me handle this, I got plans for these two." "You got that.", K.J said, then turned to Ric and Roc, "Maybe in the next life playa, but in the mean time, tell Satan I said I'm coming for him." K.J knew that if he did not repent of his sins soon, that he'd get a first class ticket to hell. "I'll holla at y'all tomorrow.", Linz said to Doe and Aaron as the crew left them to deal with Ric and Roc.

The local news covered a story about two bodies found hanging from the West End Bridge with their chest cavities ripped open and hearts removed. "It was a bloody night in Pittsburgh, the five murders are supposedly linked together, but it has not been confirmed yet. Back to you Dan.", the anchorman said.

AFTERWARDS.......

It has been three months since the robbery and killings of Royce and his two soldiers, Ric and Roc. The Four Kings, Four

Queens, and their crew seemed to have beaten the odds. They made it out of the streets alive, pulling off some of the biggest capers the city ever seen, while still maintaining healthy and loving relationships with each other. Through it all loyalty and respect remained, not even the vast amount of money changed that. Each member that took part in the heist received a total of 8.275 million a piece. Each couple had $16.5 million, not bad for a few hours of murder.

Armando and Aaron traded in the biker look for the more destinquished one of designer suits. The two looked like young stock brokers on the rise. The brothers relocated to Las Vegas. Grench had taken the killers under his wing. In the under world circles, the boys were earning a solid reputation as the best problem solvers in the business . They did whatever to whoever as long as the paper was proper. Grench named them the Janitors.

Doug and Cristal were settling into their life and home in sunny California, erasing all traces of their past life in Pittsburgh from their minds and focusing on their future together. They kept in contact with the other members of the crew through weekly phone calls, but the thought of returning there never crossed their minds.

A.P and Diamond just purchased a home in the Penn Hill's area and were in the process of having it remodeled. Currently, they were on a 21 day cruise that A.P had promised to take her on several months ago.

K.J and Jade were also house shopping, but haven't found anything yet, so they stayed at his old condo. They were currently on vacation, exploring Tokyo and the Honshu Islands with the twins mother, Ms. Iko.

The twins boutique, La Bella Dame, was doing well. It was

quickly becoming one of the cities most popular clothing stores. It had a reputation for having some of the finest clothing and sales ladies in the area. Tootie and Jeanna kept an eye on the shop while the girls were away. With Tootie being five months pregnant, she didn't want to travel, unless it was to the store and back. Stephanie was moved up to manager and placed in charge of advertising and promotions. The twins planned on opening up other stores in Monroeville, Ross Park, and Sewickly shopping centers sometime next year. Life was treating them good.

Lil Mac and jeanna were the proud parents of a little boy. Mac began to slow his roll in the streets. He was still moving pounds of dro but at a much slower pace. He decided to let a couple of his workers come up and shine for awhile. This was a good move because the streets were getting more treacherous every minute, plus he was a car thief at heart, not a dope boy. Jeanna remained his ace and was down for whatever with him. She gave up her cheating, freaky ways and settled her ass down with him.

2 Major Automotive was doing better than expected. Motorhead and crew were turning a profit at every angle. They secured an auto brokers license and was moving exotic cars like a hustler moves work on the first. Linz and K.J were getting major legal money in the auto business. They had clients on both coasts, down south, athletes, and celebrities. The buzz was super, just like their work.

Linz and Tootie were enjoying the married life and was learning together what it was like to be husband and wife. The couple was eagerly awaiting the arrival of their first child, a girl who they were naming A'Najia Tamar Lindsey.

It looks as if everyone had beaten all the odds, but at this present moment, Tootie sat in St. Judes Medical Center at her husband's bedside praying to God to let the love of her life live. Her eye's puffy from crying nonstop as she held his hand tightly.

Three days ago, Linz was shot three times outside of the doctor's office when he dropped Tootie off for her monthly check up. She could still hear the shots ringing in her ears and see his body falling to the pavement as life flowed from him. It all seemed to happen in slow motion, as soon as he stepped off the curb, shots rang out from a black Yukon with tinted windows that was parked across the street. The truck sped off once his body hit the pavement, painting the concrete red with his blood.

Linz took three shots, one to the head and two to the body. She remembered cradling his head in her bossum, screaming for help. "Nooo, God No!", she cried and begged. Inside the office of Dr. Johnson, the secretary Grace, heard the gunshots along with Tootie's screams and called 911. Without the assistance of Dr. Johnson, Linz would have been pronounced dead, but God had other plans.

Linz now laid in a hospital bed for the last three days in a coma. He is expected to make a full recovery, however, he lost a kidney and suffered a puncutured lung . His wife was by his side, were she'd been for the last three days whispering, "I love you, remember, it's me and you against all odds.", over and over again hoping he hears her voice. Her mother, Ajia, stood behind her weeping and praying for her daughter and son-in-law.

SHOUT OUTS

First off I'd like to thank God for blessing me with the talent to paint a portrait with words and for watching over me all those days and nights that I ran the streets chasing paper, trying to stack a million. I'm so thankful that I had people praying for me & angels speaking to God on my behalf.

I'd like to give a respectful shout out to to all my fellow hustlers,fallen soldiers, and friends that lost their lives in these cold streets, trying to better their situation. Clyde Lee McGhee aka "Popcorn", your were my friend & brother, we go way back to the south end projects. I still remember your first car that you copped, that black VW rabbit that was painted with house paint for $500. Man, I miss you. We had some really good times in life & in the game. They don't make em like you anymore.

Richard Rashee Young aka Rich Wally. Maaaaannnnn, they stole a good nigga when them bitches downed you. I'll never forget you fam, we used to clown. It was never a dull moment when you were around, you had the whole city screaming "wally thugs".

Brandon "B.Y." Young, man I watched you grow up. You were like a nephew to me. I still can't believe your gone.

De'ron "Beck" Thorton, dammit man!! We go back to remote control cars & pony sneaks.

Also Greer "Wise" Montgomery, Alfie "Spanky" Wade Jr., Torry "TC" Carter, my dude Suga Bae, Shaheen Thompson & Marte "Jo" Wilson, can't forget you. Y'all some of the people I came up & hustled with, y'all maybe gone but damn sure ain't forgotten.

Now to those who helped make this happen and or, believed in me before the first word was written. To my family(actual family members) thanks for being there no matter what. To my pops Lionel R. Lindsey Sr. Aka "Bo" thanks for being my role model & never giving up on me even tho I took you and mom through it. To my mom Ruby Lindsey, thanks for loving me and never turning your back on me. Even tho you cussed & fussed, you still had my back. I love y'all. To my brothers & sisters, Diane, Terry, Sherri, Robyn and Jason Lindsey thanks for holding me down through out life. I love y'all and wouldn't trade y'all for nothing in this world. Y'all my family no matter what, sure we have our disagreements but at the end of the day.....we got each others back 100%. To my cousins Derek, Dana, Lori, Scott, Chad, Donna & Betty Jean, Raymond Lindsey(its a lot of damn Lindsey's). Also my other cousins Manard, Jerome(Rome), Sabrina, Keyshia, Man Man. To my Aunt Lizabeth Reed-Brown, my Uncle Herbie & Aunt Lois Lindsey, my Uncle Leon Lindsey , y'all just don't know how much your letters, cards, phone conversations & visits meant to me. The support & out pouring of real love you give and show is priceless! Thanks for loving & accepting me as I am. To my nieces & nephews Pooney, Anthony, Shaliah, Quashon, Sha'miah, Terrence, Albert Jr.(mooshie), Ter'nashia(peachy), My'kel thanks for not forgetting about your uncle in my absence. Thanks for all the letters & pictures, I love y'all never forget that.

Special shout outs to the following, they went above & beyond to make this book happen. To Robert L. Sullivan (Rob) my brutha even if it ain't by blood, your my fam. Thanks for believing in me & my work to put your hard earned money up to make it happen. A lot of people talked about it, but you did it. You already know when I blow, you blow too. If I got a dollar, your welcome to .95¢ of it, no questions asked. Thanks for always keeping it 100 wit me.

Again to my brother Jason, sister Sherri, cousins Derek, Dana & Rome for holding me down and not turning your backs on me when I caught this sentence. Man the visits, money orders, greendots & phone cards that y'all hit me with from time to time, I truly appreciate it and your unwavering support y'all showed on this project. I love y'all!!!

To my homies who also held me down & never changed when I went to prison Shawn Ross, Brandon "Supreme" Mayo, Terrell Sayles, Terrence "Bookey" Elder, Monte "Silver" Young, Donte Wade, Tyrone Rice, Raymond "Piggy" Williams, Jermaine Thompson, Billy Murray, Greg "yogi" Harris, D'shawn "dirty" Rooks.

To my home girls that kept a brutha in thought & prayer and, didn't switch up and act like they ain't know or fuck with me when I got arrested. Adrian Bennett(Holmes), Toychica N. Williams-Harness(Tootie), Natasha Champale Haynes. My 3 amigos Quana Jones, Janee Rue, and Karla Dallas. Thanks you all for keeping real & for all the love, y'all always got a place in my heart no matter what.

It's many more people, but these are the ones that truly stand out. So, if you don't see your name please don't trip I'll get you next time. But real talk, you know if you was down for me or not. I don't have to say it, search your self and you'll find the answer.

To my homie,friends, and editors Delshawn Byrom, Salima K. N'Dulu,Sabrina Whittmon for being a friend and believing in my work. To my dude Andrew "Drew" Simmons thanks for the super tight cover design. You helped bring my vision to light. I look forward to working with y'all on the next book.

Also shout outs & much love to Laura Albea for accepting me as I am, when I was at my worst. To Roberta "boo" Taylor, La'Tiqua Acavedo thanks for being a friend, told you I was gonna shout y'all out!

To all my fellow hustlers all across the map that's still out there getting it in, get your paper & trust no one. Cause these niggas ain't the same no more, they singing like crazy out there. To my bruhs thats locked down, this is for you. I feel your pain fam. Also to a few real bruthas I met while locked down, Hot, Twinn, DirtyMoney, Stuff, Lil'Dain, Smocc(D. marchbanks) Bud, Byrd, Tall T. Snoop, Craig Shears,Kenny Moore, Kevin Love, Bug Eye(old school bugeye) Ray Mac, E(Elro Chambers).

To my hustlers in the city of Steubenville, Ohio, Pittsburgh, Pa & Columbus, Ohio stand up! We here now, this is for us.

Lastly, to all those that counted me out, turned their backs, betrayed me or just flat out said "fuck him" when I got locked up(AND Y'ALL KNOW WHO YOU ARE) I say to you FUCK YOU! Whether free or locked up, I'm still shining on you bozo ass niggas & bitches.